FOOLS RUSH IN

FOOLS RUSH IN

by

Gilliam Clarke

Copyright © 2000 by Gilliam Clarke

All rights reserved.
No part of this book may be reproduced, stored in a retrieval system, or transmitted by any means, electronic, mechanical, photocopying, recording, or otherwise, without written permission from the author.

ISBN: 1-58721-358-3

1stBooks – rev. 06/13/00

ABOUT THE BOOK

The City of Sunshine, on Florida's central west coast, perches uncomfortably at the mouth of the Hatchacootee River– the only river in Florida to boast a delta. The town is a backwater plagued by the Saved Sons Society, a seedy, chauvinistic outgrowth of the Living Witness Holy Confederation, and an ancient, leaking sewer system that has polluted everything in sight.

The city has seen its past leaders taken off to jail for various degrees of criminal activity, and its present politicians concentrate their efforts on trying to remain in office.

The dysfunctional City Council, as infamous for its bickering and backbiting as it is for the mayor's chartreuse wig, are determined to install a beach on the delta, hoping to attract more tourists. This leads to outright warfare, not only among themselves, but also with local activists, who are concerned with the survival of the Polychaete worms, and the Department of Environmental Protection.

Then most of downtown is swallowed by a sinkhole.

ACKNOWLEDGMENTS

Many thanks to the staff at Southwest Florida Water Management District, who were unflagging in their efforts to restrain my verbiage and keep the events of the book within the bounds of reality.

Special thanks to Karen Lloyd, Esquire, Len Bartos, John Parker, Bob Perry, and marine biologist Brent Henningsen of the District.

Thanks also to Paul Firmani, Esquire, and Kim Streeter, Esquire, for their legal renderings, to Bruce Kennedy, and to my husband, Silbourne, whose patience is legendary.

And undying thanks to Florida's politicians, both good and bad, who inspired this book and those to come.

CHAPTER ONE

Lila Mae Warner sighed. She did wish the mayor wouldn't wear that chartreuse wig. Especially with the black, purple, and blue-green dress. And, worse, the mayor was wearing awful lilac and black shoes.

Unaware of the critical scrutiny of her colleague, Mayor Melba Tosti minutely adjusted her yellow-green headgear, cleared her throat, flashed a smile at the local television camera, then banged her gavel. "The meeting of the City Council of the City of Sunshine will now come to order." She then looked upward and intoned, "All rise for the Invocation and the Pledge of Allegiance." After a glance to make certain the camera beamed her image, she rose.

Josephus Tyler, prominent businessman, member of the Living Witness Holy Confederation, and president of the Saved Sons Society, shook himself in preparation for the prayer. His lower face flapped like the jowls of the basset hounds he resembled. He closed his red-rimmed eyes and clasped hands beneath his layered chin. "Lord God, Maker of all things, Knower of all sins, we humbly beseech Thee to lead us to do Thy will while we attend the business of the City of Sunshine." His voice assumed the cadence of the pulpit and he squeezed his eyes tighter shut. "Help us, Lord, to avoid the terrible pitfalls of power! Guide our thoughts, Lord, to Thy ways, that we might prosper. There are those in this city who wallow in iniquity and sloth. They have backslidden until there is no hope! Stamp them out, Lord! We need Your righteous fist and Your righteous wrath–" He grunted as the mayoral foot made contact with the back of his leg. "Huh..?"

"Cut it short, Joe," the mayor whispered. "We got a long agenda."

"...and let us walk in Thy shadow all the days of our lives. Amen." He glared at Melba Tosti, pivoted to face the flag, clapped his hand to his heart, and began the pledge. The voices of citizens come to protest a zoning change rang in faltering echo behind his own.

Opening rites concluded, the councilmen sat and looked out upon those they considered to be lower life forms. Lila Mae leaned across the long desk that was built across the width of the dais, peering at the front row of seats in the council room. She could watch Dreyfus Odlum from her perch and he would never suspect it. What would have happened, she wondered, if she had married him instead of Henny? She flushed, remembering the fantasies she had had about the utilities director.

Then she thought she spied a neighbor. Putting her microphone to one side, she whispered to her right, "Is that Brownie Franks out there, fourth seat to the left on the sixth row?"

Her colleague, Gianni "Meats" Merlini, moved his microphone and answered softly, "Nah, that's old McGinnis. Prolly wants to bitch about the rezoning. It's in his neighborhood." Meats Merlini rocked back and again surveyed the chamber with a sour expression. "Ain't anyone here worth bothering about today. Just a buncha farts."

Lila Mae gasped, her eyes wide. "Meats, it's just shocking, the way you talk! How would you like it if folks called you a *poof*?"

"Poof? What the hell is a poof? I said they're just a buncha farts." He snorted loudly and smirked as the mayor's eyes flashed a warning.

"Councilman Merlini, we are in session," Melba Tosti reminded him.

"Yeah, yeah, Mzzzz. Mayor, that's why I'm here." Merlini returned his attention to Lila Mae and her bosom, wondering why she wore those flowery dresses with lace collars. They hid her boobs. She was good-looking, he thought, although in Brooklyn, blondes were always good-looking, even if they were real dogs, because everyone else had dark hair. Yeah, she was six feet tall and a killer, a real take-me-to-your-ladder-I'll-see-your-leader-later killer. But she wore the wrong clothes. She always looked like a draft horse in drag. "So what's a 'poof'?"

Lila Mae colored. "You're going to get us in trouble with Her Majesty if you keep this up. 'Poof' is the nice, southern word for what you said they were." She nodded her head toward the citizens in the chamber.

Merlini snorted again. A *nice* southern word, for chrissake! "Farts?"

"No, *poofs*."

"Jee-sus!"

"Will you please come to order?" The mayor sounded close to shouting. "Thank you. Now, Bonano, are there any items to be withdrawn from the consent agenda?"

"Yes, Madam Mayor, there is one item to be removed," answered Frank Bonano, the city manager. When he opened his mouth to speak, his right hand checked the knot in his tie, his shirt front, patted his jacket, then rose and smoothed his hair. After that, it returned to the desk in front of him, picked up a pen, and began tapping the polished wood. "Item 4C. The contract was not drawn correctly and has to be redone."

"Not done correctly?" Theodore Rainmaker stared at the city manager. "Did I understand you to say that the contract is not correct?" He turned back to the mayor, eyebrows raised. "Just how is it that our attorneys can't draw a simple contract the first time? If I've said it once, I've said it a million times, Madam Mayor..."

Yes, yes, Lila Mae thought. You've said it a million times and then some, and I wish you'd talk about something besides fiscal responsibility. I mean, it's nice and all that, but boring. We're sick of lectures on fiscal responsibility, and we're also tired of hearing about your–ah–lover, PooPoo, and what a fantastic money manager he is. How on earth did a grown man get a name like PooPoo?

"... this sort of thing is a waste of scarce public dollars. It is our duty as councilmen to be fiscally responsible. We cannot continue to dig into the public purse to pay for incompetence. Do you mean to tell me that the firm of Slugge, Crawley, and Schyte isn't capable of doing a simple–"

"You've made your point, Councilman," Mayor Tosti replied icily. "And we are all aware of how careful you are with the public purse. Never in the history of Sunshine has anyone been so careful of the public purse. But we're not wasting money, so you can relax. No need to ruffle your pretty feathers over this–"

"Ruffle my *pretty* feathers? You are out of line, Madam; how dare you speak to me that way? You're the one who insisted we keep them on, even though, in my opinion, their reputation is questionable. They never do anything right. If PooPoo ran his business like you run the city government, we'd have been bankrupt years ago." Teddy Rainmaker bored his bony backside into his chair, ready for battle. "What this city needs is an in-house attorney instead of those gold diggers. The good old boys don't run this town any more, and this patronage has got to stop. We pay Slugge, Crawley, and Schyte almost half a million a year and they can't write a contract? Maybe we should look at hiring another–"

"You shut up!" Joe Tyler almost shouted, "and keep your nose out of city business, you and that, that–thing you live with! Misbegotten perverts, both of you! The God Book says–"

"City business is my business; I am an elected official. Don't you call me names, you sanctimonious son of a bitch," Rainmaker cried. He shot from his chair, five feet, six inches of trembling, white-haired fury, and stormed off the dais. Turning back to the council, he gave them a withering look and left the chamber, slamming the door after him.

Melba rolled her eyes and readjusted her wig, realizing that she'd forgotten to pin it in place that morning. "Will this meeting come to order?" she asked in a steely voice. Then she smiled brightly at the camera, tented her fingers, and sighed. "Councilman Tyler, you got to control yourself when we're in session. Can't–"

"Well, I think Teddy Rainmaker has a point, even if he has said it a million times before," Lila Mae interrupted. "Four times this month, our lawyers have screwed up, and they charge by the hour." She leaned forward and peered at Josephus Tyler. "And you should be ashamed of yourself, picking fights here on the dais, Joe. I know how you feel about the happy people, but It ain't fitting to pick fights."

Tyler's jaw dropped. "The *happy people?* What are you talking about?"

Lila Mae looked confused and, in her distress, turned to Meats Merlini. "Aren't they called 'happy'?"

"Who?"

"You know, people like Teddy and PooPoo."

"Oh, you mean *gay.*"

"That's right, I knew it was the same thing as happy. Thanks."

"If you don't mind, Councilman Warner, I have the floor–" the mayor began.

"You have no right to complain of my actions, Councilman Warner, " Tyler burst out. "I have a duty to the God-fearing populace of this town, and as a–"

"Don't you dare start another damn sermon," snapped Merlini, peering past Lila Mae's magnificent chest to glare at Tyler, who was shaking with anger.

Maybe the jerk would die of apoplexy, he thought happily, right there. It would serve him right. Let him go and meet God, and explain to God why that stupid buncha nuts in his church refused to eat pork! He was sure that Joe Tyler had persuaded the people in his church to avoid pork simply because he, Merlini, was a Yankee. Tyler had a thing about folks from anywhere but Florida–thought they were inferior or something. Ignorant hick! That's was Florida's real failing, as far as he was concerned. The natives didn't know how to live right, didn't have a clue, and apparently didn't even care to learn from those who came into the state. If it weren't for the folks from the north, he'd never sell anything but breakfast links, for chrissake!

"You are godless!" shouted Tyler.

"And you are an–" Merlini stopped himself. "For chrissake, let's get on with business."

The gavel crashed. "Order!"

"Madam Mayor, shall I send someone after Mr. Rainmaker?" Frank Bonano asked, his right hand going through its ritual.

"Yeah, Frankie, you're right," Merlini agreed, bestowing a smile on the city manager. "I got some real important stuff to bring up under new business."

Bonano's secretary rose from her place beside him and left the room and, after some stir and whispering in the audience, the people in the room settled to listen to the city's business.

Sunshine's council chamber was vibrant with color. The mayor's first act after the building had been completed four years back had been to order the room painted a bright, cheery yellow. Her multi-hued wigs often clashed with the color of the walls, but she was blissfully unaware of the discordance. This choice of color led people to think they were overly warm, as yellow intensified upon itself to an extraordinary degree. Even in the midst of winter, those who came to hear the deliberations of the council constantly mopped their brows with handkerchiefs or shirt sleeves.

The wall at the back of the room was hung with colorful quilts from the local crafts society, while the wall behind the dais supported the City Seal, a smiling sun with wobbly rays and slightly crossed eyes.

"Lord!" sighed Lila Mae.

"I need a motion to adopt last week's minutes," Melba said.

"Got it," Merlini answered.

"Second." Tyler's voice was harsh.

"I need a motion to adopt the consent agenda, minus Item 4C."

"Got it."

"Second."

"Any emergencies we need to handle?" Melba glared at the city manger, daring him to speak.

"No, Madam Mayor," Bonano replied, his right hand hurriedly performing its duty.

"Okay, then we go on to councilmen's items. District A."

Lila Mae discontinued her study of the citizens in the audience. "I thought we were going to get the rezoning over first, Madam Mayor."

"Yeah, you're right, Councilman Warner," Merlini agreed. "We gotta get the rezoning done so these good people don't have to sit and listen to our–don't have to waste their time."

"What you got on the agenda that you don't want us to hear?" called someone from the back of the chamber.

"Order!" Melba screeched, banging her gavel. "You only have a right to speak during Public Comment." She turned to Merlini. "I wish to delay the rezoning matter until Councilman Rainmaker returns. The area lies in his district."

"Oh, yeah. That's right," Merlini agreed.

"District A?"

Lila Mae sighed. "The Orchid Club is presenting a play next Wednesday, at six o'clock. Second graders from the Trout Wee School will be performing as exotic flowers. I urge every right-minded citizen to attend the performance, since the proceeds go toward landscaping the city park." She sat straighter and looked at the people in the chamber. "There was a time when this town didn't have a city park. My mother could remember when we was only two stores and a crossroads. Now look at it; we have two motels, a little tourist industry, and a great number of residents from the north. So spread the word and support our landscaping efforts. I went to the Laurel Grove Women's Club meeting yesterday. They're getting ready to do a bake sale to benefit the Lions Club." She smiled vaguely. "That's all I have, Madam Mayor."

"Thank you. District B?"

"Nothing doing in my district, Mzzzz. Mayor," Merlini said.

"District–" Melba stopped as the door opened and Teddy Rainmaker came in. He nodded curtly, ascended the dais, and took his seat. "Councilman, I'm glad you're back. I delayed the rezoning until your return, as it's in your district."

"Very kind, Madam Mayor," Rainmaker said coldly.

"District D, Councilman Tyler?"

Tyler's voice was grim. "We have had another crime wave in part of my district–in that blight on civilization we call Mosquito Row. This past week there were fifteen, *fifteen* times when our police officers had to go down there, and those people don't even have anything worth protecting! Most of them are ignorant, thieving immigrants or blacks, and you know what that means. They're constantly at war with each other; there's knifings and shootings. There's whoring, drug deals, all kinds of godlessness. You know the decent citizen in this town is scared to walk the streets!–scared of that rabid area? The place is a hotbed of pregnancy–those people don't know how to do anything, just have babies and more babies that good Christian folks–why can't we raze Mosquito Row and run those bums out?" He began to pound the desk before him to emphasize his seriousness. "We got drugs and drunks, whores on the street! We got robberies–rapes–mayhem–death–damnation! Poor City of Sunshine! Poor citizens of Sunshine! You got to ado–write–sub–damn it!–to consider draconian measures." His voice rose dramatically. "I want this council to pass an ordinance making it a legal offense to break the law!" He sat back, glaring in triumph at the people before the dais.

Someone snickered.

"Joe, breaking the law *is* a legal offense," Melba reminded him.

He directed his glare to the Chair. "You know what I mean, Madam Mayor! As the titular hea–excuse me, no offense meant–head of this city, you should be appalled that our police, God's valiant warrior angels, have to risk their lives to deal with this rabble that we are forced to call citizens!"

"Valiant warrior angels?" snarled Rainmaker. "I think all this religion has eaten your brain. You go too far, Tyler; anyone who can describe Chief Rufus Hicks as a warrior angel is soft in the head."

"Yeah," Merlini agreed. "And just because a guy is a immigrant doesn't make him bad. My old man was a immigrant."

"I've made my point, then!" Tyler declared. "Your father should have never been allowed into the country."

"Now, boys," began Lila Mae.

"Now boys, my hind foot, Lila Mae! How can you take the part of foreigners? This is a free country and our citizens shouldn't have to support those–!"

"Hear, hear!" someone shouted from the audience. "Run all the no-goods out of town. You can start with yourself, Tyler."

"Order!" yelled Melba, banging the gavel. "Councilman Tyler, are you finished with your report?"

"Never! Not until you pass that ordinance."

"You're being unreasonable. Are you finished?"

Tyler crossed his arms over his chest, glared at the mayor, and refused to speak. But his thoughts turned in angry little circles behind his brow. He would bring down The Pervert–all those who opposed him. The Lord would understand and give him aid; He helped the righteous. He had to be mayor again, then he could drive all the sinners from Sunshine and live in a clean place, a city safe from the changes that had ruined his state.

"District C?" Melba's voice was strained.

There were times, she thought, when it was such a temptation to use the gavel as a bludgeon. Tyler's mother should have been burned at the stake, raising such an ass. Look at him now, she thought, sitting there with his self-righteousness almost bubbling out his ears. But what else could one expect from Florida crackers?

"Madam Mayor, I have nothing to report but a simply scrumptious new chicken dish at Rain–you know what a great chef PooPoo is," Rainmaker responded with a grin. "Absolutely divine, with little button mushrooms, lemon, and rosemary. But I do have something very important to bring up under new business, if we ever manage to reach that far in–"

"Madam Mayor, I object!" Lila Mae interrupted loudly. "You don't ever hear me advertising the food at my restaurant, Southern Fried, and he's got no right–"

"I was merely trying to be pleasant," Rainmaker snapped.

"Horsesh–I mean feathers! The day you just try to be pleasant will be the day that–"

"Order!" shouted the mayor.

Laughter from the citizens drowned out her further comments.

DeLeon Slugge finished his summary of the rezoning problem and smiled helpfully. "Are there any questions?"

"Yes," said Lila Mae. "Let me see if I got this straight. The builder had a permit to put up six single family dwellings, and instead, he decided to put up a six story condominium. Is that right?"

Slugge nodded.

"So all we have to do is to agree to a permit change, and everything will be all right?"

"Yes, Councilman Warner, that is correct."

"I think it's just grand, having things like condominiums in Sunshine," Lila Mae said brightly. "My mother could remember when there was just two sto–"

"And a crossroads," Rainmaker finished for her. "I suppose we might consider the change *if there is no serious opposition*."

"Has there been any opposition so far?" the mayor asked.

"Yes, a little. Mostly from the elderly folks who own those trailers near the water. They say their view will be obstructed. But, Madam Mayor, all they see is some old, gnarled mangroves and the mud flats." Slugge, which he pronounced 'Sloojay', was deferential.

"Damn right there's opposition," shouted someone in the audience.

"If all the folks who live in the area see is some mud and mangroves, why does this man want to build a condo? Surely he can find a better view for his customers than that," Rainmaker said.

"Those in the upper apartments will be able to see the Gulf, sir."

"What about those on the lower floor?"

"They'll pay less."

Rainmaker hunkered down in his chair. "Isn't it a little strange that the developer had a permit for six dwellings and he forgot about it? Doesn't anyone find that hard to believe? This man has six dwellings to build, and all of a sudden a condo appears. Slugge, who represents the developer?"

"My firm, Slugge, Crawley, and Schyte."

"Isn't that a small conflict of interest?"

"Now, Teddy, quit being so rough on poor Dee," Lila Mae warned.

Rainmaker glared at her. "I merely asked if this isn't a conflict of interest," he snapped. "He ain't seen rough yet."

Melba looked at her colleagues. "Any further questions of Mr. Slugge? No? Very well, this is a public hearing and we will allow the public to speak. Anyone–"

"Madam Mayor, I have the floor," Rainmaker bellowed. "May I finish what I'm saying?"

"Certainly, Councilman Rainmaker," Melba said through clenched teeth. The camera, she noted, was no longer following her every move.

"No, Councilman, I don't see any conflict of interest," Slugge replied. "You see, one of my colleagues, Michael Crawley, is handling that item. I have constructed a Chinese wall around myself."

"I'm *so* relieved that you're hidden by a wall," Rainmaker cooed. "I feel much, much better about it now."

He sat back, content. He had raised so much ruckus about the condo that no one could possibly think he had anything to do with it. When Fielding had gotten his permit to build those six houses, he'd taken him to task for a lack of vision.

"Who is going to buy a house that fronts on a mangrove swamp?" he had asked Fielding. "Build high, sell high, make a good profit. You know the council will make everything right. It's time to move up, my man, because the Yankees are coming and they'll all want a Gulf view."

He smiled as Merlini began opposing his remarks.

"What's the problem?" Merlini asked in a reasonable tone. "You know the developer; he's getting along in years. Prolly forgot. I forget all the time."

"Is everyone through with their questions?" Melba asked, determined to regain the camera's attention. "Very well, this is a public hearing and we will allow the public to speak. Anyone wishing to address this council will please come forward, one at a time. You are limited to two minutes each."

McGinnis rose painfully and hobbled to the lectern facing the council. He barked sharply into the microphone, then laughed as those on the dais winced. "Just wanted to make sure the dang thing works."

"State your name and address, please."

"Harold McGinnis, 2244 Flowerpetal Drive, Sunshine. Hey, I got a question for the counselor. You got a permit to build that Chinese wall?"

The citizens tittered and McGinnis turned to them and took a bow.

"Mr. McGinnis!"

"I just wanted to remind you folks that this is the fourth time the developer has forgotten what he started out to build. First time, it was those hou–"

"We don't need a history lesson, McGinnis," Tyler warned. "And you keep an abandoned car in your yard. We could give you some serious problems about that if you aren't careful."

"Okay, but I worry about whether you're as stupid as you mostly act," the old man said defiantly. "You can threaten me, but I got rights. I like looking at my mangroves and mud flats. There's a lot of bird life out there, and I don't think you got a right to cheapen our property so's a friend can make a killing. That's all I got to say."

Stony silence.

"Anyone else wish to speak?" Melba asked in a brittle voice.

"How come this comes up after the building is almost completed?" cried an elderly woman.

"If you wish to speak to the council, come forward," Melba warned.

"Whose town is this, anyway?" called another voice.

The mayor stiffened. It was that pest, Fawkins. Always sticking her nose in city affairs. Kelsey Fawkins, would-be environmentalist, who called the governor's office when they passed the ordinance banning dog poop on the sidewalks and lawns of Sunshine. She claimed that the city fathers had deprived the environment of vital nutrients. What kind of a nut would think there were benefits in dog poop? Melba muttered, "Southerners are weird."

"Did you say something?" Lila Mae asked.

Melba's thoughts drew together into a neat pile. She again patted her lime green hair and smiled. "It's your city, Mrs. Fawkins. Yours and ours. You know how I insist on public input. It's necessary to the process of democracy." She sneaked a look at the camera. Good, it was zeroed in on her. Probably a closeup; that guy was good with closeups. "This is a government of the people, by the people, for the people, and as long as I am mayor of the city, this will continue to be a government of the people, for the people, and by the people. I want all of you to remember that I keep my campaign promises, unlike some people who have served as mayor in the past."

"You'll pay for that!" Tyler bellowed. He half-rose in his seat and the camera zoomed in on him, then moved to pan the folks in the audience.

Melba's smile disappeared.

"Sit down, Tyler, and quit being an ass. Mzzzz. Mayor, are we going to vote on this?" Merlini demanded.

"Oh, for–yes!" the mayor responded. "Let's get it over with. I need a motion to approve this change."

"You got it."

"I need a second."

"Done."

"All in favor?" Ayes all around. "Motion passes." She smiled at Slugge, who bowed slightly. Then she saw with annoyance that the lone member of the press was scribbling furiously.

The mayor looked at her watch. If they didn't finish up soon, she'd have to hand over the gavel to Merlini and get going. Senator Fatigay hated waiting for anyone as lowly as a mayor.

"As there's no old business, we'll take new business next. I'd like to be quick on this; we've wasted a lot of time this morning."

Bonano cleared his throat. His right hand leaped to its duty as he began to speak. "Madam Mayor, we have some old business to discuss."

"What?" Melba snapped. "I don't see anything on the agenda that I want to discuss under old business."

"The sewer problem, Madam Mayor. It is on the agenda."

"I am damned sick and tired of your carping on the sewers. If the Department of Environmental Protection chooses to waste its time trying to make us raise taxes, they can kiss my–I am not going to raise taxes! I am not going to stand for the citizens of this town being robbed by Peter to mess around with Paul. I don't want to hear about it, is that clear?"

Dreyfus Odlum rose to his great height and went to the lectern. "Madam Mayor, three more mains have burst and there is no way to repair them. You have refused to let us raise sewage rates and I don't have the money to replace them. I'm probably going to have to cut some folks off as it is; I can't let the sewage run into the ground, as you well know. We have got to have a bond issue to replace this system. That's all there is to it. Are there any questions?"

"I told you that I don't want to hear about it!" the mayor shouted.

"Well, Madam Mayor, I do," Rainmaker said. "We are already in deep trouble about our leaky system, and this will only worsen the problem. Dreyfus, can these things be pat–"

"Point of order!" Tyler yelled. "Pervert, can't you understand English? Melba doesn't want to hear about it."

"Good grief, Joe, since when do you take up for Melba?" Lila Mae asked. She looked at Odlum and sighed. He was so– tall! In fact, when they were growing up, he was the only really tall person in school outside herself. But he'd always been pathetically shy and she had given up on him and married Henny, who was at least six inches shorter than she was.

The gavel crashed. "I will not allow this discussion; is that clear?" The mayor looked at Bonano with absolute hatred, then glared at Odlum, who was still at the lectern. "Sit down, Oddman. I don't want to hear it. Is there any new business?"

Rainmaker sat forward in his chair. "Madam Mayor, since serious matters don't interest you, I have some new business. We know that, as the leaders of Sunshine, we have to do something to develop a real tourist industry. The few fishermen and visitors we get just don't cut it. Everyone goes through Banter County like a dose of salts, heading for those beaches farther south. We need a new image, we need palm trees so the city looks like it's in Florida, and most of all, we need a beach." He folded his arms across his chest and looked at each of them in turn.

"I'd like to know what's wrong with all the beautiful oaks we have growing around the city, Teddy," Lila Mae protested. "We got some of the most gorgeous oaks on this side of the state.

Mama said people used to stop, when all we had was two stores and a crossroads, just to look at the oaks and all the Spanish moss. Lord, I used to pack 'em in at Southern Fried of a Sunday, and all they'd talk about was our—"

"Boobs—er, so they just looked at the trees?" Merlini interrupted. "There ain't anything wrong with the oaks, Lila Mae, but Teddy has a point. We don't have no tourist attractions worth mentioning. People drive through here, they don't even think they're in Florida because all they see is oaks and stuff. Folks think of oaks as being in the Carolinas, or maybe Alabama. Oaks and moss go with southern bellies, and we don't have them down here. I ain't seen one belly since I moved south." He chuckled and looked at the citizens in the chamber to see if they had caught his witticism, but the citizens merely looked puzzled. "We gotta go tropical to draw tourists. I hate to say it, but you're right, Teddy, we need some palm trees. Anyone know what they cost?"

"Plenty," snarled Tyler.

"Like how much?" Merlini insisted.

"I don't know, probably thousands of dollars each."

"They couldn't possibly cost that much," Rainmaker objected.

'Well, if they did, then you *certainly* wouldn't want them, would you?" Melba asked. "We'd have to dig a hole through the bottom of the public purse, and we all know how careful you are of the public purse."

"Madam Mayor, your sarcasm is showing. Might we ask the city manager to look into the cost of the palms? I don't want royal palms or anything fancy: just plain old palm trees."

"Sabal palms grow very well on the west coast," Tyler remarked sourly. "But I don't suppose you'd be happy with what the good Lord put here."

"I think Sabal palms are cute," Lila Mae ventured. "Like little fur balls on a stick."

Merlini winced. Lila Mae was gorgeous, but sometimes she really sounded dumb.

Frank Bonano's right hand leaped to its work in anticipation this time. "Madam Mayor, I'll get some prices for palms and let you have them next week."

"You'd better, Bonano. Any further business? No?"

"What about my new business?" Merlini demanded.

"Don't have time today, Meats. Next week."

"Jee-sus! You took Teddy's."

Bonano's hand leaped to its work. "Madam Mayor, I have an emergency."

"And I have a lunch date with Senator Fatigay," she snapped. "I won't hear it."

"Madam Mayor, this is a requirement from the state government and we must comply."

"Then bring the damned emergency next week, or stick it on the agenda, or–I want a motion for adjournment." Melba began tidying her papers.

"Got it." Rainmaker said tiredly.

"I need a second."

"Done."

The meeting was adjourned.

CHAPTER TWO

Senator Jackson Fatigay, seated at a table in Lila Mae Warner's place, Southern Fried, irritably looked at his watch, willing Melba Tosti to appear. She was never on time and she always had the same excuse: the crush of responsibilities. If she couldn't handle responsibility, why did she bother with politics? Political office was the ultimate responsibility–you had to be accountable, like he was.

He considered Melba's lack of accountability a disgrace. She was flighty–look at the way she had changed parties to win the election! A perfectly good party member down the drain. What was the use of being mayor, even of a one-horse place like Sunshine, if she compromised her very soul by joining the others?

He wondered what idiotic notion she had in her head today. The last time he'd met with her, there had been a state-wide hootenholler when the city council banned dog poop on the city streets and lawns. Sunshine had been the laughingstock of Tally, and driven the tree-huggers crazy. If the council couldn't think up better ordinances than that, he'd told her, they should just dissolve themselves and give up. The city manager had enough sense to keep Sunshine going, and he'd never waste his time on dog shit.

They didn't really need a city council; look at the fools who were elected to run cities! Even though they had enormous powers, they didn't have sense enough to use them intelligently. Usually city pols got caught taking money under the table from some favor-seeking pissant and went to jail. A real bunch of amateurs, city councils. Not like those who ran the state, nosirree. In Tallahassee you had real pros, men of substance like himself–men of accountability whom the public could trust with the future of the state. A lot of money changed hands, sure, but it didn't hurt the public because they didn't know anything about it. Hell, politics was all about money. It wasn't as if you were selling yourself, taking money from special interests. The world of commerce wrote off the expense as a cost of doing business, politicians had more money and could devote more time to their jobs, and everyone was happy. He was putting all his kids through college with the proceeds brought by a few favors.

But Melba had thrown up her hands and said it wasn't her fault, it was Joe Tyler's idea and what was she to do? Said she was looked upon as an outsider still, even after living in Sunshine for twenty years. Then she'd started in on the old boy network.

The old boy network! What did she want in its place, an all girls' network? Women didn't belong in politics; they didn't have the stomach for deal-making. Further, they were mathematical idiots who could never understand the finer points of budgetary concerns. Women should stay at home, raise their children, and look after their husbands. That's what they were meant to do, otherwise God would never have made Eve from Adam's rib. The Baptists were absolutely right, insisting that women submit to their husbands. It was God's will.

His own wife, Annie, was a proper woman. She had home-schooled their five children, baked bread every day, and still kept the house filled with cookies and old fashioned taffy and fudge. Now that the kids were in college, she had time to catch up on reading those books she loved so much, those with that long-haired fellow on the front cover tearing off some woman's clothes. When he had asked her about the lurid covers, she explained that the books were classics. It gave him great pleasure to see her sitting on the couch in the family room, a glass of iced tea beside her, reading her little classics. "Annie," he had told her over the years, "you just wait till the children are in college, and you'll have the time to continue your education." She was, in that regard, his true soul mate; he believed in improving one's mind.

The only time his wife ever appeared in public, outside of prayer meeting every Wednesday night, church every Sunday, and household shopping, was when he had been made Speaker of the House back in 1988. Tradition had it that he share the limelight with his spouse, although he still couldn't see any reason for that. What had she ever done for the State of Florida?

His reverie was interrupted by Melba Tosti, who approached through the crowded restaurant slowly, smiling at everyone, patting shoulders. Fatigay shuddered. Did she kiss babies as well? He rose, pretending a gentility he didn't feel, and seated her opposite him.

"Must you wear that lime green wig, Melba?"

"What's wrong with it? It goes with what I have on."

"But it's lime green."

She leaned across the table and patted his cheek. "The color, Jackson, is chartreuse. What a dinosaur you are! Just remember, they were lime green too."

Fatigay winced at her condescending tone and looked heavenward. It was going to be a long lunch.

The waitress took their orders, then Melba settled back with a determined look in her eye. "I need a big favor, Jackson."

"What?"

"The council is determined to develop tourism. This town has got to grow. We're Florida's bald spot where development is concerned, and that needs to change. We need something to get folks into the city of Sunshine."

"You've got some sportfishing out of here; what more do you want?"

"A beach, Senator."

Fatigay gaped stupidly for a moment, then leaned back and roared with laughter, disrupting the chatter in the restaurant. He snuffed his mirth, nodded amiably at those diners whom he caught staring at him, then turned his attention to Melba's startling statement.

Just south of the Hatchacootee River with its muddy banks and delta lay the shining beaches of Heart County, envied by all of those who lived on the west coast of the state. And Heart County's multitude of citizens kept him in office. Melba must be mad to think he would help her provide competition to his home county. Wearing those wigs must have toasted her brain. "Where?"

"On the coast, of course."

"The coastline within the city consists of mud flats and estuarine marsh that you cannot be allowed to touch. The

Department of Environmental Protection would never permit such a thing, and you'd have the owl-lovers after your head all over again. Haven't you had enough of those people?"

"We've got a wide strand of mud out there at low tide. If we covered it well with beach sand, we'd have a beach instead." Melba resented his attitude. It was going to be hard, she knew, to persuade the old fool that something had to be done. Every time she heard him speak, he referred to the fact that he was elected by Heart County. It was almost as if Banter County didn't exist for him, even though he represented a third of the county and the whole of Sunshine.

"Yes, and then folks would walk into the water and sink into the mud."

"We'd have to put sand at least a quarter mile out into the gulf, otherwise the tide would take it away. If anyone wants to try walking on the bottom that far out, well, it's their lookout."

He wondered if she had any idea what such a scheme would cost. And what hell she'd bring down on Sunshine with such a harebrained idea. "Have you spoken with anyone in Tallahassee about this?"

"No, thought I'd run it by you first." Melba shook out her napkin as the waiter approached with their food. "I'm starving. Didn't have time for breakfast this morning."

"I would never do without breakfast," he said, patting his formidable gut. "Most important meal of the day, my mother always said."

"Your mother wasn't the mayor of a city. I simply don't have time to eat."

He ignored her comment. If she planned her day, she'd always have time for meals. Instead, she ran from meeting to meeting, visited children in classrooms, sat with the old folks for photo ops–her busyness was legendary. She never accomplished anything; she just ran.

That's probably why she's divorced, he thought. Because she was so busy chasing after votes, she never stayed at home to make breakfast,. He felt sorry for her ex-husband; the man must have been half-starved. And, no doubt, he was a martyr to vanity. It was commonly known that women who went into politics were extraordinarily vain.

He hastily cut into the pile of southern fried chicken that the restaurant did so well, then stuffed a large piece into his mouth. "Have you ever had this chicken?" he asked around the food.

Melba watched his greedy mastication with disgust. He attacked food as if it were a mortal enemy, she thought, as he snatched a biscuit from the basket and sent it after the chicken. Even though he and his best friend, Joe Tyler, lectured at every opportunity on the evils of excess, both were grossly overweight and ate everything on the table, right down to the parsley used to dress up the plate.

She despised Jackson Fatigay and his cronies. As a rule, they were ignorant and pompous. All were members of the Saved Sons Society, a so-called prayer group that touted keeping women in their places, wanted public whipping as a deterrent for infractions such as disobedience to parents, and advocated a return to making prisoners bondmen, sort of a legal slavery, which was supposed to solve the crime problem.

She had made up her mind to divest them of their hold on Sunshine. Retirees had a right to government like they had up north–responsible government, not a clique of good old boys who grabbed everything for themselves and cleaned the pockets of the retirees for their own benefit. The prices in the Stop N' Shop department store were proof of the native greed.

But she needed the Senator's pull in the state capital. He was enormously powerful, having catered for years to any lobbyist with a sackful of dollars to fill his bottomless pockets. And he was as dirty a campaigner as she'd ever seen. Even though no one stood a chance of beating him in a race, those who dared to try found their private lives picked apart, their reputations ruined by baseless innuendo.

Melba toyed with her salad. "Of course I've eaten the chicken; I don't always dine on frogs' legs. As much as I hate Lila Mae's airs and her awful drawl, the place makes great chicken. She has a good chef."

Fatigay laughed shortly. "Chef? Hellfire, Melba, you can't call Henny a chef. He learned cooking' back in the old days when folks knew how to cook. Chef? He'd be insulted." He snatched another biscuit and crammed it home. "He makes damned good fried mullet too, and some of the best barbecue in the world."

"Mmmm. What about our beach, Jackson?" she asked.

"Never talk business when you're eating, Melba. Makes you dyspeptic–that's what's wrong with the world today, too many 'power' meals."

Melba bit into a frog's leg and munched reflectively. "Of course, I know we couldn't get a beach right away, the environmental study and all that crap has to come first. But we need money for that, then next year, we might get somewhere in Tallahassee."

The senator looked at her long and hard, then attacked his salad, generously dousing it with ranch dressing.

"Wouldn't take more than a couple hundred thousand for the studies."

Through lettuce and red cabbage slices, he asked, "Who you plan to use?"

"Naturally, we'll put out bids, but Fyndar and Ramirez will get the business."

Fatigay nodded vigorously in the affirmative. "Good, God-fearing men. You couldn't do better."

Both of the consultants, whose fees far surpassed those of any other consultant in the county, were members of the Saved Sons Society, therefore snaring every city contract because they were "connected."

Melba relaxed somewhat. Perhaps he would be cooperative, after all. She sipped tea and watched as he slathered his fried potatoes with a combination of mustard and catsup, then began to devour them. "Well, if you think they can do the job–"

"Of course they can do the job! Who else is around that has their track record? If you want some special findings, Fyndar always comes up with them. There's no point paying good money for a consultant if he don't find what you want, is there? You certainly wouldn't want to hire those fools who feel they have to protect their good names." He leaned forward confidentially. "If you want to get ahead with your project, then you hire them. I have an arrangement with them." He looked around the room, spied the waitress, and waved her over. "Did you see that lemon pie when you came in?" he asked as the waitress threaded her way between the diners.

"No, I didn't have—"

"Right, you didn't. You were too busy politicking. Take my advice, Melba. Quit trying to be everybody's friend and look out for Number One. You ain't getting any younger, and you won't have a husband to take care of you when you get old." He beamed at the waitress, "Let me have a double order of that lemon pie, you sexy little sugar. Then you can tell the old senator your telephone number."

Melba cringed as the girl left them. "Jackson, you should be ashamed."

"What the hell, Melba. I'm just giving the girl a thrill. She needs one; she looks like a cow with the colic."

Meats Merlini proudly displayed the architect's rendering of the museum he wanted to have built in Sunshine. "So what do you think of the concept, huh? It's mind-boggling, right? That's the problem with most people, Sandfly, they don't have any imagination. Can you believe that most people go through their lives, eating all kinds of meat products, and never giving a damn about the history of meat?"

House Representative Henry "Sandfly" Bates looked at the drawing with a solemn face. "What's this sausage-shaped thing out in front?"

What the hell do you think it is, Sandfly? It's a bronze sausage sculpture, for chrissake. How can you have a museum dedicated to the history of meat without pointing out the importance of sausage in the history of mankind? "It's a sausage, Sandfly. Do you realize that over the history of man, every nationality has developed their own sausage? You got Spanish chorizos, you got liverwurst, bratwurst, all the German sausages, Polish sausages, English sausages. Even the southerners know about sausage; look at blood sausage and liver pudding. The Chinese got sausages, and the French got them too! The whole world lives for sausages, Sandfly."

"You're right, Meats, but my question is whether the vacationing public will give a hoot. If you were escaping the winter snows of Minnesota, would you come to Florida to visit a meat museum or would you go to Orlando to the Mouse? If you had a choice as a weekend tourist, would you prefer Busch Gardens or a museum glorifying the one thing vegetarians hate? Suppose the animal rights folks come down on you? They're all over Tallahassee this year." He threw back his head as if having a vision. "I can see it all now, picketers in the streets crying that the city of Sunshine advocates bloody slaughter of innocent animals who want nothing more than to munch on grass and lie under trees in the shade–normal, thinking animals who're our brothers, etcetera. Can you appreciate what I'm saying? The vegetarians would object to the thing, and their numbers are growing. What I'm trying to tell you is that the public interest angle seems to be missing."

Although he'd lived in Sunshine for the past quarter century, and had studied the humans who inhabited the little city, Bates could not understand how the citizenry chose to elect Meats Merlini to the city council. Merlini, for starters, was from Brooklyn.

And he was slightly mad. The man spoke of meat products as though they possessed souls, were sentient beings.

"Of course the public will be interested, Sandfly," Merlini insisted. "You remember that television show years back where they showed sausages being made, and sales plummeted? That's because folks didn't really understand what they were seeing. I remember some broad saying that she didn't know how I could eat my own products, for chrissake! The TV people went to a cheap outfit, is all. Making sausage is an art form." Merlini's hands and arms began to talk, Italian style. "First, you gently cut the fat from the skin. You gotta be careful not to bruise the fat, because you want it nice and plump, see? There's some stuff I make where I actually dice the fat by hand, can you imagine that? If the fat ain't right, the sausage ain't right." Merlini's stomach growled loudly in agreement.

"What's this?" Bates pointed to the drawing.

"That's the ancient history wing, where you have cave men chasing a mastectomy, or whatever they were called."

"They were called mastodons, and they still are. So cave men made sausages?"

Merlini looked thoughtful. "I don't know, because sausage don't leave no artifarts behind. But they prolly did; those big animals had plenty of guts for stuffing." His eyes opened wide in awe. "Can you picture the sausages they had from elephants? Think of the amount of meat that you have in an elephant, and the fat, and the size of the gut! You could make enough sausage to—oh, man, what a feast!"

Bates nodded and stifled a smile. "Things that are dug up are called artifacts, Meats. What's in this wing?"

"It's like a photo album with big pictures of the meat dishes that have been eaten through the centuries. You know, great standing rib roasts like the kings in England ate, then threw the bones to the dogs under the table. And some of the funny French dishes where they put lace drawers on perfectly good lamb. Man, the French are really weird! Bratwurst with sauerkraut, polish sausage with dumplings, steak with french fries, that kind of stuff."

"No hamburger?"

"Of course; you got to have hamburger. You crazy? And hot dogs with mustard and beer!"

"And what do you want me to do, Meats?"

"Well, the Legislature is in session now; that's why I had to see you today, because you're going to be gone for the next couple of months. I want you to run a little bill for us, get us the dough to build this thing. Maybe you could even go after some federal funding, or something like that. We got to put this town on the map, Sandfly."

"Perhaps I could try for a grant from the National Endowment of the Arts. You did say that sausage-making is an art form, didn't you?"

"Yeah. Great idea! Then you could really bring home the bacon." Merlini guffawed at his own wit.

"I'll make a deal with you, Meats. You bring me a resolution from the city council that they want this museum, and I'll see what I can do."

"You got a deal, buddy!" Merlini opened the door, then turned back to Bates. "Thanks again, Sandfly. I always knew you was a winner."

As Bates stared after Merlini's departing figure, he grinned. Meats would have one hell of a time getting a resolution, of that he was certain. The other council members would see right away that such an attraction, if one could call the thing an attraction, would never bring any attention to themselves. As far as he could make out, that was the reason that most of them had run for public office, to bask in imagined limelight.

Joe Tyler had his own agenda, that was true, but some of the others!

Merlini was right in one respect. Sunshine was a sad little place; there was absolutely nothing to do but fish or wander along the river banks and look at wading birds. Or residents could seek amusement in the Stop N' Shop, but Joe Tyler's emporium lacked a great deal. The town was a backwater even though it was located in a perfect spot for development.

Part of the reason Sunshine had never taken off was local politics. The races for public office were nasty in the extreme– either that or downright silly. Over and over, the city fathers made state-wide news with their infighting or their battles with citizens who were naive and expected good government. Until Frank Bonano had been hired after the last bunch of councilmen had gone to jail, the place had been a madhouse.

But he liked the little place; it was peaceful and, being on a river, relatively cool in the summer. He wanted to do something for Sunshine, but every time he brought up the subject in Tallahassee, he was laughed at. The state capital looked on Sunshine as a joke.

"I'm sorry, Merlini," he muttered, "your museum is one pig that will never fly."

"You got to help me, Lila Mae," Joe Tyler insisted. "You're one of us, you ain't some damned Yankee import that's come into Florida to try and make good."

They were seated beneath a tattered umbrella by a little fenced swimming pool just off U. S. Highway 15-B, the main road that led into Sunshine. About them, plastic pink flamingos at gravity-defying angles staggered across the mangy grass. Across the lawn, partially hidden behind oaks and curtains of Spanish moss, squatted the little cypress log shacks that made the Pink Flamingo Motel the favorite stopover for visiting fishermen who sought to drink with the boys and fish for grouper and snook from the city's six charter boats. There was even a fake outhouse with a sickle moon carved in the door to one side of the building marked "Office." The place was owned by another Saved Son, Tom Fellows. The only other motel on the highway was the Fisherman's Paradise, even more scrofulous than the Pink Flamingo.

Lila Mae's interest perked up considerably when a car drew up before the dilapidated blue building across the highway, the Sunshine Gentlemen's Club. "Do you recognize that car, Joe? Sure is a strange time of day to go to a house of ill repute."

"The place should be shut down and those sinners run out of town, Lila Mae. It's a disgrace to the city, that whorehouse. For the life of me, I can't see why we allow it to exist. Remember what the God Book says–"

"I always get a generous contribution to my campaign fund from Zona. Shoot, as far as I'm concerned, she's a good neighbor. Keeps the fishermen happy, prostitutes off the street, and her taxes are paid in full. Half the citizens of this town don't do as much for Sunshine. But then, being a woman, I guess I look at things different from you."

"Well, since you admitted it first, I get a big contribution from her too, every year. At first, I–I thought about returning the money, because it is literally the wages of sin, but Zona swore that it didn't come from her, and she's right in a way. I look at her money as coming from her customers, which is different. There's been a lot of noise at the church lately about them, but if we close her down, we'll lose a lot of the fishermen, so I persuaded them to leave it be for the sake of the city."

"I don't much care where my contributions come from, Joe," Lila Mae explained. "Now, did you ask me out here to talk about the Sunshine Gentlemen's Club, or was there something else on your mind?"

"Palm trees. I want to talk to you about palm trees."

"We're probably going to vote on this, Joe, and we'll be breaking the Sunshine Law talking about–"

"Sunshine Law be damned. We can't possibly be discussing anything out of the sunshine, because we live in Sunshine. I don't know why this city should pay out one thin dime for palm trees. We need to fix up some of the potholes in my area, and–"

"Teddy thinks it'll make Sunshine look more like, well, like tourists think Florida looks like."

"You mean if we plant palm trees, they'll think they're in Miami? I don't think so."

"To tell the truth, Joe, I wouldn't mind a few palm trees, as long as they don't cut down the oaks. I love oak trees. Palm trees don't have any moss."

"Where would they be planted? I certainly don't want any in my neighborhood. Our grounds committee would never allow such a thing."

"Probably along the waterfront, and maybe out here where folks will see them when they come into town. Might make them want to stay a little longer."

"We must stick together, Lila Mae, and teach that pervert a lesson. I know you were running short on your last campaign, and if you side with me on issues like these, I can make the pot a lot sweeter when you run again."

"Joe, I ain't like Zona's girls. I ain't for sale. Now, drop the subject and I'll try and forget that you tried to buy me."

"That's not so! You been hanging around Pervert too long, Lila Mae."

"Now, Joe, just because he's a little queer–"

"That's like being a little pregnant."

"You know what I mean. You think Her Majesty will go along with Teddy or with you?"

"If she knows what's good for her, she'll cooperate. The Saved Sons Society won't tolerate this Yankee nonsense much longer, and if she thinks–"

"Oh, my God!" Lila Mae's eyes were enormous. "Will you just look at that, Joe. It's Gavel Strike coming out of Zona's place. You suppose he and Kelsey are having a lovers' quarrel?"

"Maybe he went in there to hug a tree," Tyler quipped. Then he said darkly, "Guy Fawkins ought to stop the carrying on between those two. You'd think he'd get the message, with all the gossip about them. I read in the paper this morning that Strike and Kelsey are even planning a trip to Tallahassee this session. Kelsey Fawkins is a married woman, and the God Book says that adultery is a sin. It's one of the Commandments. Besides, the Judas is supposed to be Fawkins's best friend."

Strike paused before getting into his car and stared across the road at them, then he smiled and called, "Naughty, naughty. Remember the Sunshine Law. Are you two being bad?"

"There are times, Lila Mae, when I am sorely tempted to cancel my insurance with him. But I don't want to take my business into Heart County."

"I just hope he don't run his mouth, Joe," Lila Mae replied.

"You shut up!" Tyler bellowed. "Just remember we saw you come out of there, Mister."

"Gee, Councilman, even ladies of the night need insurance," Strike retorted.

CHAPTER THREE

Op/Ed				The Sunshine Bulletin				Page 6

EDITORIAL

COUNCIL MEETING MARRED BY SPATS

Responsible government took a back seat on Monday to shouts and name-calling. Ted Rainmaker lost his temper and stalked from the room while the Mayor, wearing a lime green wig, blissfully preened herself before the camera.

The in-fighting began immediately after the invocation, when the Mayor interrupted a private conversation between councilmen Merlini and Warner, who seem to believe that conversation out of the sunshine is fine as long as they are on the dais. The meeting went downhill from there.

When Rainmaker questioned another mistake by the city's attorneys, Councilman Tyler called Rainmaker a pervert and told him to keep out of city business.

Rainmaker is right in questioning what goes on in City Hall. Mistakes are routinely made in simple contracts by the city's lawyers, who are paid by the hour. Further, Brantley Fielding managed yet again to forget that he had a permit to build six single dwellings. Now that Fielding has erected a multistory condominium instead, his attorneys asked that the Council forgive the indiscretion.

This is the fourth time that Fielding has "forgotten" what his building permits allow. But rather than demanding straight answers, our councilmen again voted to gloss over the affair.

The firm of Slugge, Crawley, and Schyte, who represent the city, also represent Fielding. DeLeon Slugge calmed any thoughts of impropriety the council members might harbor by assuring them that he had built a Chinese wall around himself. According to him, there is no conflict of interest.

The city's ancient sewer system is disintegrating and badly needs replacing, but when City Manager Frank Bonano and

Utilities Director Dreyfus Odlum attempted to bring the subject before the council, Mayor Tosti began screaming that she did not want to discuss the subject. Is this responsible government?

Tosti also refused to hear an emergency brought by Bonano, even though the city is out of compliance with the state mandate for disaster management staff. If the mandate is not met by the tenth of March, which is the council's next meeting date, a heavy fine will be imposed.

Mayor Tosti ended the meeting without completing the agenda. This behavior, too, is becoming as commonplace as the city attorneys' mistakes and Fielding's flouting of the city ordinances.

Teddy Rainmaker stared at the front page of the local paper with disbelief. "PooPoo, this coverage is a disgrace. Why doesn't that fool of an editor jump on Tyler for his constant disruptions of our meetings? Every time we begin to discuss a topic, the Lord's hootenholler erupts into apocalyptic threats or misquotations from the Bible. I'd give anything to catch him in some violation of the law. By God, I'd hang the bastard."

Tarkington Pickles, known to all as PooPoo, looked up from his desk and brushed his salt-and-pepper hair from his eyes. "Now, Teddy, don't lose your temper. You've known from the day we moved here that you're dealing with cretins. Since the Tyler family and the rest of the Bible-babblers have lived here for three or four generations, they think they have Mayflower status."

"I'm getting a little tired of being referred to as a pervert."

"But, darling, you are a pervert and I love you for it. Honestly, Teddy, lighten up."

He looked fondly at Rainmaker, picturing him as he was on the day they met, over a quarter century ago. For him, it had been love at first sight. Even though Teddy was short, he had the lithe, muscular body of a dancer. And he was so assertive!

He had been sitting in a gay bar in Miami, drinking a margarita, when Teddy walked up and introduced himself. He'd been distant and retreated from Teddy's touch. He certainly didn't want this forward shrimp to think he was easy; he *hated* tarty men! At the same time, though, he had felt almost like swooning.

"You're mine," Teddy had said. "Now, tomorrow, and always. Got it?"

They had been together ever since.

Things had been tough in Miami because the mob controlled most of the nightclubs and restaurants, so after he had graduated from chef school, they'd decided to settle on the west coast. It had taken a while to build a clientele for his restaurant, Rain, but now folks came from far and wide to sample his delights. Everyone told him that he had a genius for mixing things– people, spices, decor. He adored what he was doing as much as he adored his partner for life.

"What are you working on?" Teddy asked.

"I want to do a new menu; this one's boring. I was thinking of a Caribbean and South Seas thing, lots of spicy meats and seafood, rice pilaf–something colorful."

"The present menu is quite popu–"

"I know, but I've noticed some of the folks from Heart County aren't coming as often and that usually happens when they get bored with the menu. It's been at least two weeks since their county commissioners have snuck away for a private confab. I've been meaning to ask you, Teddy, isn't that against the law?"

"What?"

"Their meeting over here to discuss business they're going to vote on."

"Of course it's illegal. The Sunshine Law forbids elected officials discussing business they're going to vote on outside publicized, formal meetings. But it's done all the time. Every time I bring up the law with Tyler, he pops back that we live in Sunshine, therefore everything we do is in Sunshine. He's so full of–"

"Did you have to mention him? I'm sorry I asked the question. Margie Noessit got anything good today?"

Rainmaker looked at the page opposite the editorial page. "Yes. She's writing about Melba's behavior with Frank Bonano, which is getting out of hand. I wonder what's behind her bitchiness?"

"I think she's got an itch that he refuses to scratch."

"She's older than he is by ten years, at least, Hon."

"Doesn't matter. Women don't get that nasty unless they've been spurned." He rose from his desk, took Rainmaker's hand, and led him through a curtain of wooden beads from the office into the restaurant proper. "I'm going to redo the main dining room. Found some fantastic wet-look vinyl that looks exactly like a stand of bamboo after a rain. I've ordered a dozen double rolls."

"Sure you won't be overdoing it?" Rainmaker looked fondly over the room, where groups of life-like *papier mach*é palms leaned gracefully over the tables, almost obscuring the ceiling. At the entrance, guests threaded their way through a defile between plastic boulders partially hidden behind rain forest flora. At the far end of the enormous room, a small waterfall plashed into a tropic pool. The walls exhibited stills from "Rain" starring Rita Hayworth, who played Sadie Thompson. Everything was understated, restful, fresh, even after so many years.

Their biggest enemy in the early days had been dust–paper and plastic seemed to create dust at an alarming rate. They had spent a small fortune on special filters and air conditioning when the dust mite phobia became popular with their feminine clientele. It had been a good investment; the air always smelled fresh and dewy. Women flocked to the place.

"No, Teddy. Leave it to me. The background of bamboo will actually emphasize the South Seas ambience. Besides, you know I adore interior decoration."

"You're changing the menu, you're redoing the decor. Do you intend replacing me as well?" Rainmaker kept his voice deliberately light.

"You silly savage!" PooPoo gave him a quick squeeze. "I've been thinking of opening up a little interiors shop across the street in the mall. There's an empty place there."

"Somehow, I can't see interior decoration taking off in Sunshine."

"Well, with that condo going up–"

Rainmaker grinned. "You're right, as usual. I can see our dear mayor now, decorating her place with all those hideous wigs she insists on wearing. She'll paint the walls hot pink, screaming green, and purple. And she could have special incense made to perfume her quarters–"

"Yes, essence of would-be-virgin garlic! Tyler would do his apartment in hair shirts," PooPoo laughed. "But his *piece de resistance* would be a tinsel cross over the mantel. I can see it now! Ghastly red orange velvet drapes with gold tassels at the windows overlooking the gulf. I'll do his bedroom in black and red to give him a foretaste of hell–"

"Merlini is certain to buy an apartment. He'll have large, plump leather sausages grouped around the fireplace, and sheep bladder bar stools–" Rainmaker had joined in the laughter now.

PooPoo threw an arm across Rainmaker's shoulders. "Darling, the Yankees are pouring into the state, the counties to the south are filled to the brim, and it's our turn. You just wait and see. Growth is going to hit Sunshine at last, and you and I will make a killing."

Suddenly, Rainmaker sobered. "Not if we don't have a beach."

Alvin McDonald indicated a chair in the small conference room at the newspaper office, then sat facing Kelsey Fawkins.

"You are in deep trouble with the powers that be," she remarked.

"Do you think I'll be drawn and quartered? I've had two phone calls from Madam Mayor, one from Joe Tyler, a real lulu from Teddy Rainmaker, and Meats is threatening to sue–says I accused him of breaking the law."

"I ran into Lila Mae at the Stop N' Shop, and she was ready to tear your hair out. Said that all she and Merlini talked about were ordinary things. Apparently he refers to all of us in the chamber as farts, and Lila Mae finds that offensive. She wants him to refer to us as 'poofs'."

"What are 'poofs'?"

"Apparently that's Lila Mae's nice word for farts." Kelsey removed a little notebook from her purse and put it on the table, then leaned back in her chair and smiled at McDonald.

Next to her husband, Guy, she considered Al McDonald the most attractive man in town. He reminded her of Robert Redford, short and sexy, with great blue eyes and hair she wanted to run her toes through. His prime attribute, however, was his delight in pulling the public leg. For years he had written a gossip column about the denizens of Sunshine under the pseudonym, Margie Noessit. Some of what he wrote was positively outrageous. But no one outside herself had ever figured out who Margie Noessit was–not even the publisher; all he knew was that Margie Noessit sold papers every week, and that helped advertising revenues.

"Do you have any idea what Merlini's new business was? Melba ended the meeting so abruptly that we didn't find out. And Merlini isn't talking. Told me to mind my own goddamn business or he'd make sausage of me." McDonald picked up his pencil and began tapping it.

"He certainly has become arrogant since being elected for a second term, hasn't he?"

"Arrogant, more intransigent, and a little crazier. The only thing that interests him is sausage, and he such a recluse, you have to wonder how the guy got elected in the first place."

"That's easy. He's peculiar, but he's all over the place selling his sausages, and his products are good, so folks like him. Says a lot for the average voter, doesn't it–electing someone because he makes good sausages. Gavel went to see him last week about renewing his liability insurance, and he caught hell about the affair he's supposedly having with me. I wasn't aware that such gossip was making the rounds."

McDonald grinned at Kelsey. He liked her; she was straightforward. But, like so many young women who had grown up on the west coast before the boom turned cypress swamps into tract housing, she was naive and still considered herself still surrounded by a loving and understanding extended family. Reality, he knew, was something quite different.

Guy Fawkins, her husband, was a born-in-the-bone environmentalist. But he was also an accountant and he knew that the locals looked down on environmentalists. He spent his weekends picking up roadside trash, or searching the mud flats along the Hatchacootee River for refuse that might harm wildlife, always dressed to disguise his identity. He encouraged Kelsey to take the public role of tree-hugger. She was the one who attended all the meetings, subscribed to the environmental journals, and when townspeople made snide remarks, he'd roll his eyes, shrug, and reply, "Women!"

"That gossip is actually quite old, Kelsey. I'd say it's been around for a good six months."

"How come I haven't heard it?" She looked as if she were really shocked.

"Do you expect Frank Bonano to come up and ask you if Gavel is good in bed?"

"If Gavel ever took anything to bed, it would have to be an endangered species. Sometimes—"

"I can see the headlines now, 'Gavel Strike caught in *flagrante delicto* with bald eagle!'"

Kelsey relaxed somewhat and sighed. "Poor Gavel, he's so serious about the environment. He spends all his time worrying about the increasing lack of biodiversity. I get a lecture every time we drive anywhere together. He says that even man is endangered now. And speaking of endangered species, he gave me a tidbit to pass to you relating to our city fathers. Maybe Margie Noessit could have some fun with it." She took a sheet of paper from her notebook and handed it to McDonald, who quickly read it.

"What is this?"

"Zona gave it to Gavel. She didn't want to be seen consorting in public with someone as shady as an editor. It's a list of all the donations she's made to the city council members and people like Jackson Fatigay during the last three elections. Told Gavel they really put the bite on her. She's been told to shell out or get out."

"Joe Tyler takes money from her? And Senator Fatigay? Even Lila Mae? I'll be damned."

"Yes, all of them. I was really surprised by Joe Tyler. You'd think that, being the richest man in town, he'd lay off hard-working ladies of the night. Talk about hypocrisy."

"What about Sandfly Bates?"

"Zona says he and Rainmaker are the only honest ones in the whole bunch. Never asked her for a dime."

Al jumped up and gave Kelsey a bear hug. "Thank you, sugar pie! Now get out of here so I can concentrate on making this public."

"To tell the truth, Frank, I haven't a clue where to go from here. No matter what I do, nothing seems to work." Mary Lee Mince, Sunshine's tourism guru, held her breath in anticipation of what Frank Bonano's right hand might do.

During each meeting of the council, she sat across the room from him and watched his right hand go through it's ritual. As it unconsciously checked the knot in his tie, his shirt front, patted his jacket, then rose and smoothed his hair, she could almost feel that same hand caressing her face, her hair, her–she shook herself and forced her mind to the subject at hand.

"Mary Lee, you have the most thankless job in the city administration. How you're supposed to conjure up tourists outside sport fishermen, I don't know. Maybe we could persuade the county commissioners to let us use their sewage treatment ponds as fishing holes so we could start some eco-tourism?" He tilted back his chair and gazed at the ceiling. "Tell you what." He thumped back to an upright position. "Get me some prices on palm trees. Price a couple of kinds, like royal palms and coconut palms, you know what to do. Then prepare a report and you can give it to the council at the meeting next week."

"I had an idea, Frank, that I'm not sure–" She looked at the floor. "I–"

"Speak up, woman."

He wondered what kind of man would appeal to Mary Lee. She was mousy in an attractive way that really turned him on, rather like a Julie Andrews with no makeup. She was efficient when she had something to do, and normally she handled people well. But when she was in his presence, she quivered like a bow string when an arrow is released. Did he scare her? He tried not to. Tried to be gentle and polite, like he was with everyone, but the gentler he got, the harder she quaked. It wasn't a noticeable shake, like the DT's, but a shake nonetheless. Could she be attracted to him? Did he dare explore the possibility? After all, she was a city employee and you just didn't mess around where you worked.

"I've been thinking that we might start something–a festival of some kind. Since we don't have anything but fishing, what about a snook catching contest or a prize for the biggest grouper during festival week. It's not much, but what do you think?"

"Before we put it before the commission, we have to come up with some snappy name, and contest rules, all that crap. You know how they are; they couldn't think a problem through and make pertinent suggestions if their lives depended on it. Give me a good name, outline the idea, and we'll take it from there."

"I'll get some back issues of fishing mags and see how to structure a festival. It certainly isn't an original idea, but then, we don't really have much to work with." She sighed mightily. "I wish we had a beach."

"Melba the Mayor hinted to me just this morning that she had spoken with Senator Fatigay about just that project. She's sure the senator will come up with the money in Tallahassee this year." Bonano's hand leaped to its routine at the mention of the mayor.

Mary Lee wondered about that; his tic never exhibited itself when he was engaged in private conversation. She wondered if the poor darling found his job unbearably stressful, and she yearned to give comfort. Emboldened, she leaned closer. "Frank, there's nowhere to put a beach. We can't even have a river beach because of environmental concerns. Remember when that old man, Flossul, tried to put in some sand in front of his place so he could wade out and fish without going up to his waist in mud? The Department of Environmental Protection and the water management district came down on his head. The man paid a small fortune fighting them in court, lost, and then he had to pay for the cleanup of the sand. I shudder to think of what would happen if Sunshine were to–"

"Madam Queen is of the opinion that the entire gulf coast that's within the city limits can be turned into a shining white strand that will result in a blizzard of tourist dollars. She thinks Fatigay can fix it all. Personally, I don't think the senator is capable of buttoning his shirt without help. But that's my opinion; people in Heart County keep putting him in office."

"What color wig is she wearing today?"

"Hot pink. She was wearing a new suit visible from a mile away. When she came into the office, I damn near called the fire department."

The telephone rang and Mary Lee jumped, then rose to leave. Bonano motioned for her to remain, but she shook her head. "You're busy. I'll keep you informed."

"Call me any time," Bonano said softly. She looked back at him and blushed when he winked. Whistling softly between his teeth, he reached for the telephone as it again demanded his attention.

It was the mayor. "I want you to come to the house this evening, Frank. I have some city business to go over with you and I–"

"Madam Mayor, I have told you before that I think it unwise for me to come to your home after hours. We have your reputation to consider, and furthermore–"

"Since when did you give a damn about my reputation?" she snarled.

"Since the day you were elected mayor, Melba. What's the business you want to discuss? I can go into it right now. Want me to come to your office?"

"I–no, I have an appointment in about fifteen minutes and won't have the time. Come on, Frank, bend a little. This is important."

"Then tell me what it is so I can familiarize myself with it, and we can talk tomorrow." He stared at the ceiling, wondering how many times they gone through this charade. Melba had once thrown her arms around him at some public celebration and then groped him. He'd been shocked; the woman was his senior by at least fifteen years. Then, one evening, he'd had to go to her place to deliver some papers and he'd ended up actually fighting her off. It had not helped his relationship with her.

"One of these days, Frank, you'll be sorry," she said in a tight voice.

"Madam Mayor, as an employee of the city, I am entitled to a private life. I intend to keep it that way, and will never do anything which might compromise you. Okay?"

"Bastard!" she spat. The line went dead.

Gavel Strike tidied the papers on his desk, put them in a file folder, and looked sternly at the senator. "You have to appreciate the damage that so much sewage can do to the Polychaete worms, Senator."

"To what?"

"Polychaete worms."

"I have District 32 to worry about–one of the most fractious districts in the State, this is an election year, and you want to waste my time talking about some damned *worms?*"

"Senator, I don't think you realize how vital they are to the food chain of endangered species! Our wildlife is going to disappear if this filth at the mouth of the Hatchacootee is allowed to continue. Man, Sunshine is dumping crap into the estuary and you don't even care." He glared as the senator looked at him over his half-glasses.

Scrawny, bug-eyed, round-headed ass! Fatigay disliked Gavel Strike intensely, detested everything he espoused. Strike was so weird that he even had square eyebrows!

Every time the word "environment" was spoken, he pictured Strike bound to an oak tree, passionately defying the homeowner who planned to remove the tree from his yard. The incident had made every paper in the state. Police had to remove him by force and threaten him with a serious jail sentence to keep him out of the man's yard.

But Strike was the only insurance agent in Sunshine, and it was easier to keep his private business in a backwater than to risk possible gossip about his net worth in Heart County, his home and most important constituency. He was forced to deal with the idiot.

"How do you know they're dumping into the estuary?"

"By walking along the river bank. The smell of raw sewage is overpowering."

"You contacted the utilities director about this?"

"You know the mains are rotten."

"I *don't* know that the mains are rotten, and I don't care. Nor do I know the utility man; I avoid people like him. As far as I'm concerned, utility directors are very strange people; look at the stuff they deal with. And as a state senator and a resident of Heart County, I–" Fatigay stopped himself in mid-sentence. There was no point arguing with madmen. He resorted to his usual attack stance. "Speaking of sewage, isn't it time you and that Fawkins woman stopped your scandalous affair? It's an abomination in the sight of the Lord, and furthermore–"

"What are you talking about?" Strike's voice was rising.

"Oh, you don't know what I'm talking about, is that it? Well, let me give you a hint. Adultery is a sin, young man."

"Who is committing adultery?"

"It's common knowledge that you and the Fawkins wo–"

"That's a damned lie!" Strike shouted, leaping to his feet. "How dare you even suggest such a thing? Guy Fawkins is my best friend!"

"All the more reason to stop your disgraceful behavior. You can protest until you're blue, but where there's smoke, there's fire, Strike. This talk has been ongoing for at least half a year. Don't try to pretend you haven't heard it, and don't play innocent. You are not a convincing liar."

Gavel Strike looked as if he might burst. "Get out, Fatigay. If you want to take your business with you, that's fine. But if I hear of your spreading this rumor, I'll–"

Fatigay's eyebrows shot upward. *"I spread a rumor?* Don't be silly, you're not running against me." He ponderously rose to his feet and left Strike's office, closing the door gently after him.

As the senator strolled back to his Lexus, he pondered environmentalists. What was wrong with those people, he wondered, that they should concern themselves with the safety of worms, the life style of the birds, the social mores of dung beetles? Was the upcoming generation completely mad?

Technology was probably the criminal in this aberration among humans, he thought. Television dulled the senses and computers loomed as a mortal enemy. They could think; he was convinced of that. Too much was changing too fast and, human nature being what it was, the changes were driving people crazy. Folks could sense that sooner or later, the machines would take over. Man, God's proudest achievement would become the drooling slave to an electronic monster. Yes, that must be the answer. Folks were going mad. How else could any sane person explain a Gavel Strike?

CHAPTER FOUR

Melba Tosti stopped in the entrance of Rain and peered into the room. It was mid-afternoon and she was surprised to find four customers from out of town. One of the men looked at her and then turned quickly away, shaking with obvious laughter. The others turned to see what he found amusing. Melba's hands automatically went to her head to see if her wig was straight. It was. She resented the man's mirth. If she wanted to wear wigs rather than wasting time on her thin, straight hair, it was nobody's business but her own. And no one laughed if a woman wore a hat to match her outfit, did they? Hell no, they didn't.

There were times when she regretted having moved to Florida. Were she in New York, she could have walked into the room naked and no one would have noticed. But down here in the sticks, well-dressed, good-looking women drew rude stares. Why didn't they stare at the old fogies who wandered around in baggy shorts, flip-flops, and faded tee shirts?

She looked around curiously. It had been a while since she'd been here; she couldn't take PooPoo's la-di-dah. He was certain he was adorable and he just *loved* fussing over people. It was enough to make one ill. The sad thing was, everyone ate up that artsy-fartsy crap. His year-round clientele would have pleased the Four Seasons; he really packed in the customers.

She did like the ambience, though. The place genuinely looked like a slightly seedy South Seas eatery–at least what Hollywood had portrayed as the genuine article. The palms were nice and the fake boulders that one walked around to get into the restaurant proper were great. She almost expected Johnny Weismuller to swing in from the ceiling and dive headlong into the little pool at the back of the room.

Perhaps she should have called Teddy. Maybe coming to the restaurant wasn't a good idea after all. But it was too late to change her mind.

"Melba, darling!" PooPoo had come in from the kitchen, spotted her, and came hurrying across the room blowing kisses. "Whatever brings you here? Come for a taste of my new chicken dish? It is good; I'm using Pinot Grigio and rosemary. The two together are absolutely *divine!* Of course, I hate using such a good wine for cooking, but it simply makes the dish. I tried a Gewurtstramminer, but it was just not right. Do you know Gewurtstramminer?"

"Wasn't he executed as a Nazi war criminal?" Melba smiled and edged deeper into the room, drawing PooPoo away from the diners. One never knew when someone from out of town had local contacts. "I need to see Teddy. Is he around?"

"He's at the house. Want me to call him?"

"Yes, please, it is important, and I don't dare go to the house–your neighbors might see me."

"Well, what if they do?"

"I–well–I'd rather meet Teddy in a public place. That way, if we're seen talking, it will look like a casual encounter rather than a–never mind. I'd just like for him to come over as soon as possible."

"Darling, how stupid of me. You're talking about that silly law they named after our town. Don't you worry; I won't breathe a word." He tripped to the cash desk and picked up the phone, quickly dialing the number. "Teddy, can you come over right now? Melba is here and wants to talk with you. Okay, 'bye, love." To Melba he called, "He'll be here in about ten minutes. Can I get you something to drink, or a bite to eat?"

Melba smiled over her shoulder as she headed toward the back of the room. PooPoo caught up with her. "If you don't mind, I'll sit here near the pool and wait. Yes, I'd love a glass of white wine–some of the Pinot Grigio will do just fine."

At the front of the room, the diners rose to leave.

"Excuse me for a moment, darling, and let me get these folks on their way."

Melba sat and stared into the pool at the base of the little waterfall. She should have arranged this meeting in Heart County, away from prying eyes. The commissioners from Heart met regularly here at Rain for their *sub rosa* conferences. But then, Teddy was so damned stubborn he probably wouldn't have agreed to meet her out of town. He'd bitch about breaking the law, but that was meaningless. She had to have someone to back her idea, and there was no one else on the council she could trust. Teddy might posture, but he wouldn't snitch.

If the two of them could find another vote, she'd get her beach. They wouldn't dare approach Merlini, he was too crazy to be trusted. You never knew what the man would do next. Lila Mae Warner was too stupid to see the enormous growth and prosperity that a beach would bring to Sunshine. All she ever spoke of was how her mother could remember Sunshine as a crossroads with two stores, and wasn't it marvelous that they now had a Piggly-Wiggly Food Store instead of having to cross the river to the strip-mall infested stretch of U. S. 15-B that ran the length of Heart County. Besides, she was a native Floridian who longed for a return to the days before the state was developed.

Joe Tyler wasn't even a possibility. She did wish she had something to hold over Joe. Surely the sanctimonious jerk had done *something* illegal in his life. So far, she'd been unable to discover his Achille's heel, but she would never quit trying. Knowledge was power.

Teddy was another matter. She'd hired a private detective to do a run-down on him. The man found that Teddy was a silent partner in a number of local enterprises that disqualified him for voting on almost every matter that came before the council. Of course, he never recused himself. It was all PooPoo's idea, Teddy's putting forth financial tentacles, but PooPoo should have had enough sense to put the holdings in his name instead of Teddy's. Still, culpability had its uses.

"Teddy," she'd said after a council meeting last year, "how did you have the gall to vote on Fielding's building permit change when you own part of his business?

He had gone so white she was afraid he'd have a heart attack, but that passed quickly. He stammered and stuttered about all kinds of crap, but she'd put out her hand to stop his speech. "I will never say a word, friend. Just remember that when I ask you a favor."

"You unutterable bitch!" he had replied.

But that was a year ago. Now she and Teddy got on beautifully, with just an occasional clash of egos. All it had taken was a little understanding.

PooPoo came back to the table carrying a bottle of Pinot Grigio, two glasses, and a small plate of cheeses. He set them on the table, opened the wine, then went back for the chiller. Then he sat. "I do hate white wine that isn't chilled properly, don't you, darling?"

Melba flashed him a smile, then sipped from her glass. "Absolutely."

She wouldn't know properly chilled wine if it was poured over that ridiculous hot pink wig she was wearing, he thought. The wig fought her pink and yellow flowered dress and he wondered fleetingly if she might be color-blind. But his knowledge of Melba overruled the thought; she just didn't have any taste.

He considered the mayor monumentally ugly, with her hard little brown eyes and enormous nose with the mole on the left nostril. Why didn't she have the mole removed?–in fact, why didn't she have a nose job and a new face and be done with it? But her mouth was her worst feature. Her lips reminded him of veal liver–brown-pink, slick, and glistening. He *hated* liver! When she spoke, her mouth slimed across her lower face like some pernicious leech. Bela Lugosi should have had such a mouth; it was made for vampires.

She did have a good figure for her age, he had to give credit for that. But what good was a nice body if your head needed a bag over it? He had heard that she was divorced and he really couldn't blame the guy. What must it be like to wake up each morning beside that nose and mouth? Did she wear those awful wigs to bed? Maybe she had one made up with rollers in it, or pin curls.

He watched as Melba again raised the glass to her horrible lips, and shuddered delicately when he noticed that her pinky was straight up in the air. *Why* didn't people who lived public lives read a book on etiquette? The fact was, the creature had no class.

"Naughty you, you haven't tried the cheese, and it is divine."

"I'm watching my cholesterol." Melba glanced at her watch. "Teddy's taking his own sweet time."

"He might have had to dress. I encourage him to take a little nap in the afternoon; he works so hard."

"Yes," Melba said cattily, "he does have lot of business interests, doesn't he? I'm surprised that he has time to serve on the council, he's so involved in business. I thought that was supposed to be your forte."

PooPoo was modest. "I do advise him from time to time."

"So where did you two get the money to start this restaurant?" Melba asked bluntly. "Bank loan?"

No class whatsoever! "Well, I did dabble in the stock market rather successfully," he replied. "And Teddy was in real estate in Miami during the boom. He did quite well."

"Still play the market?"

"I have a modest portfolio."

Her teeth ached from having to carry on polite conversation with PooPoo; she was accustomed to aggression. His modest portfolio! Since her divorce from Antonio, she lived in greatly reduced circumstances. She had been forced to trade her beloved Jaguar for a car that cost less to maintain. That had really hurt; the Jag had made a statement about who she was, but the ensuing years had dulled the pain. She was still bitter about having to scrimp, though. It savaged her pride.

Recently, Teddy had told her of Fielding's plans to build the condominium, and arranged for her to have first choice of the units if she'd go along with the zoning change. As the house she rented was a dinky retirement hovel with only two bedrooms, she had finally made herself sell some of her jewelry to make a down-payment on one of the apartments. Top floor, of course, with a small roof garden and a marvelous view. At last she would live in something befitting the mayor of an up-and-coming city.

Her thoughts were interrupted by Rainmaker's arrival from the kitchen. She was relieved that he'd come in the back way–suppose some of the nosebodies saw him come in the front entrance after seeing her enter the restaurant. Damn the Sunshine Law; it made doing back room deals so difficult!

"Sorry I took so long; there's a traffic jam on 15-B. Some idiot turned left from the right lane and about eight cars are piled up there." He slumped into a chair. "Got another glass, hon? I'm in need of sustenance."

PooPoo rose and ruffled Rainmaker's hair, then went to the bar to fetch a glass.

"What's up, Melba?"

"I had lunch with the senator after the meeting the other day, and he's agreed to see about funding a study to turn our mud flat into a beach. Isn't this exciting?"

"No, it's not. In the first place, the beach was my idea and you stole it. Why don't you wake up and get some ideas of your own, Melba? I'm tired of doing all the thinking." Rainmaker's voice was sharp. "Secondly, you just had to talk with Fatigay, didn't you? Know what he'll do? He'll go straight to the commissioners in Heart County, tell them all about your little plan, and they'll laugh themselves silly, put their lobbyists to work, kill any funding for a study, and that will be the end of it. You and your bi–!"

Melba bridled. "What the hell did you expect me to do, go to Tallahassee myself? I am not accustomed to begging for money. It's hard enough to ge–"

"I expected you to have sense enough to keep quiet until we figure out a way to let Tally know we're serious. But no, you have to go and preen yourself before the Great Blowhard from Heart County. Had to show him what a big shot you are! The way you're going about it will abort the entire thing." Rainmaker was almost shouting.

PooPoo hurried across the room making soothing noises that did nothing to quell Rainmaker's temper. He poured a glass of wine and handed it to his lover, then quipped, "Get Joe Tyler and his group to work on it. You know they hate abortion."

Rainmaker laughed shortly. "Not a bad idea. At least he'd have sense enough not to blab to Heart County. Are you on the take from them?"

"I resent that!" Melba half-rose, thought better of it, and sat down again. "No, I'm not, but I have to find some way to make more money, Teddy. You're going to have to cut me in on some of your deals."

"Tough shit about your finances. Maybe Zona could use some expert advice."

"You smug bastard! Men make me sick." She controlled her fury with effort. No point alienating her one ally. "So let's hear your great plan." She crossed her arms and leaned back in her chair.

"What great plan are you talking about, Melba?"

"What we have to do first about the beach."

"That's obvious. First, we have to see if the tide will let beach sand stay there."

"And how do you propose to do that?"

"By taking several truckloads of sand down there, spreading it around a little, and watching to see what happens."

Melba, eyes squinted as though sand were being blown through her mind, tapped her wine glass. "Could I have a refill on this?"

PooPoo filled the glass and sat gingerly, unaware that he was holding his breath. He did hope they wouldn't quarrel. It would just ruin Teddy's mood for the rest of the day.

"Where you going to get the sand?"

"From Fielding, who else?"

"Of course, your partner in crime. Suppose someone sees him, then what?"

"No one is going to see him, he's dumping tonight. Everyone will be at dinner–not an environmentalist in sight. And if he does get caught, DEP will make him clean it up. Big deal. But we have to know whether a beach can live there."

"I hate to admit it, Teddy, but you have a point," Melba conceded. Her pinky rose as she picked up her wineglass.

PooPoo shuddered.

"Amen!" Joe Tyler opened his eyes and surveyed the "club room" at the Fisherman's Paradise Motel, where the Saved Sons Society met weekly to call upon God to do their bidding. They begged damnation for all those who had offended, and discussed local items that needed their attention.

It was a scruffy room in need of refurbishing. Green and purple flowered wallpaper at the far end rendered almost invisible a dilapidated sofa that had been navy blue. At the other end of the room, above the large round wooden table and mismatched chairs, a cross of driftwood, a gift from the Hatchacootee River, leaned drunkenly outward from the wall.

Their membership was small, fifteen altogether, but select. As Joe Tyler was fond of saying, the God Book plainly stated that many were called but few were chosen.

"I wish there was some way we could run that damned Al McDonald out of town, Joe," said Tom Fellows, who owned the Pink Flamingo Motel. "He's got no right accusing you of breaking up them council meetings."

"I don't worry about McDonald; he's small stuff. Besides, tourists think that if a town has a paper, it's got some substance. What we need to do is rid this city of all iniquity, and I believe that God has shown me the way to get rid of all those low-lifes who live down at Mosquito Row."

"At the last meeting, Pervert Rainmaker brought up one of his idiotic ideas; he wants to buy palm trees to make Sunshine look more like Florida. We live in Florida, and he's worried that visitors won't think they're in the state unless they see some palm trees!" Joe's expression grew crafty. "But, if the city buys that land in Mosquito Row and turns it into a park or something, then we can run all those immigrant types out of town. There will be no more greaseballs in Sunshine. So maybe we need some palm trees after all."

"Don't you own most of that land, Joe?" Ferdy O'Doole, proprietor of the Fisherman's Paradise Motel, took a cheap cigar from his shirt pocket, bit off the end, and began to light it.

"Yeah, I own a fair amount, but I lease out most of it. All those cheap rental units that Fielding put up are built on leased land."

"How you going to get out of the lease?"

"What can any man do if the city condemns his property?" Tyler asked, his expression injured innocence. He shrugged. "Besides, Fielding owes me a few."

"But then where will all the poor folks live?" Fellows inquired. He waved away the cigar smoke that threatened to engulf him.

"The whole point of taking over the land, Tom, is to move them out of Sunshine for good."

"Shit, Joe, if you get rid of all the immigrants, who'll do the housework and baby-sitting? You got to have that type in town to serve everybody else. Want all them working mothers to come down on your ass?" O'Doole took the cigar from his mouth, licked it, and stuck it back between his lips. "Almost half the working population of the town depends on having their kids watched by someone from down there."

"Well, we could put up some trailer park outside the city limits for 'em," Tyler conceded. "I just don't want that type of folks in the town where I live. I want to be able to sleep clean at night, not have to worry about being surrounded by sin."

"Who else owns land down in that area?"

"I think Pervert owns some, and we can find out who owns the rest." Tyler looked up as Rufus Hicks came into the room. "Evening, Rufus. You off duty?"

Chief Hicks pulled out a chair and dropped into it. "Yeah, just got off."

"You keeping up the raids on Mosquito Row?"

"Joe, I'm doing as much as I can to make it look like there's trouble down there, but we got real crime to deal with too, and you got to understand that."

Tyler reared back. "Real crime? What kind of crime?"

"Hell, old man down on Monroe Street took a shovel and beat his wife in the head with it. He's senile and she ain't much better, but her head is really in a mess now. What are you boys up to?"

"We're talking about making a park out of Mosquito Row when the city condemns the land," Fellows explained.

"If the city condemns the land, how you going to get a decent price for it?" O'Doole asked curiously. "You know how tight the city is—well, I mean, where's the money coming from?"

"We can raise the money, don't worry. Probably have to cut Melba in for a few percentage points, but if we agree to do that, she'll get it through. Slugge, Crawley and Schyte will handle everything and make sure we don't get gypped. They pretty much do what I tell them, anyway. Slugge knows what side of his bread has butter."

"Yeah, but with that pervert, and the looney, you're going to have a hard time convincing the council that they ought to condemn the land," Ferdy O'Doole drawled. He sucked again on his cigar.

Tyler scratched his head. "You know as well as I do that if we pay Melba off, she'll do anything. I mean, anybody who will switch parties just to get elected will stoop however low you need them to go. I'm pretty sure I can get Lila Mae to go along with it; she's local. You know what she does?" He slapped the table for emphasis. "She takes campaign contributions from Zona Flores and her girls!"

"What?" Fellows turned to O'Doole. "How about blowing that stinkweed in the other direction? How you know she takes money from the madam?"

"She told me the other day when we were at Tom's place."

"I'll be damned! You wouldn't think a southern lady like Lila Mae would touch dirty money."

"I was shocked myself," Tyler admitted, his eyes downcast. "There is no end to abomination. You know, maybe the church should pick up a few lots down at Mosquito Row. I understand there's two or three for sale. Make a nice addition to the building fund when the condemnation goes through. Those two just this side of the Lightning Bug Bar would fetch a nice price."

"Shit, I might just pick them up myself, make a profit, and give some of the money to the church. I can always use the extra tax deduction." O'Doole scratched his ankle, took a last puff on his cigar, and ground it out in the cheap astray on the table.

"Well, let's keep this to ourselves, fellows," Fellows suggested. "Ain't no sense spreading too much joy around. Not where money is concerned."

"Amen!" Tyler intoned. "If we ain't careful, the Yankees are going to take over the town. Won't be anything left for an honest man."

Frank Bonano leaned back in his chair and stretched. "I'm tired of problems, Oddman. Just when I think I've got most of the albatrosses off my neck, Sandfly Bates calls me about sewage at the mouth of the Hatchacootee. And he's truly hot about it. No wonder they call him Granola. Said Strike has had the water checked and it's real high in E coli and all those other niceties. We got *another* leak?"

"Yeah," Dreyfus Odlum answered in his most funereal voice. "The lines are too old, and after that last bad rain, four more of them cracked little. I had them patched."

"Apparently the patch isn't working. I know we need new sewer lines; we need a whole new system, but where the hell is it going to come from?"

Odlum slumped into a chair and sighed. "How do I know? You heard Melba the other day. She doesn't want to hear about it! What's wrong with that damned woman, Frank?"

"She needs a roll in the hay."

"Jee-sus! Can you imagine making love to that? I don't know what to do. If I up the rates to pay for improvements, and it's going to cost a bundle, believe me, the old folks will go to city hall and raise hell about how they can't afford it, then the city fathers come down on my neck and drop the rates again. Hellfire, the retirees can afford to travel to New Orleans to gamble, how is it they can't afford to clean up their own mess? I had that old bat, Norma Schliken, in my office yesterday. She was going on about how she's starving because of the utilities rates, and how if they don't get lower, she's going back to Michigan. I was real tempted to tell her where Highway 15-B is." He jumped to his feet and began to pace, agitated. "We got nineteen million people in this state now. You know how much sewage they create every day? What are we supposed to do with all this crap, drown in it?"

"Calm down, Oddman, I'm not blaming you for this."

"I know you aren't, Frank, but dammit, I'm up to my eyes in shit and don't have a straw to breathe through. Where is the money going to come from to rebuild the sewer system? You hold your breath until those tightwads on the council agree to float a bond issue, and you'll be older than King Tut before you can ever breathe again. They don't give a damn about the city, all they care about is staying in office."

"Hey, you're getting worked up about this; stop it. I don't want to call 911 and tell them to put you on a gurney." He chewed his lip. "I'll talk with Melba, see if she won't approach the matter in her usual delicate manner. Why don't you speak with your lady love?"

Bonano usually resisted the urge to tease Odlum, who had yearned fiercely for the affections of Lila Mae ever since high school. But Odlum, painfully shy, had never found the nerve to confess his passion. He had wept when Lila Mae married a man much shorter than she was.

As much as he liked Odlum–the guy was honest and easy to work with–he did wonder if Lila Mae would have repulsed her admirer. Odlum was six feet, seven inches of gloomy countenance. His face was more Coleman lantern than human, and his awkward, lurching gait reminded folks of Frankenstein's monster.

"You keep Lila Mae out of this. She's a lady, Frank, a real lady. You don't talk shit with a lady!"

CHAPTER FIVE

Local/County   The Sunshine Bulletin   Page 1A

THE WAGES OF SIN
by Margie Noessit

Most of our City Council members are the worst kind of hypocrites. Heaven forbid! said I when I received proof; but it is true. Believe it or not, these goings-on in Sunshine are inspired by Shakespeare. Talk about a pound of flesh! It would seem that the stellar leaders of our fair city have been plunging their greedy little fingers into the profits of our local fleshpot.

During the last three elections, our city fathers have bitten Zona Flores for over eighteen thousand smackeroos. Yes, eighteen of the big ones. And you'll never guess the winner of the Extortion Award. Our mayor, Melba Tosti, has hit up the ladies of the night for a whopping seven grand. No wonder her wig wardrobe increased.

Next in the award lineup is Josephus (Holy! Holy! Holy!) Tyler, who received six thousand. Sunshine's department store tycoon, leader of the Saved Sons Society, and pillar of the Living Witness Holy Confederation is always hot on the scent of corruption, but leaning on the members of our oldest profession is apparently okay. What do you want to bet that none of the lolly ever found its way into a collection plate?

Third in at the gate is Gianni "Meats" Merlini, who stuffed two thousand, seven hundred into his sausage casings. Could it be the girls weren't eating enough of his product?

Running last, as always, is Lila Mae Warner, who took a mere twenty-three hundred over the years. Get the message, Merlini? The Sunshine Gentlemen's Club prefers southern fried chicken to bratwurst. Chickens don't eat so much of the green stuff.

"I don't think it's fair," Zona said recently in an interview. "Whoring ain't easy work and my girls is good girls and they work hard. What the councilmen take comes out of their earnings. I got the message loud and clear–if we don't pay up, they'll close us down. You'd think that the ladies, at least, would have some compassion for their sisters, but it ain't so."

The only councilman who isn't on the bread wagon is Theodore Rainmaker. I asked Zona why.

"Well, Teddy's different. I guess, being as different as he is, he don't consider whores as easy pickings."

Perhaps it's time for our citizens to wake up to the fact that this city is run by a clique of money-grubbing, power-mad yo-yo's who should never be given any job as responsible as dog-catcher.

Who will they hit when next they seek election–the halt, lame, and blind?

"I am going to kill whoever wrote this," Lila Mae declared. "I swear, I'm going to find out who Margie Noessit is and strangle her. Saying I ran last, *as always*. She's got some nerve!"

Her husband, Henny, looked up from the comics section of his *Tampa Tribune*. "What's it about?"

"Our taking campaign contributions from Zona," his wife explained patiently. She avoided looking directly at him at breakfast; mornings were not Henny's best times. His hair poked up here and there on his little balding head like broken reeds, and his normally florid complexion was pallid and pockmarked. Hunched over the table in his oversized bathrobe, peering nearsightedly at the newspaper, he reminded her of an armadillo.

When they had been courting, the only way she could look into his eyes was by sitting or lying down. He was a good half foot shorter than she was. Of course, right after her marriage, she'd really enjoyed the lying down part, but that ecstasy had been short-lived. Even though she had suspected that sex was overrated, copulation with Henny was really underdone, like a half-minute egg.

And she'd had to give up high heels. He insisted that she wear those horrible flats so she didn't tower over him quite so much. She loved high heels.

"Margie Noessit claims that we made Zona give us money, or we'd throw her out of town. I never said anything about her leaving town. I went along because everybody else was getting some. Listen to this, 'Running last, as always, is Lila Mae Warner, who took a mere twenty-three hundred over the years.' If I'd known she was shelling out money like she did to Melba, I darn well wouldn't be running last. This past election, I could have used another five or six thousand for posters. That way, the race wouldn't have been so close."

"Mullet's running."

She gasped. "Against one of us?"

"Mullet's running. Got a call this morning, so I ordered a hundred pound. Wholesale cost is five cent a pound higher than it was last season. Have to add fried mullet to the menu and raise the price. Second time I raised the price in two years. Customers are going to bitch, and that's for sure."

"For God's sake, Henny, can't you think about anything but the restaurant? I been insulted all over town and you talk about mullet."

Henny lay down his paper and grinned evilly at his wife. "Didn't I tell you when you decided to go into politics that you'd be called names? Didn't I? If you'd stayed on and helped me in the kitchen, like a proper wife, you'd have been a lot better off than you are consorting with those northerners."

He seldom saw her any more. She was always off to one meeting or another, and there were times when he'd swear that she was gone just to avoid him. Since she got so high and mighty, she seemed to be ashamed that he cooked for a living. Hell, he'd even heard that she was seen occasionally in that fag place, Rain. It wasn't right, her straying from his side. A wife belonged by her husband. A wife was supposed to be a helpmate, not a politician–all the boys at the Saved Sons Society said so.

"Joe Tyler ain't a northerner. He's the richest man in town."

"No, he ain't a Yankee, but he's a son of a bitch, and that ain't much different."

Lila Mae sighed and stared out the window at the oaks in her yard. "Henny, you just don't understand. What do you mean, like a proper wife? Don't I circulate and bring in paying customers? I've spread the word about how good Southern Fried is all the way to Tallahassee and as far south as Venice. Business wasn't nearly as good before I got on the council."

"It was good enough for you back then. But back then you didn't need a new dress every week to keep with that green-haired witch, so I didn't need to make as much money. What you make as councilman don't amount to a string of farts."

For the first time since their marriage, she regarded him with heartfelt dislike. In far too many ways, he was *so–so–short!* "You are being crude, and I ain't going to argue with you."

Henny would never understand why she had to be in politics; he was capable of deep frying, but incapable of deep thought. It certainly wasn't the money; it was the *power!* He had never sat on a dais and looked down on people, and since he had no imagination, there was no sense trying to explain it. It did something to your head, sitting up there above the citizens; it made you feel godlike.

She had never aspired to anything more than a husband, and maybe a child– certainly not to greatness. But by assuming a position on the dais, she automatically became a part of greatness. She was now a fact in the history of man, not just some faceless slob who lived and died with no one to mark his passing.

She'd never forget that day she'd made up her mind to run for the city council. She'd been there to talk about garden club activities to them, to ask them for a little help, and suddenly she had seen her own face peering back at her from the very chair she now occupied. That vision had changed her life! But her husband was not destined for higher things, and he would never understand.

She rose from the table and carried her plate, cup, and saucer to the sink. "I got a meeting to go to. See you at lunch."

Henny sniffed, then turned his attention back to the comics. "Right. You going to want some of that fried mullet?"

Lila Mae sighed.

Meats Merlini was seething. That creep, that faceless creep, Margie Noessit, had written that southern fried chicken was better than his sausages! What was Al McDonald thinking of, printing such crap to begin with?

He'd demand to see the evidence, by God. What evidence could there be? Zona always paid by check, every time, and she wouldn't keep canceled checks, would she? She couldn't! She was only an ignorant broad who ran a whorehouse. Women like her didn't have good sense. Noessit was making it up. Besides, wouldn't Zona's blowing the whistle on the councilmen hurt her credibility? Hell, a local man wouldn't be safe going to the Sunshine Gentlemen's Club if she sang like a canary to that thing who wrote the gossip column. She must be one dumb broad, hurting her own business.

But that anonymous creep, Noessit, she was something else. He was going to find out who she was if it killed him. Fried chicken better than his sausages! What these southern hicks didn't realize was that sausage was an art form. But the time was coming when they would finally see the truth.

His heart began to pound, as it sometimes did, so he sat down, put his elbows on the table, closed his eyes, and concentrated on his fixation to calm himself. As he pictured delicate white pearls of back fat blended lovingly with misty hues of sage and rich, pink meat, he began to relax a little.

Sausages! Shy peppercorns peeped coyly from amongst little nibblets of prime pork. Snowy white bratwurst, capicola, hard salamis, Genoa Salami. Rich red and smoky brown sausages, deep and pale pink sausages–mortadella, pepperoni, kielbasa, garlic sausage, Italian sausages, hot and mild, Mama Mia! Hard and soft, chewy and tender, fatty and lean sausages, cold or sizzling in a hot pan with peppers and onions, then served on good Italian bread.

When he set up business in Brooklyn back in '69, he had used the bible of sausage-making. He had practically measured every grain of salt, for chrissake, so that each of his products would be perfect. He cut the fat by hand. Each link was a masterpiece. Of course, he made his real money on breakfast sausage; they were what paid for his retirement in Florida. He could cheat with breakfast links, run everything, even the fat, through the grinder, because they were common sausages. They weren't folk sausages.

Folk sausages were probably the most important thing a person could eat. When immigrants came from the old countries to New York, they had to eat their native sausages, didn't they?– or their brains would get damaged from too many changes. He, Merlini, had performed a vital function to the mental health of one of the world's largest cities.

And what Creep Noessit didn't know was that, in addition to the checks for his campaign funds, Zona shelled out each week for thirty pounds of sausage. The girls loved 'em. Fried chicken was better? Shit!

He couldn't wait until the next meeting to unveil his plans for the museum. Sandfly Bates wanted a resolution?–he'd get a resolution. The museum would be built, Sunshine would finally be put on the map, and his name would live forever as the benefactor of the city. Not bad for a second-generation Wop, even if he did say so himself.

But where to build the museum? There wasn't a decent place in the downtown area that wouldn't require the destruction of what the folks in Sunshine considered historical buildings– rickety old wooden things with big porches on them. One had a little gingerbread across the front and every time he passed the place, there was some old biddy standing out front admiring the joint.

He could hear Lila Mae now, see her magnificent, heaving bosom as she defended those miserable shacks. Yeah, yeah, so they were here when Sunshine was only a crossroads with two stores. Who cared?

It was a shame that the river frontage was so ugly. And with the constant sewer leaks, the banks at low tide reeked like a slaughterhouse. The museum would look nice on a river, if only there were a proper river in the state of Florida. When compared with the majestic Hudson, the Hatchacootee looked like an unfinished gutter in Brooklyn.

But wait, wasn't Rainmaker talking about bringing in some palm trees to try to make the place look more like Florida? Where did he plan to put them? Certainly not on the road coming into town; no need to waste good palm trees on jerks driving through to Heart County. Now, if they were planted along the riverbank, and they could raze Mosquito Row, then they'd have made some progress and the museum could go up there.

Merlini got to his feet and shuffled into his living room to the telephone. "I gotta talk to Joe," he muttered. "Sunshine Law be damned."

"I want this woman identified and I want her sued," Joe Tyler told Michael Crawley. "This is slander of the worst sort."

"No, it isn't; it's libel."

"Slander, libel, what's the difference? She has accused me of the lowest kind of behavior." Tyler glared across the desk.

"Is it true?" Crawley asked.

"Why should I turn down a campaign contribution just because it comes from fallen women? I have a duty to this town; no one knows better than I do how far we've come since the turn of the last century, and my family was here then to lead the city into this bright future we now share."

"So it's true. Did you threaten to run her out of town?"

"Of course not! I did tell her that the Saved Sons Society looked on her sins with a jaundiced eye, and that a modest contribution to my campaign might help them realize that she was not as bad as she seemed. That's not a threat, and I resent the impli–she used that word, 'extortion.' It has a filthy sound, Michael."

Crawley quickly looked down at his desk, then cleared his throat. "Joe, you realize how many folks have tried to identify this Margie Noessit? It sure as hell isn't Al; he'd never dare write such trash. The publisher would toss his ass out the door. Furthermore, the law allows a newspaperman to keep his sources private. As much as I appreciate how the article offended you, if what's written there is true, then it isn't libel."

"Of course it is."

"No, it isn't."

"Then why isn't it slander?"

"Because slander is spoken, not printed."

"That doesn't matter. I have been publicly humiliated."

"That's true, but you asked for it by taking money from her. You don't have a case that will stand up in court."

"You mean I'd be found guilty?"

"No, I mean your claim that you have been slandered or libeled, or whatever, would be thrown out by any judge with a minimal knowledge of the law."

"That's not fair! We could take it before Meekins; he's a cousin of mine."

"Wrong court."

"Dammit, there must be something we can do."

Crawley stood and stared out the window behind his desk. Below, Hatchacootee Boulevard stretched westward to the Gulf. Two blocks away, he saw the Stars and Stripes waving bravely over a used car lot.

"You're not paying attention to me, Michael," Tyler complained.

"I am thinking."

"You should hear my wife. She's been at me since dawn about what the ladies in the church will think. This could really hurt. I'm running for Lay Speaker this year."

"I thought you were running against Tosti."

"Of course I am, but I'm also running for Lay Speaker."

Crawley turned to face his client. "What does a Lay Speaker do?"

Tyler smiled briefly. "The Lay Speaker writes the sermon every other Sunday. It gives Learned Speaker some relief. I've been Lay Speaker before, and have delivered some powerful sermons, Michael. One Sunday a woman actually fainted, she was so moved. But to win the post, you have to be saintly."

"Oh, and this renders you less than."

"Less than what?"

"Saintly." Michael smoothed his hair and again looked out the window.

Tyler watched his back resentfully. Why was it that lawyers always faced away when they were thinking? Dee Slugge did the same thing. Was it because they were avoiding distractions, or was it because they were secretly laughing at him? They'd better not be laughing at him, if they knew what was good for them.

"The fact that you're running for office changes everything," Crawley said. "If you're running for office, then we can sue for libel because Noessit might have hurt your chances of being elected. Or, if not libel, we could probably bring a case of malice in fact."

"What's that?"

"The intent to do harm. If we can ever find out who she is."

"Hell, sue her in whatever you call it when you don't know who the person is."

"That might be difficult, Joe. But let me work on it. I'll try to figure out some way to bring the case before Meekins and I'll get back to you. Anything else?"

"Yeah. I'm going to get the council to condemn Mosquito Row so we can plant palm trees down there and turn the area into a riverfront park. Make sure I don't get stung when the deal goes through, understand?"

"Let's get DeLeon to take care of that, Joe, since I'm representing you on a personal matter. We'll build another Chinese wall."

"Build whatever you have to, Michael, just make sure I get a top price for my land."

"What about the other landowners?"

"A couple of immigrants own some land, and as far as I'm concerned, the godless heathens can go to hell. The only other owner, as far as I know, is Pervert Rainmaker. Whatever losses he suffers don't matter; it's God's will. The God Book says--"

"I'll pass the word to Dee."

"God bless your endeavors, Michael," Tyler intoned.

"Amen," said Michael Crawley.

"Kelsey, the most awful thing has happened," Guy Fawkins said as he stripped off his sweaty shirt. "Some fool has dumped about six loads of sand down at the river mouth, and spread it around."

"Who would do something like that?" Kelsey asked. "The place is full of migratory birds and they need every bit of feeding ground they can get."

"I went over to the delta island and looked around. At least that hasn't been tainted by sand. I spotted about a dozen wood storks." Guy toweled his torso and threw the towel into the hamper. Then he grabbed a fresh shirt from the drawer and pulled it over his head.

Kelsey watched her husband, wondering if this was the right time to bring up the subject of the gossip she'd just heard about. When Al told her, she'd felt really sick inside. But she had to know if Guy had heard it, and if he had, what his reaction was. She was proud of her marriage and her husband, and anything that threatened either gnawed like a starving rat at her sense of well-being. She *hated* gossip. But maybe this wasn't the time; Guy was upset.

"Did you get photos of the sand?"

"No, I didn't think to take the camera, however, now that I'm cleaned up a little, I'm going back down there with a camera and shoot a couple of rolls of film. DEP needs to see this. I might even call in the Feds."

"The EPA?"

"Yeah." He looked at her closely, noticing for the first time the little worry lines between her eyebrows. "You don't think it's a good idea?"

"Yes, I do. I think they need to be told," Kelsey said.

"Then why the frown?"

Kelsey put her arms about her husband. "You've been so distant lately, Guy, and I just wondered--"

"Been working on taxes, honey, it's that time of the year. Don't worry about it."

"It's not me, or something I've done?"

"You? Well, I don't know about you, but I love my wife and am very happy with her. Why would you even ask? Hey, what's the matter?"

Kelsey's arms dropped to her sides. "Al told me about some gossip over Gavel and me, and–"

"Oh, that."

"I didn't have a clue such things were being said. I mean, simply because two people work together on environmental issues doesn't mean that–I hope you don't believe all that crap!" she wailed.

Guy chuckled. "Don't give it another thought, honey. It gives the bastards something to do, talking about you and your supposed affair with Gavel. I know perfectly well that he would never think of carrying on an affair with you; it would interfere with his love for the scrub jay." He gave her a hug. "What you and Gavel are doing is important. Keep it up and damn the torpedoes."

She smiled ruefully. "When Al told me, the first thing I thought about was how distracted you've been lately. It really had me going."

"Have you heard that you two are shacking up in Tallahassee next month?"

Kelsey gasped. "How dare they?"

"They dare; but they'd never dare go to Tally and find out the truth. How about calling DEP down in Heart County. Tell them about this sand. Tell 'em I'm taking pictures and will send them a set of the prints within the next couple of days. New moon is just about due, and the currents get weird. Might take the sand out into the Gulf and we'll never know who did it. At the same time, remind DEP that they were supposed to make the city council do something about the sewage leak. It's getting worse; the stink is overpowering. I don't know how the birds stand it."

"Know what I saw this morning when I left Piggly-Wiggly? I went through Mosquito Row because Tyler is raising so much Cain about drug dealing and so on, and Dee Slugge was sauntering along in back of some of the rental units, making notes. He isn't the slumming type. What do you suppose he was doing there?"

"Call his wife and see if you can find out. It certainly sounds strange; he hasn't been near that place since he moved here fifteen years ago."

"Okay. I'll arrange a little lunch at Rain. Then I'll clean out Sally's brain."

"Just be careful you don't clean too hard, there won't be anything left."

"Guy!"

"I'm not joking. Any woman who would marry something like DeLeon Slugge is bound to have fewer brains than a dinosaur."

"Dee's not so bad, Guy. He's just a lawyer."

"Kelsey, there is something wrong with Dee Slugge, something bad. I know more about him than you do. Just make certain, when you're dealing with Sally, that you don't end up dealing with him. Understand?"

"What could he do to me?"

"We don't want to find out."

CHAPTER SIX

"There is no excuse, Joe, for giving the Saved Sons Society a bad name. I don't belong to many clubs, and I want the ones I am a member of to be clean." Jackson Fatigay was grave. "If you accept money from Zona, that's one thing, but did you have to get caught? You have brought the taint of corruption to our group, and that–"

"You got one hell of a nerve, Jack, lecturing me," Tyler snapped. "I went to the paper and demanded to see backup information, because I have every intention of suing. Al showed me a list that Zona had given to Margie Noessit. I know it's real because I recognized Zona's handwriting. She writes checks at the store all the time. And your name was there in black and white, along with the figure of three thousand, five hundred for the last election alone."

"Maybe, but my name wasn't in the paper, and she had no right–!"

"Rights or not, she sure has hurt us." Tyler grunted, then slumped back in his chair. "This couldn't have come at a worse time; I'm running for Lay Speaker this year, and you know how strict the church is about that. Learned Speaker will have a fit. And I'm running against Tosti."

"Sure you can handle both jobs? You ain't getting any younger, Joe."

"Of course I can, Jack. I'm in the prime of life. If I get elected Mayor and Lay Speaker, I can pretty much control the morals in this town–turn it around and make it a God-fearing place like it should be."

Fatigay picked up a piece of paper from Tyler's desk and folded it into a plane. He studied it for a moment, then laughed shortly. "You got your work cut out for you, trying to make any place God-fearing any more. When you got live sex coming through computers, and all that cra–"

"Speaking of that, Sarah has locked me out of our bedroom."

Fatigay launched the paper plane across the room. "Why? You didn't do anything but take money, did you?"

"No, but she acts as if I did. She and the women of the church are making my life hell. The other day I was their hero because of my stand on razing Mosquito Row. Now I'm–"

"I told you a long time ago, you folks need to adopt the submission doctrine that the Baptists have. Women get uppity, you teach 'em a lesson."

"*You* teach them a lesson. I'd rather tackle a hundred octopuses than take on a bunch of females." Tyler sighed. "When the octopuses get through with you, at least you're dead. With women, you're dead meat."

They were sitting in his office on the second floor of the Stop N' Shop Department Store, overlooking Hatchacootee Boulevard. The furnishings were scarred and worn, relics from the days of Tyler's grandfather, who had built a general store on the spot many years before, torn that down, then put up the modest brick edifice that would later grow to become the Stop N' Shop Department Store, "Dry goods are our specialty."

Fatigay shifted his enormous rear uncomfortably in the narrow wooden chair. "I'd like to see my wife try to lock me out. She'd change her mind real quick."

"Sure she would. You'd disappear to Tally and after a while, she'd miss you and ask when you're coming home. You got an excuse for leaving home. I don't."

The senator nodded in agreement. "You just don't know how to handle women, Joe. Never did. But what I wanted to see you about is Melba's screwy idea. You and the council need to kill it so Sunshine don't become a laughingstock. You'll probably pick up quite a few votes when this latest nonsense comes to light. You running for mayor, and with all the Yankees in town now, you need all the admirers you can find. Especially after that stuff in the paper. You talk to the lawyers about making Al tell you who she is?"

"Yeah, and there isn't any way. But I am going to sue."

"How can you sue someone when you can't identify them?"

"I don't know, but Michael Crawley is a smart boy and–"

"You should have used Schyte for that kind of work, Joe. There ain't anything he won't do. He's dirty."

"Is there anyone in that firm who's clean? Schyte will be tied up in Tallahassee for the next few months and I don't have that much time to spare. But I'm not ready to go to war with Melba yet, Jack."

The two men glumly stared at each other, then Fatigay cleared his throat. "Joe, I ain't kidding; you got to kill this brainstorm she's come up with. If you do, people will fall over themselves to vote for you."

Tyler nodded. He had felt diminished when Melba beat him in the mayoral race. Felt like the town didn't really appreciate all he and his family had done over the past generations to put Sunshine on the map. The campaigns had been rancorous, northerner against native–progress against stagnation, that sort of thing.

She had asked all the folks who had moved into Sunshine, those retirees from the north who outnumbered natives ten to one, to vote for her *so they'd feel at home again!* She had accused his administration of picking on those who came from out of state. She had said that he was ignorant and arrogant. There had been snide remarks about the Saved Sons Society, male supremacy, and narrow minds. He had never heard that kind of talk in Sunshine before. But they had voted for her!

Of course the retirees felt put out–all the good land was owned by those long-suffering people who had lived in Florida before air conditioning and mosquito control. Those landowners who had good sense were holding off for the rich developers to come in, so they could get top dollar and get out. And they deserved every cent they could make, the sons of the pioneers who had tamed this snake-infested, insect-ridden, mildewed wilderness, and made it a wholesome place to live. They had suffered long enough; let someone else fight the climate.

The tract housing that developers like Fielding built was on low ground that flooded if it rained too hard, or dropped out when sinkholes showed up. The sinkholes really rattled the newcomers, but what did they expect? When the ground gave way, it was God's will.

There had been some idiotic talk about the aquifer in the area being over pumped to supply water for new growth, but what did scientists know? Anyone with good sense knew that killer storms, earthquakes, blizzards, and sinkholes were Acts of God. Even insurance policies referred to Acts of God; they were a fact.

After winning the first time, Melba had gone on a binge. She started to lure more aliens into the area. The population of Sunshine, normally around ten thousand, exploded to ten times that many during the winter months. The snowbirds flocked into hundreds of trailer parks that littered the west central Florida landscape. They blocked the roads, they stuffed the restaurants, crowded the tiny Museum of Shuffleboard that had been created by the City Council under his stern fist. They drove around slowly looking at nothing, because there really wasn't anything to see. But they spent money, hallelujah! That was their only saving grace.

He had prospered greatly from the influx, but enough was enough; he had lost control of the town. Progress had to come to a screeching halt; the town was going to the dogs. A lot of younger working couples were crossing the Hatchacootee and making their homes in Banter County, where taxes weren't so high. Large numbers moved into Sunshine, because it was near to Highway 15-B. But these young professionals came from a dissolute society. They didn't have the right attitudes, didn't know about how things were supposed to be. They had grown up on television, and everyone knew that TV fried the brains and left robots who couldn't really think for themselves. Even the young professionals approved of Melba, which proved his point about their having fried brains.

If he and the others could make Melba look like the fool she really was, he'd win the next election. It was his *right*, being mayor. Wasn't he the richest man in the city of Sunshine? Didn't he own the only department store?

She had even accused him of keeping progress from Sunshine by making it almost impossible for any competition to move into the city. What did she expect? Business was business, and the *business* of business was to control the market and to make money.

Tyler slapped his desk and stood. "You're right, Jackson. Once the electorate see how stupid Melba really is–uh, what's she got planned?"

Jackson Fatigay gave Joe a Mona Lisa smile and said nothing.

"Okay, quit being so mysterious and tell me what she wants," Tyler insisted. He sat back down and picked up the letter opener, hefting it.

"She wants a beach."

Tyler gaped. "A *beach?*" The letter opener clattered to his desk. "I thought the Pervert wanted the beach, so I didn't say anything."

The senator chuckled. "No, Melba wants the Legislature to fund a study to cover the gulf coast within the city limits with sand. A quarter mile out into the Gulf, too, so that folks don't step in the mud."

"I always knew that wearing those things on her head in the heat of summer would melt her brain."

"She's very serious. Plans on asking Fyndar and Ramirez to do the study."

Tyler began to laugh out loud, his great belly heaving with the unaccustomed effort. "She has stolen Pervert's idea, by God! This will be her downfall. You ever been out to that mud flat on a full moon?" he asked when he had controlled his mirth.

"I got better things to do with my time. Why?"

"The tide gets funny at full moon. Takes anything on that flat plumb away. Gone. Kaflooey!"

Then Jackson Fatigay threw back his head, hee-hawed, and the two of them bellowed with laughter.

"This is the way I started the week," Odlum said as he tossed the letter onto Frank Bonano's desk. "Someone has cranked up DEP about the leakage, and they're threatening to sue if we don't clean it up."

Bonano unfolded the pages carefully, still looking up at Odlum. "I don't need this."

"Nobody needs this."

Bonano read quickly, tearing the front page as he went to the second. "Jee-sus! They really are threatening to sue!"

"Yep."

"How? I mean, how did we get this so quickly? The latest leak occurred on Tuesday, I heard about it on Wednesday, and it's Monday morning and we have a letter on it? Hell, the last time I asked the Department of Environmental Protection for anything, it took them six months, *six months*, to get around to an answer. I wonder who's behind this?"

"Damned if I know."

"You spoken with Lila Mae about it yet?"

"I told you, Frank, that I won't discuss such a nasty thing with Lila Mae; she's a lady."

"She ain't that much a lady, Oddman. If she doesn't take up this cause, we're in deep shit, literally. She's popular with the old folks and can get them stirred up if she wants to. The retirees could demand that the sewage system be rebuilt."

"You forget that they have to pay for it, and they're on pensions. Why don't you speak with her?"

"Because I'm the City Manager, not the Utilities Director. I already pester them enough. It's time someone besides me took some fla–"

The telephone rang.

Bonano grabbed the receiver and barked, "Bonano." Then he stopped breathing and began to softly pound his desktop with a bunched fist. "Yes, Commissioner. I–that is–I–we *are* doing something about it, I can assure you, but these things take time and–yes, ma'am. I will certainly pass on that message. And I'm sorry you couldn't reach the mayor. Thanks for calling." He slammed the receiver onto the cradle. "Shit!"

"Who was that?"

"Chairperson Heliotrope Engelhardt from the Heart County Commission."

"What does she want?"

"She received a tip that our leaky sewer pipes are contaminating the Gulf. She has contacted EPA and the DEP, and she's threatening to bring in the President if we don't do something about this–fast. She is concerned that we might pollute their pristine beaches, and further, she's going to ask advice of their attorneys about whether they should sue Banter County and the City of Sunshine."

"Oh, hell, hell, hell!" Odlum groaned. "I'd rather deal with a nest of poison spiders than that bunch down there. We really have to do something or they'll get all the papers on it and we'll be accused of playing fast and loose with public health and safety." Odlum groaned again. "I guess I'll have to talk to Lila Mae. I'll do it this afternoon."

"Yeah," Bonano agreed. 'And you do whatever you have to do to convince Lila Mae that she's got to bring it up at the next meeting. Melba will kill me if I bring an emergency; we've had another misunderstanding. Christ, I wish she'd get a lover! Besides, she, Merlini, and Teddy all have special pet projects to fight about."

Odlum shuddered. "I feel for you, Frank. God, I'm glad I don't appeal to her."

Kelsey threaded her way through the tables, following PooPoo as he led her to a secluded table by the waterfall.

"Who's meeting you, darling?" he asked as he seated her.

"Sally Slugge."

"Slumming, are we?" He was arch. "Kelsey, the gossip about you and Gavel is funny, but if they start on you and Sally fighting over him, oh my God!"

She laughed. "You are silly, PooPoo. Why would Sally Slugge fight with me over Gavel, even if he and I were having an affair?"

"Because she absolutely *adores* Gavel, but is too afraid of DeLeon to leave him."

"PooPoo, you're making all this up. How could any woman ever adore Gavel? His looks alone would discourage any female who wasn't blind. He looks sort of like a mongoose with horn-rimmed glasses. And he's so skinny that if he took off his clothes to hop into the sack, he'd disappear."

He laughed. "I always heard that women were hard on their lovers, darling, but you take the cake!"

"Go to hell."

He patted her shoulder. "You take old PooPoo's word for it, darling. I got it straight from the horse's mouth."

Kelsey was shocked. "She told you she's got a thing for Gavel?"

"She certainly did. Said that if DeLeon had the balls that Gavel has, she'd be a happy woman. Well, she didn't put it in exactly those words, but the message was loud and clear. Now, what does that tell you about DeLeon Slugge, Esquire?"

Kelsey laughed. "I never suspected that she–PooPoo, having balls–I mean–maybe she's an environmentalist at heart."

"Darling, I can assure you, the only environment she's interested in is Gavel's *terra firma*. Oh, my, there she is. Now you girls keep it quiet and clean. I don't want to have to referee." He hurried toward the front of the restaurant.

Kelsey watched as PooPoo led Sally through the crowded room. Sally was a slight, colorless blonde with enormous blue eyes that looked at the world in apparent confusion. She was pretty in a vapid way, but she lacked presence; she could enter an empty room and it would still seem uninhabited. She wondered if anything would ever change Sally, but she doubted it. Dee Slugge kept everything in his domain firmly beneath his heel.

How could any female possibly be attracted to Gavel Strike? He was a dear; she was very fond of him, but his looks! Gavel did have passion, though; perhaps that was what drew Sally to him. DeLeon's personality was like the iceberg that sank the Titanic.

She didn't know Sally well. Even though they were both members of the Sunshine Women's Club and the Blossom Garden Club, they had never worked on the same committees. She wondered how to begin the conversation. Picking someone's brain about their spouse's doings was a new experience.

Sally thanked PooPoo and seated herself, smiling hesitantly at Kelsey. Her pale blue skirt and sweater gave Kelsey the impression she could see through her. "Thanks for asking me to lunch, Kelsey," she said in a soft voice. "I'm terribly interested in your environmental work, but I don't know how I can become involved–or, or if I'd be welcome. I'd like to help but I don't want to tread where–I mean, you and–"

Kelsey caught her breath; PooPoo had been right! "You've heard the gossip that's been making the rounds? About Gavel and me?"

Sally blushed. "Well, yes, but I didn't mean to imply that–"

"There's nothing to it but hot air, Sally."

"Oh, I know, I mean, I never believed it. I think Gavel is far too heroic to stoop to such things, and besides, Guy is his best friend."

"He's also a good friend of mine. Period. Sure you want to be known as a tree-hugger?" Kelsey asked lightly.

"I need something to hug, Kelsey. I can't have children, and–"

PooPoo, who had flitted away, was back with menus. "Now, ladies, I must insist on my new chicken dish and a small bottle of Pinot Grigio. And next week, I'll have an entirely new menu for you to enjoy."

"Oh, what?" Sally asked.

"South Seas cuisine, with a little of the Caribbean thrown in."

"Sounds dishy. I just want a small salad," Sally said. "And iced tea."

"Nonsense, darling. When in Rain, do as Sadie did! Chicken it is. Kelsey?"

She laughed. "I'm not going to fight with you, PooPoo. Chicken. And Pinot Grigio. We might as well live it up, eh, Sally?"

Sally flushed. "If he insists. But I don't usually drink wine with–"

"Neither do I, but what the heck." Now that she was certain she would dominate the meeting, she knew she could persuade Sally to tell her all–if she knew anything. Somehow, she couldn't picture DeLeon telling anyone what skulduggery he was up to, especially his doormat wife. But then, men were strange creatures.

During the meal they spoke little, concentrating on the luscious melding of rosemary, wine, and chicken that PooPoo had brought them. A tiny salad and delicate cloverleaf rolls made in Rain's kitchen finished the meal.

Kelsey dabbed at her lips with her napkin and took a sip of wine. "Oh, that was good. I wish I could cook like PooPoo, but if I did, I'd be fat."

"Mmmm," Sally replied, putting down her fork. "So would I. I don't do much cooking at all because Dee is seldom home in time for normal meals. He eats out, and I make do with something simple, or takeout. Sometimes I wish—"

"You can't survive on fast food," Kelsey exclaimed. "You'll die of boredom."

"Oh, I drive over to Heart County and get Chinese or Italian. I've had enough of Southern Fried to last a lifetime. I wish we had foreign foods on this side of the Hatchacootee, because I can't eat at Rain all the time."

Yes! Kelsey thought. Right on the button. "Maybe there's a plan afoot to develop the river bank," she said offhandedly. "I saw Dee down there the other day, wandering back of the shacks. He looked pretty lost."

Sally giggled. "He was. He was actually in a good mood that night and told me that he's never been down there before. But nobody that I know of is going to develop it. Not that way, at least. I think someone on the city council is interested in tearing down the houses and making the place into a park."

"But where would the folks live whose homes are destroyed?"

Sally shrugged. "I don't know and Dee doesn't seem to worry much about that. He said his concern was getting a good price for some of the landowners."

"Oh," Kelsey said, nodding. That was an interesting piece of news. Joe Tyler owned a lot of land in that part of town; in fact, there were some newcomers who referred to him as a slum lord. "I sure am glad I don't own land there—all that smelly mud." Now that lunch was over and she had the information she had come for, she was anxious to tell Guy what she'd learned. But Sally had other ideas.

"Tell me about Gavel and his wonderful work," her guest demanded. "I want to hear about everything he's ever done for the world we live in." She rested her elbows on the table and, chin cupped in her tiny hands, gave Kelsey her undivided attention.

Lila Mae peered around the car park, searching for Odlum's Oldsmobile. It was a late model Aurora, dark green, and she finally spotted it. Then she saw Odlum rising from it's silhouette like some tree against the horizon. She hurried to meet him, looking forward to being with someone taller than she was.

"Oddman, what on earth is wrong? I got a meeting at four, and—"

"Lila Mae, I need to talk to you—in private. Get in the car. I have something to show you, we have to talk about it, and there's too many folks around the Piggly-Wiggly for my taste."

She got into the car and settled back, then looked at the utilities director. Lila Mae was surprised to see that, in profile, he was quite nice-looking. The Coleman lantern countenance disappeared and a strong-willed, masculine look took it's place. She wondered that she had never noticed this before, having known Dreyfus Odlum all her life.

He felt her scrutiny and colored slightly, cleared his throat, put the car into gear, and drove from the lot and along Hatchacootee Boulevard, heading west.

"Where we going?"

"Like I said, I got something to show you."

His voice was choked, as if he were holding back some terrible emotion. She touched his arm, concerned, and he jumped as if she had bitten him. "Oddman, what's wrong?"

"Everything's wrong," he cried in anguish. "I don't want to do this, Lila Mae, but I got to. Even though Frank's been after me, I didn't want to involve you in something so–so *dirty!* But everything's coming apart and I need you—need your help. Swear you won't hate me for this. I mean—do you understand?"

She nodded gravely. "I understand."

She was overcome with pity for the tall, gangling man. She had known for years that he was hopelessly in love with her, and that had buoyed her ego, which sank to nothing each time she looked at her husband. Many nights, lying beside Henny, who dropped into bed like a stone and fell asleep without saying a word, she would pretend that she lay beside Oddman–the only person in town who would be capable of making love to all of her at once. She had, at times, imagined his bony frame covering her body, and his pent-up passion rising, and she had reveled in the unbidden warmth that suffused her.

Now she understood that his love for her had finally burst free of its bonds, had overridden his reluctance to speak out, and she waited breathlessly to see what would happen next.

They drove past the nicer homes that crowded as close to the Gulf as they could without being offended by the harsh salt stink of estuarine mud at low tide. Within two blocks of the marsh, the lovely houses gave way to shacks amid intermittent oaks. Beyond the shacks lay the tangle of mangrove that protected the river mouth from erosion during the frequent storms. Then human habitation disappeared, confronted with the mud flats and marsh that made up the mouth of the Hatchacootee.

Odlum parked in the big turnabout at the end of the road, got out of the car, and came around to open her door. He quickly stepped back as she left the car, avoiding physical contact.

The sky was the clear, brilliant blue found in Florida during the dry season, with a few perfectly white clouds in the distance. The scene was desolate except for the hundreds of migratory birds who placidly browsed the mud; there was not a soul in sight. Lila Mae smiled up at Odlum and inhaled deeply, then gagged. The air was crisp, electric. And it stank like a polecat.

"Oddman, what is that awful smell?"

"Sewage."

"What's it from?"

"All our sewer pipes leak, Lila Mae, just like I've been telling the council. There's nothing I can do about it! We got to put in an entire new sewage system and there's no way I can raise the funds unless a bond issue is approved by the Council." His voice was filled with despair.

"Oh, honey, that's terrible. Of course I'll help you. Any way I can." She touched his arm again. He froze, then she suddenly found herself in a crushing embrace. Her knees went weak as Odlum's mouth covered hers and his hands roamed roughly across her body. She felt her hands tearing at his shirt, at his pants.

I'm going to commit adultery, she thought, but I don't give a damn. She ripped off her blouse and yanked off her skirt.

For the first time since she'd been elected, she missed an appointment.

10 Times _ Monday, March 15, 2—

HEART COUNTY THREATENS LAWSUIT OVER SEWAGE

County Center: Heart County attorney, Maydew Crabtree, said today in an interview that unless Banter County and the City of Sunshine clean up the sewage leaks that are fouling the Gulf of Mexico and threatening their beaches, Heart County will sue.

"The City Council in Sunshine have known for years that there is a problem, and they steadfastly refuse to do anything about it," Crabtree said. "Our County Commission has a duty to the people of Heart County to see that they can use their beaches in perfect safety. Sunshine's sewage is fouling our beaches."

"Not so," said Sunshine's mayor, Melba Tosti. " Every time I have spoken with Chairperson Engelhardt, she talks about sewers. The real problem is that Heliotrope Engelhardt has a dirty mind and a dirtier mouth. I think the woman has a fixation that needs to be fixed."

Chairman Fowler Dayes of the Banter County Commission says that the sewage leaks are the problem of Sunshine, not Banter County. "It should be apparent to anyone with good sense that Sunshine will always be a problem until the people elect sensible government officials."

CHAPTER SEVEN

Mayor Melba Tosti cleared her throat, flashed a smile at the local television camera, then banged her gavel. "The meeting of the City Council of the City of Sunshine will now come to order." She then looked upward and intoned, "All rise for the Invocation and the Pledge of Allegiance." After quick glance to make certain the camera beamed her image, she rose.

Josephus Tyler shook his jowls in preparation for the prayer. He closed his red-rimmed eyes and clasped hands beneath his layered chin. "Lord God, Maker of all things, Knower of all sins, we humbly beseech Thee to lead us to do Thy will while we attend the business of the City of Sunshine." His voice assumed the cadence of the pulpit and he squeezed his eyes tighter shut. "Help us, Lord, to avoid the pitfalls of absolute power. And Lord, there are those in this city who would slander your humble servants. There are sinners in this town, God, who know not the ways of righteousness. Bring down Thy wrath on Margie–"

Melba kicked him in the back of the leg.

He opened his eyes, glared at her, then closed them again and, in a voice laden with a sticky mixture of intransigence and piety, continued. "Bring down Thy wrath-- "

"Shut up!" Melba whispered, "Right now."

"How dare you interrupt my communion with the Almighty?" Tyler snapped at the mayor. "The invocation is *mine,* damn it! You assigned it to me during my first term as councilman, and I am the only person on this board worthy of speaking with the Lord." He closed his eyes again and raised his voice. "I beg you, Lord, bring down Thy–"

Melba sighed with exasperation, turned to face the flag, and began the pledge of allegiance in a loud voice and, when that was done, she shouted, "All be seated. Is everyone present? Fine." She gazed in both directions along the dais, then glared in triumph at Tyler, who was still standing, eyes stubbornly closed and hands clasped beneath his chin, praying. He was pale with anger. "Councilman Tyler, please have a seat so that we might go on with the meeting. It's a poor pot that can't keep the kettle black."

While Tyler made up his mind about whether to capitulate, Melba adjusted her new navy blue wig, a bouffant creation sprinkled with minute sequins, smiled at the camera, and tidied her papers.

"You know," a smiling Lila Mae whispered to Merlini, shoving her microphone aside, "one of these days Joe's going to kill her."

"Why?" Merlini watched Lila Mae closely. There was something different about her, but he couldn't fathom just what it was. She had more color, and where she usually sighed, she was now smiling. Then the thought that perhaps Henny had given her a nice, fat mullet occurred to him; he had heard that they were back on the menu. He snorted loudly.

"Councilman Merlini, we are in session," Melba said sharply.

"Yeah, yeah, Mzzzz. Mayor, that's why I'm here." He returned his attention to Lila Mae and her magnificent boobs.

"Because she keeps interrupting his prayers. He thinks he's the only person in town who knows how to pray."

"You heard he went to see Crawley about suing the Noessit dame?"

"No, who told you?"

"I got my sou–"

"Councilman Merlini, do you mind?" Melba banged the gavel.

"Oh, for chrissake, let's get on the meeting instead of sitting here like a buncha dummies while Joe makes up his mind whether he's gonna join us." He gave Lila Mae a look of triumph.

"Better'n a zoo," came a voice from the back of the small auditorium.

Tyler glared in the direction of the voice, then seemed to remember something and abruptly sat. His chair shrieked in protest.

Melba smiled at the camera. "I need a motion on the minutes of the last meeting."

"Got it," said Merlini.

"Second," Tyler snapped. He glared at the citizens in the chamber, daring them to laugh.

"All in favor?" Ayes all around. "Motion passed."

"Any financial matters to be discussed?"

"No, Madam Mayor," Bonano replied. His right hand leaped into action, completed the inspection of his person and picked up the pencil on the desk.

"Any items to be pulled from the consent agenda?"

"No, Madam Mayor," Bonano murmured. His hand hesitated, then began to tap the pencil.

"I'll be damned!" Merlini whispered to Lila Mae. "You see that?"

"What?"

"Frankie must be losing it, either that, or his hand is on strike."

"Councilman Merlini, do you mind?"

He nodded, affable. "Not at all, Mzzzz. Mayor, go right ahead."

Melba looked as if she might explode. "I need a motion to accept the consent agenda."

"Got it."

"Second."

"Might I ask if Item 4C that we pulled because of mistakes last week has been corrected? I don't see it in the consent agenda, but no doubt there's another legal bill from our attorneys." Teddy's voice was nasty and he glared at DeLeon Slugge as he spoke.

"Yes, Councilman," Bonano replied. His hand was busy again. "I was just going to bring that up. We got the correction back too late to make the agenda, and the matter needs to be finalized."

"So our attorneys are not only incompetent, they are slow." Rainmaker sat back, smiling.

Melba leaped into the exchange. "That doesn't matter. We need to vote on Item 4C. Do I hear a motion?"

"Got it."

"Point of order, Madam Mayor: it has to be put on the agenda," Lila Mae insisted.

"Why?" Tyler growled.

"Because that's the procedure," Lila Mae said stubbornly. "I ain't going to vote on anything that isn't on the agenda because I think it's illegal."

Melba smiled at Dee Slugge, inviting him to speak, but he simply smiled in return. She frowned. "Bonano, what's the procedure here?"

"You could bring it as an emergency, Madam Mayor, and replace it on the agenda."

"Wait a minute, here," Merlini intervened. "You're confusing me. You can't bring this as an emergency; it was on the agenda last meeting. How can a thing that wasn't an emergen–"

Lila Mae patted his hand to calm him down. "Meats, it was late getting here, and you know how late things can get real urgent? Well, this is urgent."

"Oh. Okay. I vote to hear an emergency because it's urgent this week."

"Second."

"All in favor?"

"Might I ask if anyone even remembers what Item 4C concerns?" Rainmaker asked.

Melba looked flustered. "All in favor?"

Four ayes. One nay.

"Motion passed." She favored Teddy with a nasty smile. "Now, Councilmen's items. District A."

Lila Mae grabbed her mike and adjusted it. "Madam Chairman, I have a grave issue to bring before this council, even though the matter isn't in my distri–"

"Then you have no right to interfere!" Tyler almost shouted.

"Oh, shut up, Joe, you don't even know what I'm talking about," Lila Mae said tiredly. "I suppose I could bring this up as an emergency, but I think we've had enough of those for this morning." She looked at the mayor and saw that Melba was impatient. "What do you want me to do?"

"Get it over with!" said Rainmaker.

"Point of order, Teddy. You aren't the Chair. And besides, the problem is in your district, so you should rightly be bringing it to our attention, but no doubt you've been too busy with PooPoo's special recipes to bother wit–"

"Madam Mayor, I object!" snarled Rainmaker. "Are we going to have a bitch kitty session or are we having a city council meeting?"

The townspeople in the chamber were laughing out loud.

"Order! Please finish, Councilman Warner," Melba said.

"Our sewer system is shot and we're leaking doo–I mean–well–poop and it's polluting the riverbanks, and putting E. Coli into the Gulf."

Merlini's jaw dropped. "Where did you get that information?" he blurted.

Lila Mae blushed. "From Mr. Odlum," she said. "And I went out to the mud flats and saw, or rather smelled it, for myself. We're polluting everything in sight. Isn't that against the law?"

Merlini scratched his head. "And you believe all this shi–this nonsense?" Why would a sewage leak make Lila Mae smile like that? "I don't think we can take your word for this, Lila Mae. We have to have a study, don't we?"

"Madam Mayor," Bonano interrupted, "please excuse the interruption, Lila Mae–Mr. Odlum received a letter from the Department of Environmental Protection about this matter. Someone has reported it to them and they, in turn, have written us warning that the leakage must stop. I'm having Mr. Odlum compile a report for you for the next meeting, giving us some figures on what it'll cost to repair the mess."

"And why wasn't I informed of this letter immediately?" Melba asked sharply. "As Mayor of Sunshine, I wish to know–"

Bonano's hand was busy. "We received the letter late on Monday, Madam Mayor, and I got Odlum on it right away. I was going to inform you yesterday, but you were unavailable. I also got a call from Commissioner Engelhardt in Heart County. She is concerned about the possible pollution of their beaches and has informed the DEP and the EPA of the problem."

"That bi–!" Melba snapped her mouth closed, adjusted her navy blue blouse studded with silver nailheads and pulled her wig a little tighter to her head. "In the future, Bonano, I want to be kept abreast of developments like these, even if you have to track me down in China. Why haven't we been told of this sewer problem before?"

Lila Mae sat up straighter. "Madam Mayor, we've heard about it a thousand times. It ain't Frank's fault, and it ain't Oddman's fault that this happened. We've had leaks like this before, and the pipes got patched and everything was fine. It's just that the pipes are too old to be patched now, and we got to float a bond issue to put in a new sewer system. Every time Frank and Oddman try to bring it up, you start screaming just like you did last week. No point putting your head in the sand any more." She drew in a deep breath and glared at the mayor. "And if you didn't spend so much time shopping over in Heart County, they might have been able to get hold of you."

"How dare you!" Melba seemed ready to burst.

"Councilman Warner is right," Joe Tyler said hotly. "I been trying to reach you all week and you haven't been around. The mayor of Sunshine needs to be available to the citizenry and–"

"You're not on a soapbox, Joe," Rainmaker warned. "Get off Melba's back."

"Don't you tell me what to do, you–!"

"Order!" shouted the mayor. The gavel crashed. "Mr. Bonano, I apologize if I sounded too rough." An icy smile. "The matter certainly is not your fault. We will look forward to Mr. Odlum's report next week, and please let the DEP know that we're right on top of the matter."

Bonano nodded. His right hand extracted a handkerchief from his jacket and wiped his brow.

"District B?"

"Is that all?" Lila Mae asked, incredulous. "We're polluting the whole world and we're going to sit around doing nothing until we get a report? We need to get busy right now to try and persuade our citizens to help us. They're the ones who'll have to pay for the–"

"Councilman Warner, if you want to persuade our citizens to support another bond issue, go right ahead. You'll lose the next election," Melba said nastily. "And you are out of order. Mr. Merlini has the floor."

Merlini smiled apologetically at Lila Mae. She was really beautiful when she was angry. "I have something really important to bring to the council," he began. "I already spoke with Sandfly–Representative Bates about this, and he's promised to find funding for this project if he gets a resolution from this council."

"Isn't this new business?" Melba asked.

"Yeah, but you haven't been finishing the meetings lately, so I'm doing it now." He waved an arm towards the back of the chamber and Mary Lee Mince came hurrying forward, a display board in her hands. The board was awkward and she stumbled. Bonano shot to his feet and hurried to help her. Between them they set up the board on a stand. Bonano took his seat as Merlini came from the dais to stand facing his colleagues.

He smiled in triumph as Lila Mae peered at the rendering of the museum, her lips making a beautiful O. "This, Councilmen, is what is gonna put Sunshine on the map–the world map. It will be the only museum in the entire world devoted to the history of meat."

He stepped back, whisked a pointer from the tray on the stand, and indicated one of the wings. "This, ladies and gentlemen, is the history wing, showing man hunting the animals like the mastec–mastodon, the tiger, the bear, all those things that he ate. And this wing," the pointer moved, "will be like a giant photo album, with enlarged pictures of all kinds of meat dishes–sausages, hamburgers, steaks–all kinds of stuff. And here," the pointer zipped to the center of the building, which closely resembled a boomerang, "will be a thirty-foot high bronze statue of a sausage!" He bowed slightly as one of the onlookers in the back of the room applauded. He smiled at the appreciative citizen, then lumbered back to his seat on the dais.

Grinning wolfishly, Rainmaker watched Merlini take his seat. "Councilman Merlini, am I to understand that you're serious about this piece of nonsense?"

"Whaddaya mean?" Merlini ground out.

"I mean I am hopelessly, utterly underwhelmed."

"I didn't expect anything else from you, Teddy; it ain't your idea."

Melba turned to Merlini. "It certainly is a different approach, Meats."

"Do you know how many tourists this museum will bring into Sunshine?" Merlini demanded.

"I have a feeling we would achieve a negative figure," Rainmaker said.

"Go to hell, Rainmaker," Merlini snarled.

"Order!" shouted Melba. She banged her gavel and smiled at the camera simultaneously.

Lila Mae pulled her microphone close. "Meats, you are so knowledgeable! I never knew that people ate tigers. When?"

"Back in the old days."

"When men were men and smelled like mice," Rainmaker quipped. "They'd all get together behind a big boulder, and since they smelled like mice, the tigers would come stalking them, then they'd all jump out–"

"Councilman Rainmaker, if you please!" Melba begged. The camera had moved to cover the people in the chamber, who were laughing. "Meats, do you have any idea how much this museum would cost?"

"Yes, Madam Mayor, I got the figures right here. Of course, we haven't put it out to bid yet, unnerstand, but–"

"What's the estimate?" Rainmaker asked.

"Only a million and a half," Merlini replied. "Of course, that's just the building; it don't include the art work or the exhibits."

Melba blanched. "And what would the art and such cost, do you have any idea?"

"No, I ain't got the estimates on that, but I did get in touch with a guy who does statues, the same one that did that stick and ball thing in Tampa, and he said–"

"He said that he doesn't sculpt sausages?" Rainmaker asked innocently.

"How'd you know?" Merlini asked. "Said that sausages wasn't really art. You bet your booties I told him a thing or two."

Melba sighed. "I think we have to mull over this proposal, Councilman Merlini. It's so—so—different, you see, and I—"

"Sure, you guys think about it as long as you want, but we ain't got that much time. Legislature is already in session, and they wind up their show in May." Merlini was expansive. "Tell you what. I'll even keep on trying to find a real sculptor."

Melba banged the gavel when laughter broke out again at the back of the room.

Sally Slugge put her hand over her mouth and looked at Kelsey with watering eyes. Kelsey shook her head in warning.

Beside them, Gavel Strike sat erect, trembling with anger. "Did you hear the way they just ignored the sewage leak?" he whispered. "They don't give a damn!"

"Gavel, they have to wait for the report from Oddman," Kelsey said.

"Wait, my ass! You don't have to know what it's going to cost to order repairs made immediately. This is serious."

Sally pulled on Kelsey's arm. "What was Teddy Rainmaker saying about the city attorneys?"

"He isn't too pleased with the way Dee makes money," Kelsey said shortly. "I didn't hear just what he did say, but you can bet it wasn't too complimentary. He's always down on Slugge, Crawley, and Schyte."

"But why?"

Gavel leaned forward. "Because Dee is constantly screwing them."

"Gavel!"

"Kelsey, if Sally is going to do any good at all, she's got to know the truth."

"Yes, Gavel, but you're talking about her husband."

"He's a shit."

Sally covered her mouth again, nodding in agreement. When she stopped giggling, she looked at Gavel with pure adoration. He was so wise! "Gavel's right about Dee's screwing them," she said to Kelsey. "He brags about it all the time, about how stupid the councilmen are and how much money his firm makes from the city. I think it's a disgrace, the way he carries on sometimes."

"As there are no public hearings scheduled today, we'll go on to old business," Melba said brightly. "I don't believe there is any old business."

Tyler glared at her. "I beg to differ, Madam Mayor. Last week I asked that this council pass an ordinance making it illegal to break the law. Nothing has been done; our attorneys haven't been asked to write a thing. You are shirking your duty to the citizens of this–"

"Aw, for chrissake!" Merlini cried.

"You shut up, Meats," Tyler warned. "You just had the floor with that mad idea you've–I–I–sometimes I think you're crazy, talking about such godless things. But now I have the floor!"

"My museum would sure be better than that stupid little shuffleboard thing you built when you were mayor," Merlini retorted. "People *eat* meat."

Tyler would not be drawn into argument. He crossed his arms and glared at Melba. "I have the floor! I am waiting for either a discussion on the matter I've just raised, or a vote."

Rainmaker put his hand on Tyler's arm. "Joe, it *is* illegal to break the law. We don't have to do anything."

"Get your hands off me, Pervert."

Melba was flustered. "Mr. Slugge, can you make any suggestions?"

DeLeon stood and approached the lectern, smiling. "My firm could make a study of the matter, Madam Mayor, and report to the council at the next meeting."

Rainmaker reared back in indignation. "I have never heard such a ridiculous suggestion in my life! If it isn't against the law to break the law, where did the word 'felony' come from? What is a misdemeanor? Why do we have courts, judges, police? Please, Madam Mayor, the general public often call us fools; must we insist on proving them right? And does our learned counsel think we're idiots? A study! If you have any integrity left, Slugge, you'll tell the councilman that it is not necessary to pass an ordinance such as he suggested."

Lila Mae sighed and whispered to Merlini, "Here we go. We're going to be here all day."

"Must I be insulted, along with the rest of the council?" Slugge asked with great dignity.

"Of course not," Melba assured him, her voice pure honey. "Teddy, you're out of order. I need a motion on the study."

"Got it," Tyler said, slightly mollified.

"Second."

"Done," Lila Mae sighed.

"All in favor? The vote is four to one. Mr. Bonano, kindly put this item on the agenda for our next meeting. Any further old business?"

"You are forgetting that we asked Mr. Bonano to look into the price of palm trees, Madam Mayor," Rainmaker said.

He was so disgusted with Melba that he felt like throwing in the towel. How far would she go? Certainly, it was election year and she was using her position and the city's money to make her opponent look even more idiotic than he was, but her actions reeked of fiscal irresponsibility. And Slugge was getting just a bit large for his britches. He was the city attorney, not some elected official. *Did he have to stand there and be insulted?* Hell, yes! And again, hell yes!

But he wanted the palm trees and was therefore compelled to bow to the forces of idiocy. When dealing with complete fools, one had to compromise. Sadly, he reflected that the public actually voted for people like his colleagues.

"I had made a note of it, Teddy," Melba said defensively. "Bonano, did you get those prices?"

Bonano nodded and looked toward Mary Lee Mince, who began to tremble. "Miss Mince has done the work, Madam Mayor, and she will give you the report." He nodded again and Mary Lee came forward to take her place as the lectern.

"State your name and address," Melba instructed.

"Mary Lee Mince, Tourism Director, City of Sunshine." Mary Lee cleared her throat, glanced at Bonano, received a second nod, and began. "Councilmen, Madam Mayor, I have found that we may obtain two types of palms other than the Sabal palm that is native to this part of the west coast of Florida. I dealt with local nurseries rather than going out of the county, simply because of transport costs. We can purchase queen palms, which grow to about forty feet maximum height, for fifteen dollars a foot. They are sold beginning at twenty feet high, which would make each palm cost approximately three hundred dollars plus transport and planting. You need special equipment to plant them, I understa–"

"Why is the cost approximate?" Tyler asked.

"Because the trees vary in height, I suppose," Mary Lee explained. "Coconut palms are also available locally. They reach a maximum height of fifty to eighty feet, and are sold when they reach twenty feet. They're only ten dollars a foot, which would make each tree cost us about two hundred dollars plus transport and planting."

"Would you plant coconut palms, Miss Mince?" Merlini asked. "Seems to me they'd be dangerous in a hurricane. You'd have nuts flying all over the place."

"Personally, I don't think they'd be a good investment, Mr. Merlini. We're a little too far north for them to thrive. But that's my personal opinion."

"So you're recommending queen palms," he said.

"No, sir, I'm only reporting on the cost of them."

There was no way he was going to trap her into making a recommendation. Palm trees died. The last city employee who recommended something lost his job when the council ignored him and things went wrong.

The Council had voted to buy an "instant" incinerator to dispose of all the city's garbage. He'd suggested that they take the thing on trial for six months, but they decided to buy it outright, even though it had never been tested on the market. It didn't work. It had cost a bundle, and he was blamed for the fiasco.

"I love the Sabal palms, myself," Lila Mae said. "They look just like little fur balls on a stick. But the queen palms are pretty too."

"How many palms did you have in mind, Councilman Rainmaker?" Melba asked.

"No specific number, Madam Mayor. Enough to do the job."

"And where are they to be planted?"

"That's for this council to decide."

Tyler grabbed his microphone. "I know just the place, Madam Mayor. And, Rainmaker, I want to thank you for bringing this matter to our attention. Your idea is a good idea and I will support it fully."

Rainmaker tensed. Something was seriously wrong.

"My God," whispered Lila Mae, "the world is coming to an end!"

"Nah, he's prolly got some way to make money out of the deal, is all."

"Councilman Merlini!" Melba warned. "You are talking on a matter on which we will vote and you're off microphone. Remember the Sunshine Law."

"We wasn't talking about the palm trees at all," he retorted.

Rainmaker looked at Tyler, surprised. "Do you have some spot in mind to plant with palm trees, Joe?"

"Yes. We can use our right of eminent domain to condemn the area along the riverbank that is now occupied by Mosquito Row. The buildings can be razed, and we can turn that eyesore into a lovely river front park. Such a park would be a boon for all our citizens, a sanctuary of calm and beauty away from the noise and bustle of the city–"

"Joe, I can see your point," Lila Mae interrupted, "but I don't think there's a bustle in town. They went out of style years ago." She smiled and whispered to Merlini, "It'll take him a while to figure that one out."

Merlini laughed shortly. "Who owns all that land, Councilman Tyler?"

"Well, I own some of it. I lease it out. And there are other owners, but I am willing to make the sacrifice, even though river frontage is extremely valuable, to see a river front park for this city."

"Oh," Merlini said nastily. "For a while there, I thought you'd figured out some way to skin us."

Rainmaker nodded; he'd been right. If the city condemned that land, he would not only lose his investment in land–at some time in the future, if they ever got the sewage problem solved, the land would be valuable–but he'd lose the income he received as part-owner of Fielding's business. They rented out over a hundred units.

"I really didn't have a park in mind when I recommended palm trees, Mr. Tyler. Such a park wouldn't be seen by those who pass through Sunshine, and would not serve as a tourist attraction. My original intention was to bring more tourists into the city. I suggest we table this item for further study."

"Is that a motion?"

"Yes, I make a motion that we table this for further study."

"Is there a second?"

"Got it." Merlini smirked at Tyler. If he wanted to make money on the deal, then Tyler would have to support the museum.

"All in favor?" The vote was four to one.

Melba positively beamed at the council as she announced, "There is new business to consider."

"If she's so happy about it, it must be a doozy," Lila Mae whispered.

"I spoke with Senator Fatigay about this matter before I brought it before the Council, because I wanted to test how our neighbor from Heart County might feel about some stiff competition."

Tyler's heart leapt, beating so wildly he thought he might faint. She was going to do it after all; she didn't know about the tide! He began to laugh.

Melba looked shocked, and then confused. "Councilman Tyler, I fail to see any humor in what I've reported so far. The Senator has agreed to try to get funding for a study to see if we can turn our gulf coast into a beach. Isn't that just peachy?"

"Now you're talking, Mayor!" someone shouted from the back of the room.

"Who would do the study for us?" Rainmaker asked.

"We would put out bids, naturally," Melba told him.

"Oh, Fyndar and Ramirez," he muttered.

"Do I have a motion on a resolution to send to the Senator?"

"Got it." Merlini smiled. A beach would be a much better background for the museum than the river bank. He pictured the bronze sausage against a clean blue sky. In the distance, graceful palms would sway, framing the beautiful beach owned by the City of Sunshine.

"Is there a second?"

"Done," Teddy said.

"All in favor?" The vote was four to one, with Tyler dissenting.

The mayor gave Tyler a dirty look, smiled brightly at the cameraman, then tidied her papers. She glared as Bonano interrupted her.

"Madam Mayor, this is the final day for the council to vote on increasing the staff in the Disaster Preparedness Department. If we don't handle it today, the state will fine Sunshine heavily."

"And why hasn't this matter been brought to my attention before this?"

"Frank tried to bring it up last week, Melba, and you were in one of your moods," Rainmaker snarled. "I don't care how much you dislike Bonano, or why you dislike him, when your personal feelings interfere with our duties—"

"Are you accusing me of incompetence, Councilman Rainmaker?"

"No, I am merely pointing out that your frustrations should not affect the way we perform our duties, Madam Mayor." He stared at her.

"I have no idea what you're talking about," she snapped. "Bonano, get on with what you want to say."

"The state has mandated that we increase our Disaster Preparedness staff by at least three. This is a mandate; you have no choice. Today is the deadline for compliance. What we need from you is a vote approving the addition of three staff members to that department."

"This is ridiculous!" Tyler objected. "We haven't had a hurricane in years, and with the present wea—"

"Joe, Frank said we don't have any choice," Lila Mae interrupted. "You going to argue, pay the fine out of your own pocket, then have to hire them anyway?"

"Who said anything about my paying a fine?" he snarled.

"If you're going to sit there and bluster about it until midnight," Lila Mae said, "then we're going to be out of compliance and it'll be your fault."

"Order!" The gavel crashed. Melba looked up at the ceiling, then sighed mightily. "I need a motion to increase the staff in the Disaster Preparedness Department."

"Got it," Merlini said.

"Second." Four ayes, one nay. "The motion passes. Now can we get on with the real business of the council? We're ready for public comment. Is there anyone who wishes to speak?"

Several hands went up in the back of the chamber.

"Please come forward, one by one, state your name and address, and limit your remarks to three minutes."

Old man Flossul came hobbling to the lectern. He had lost part of his foot years before to an alligator that had made the mistake of coming up the Hatchacootee. Flossul won in the end; he ate the alligator's tail.

"Ned Flossul, Riverbank Acres. I don't think you all have any right to try and put a beach on our gulf coast, Mayor. When I dumped a little sand on my riverbank to try and cut down the mud, the water management folks made me clean it up. As a taxpayer, I ain't about to see you waste money dumping something you gotta clean up as soon as it gets there. I vote no."

"Thank you, Mr. Flossul. We will certainly take your comments to heart." Melba's voice was melting. Flossul had given a big donation for her campaign.

Gavel Strike made his way to the lectern. As he glared at the councilmen, he stated his name, address, and occupation. He adjusted the microphone to suit his height, then began. "You have done some incredibly stupid things since the last election, but dumping sand on the flats at the mouth of the Hatchacootee is the most–the most–I–it is criminal!

"The Hatchacootee is a special river; there is none like it in the state. It is a river that has existed since the beginning of our peninsula for one purpose--to feed the migratory birds that depend on its bounty to survive. Our river is the only one in the state with a delta. That delta is an important estuarine marsh. The mud plain of the Hatchacootee on which you have dumped sand–that nasty, viscous mud you love to hate–is home to millions of some of the most important creatures I can think of– the Polychaeta." He turned to look at the people in the chamber, some of whom were whispering, then resumed.

"What are the Polychaeta, you ask? They are worms. Do you know the diversity you would destroy for the benefit of idiots like yourselves who come to Florida in order to advance their skin cancers?"

At the back of the chamber, Sally Slugge sat peering at Gavel Strike, her eyes alight with admiration. "Oh, Kelsey, he's so manly!"

"If he keeps up in that vein,"Kelsey said sourly, "he'll get us all thrown out of here. The mayor doesn't like to be called a fool in public, even if it is the truth."

"They wouldn't dare throw me out," Sally protested. "Dee would never stand for it."

"Don't bet on it, Sally. His business is making money, not defending his wife from dummies."

They both jumped as a particularly strident howl came from Joe Tyler.

"You got no right to speak to your betters that way, you miscreant. How dare you insinuate that we don't know what we're doing?" Tyler had half risen from his seat and was shaking his fist at Gavel. "It's people like you who are ruining this town, do you hear? We have important things to see to, no time for such godless things as sprocketeet worms!"

Gavel laughed. "Polychaete, pronounced poly-keet, Tyler. Not sprocketeet, whatever that means." He leaned forward, earnest. "The tube worm, in case you're interested, is an incredible creature. They're found all over the world. There is even one type of Polychaete that lives where sewage is dumped, that thrives on the waste poured into our rivers and oceans. Do you know that with their little jaws and saliva, they build their own homes? And their homes are castles, things of beauty undreamed-of by man. Some of them will use only one size of sand grain to construct their homes. These are palaces, delicate beyond our wildest dreams!"

Rainmaker looked down at the desk, turned his microphone aside, and muttered, "God, give me strength." Then, to Melba, "Is his three minutes almost up?"

"These are the wonders you would destroy with your beach. You would kill the food for our wild birds; there would be nothing left to sustain them. But you don't care, do you, as long as you think you can make money from such destruction. I tell you–"

The three minute buzzer sounded. Strike looked around, then back at the councilmen. "I haven't finished what I have to say."

"Mr. Strike, I doubt you ever will," Melba said brightly. "Thank you so much for your comments, and as you are so terribly concerned, please put your arguments into writing and submit them to the city manager's office for our consideration."

"But–"

"Thank you, Mr. Strike. Any other public comments?"

An elderly woman who lived in an older house one block off Hatchacootee Boulevard rose and went to the lectern.

"Your name and address, please."

"Rosa McIntyre, 122 Tyler Street. I want to know what you all are going to do about these earthquakes we keep having. There's something wrong in Sunshine, and you need to find out what it is. That's all." She resumed her seat and glared at the council members.

Melba Tosti rolled her eyes. "Any further comment?"

Kelsey rose and approached the lectern, facing the nasty looks that were aimed at her. "Kelsey Fawkins, 10 Lavender Way. It's a shame that you don't want to hear what Gavel has to say; it's important. Instead of listening to folks who know what they're talking about, you sit up there fighting among yourselves, trying to make brownie points with the voters. Well, you don't make brownie points–you don't even make sense half the time. And you're all guilty of telling lies to the public. Do you believe the things you say? If you do–"

"You sit down, adulteress!" Tyler screamed.

Kelsey reeled back as if she'd been struck in the face. "I'll sit down, Mr. Tyler, but I warn you that what you just said is actionable. And it is quite possible that my husband will be inclined to sue." She turned and walked back to her seat, rigidly calm.

No one stirred except Gavel, who sat muttering under his breath.

Melba's voice was bright and chirpy. "Since there is no further comment, do I hear a motion to adjourn?"

"Got it."

"Is there a se–"

"Done."

"The meeting is adjourned." Melba rose, jerked her wig closer to her scalp, grabbed her papers, and stalked from the room.

"She's in a real beachy mood, isn't she?" Merlini quipped to no one in particular as Tyler grabbed his things and stormed from the dais. He leered at Lila Mae.

"Lord!" sighed Lila Mae. "Meats, you're becoming a dirty old man."

Merlini snorted with amusement.

CHAPTER EIGHT

In the offices behind the council chamber, Melba turned on Joe Tyler. "It's bad enough having to listen to the public raving. I won't have you acting like an ass during the Invocation, is that clear?"

"I have the right to–"

"You have the right to say a little prayer, and that's all. The Invocation isn't a bully pulpit. Keep it up, I'll give the Invocation to Meats."

Tyler glared at her. "You would turn the Invocation into a sausageburger just to spite me, wouldn't you? I am a Christian and have the right to pray; Merlini is an ass."

Melba rolled her eyes. "Merlini might be an ass, but you're going over the edge, Joe. Watch it or you'll end up talking to those palm trees you want to plant at Mosquito Row."

Tyler looked at her warily. It was time for persuasion, he decided. "We need to talk about that, Melba. I know why Pervert wants the matter tabled; he's afraid he'll lose money. He and Fielding have a lot of rental units down there."

"You own a lot of the land yourself."

"Well, yes. But I'm willing to give it up for the benefit of Sunshine."

"Give it up?" Melba smiled nastily. "For how much per acre? I'm certain you've spoken with our attorneys already to make sure you get top dollar." She flushed with triumph as he blanched and began to protest.

She had him; her guess had been right! Who would it be, Slugge or Crawley? She was pretty sure that Slugge would never get involved with Tyler; such a connection would be too obvious. Sally Slugge was one of Tyler's nieces. He'd have to build an entire Forbidden City and Great Wall of China around himself to explain that one. Schyte was a worm, but he was in Tallahassee, ostensibly lobbying for the city as well as a few other business interests. He'd better be lobbying for the city, she thought grimly; they certainly paid him enough.

So Joe was doing a deal with Crawley, was he? If she could get proof, she might get her condo paid for yet. "You only think I don't know what goes on in this town," she said teasingly. "I have my sources. But, Joe, let me warn you, tread softly."

"I don't know what you're talking about, Madam Mayor," he said.

She grinned and patted his cheek. "Be a good boy, will you? Let's have lunch over in Heart County next week. We might be able to work something out."

"You mean–"

Merlini came bumbling through the door from the chamber. "Naughty, naughty, girls and boys, remember the Sunshine Law."

"We're talking about your museum," Melba answered smoothly.

"Oh, that's different." Merlini smiled, "You like the idea?"

"I think it's grand," Melba lied. "When are you meeting with Sandfly next?"

"I was thinking of going to Tallahassee Thursday to talk to him some more, but since we haven't passed the resolution yet, I'll postpone the trip. I hate Tallahassee during session."

"You need to talk to Senator Fatigay too, about your project; he's probably on Appropriations this year. I'm sure you know what it takes to get his attention."

"Yeah," Merlini scratched his head and said sadly, "half your retirement fund."

"Come, come, Meats, he isn't that expensive." Melba laughed.

Money, money, money, she thought. Jackson Fatigay's patronage was easy to come by; one simply passed money under the table. Had she possessed the lolly, she could have bought most of the state. But she was on the bottom rung of the ladder and needed real name recognition before she could run for the Senate. Mayors didn't make much on the side, especially mayors of little dumps like Sunshine. Though she certainly had not become involved in politics for the fun of it, she was content to bide her time.

Yes, money was what made Tally run. In the hinterlands lurked developers who would pay handsomely for a little help from those in the Legislature. And business was always anxious to increase profits and lower costs through "little" bills that left John Citizen out in the cold.

Once one made it to Tallahassee, things went smoothly. The public did their part by dutifully voting the same folks into office, year after year. It mattered not whether offenses were committed. If legislators served time for being caught with their fingers in the till, that was okay. Florida was a retirement village–most folks who bothered to vote had no real interest in the future of the state. A large number of people had come to Florida hoping to make a fortune in one way or another; she was one of them, and she secretly admired those law makers who pulled fast ones and got away with it.

She'd never forget a long-time senator from the east coast who was amiably chatting with a group of lobbyists. "Yes, boys," he had said, "everyone is happy when we're in session. You all make money, I make money–just got to keep it flowing, right?"

There were a few honest legislators like Henry Bates in Florida politics, but they were the exceptions to the rule.

Lila Mae came through the door from the chamber, lost in thought. She ran into Melba, treading on her toes. Melba blanched. "Lord, I'm sorry, Melba, didn't even see you. Is your foot all right?"

"I'm certain there's nothing broken, if that's what you mean," she replied ungraciously. "Look where you're going."

"I was thinking about the sewage going into the Gulf," Lila Mae explained. "It's just awful down at the river mouth, the smell is sickening. And you know what else? Gavel's right; someone has dumped a bunch of sand further along the mud flat. It's just above the high water mark. Ain't that illegal?"

"I don't know. I'll ask Slugge to look into it."

"Why can't someone we already pay check it out? I get tired of seeing Dee Slugge pocketing all the money he does. And we're the ones who get yelled at when he makes a mistake."

"The city doesn't have an in-house attorney, Lila Mae," Melba explained patiently. "We have to farm out the legal work."

"Sometimes I think Teddy's right. It would save us a lot of money–"

"My god, Lila Mae, don't tell me *you're* going to lecture on fiscal responsibility." Melba looked at her watch. "Got to run; I have an appointment." She hurried down the hall towards her office.

Office of the Chairman
Heart County Commission

16 March, 2—

Ms. Melba Tosti, Mayor
City of Sunshine
2344 Hatchacootee Boulevard
Sunshine, Florida 3766500

Dear Mayor Tosti:

It has come to my attention that sewage leaks in the Sunshine system are polluting the mouth of the Hatchacootee, thus placing all who live on the coast above and below your fair city in grave danger.

At our meeting last week, the Heart County Commission passed a resolution calling on the Department of Environmental Protection and the Environmental Protection Agency to look into this matter.

This is not the first occurrence of leakage from your sewer pipes; E. Coli has been found in the Hatchacootee on numerous occasions, and on at least two of those, you were required by the DEP to take corrective action expeditiously. While we appreciate that replacing sewer mains is an expensive endeavor, it is your statutory duty to maintain the standards set out in the Cleaner Water Act for public health and safety.

We ask that you move quickly to bring to an end this totally unacceptable situation. As good neighbors, we would be loathe to take your city into court for failure to conform to standards promoting good health. But as our attorney said in the paper, we will sue if something isn't done NOW.

As you know, Heart County is home to a million retirees who depend on its famous beaches to enhance their quality of life. Age and frailty go hand in hand, and it is our duty to protect our citizens from polluted waters.

With kindest personal regards, I remain

> Yours sincerely,
> Heliotrope
> Heliotrope Engelhardt, Chairman
> Heart County Commission

"I swear, I'll eat her heart!" Melba exclaimed. She threw the letter on her desk and picked up another envelope, slit it, and pulled out the contents, scanning the signature. "Another one from that–! What's going on around here?"

At least this latest missive from Heart County was on personal stationery. That boded well. She began to read.

Dear Melba,

A quick note–I do hope you appreciate how busy the days are.

Jack Fatigay told me about your proposal to turn the mud flat within your city limits into a beach.

Darling, you know that Heart County won't tolerate this nonsense–why do you even waste your time on it? By the time you get through with all your little studies and attempt to get permits to destroy a mud flat that feeds thousands of migratory birds, we'll have ruined everything for you in Tally. Don't forget, Melba, dear, that we are the second most populous county in the state, and have enormous influence among the legislators. I'm certain they'll find your idea as silly as I do.

If you're wise, you'll clean up your sewage act. There are studies which show that the Red Tide is a direct result of sewage disposal in the Gulf, and Sunshine wouldn't want to be accused of such a heinous act, would it? It would simply kill your reputation and your political career.

I know it's difficult being mayor of nowhere, but be patient. You can look forward to development in the future; we're running out of space. In another ten years we'll be built out, and then you can devise some way to attract those who like deadly boredom–and mud.

Heliotrope

Cursing savagely, Melba balled up the letter, threw it into her wastebasket, and stormed from her office.

"What brought that on?" her secretary wondered out loud.

PooPoo came through the diners at Rain, smiling broadly. "Frank! This is a pleasant surprise. A table for two?"

Frank nodded and stood aside for Mary Lee Mince to follow PooPoo. He brought up the rear, watching with appreciation the action of Mary Lee's hips under her mauve jersey dress.

He had used the fishing contest as an excuse to ask her to lunch, suggesting that they seek PooPoo's advice as he was so creative. She had been hesitant and had gone all a-tremble when he mentioned their dining together, but he had overcome her scruples by reminding her that the purpose of the luncheon was strictly business.

Her trembling still fascinated him. He had spent the past week studying her in the presence of other people and she trembled not at all unless he spoke directly to her. Perhaps he should ask if she were afraid of him and see what would happen.

She glanced back at him and blushed, suddenly aware of his scrutiny of her behind. He winked at her and then began to whistle softly. Maybe he should ask her to dinner–strictly business, of course. He'd have to think about that. Then he mentally shook himself; he'd been thinking about it for too long. It was time he made up his mind and did something.

PooPoo seated them near the waterfall and gave them menus, promising to be back in a few moments.

Mary Lee watched his retreating figure. "That is such a waste," she sighed.

"What?"

"He's so good looking. I just love PooPoo, don't you, Frank?" She looked at him directly and the trembling began. She put her hands in her lap to hide them, thankful that she was seated. At least when she sat, her knees didn't get weak.

"I don't think I could truthfully use the term "love," Mary Lee, but he's a nice guy. He's got more ideas than the rest of the county put together."

"I've often wondered how he can put up with Rainmaker. Teddy's so crotchety."

"Teddy isn't that bad; he's just frustrated. Suppose you had to deal with us, how would you feel?"

"I don't think the city has such a bad staff." She looked at him seriously.

"Not now, but when I came on the job, we had some real characters. There was one old lady in Code Enforcement who got even with anyone who crossed her–and as far as she was concerned, if you disagreed, you crossed her. She would sign up the unfortunate victim for magazine subscriptions. One fellow got bills for over fifty magazines. Took a long time to find out who the culprit was, but we finally caught her in the act. I was forced to let her go. Then there was another who sent anonymous threatening letters to elderly ladies. He got the can too. Can't have the city employees making war on the tax payers."

She laughed. "When you describe those folks, the city council looks almost normal."

"You are speaking heresy, my girl," he warned. "The council members are all-knowing and all-powerful."

"And all stupid," she rejoined. "I've never seen such idiots in my life. How the city has lasted this long is a miracle."

When he had asked her for lunch, she had made up her mind to let him see the real Mary Lee Mince. She had been determined from the day she first met him that he would have to be the one to make the first move, but he was so backward! He must have had a terrible marriage the first time around to be so put off by women. Or maybe he was put off by her, by Mary Lee Mince and her idiotic trembling. She couldn't help it; every time she was near him, she just began to shake. She wondered if she would ever get past that, ever get beyond getting weak in the knees whenever he appeared.

Bonano laughed softly. "When I was hired, the mayor and three council members had just been jailed for corruption. The ex-mayor, Plante Slugge, is still in prison. He's a third or fourth cousin of DeLeon and—"

"So it runs in the family," Mary Lee quipped.

"What?" Bonano asked.

"The love of money and the taint of corruption. I'm convinced that DeLeon would commit murder if he thought the council would hire an in-house attorney and take away his sinecure."

"The Slugges have always lived well," Bonano said. "Every one of them has an off-shore bank account. I expect that Dee follows in the family footsteps." He leaned forward, looking into Mary Lee's eyes. As he expected, her trembling increased. "Let's talk about something other than Slugges. I want to ask you something personal, Mary Lee. I hope you won't take offense. Why is it that whenever you're near me, you start to shake?"

She blushed. She hated blushing, but had never learned to control it. "Because you affect me that way."

It was his turn to redden. "I do?"

"Yes." She held her breath. Perhaps she'd been too forward and he'd go all cold and businesslike; she had seen him turn icy before.

He grinned delightedly. "Tell you what, Mary Lee. Let's explore this phenomenon–strictly on the quiet. I don't want the lunatics who control this city to get wind of the fact that we're seeing each other. Think you can carry it off?"

"Mr. Bonano, I think I can manage that," she replied.

"Now, darlings, let's get down to business," PooPoo caroled as he approached their table. He sat down and looked at them expectantly. "What is it that we have to do?"

Mary Lee snapped to attention. "PooPoo, I need a name for a fishing contest. So far, my brain is dead. We want to start some sort of week-long fishing thing to bring in tourists. Got any ideas?"

"Fishing for what?"

"Snook and grouper, something like that? I have to come up with something exciting to earn my keep, but it's really hard."

PooPoo laughed. "It's almost impossible to turn up anything exciting in this burg, darling. Of course, we could possibly hire a detective to videotape the sexual escapades of Joe Tyler or Meats Merlini–"

Bonano chuckled. "Joe is so holy, I wonder he managed to have children. Thought he'd demand that his wife remain a virgin."

"Frank, he couldn't always have been such a prick," PooPoo murmured. "He's bound to have had hormones when he was younger."

"Was he ever?" Mary Lee asked.

"You both be quiet and let me think for a moment," PooPoo said. He brushed his hair from his eyes, stared into the pool at the base of the waterfall for a moment, then looked back at them, his eyes sparkling. "Let's have a week of tournament fishing to begin with; that will give the party boats a boost. But let's not base the festival or whatever on fish, let's be realistic. Call it the Sunshine Liar's Festival. The prizes go to the fishermen who can make up the best stories about how they caught the fish and its size. What do you think?"

Bonano shook his head in wonder. "PooPoo, I think I love you after all."

Mary Lee laughed and clapped her hands with delight. "Splendid idea, absolutely splendid. And I know just the judges for the event."

"Who?" Bonano asked.

"Our city councilmen, who else? You know perfectly well that they're experts on the subject."

Local/County   The Sunshine Bulletin   Page 6

COUNCIL IRRESPONSIBLE
by Margie Noessit

This week's City Council meeting was, as usual, a farce. But those elected to govern the City of Sunshine have gone beyond mere farce; they have leaped into the realm of fiscal irresponsibility.

While it is laudable that the council wishes to bring more tourists into the city, the epidemic of silliness that has afflicted our city fathers should alarm the tax payer.

Gianni "Meats" Merlini wants to build a museum dedicated to the history of meat. This would cost at least two million before any of the exhibits are put in place. And what would these exhibits be? the public might ask. Pictures of cave men chasing tigers and mastodons, our artful councilman explained. Photographs of roast beef with Yorkshire pudding, perhaps? But the *piece de resistance* is to be a bronze sculpture some thirty feet high. Great art will come to Sunshine! Will the public be able to gaze on something akin to Venus de Milo? No, no, nothing so uplifting. We will be faced with a thirty foot high SAUSAGE! Made of bronze, yet. We can't even have a public feast on this thing, although I suppose it could be used as a gong to summon the public when the council comes up with other bright ideas.

Second on the latest list of stupid proposals is Josephus (Holy!Holy!Holy!) Tyler's idea to raze Mosquito Row to make way for a city park. No only will such a project disrupt the lives of a number of our citizens, but tax payers would be forced to picnic surrounded by the stench of untreated sewage. We need to look farther to see who will benefit from this. I suggest that His Holy!Holy!Holy!ness Tyler is after your money and mine for what is essentially worthless land. In most locales in Florida, waterfront property is considered a real asset. Not so in Sunshine. Compared with the banks of our Hatchacootee River; septic tank frontage might be a better investment.

Councilman Rainmaker runs third on this list; he doesn't think that Sunshine looks like Florida and wants to add palm trees to our landscape. At least he wants to plant trees, rather than erecting a thirty foot sausage made of bronze, but this is still a silly waste of tax dollars.

So far, the ladies on the council have refrained from stupidity, but Margie has a feeling that Melba Tosti is busy behind the scenes. Given her predilection for self-promotion, we had better be prepared for total preposterosity.

These latest idiocies should help our taxpayers to appreciate Councilman Warner's mediocrity. She did question whether cavemen had actually eaten tigers.

Joe Tyler hated being nervous. His hands were sweating, his chest felt constricted, and trickles of sweat itched down the center of his spine. When Learned Speaker had called him the night before, he had been certain that the holy man was going to offer his assistance; there were five other brothers in the church who were in the running for Lay Speaker. But Learned Speaker ordered him to attend a meeting. A very important meeting, Learned Speaker had said. And his voice had been cold, accusing.

Joe had been up most of the night, pacing through the kitchen, into the living room, the dining room, the family room, back to the kitchen, trying desperately to recall what, if anything, he had done to deserve Learned Speaker's wrath. He could remember nothing; his conduct had been Christian and impeccable at all times.

All the Tylers had been Pentecostal until he had broken the mold. Even though his father had passed on, Pappy was still his model. Pappy had been righteous, rigid in his beliefs. Never once throughout his long life had he ever uttered the word "liberal."

Learned Speaker was also a rigid Bible man; that was why Joe had followed him. What was in the God Book, as Learned Speaker called it, was the map which all mankind must follow. Under the tutelage of the God Book, man would grow even wiser, holier, more Christ-like. Learned Speaker's interpretation of the God Book was faultless, and he demanded of his congregation the same dedication to the word of God that he offered to the Father.

No one knew just where Learned Speaker had risen. Physically, he had come down I-75 from Ohio twenty years before, and had come to the Stop N' Shop Department Store looking for work. On his job application form, he had written that he had come from The Word, and that he had come to Sunshine to spread the joy and beauty that came from a full knowledge of The Word.

Joe had looked at the application, balled it up, and had actually aimed for the wastebasket when a voice inside his head whispered, "He is a Holy Man!" From that day, he had followed Learned Speaker, tithing, spending most of his free time searching for lost souls to bring into The Truth. The Living Witness Holy Confederation was now an army of Christian souls almost two thousand strong. He had been the perfect disciple.

Now he sat outside Learned Speaker's office in back of the church, reduced to a sweating jelly. He looked at his watch. He'd been ordered to be here at noon, and it was now 12.30. Just as he began to consider a fervent prayer to the Almighty, the door to Learned Speaker's office opened and he was invited inside.

Joe silently stepped into the sunlight that flooded the chamber, smiled uncertainly, then sat as Learned Speaker indicated a chair in the center of the room. He watched as Learned Speaker came to stand before him, his hands clasped at his waist, his countenance grave.

"Brother Tyler, I have long considered you my foremost disciple, but you have fallen on evil times and my heart is sore."

Fallen on evil times? What could he possibly have done that might be considered *evil?* "Learned Spea–"

The holy man stopped him with a look of such reproach that Joe cringed. "I have prayed and deliberated over this problem, Brother Tyler, and there is nothing I can do but to condemn you for your behavior. I have put this from me, but you are not a fit person to become Lay Speaker; you will not have my support in the coming election."

"Learned Speaker, what have I done?" Joe cried in anguish.

"You have sinned against the God Book; you have ignored the words written by the Hand of God, and you have clothed yourself in arrogance and iniquity." Learned Speaker pulled up a chair and sat beside Joe, then looked into his eyes. "I thought you could soar like an eagle, my son, but you have remained earthbound."

Joe started to protest, but again Learned Speaker silenced him. "It often happens with those who seek public office; they wear pride and arrogance like armor, and nothing can penetrate their scaly skins. But pride and arrogance are forgivable. What you have done cannot be forgiven. You have turned your back on God's words."

"What did I do?"

"'The laborer is worthy of his hire,' Luke 10:7," Learned Speaker almost snapped. "I was shamed by your actions; the entire congregation was tainted by your act."

"What act?"

"Your act of extortion. I read in the paper that you forced those fallen sisters to contribute money to your campaign. Shame, Brother Tyler, shame!"

"Every one of us took money from Zona's girls," Tyler protested. "And they should have contributed to our campaigns; don't we tolerate their presence? Don't we let them stay in business? How could you–?"

"'The laborer is worthy of his hire,'" Learned Speaker repeated. "You took money from sinners who know no other way to live. They are sinners, yes, but they have labored and earned their bread, which you have taken from their mouths. I have spoken; you are condemned. Leave me."

Heartsick and utterly confused, Joe rose from the chair and tottered from the room, his righteousness in a shambles.

Tuesday

Dear Jackson,

For no good reason, Learned Speaker has turned against me. He claims that I turned away from the Word of God by taking money from Zona's whores. He quoted Luke, "the laborer is worthy of his hire.," as his reason for condemning me.

You and I have worked hard to raise up the standard of the Living Witness Holy Confederation, and you and I have got to stick together on this matter. If Learned Speaker will condemn me for this, he will also condemn you. With both of us up for election this year, his action will cost us a bunch of votes.

Learned Speaker's taking up for whores raises a lot of questions in my mind. Has he become lecherous? Why would any decent Christian take the part of women who sell their bodies and wallow in sin? Let me hear from you on this, old friend. I can't fight this alone.

Joe

CHAPTER NINE

"What did you want to see me about, Gavel?" Rainmaker asked testily. "I'm busy as hell today, so make it quick."

"Teddy, you're the only one on the council I can talk with," Strike began. "The rest of them are idiots and–"

"Must you overstate the obvious?" Rainmaker snapped.

"Oh, for–we need your help to find out who's dumping sand on the flats. There are so many endangered–"

Rainmaker slapped the desk with the flat of his hand, causing Strike to jump. "I don't have time to worry about the endangered species, Gavel, I warn you. This town has got to develop, has to attract more tourists in order to survive, and we need a beach to do that. You want to know who dumped sand on the flats? How do you propose I find out? Do you want me to camp down there with an infra-red camera to catch the dastardly perpetrator? Maybe God dumped sand on the flats. Stop wasting my time on nonsense."

"Those flats feed thousands of birds, Teddy. We can't allow tourist dollars to blind us to the needs of species other than our own."

He looked around the tiny room that the councilmen used when meeting members of the public. The walls were dyspeptic green below the chair rail, and institutional tan above it. The desk, brought from the old city hall, was scarred from years of abuse by both frustrated citizens and councilmen trying to make themselves understood. On it were a telephone, a memo pad, and a pencil. Other than three wooden chairs, there was nothing else in the room.

"Screw species, man! The birds can always find somewhere else to go. Let 'em feed on the river banks if it comes to that; the water management district won't let us touch those. If this town grows, we'll all prosper. Do you want to live hand-to-mouth for the rest of your life?"

"I would hardly describe the way I live as hand-to-mouth," Strike replied coldly. "And no one could possibly accuse you and PooPoo of that; you're rolling in dough. What more could you possibly want?"

He hated Rainmaker at that moment. Couldn't the one intelligent member of the of council see what would happen to the river mouth if the flats were contaminated? The sewage leak was problem enough without adding beach sand to the equation. The beach sand would kill the worms–didn't anyone care about the worms?

He remembered little Ozzie, a Polychaete worm he'd studied in one of his marine biology labs. Ozzie was a very particular creature; nothing that he used to build his tube was anything less than perfect. Each particle of his construction was precisely uniform. He had built his tubes from corn flakes or whatever material handy in his Petrie dish, using his saliva and his microscopic jaws to create gothic palaces worthy of being shown in museums. His creations were art, true art.

Ozzie had not been one of the more spectacular tube worms like those found in tropical waters. He was a commonplace sort of worm, but Gavel had never lost the sense of warmth and wonder that the creature had wakened in him. Since leaving the marine biology lab, he'd wondered what happened to the lab worms he had known.

From early childhood he had wanted to be a marine biologist. The Gulf of Mexico and its denizens fascinated him. But even though he held a bachelor's degree in science, his father had insisted that he come into the insurance agency that had provided so amply for the family, even during the hard times. Common sense had won out; he really didn't wish to leave Sunshine to find work, and further, he enjoyed small luxuries like the latest in SCUBA gear.

"Our standard of living is no business of yours," Rainmaker said nastily.

"I didn't mean that the way it sounded," Strike replied. "I mean that we can't destroy the entire ecology of this area for tourist dollars, that's all I meant." He planted his palms on the desk top and leaned over, nose to nose with Rainmaker. "If the wildlife cannot survive here, it won't be long before *we* cannot survive. Can't you see that?"

Rainmaker leaned back in his chair and sighed. "Gavel, the history of Florida is a history of ecological destruction. How else could the state develop? A great deal of it was under water and we needed farmland. Hell, the history of the United States follows the same logic." Strike opened his mouth to speak and Teddy waved his hand. "Let me finish, please. Just this once, let me complete a sentence before you jump in spouting about some endangered—"

"*Logic?* Are you mad?" Gavel realized his voice was rising and struggled to bring himself under control.

"Yes, logic. Nature abhors a vacuum and business abhors an Eden; that's the way things are. There's nothing we can do to stop the advance of growth, nothing to stop the influx of people into this state. But, as a city councilman, it is my duty to see that some of the new growth comes to Sunshine." He smiled at Strike persuasively. "You're not getting any younger, Gavel; you're going to need a nest egg to retire on unless you plan on peddling insurance until you drop of old age. Everyone will benefit from growth here in Sunshine, including you."

"I'm not worried about my future, Teddy. Insurance is a necessity of life and I'm the only agent in town—"

"Well, you won't be the only agent in town for long. When that beach comes in, friend, this place is going to explode with newcomers, including insurance agents."

Rainmaker stood and looked at his watch. "You have made me late, Gavel. Not a friendly gesture at all. Sorry, but I have to run." He grabbed his jacket from the back of the chair and left the room, waving two fingers in farewell.

Gavel's antenna were buzzing. *When that beach comes in?* So Rainmaker did know who dumped the sand. This lunacy had gone farther than he thought. He and Guy would have to figure out a way to stop it.

Kelsey set a chef's salad before her husband and sank into her chair. He picked up his fork, then noticed the opened envelope beside his wife's plate. "What's that?"

"It's an invitation to a party that Dee Slugge is giving on the first of April. Apparently he and Sally throw an April Fool bash each year."

"And we're invited? He must have enjoyed his little effort at slumming, since we're being invited."

"I can't imagine him throwing an April Fool party, unless all his guests get together and tear wings off flies or something equally grisly. I would have thought Halloween a more likely time for him to entertain. Shall we go?"

"Sure, if you want to. I have a suspicion that Dee doesn't know anything about his wife's personal guest list. Think she'll invite Gavel as well?"

"Probably. She seems to have a bad case of hero worship." Kelsey speared a piece of lettuce. "Gavel said he didn't get anywhere with Teddy. In fact, he thinks Teddy is involved in the sand dumping because he was talking about the need for Sunshine to have a beach. Think I should talk to PooPoo? Usually PooPoo will listen."

"Sure, have a word with him. We have to find out what's going on."

Guy watched as Kelsey cut up a piece of tomato. When she looked down, her incredibly long lashes showed to their best advantage. Those lashes had been his downfall; they reminded him of his childhood pet, Toby. Toby had been the most beautiful ostrich he had ever seen. He had thrown tantrums and begged incessantly until his parents had brought her home to him.

His father had made a fuss about fencing in the yard so the ostrich couldn't escape, but his mother had prevailed. Then, as Toby had grown larger, the fence just hadn't been enough; the ostrich had escaped and terrified the neighborhood. Toby was sold to an ostrich farm. Only maturity had brought him the realization that ostriches didn't make good pets. But he had never forgotten Toby's beautiful eyelashes.

He didn't think that comparing his wife's eyes with those of a ratite bird was strange; he adored animals. Animals had personality; they were graceful and mysterious–and honest.

The first time he'd seen Kelsey was at the pier in St. Petersburg. He'd been in the city to see a client–he was a CPA. After finishing up, he had gone to the pier to escape profits and losses. Gazing at the circling birds, he had turned when she called out, thinking she was calling to him. But she had gone past him, giving him an apologetic smile, and embraced an elderly man standing farther along. He had felt cheated. On her way back, she grinned at him, and he stepped in front of her.

"Hi, I'm Guy Fawkins," he had said.

"Oh. Hi. So how can I help you?"

"So I want to know your name, if you're married, your telephone number, and last of all, whether you'll have dinner with me tonight."

She had looked down, blushing, and he had seen those lashes and fallen in love.

His wife was a honey girl, with honey-colored hair, light brown eyes, and the kind of skin that held a honey tan year-round. She was sweet by nature, intelligent, and possessed a sense of mischief that never ceased to delight him.

Now Kelsey put down her fork and stared at him. "Guy, what if some of the council members are involved in the sand business. What are you going to do?"

"I'll drive to Tampa and talk with the DEP, for starters. Then I'll go to the water management district and talk with them. If necessary, I'll fly to Atlanta and get the EPA involved. If they start messing around with estuarine lands, they'll find themselves in more trouble than they ever dreamed of."

"You know what Teddy said to Gavel? Said that the history of Florida is a history of environmental destruction. How's that for callousness?"

"Pretty normal for those in office, I'd say. Once people are elected, they immediately start to think like politicians. Some are just better than others at hiding their concern about remaining in office for a long time." He chewed reflectively, then said, "Who would dump sand for Teddy, Fielding, perhaps?"

"Probably, but do you think he'd risk asking Fielding to do something illegal?"

"Of course he would. They're in business together, you know."

Kelsey's fork clattered to the plate. "Teddy and Fielding? But he votes on–"

Guy chuckled at his wife's naivete. "You thought that because he's gay, he'd stay clean? There isn't a member of the council who's squeaky, not even Joe Tyler."

It was Kelsey's turn to laugh. "The first thing I wonder about when someone spouts off about being a Christian is how many dirty deals he's involved in."

"I never knew you were so cynical, Kelsey. But you have given me an idea. I'm going to borrow an infra-red camera from one of my clients, set it up somewhere down at the river mouth where it won't be seen, and see what fish I catch."

Kelsey made a face. "Poor camera. I hope it doesn't have a sense of smell."

Mary Lee Mince came through Bonano's office door, her arms filled with rolled posters and handbills. She plopped them down on the tiny conference table across the room from his desk, straightened, and grinned at the city administrator. "Here it is."

Bonano rose and crossed the room. "Show me."

She unrolled a poster and weighted the corners with ashtrays and a paper clip dispenser. "Like it?"

"How big was it, really?" asked yellow letters spread across a background of sparkling aquamarine water. "Tell the biggest lie and win a free three day fishing trip aboard the *Suncoast Susie*." In smaller type, the particulars of the contest were spelled out, and at the bottom of the poster, international orange lettering screamed "Sunshine Liar's Festival."

"I wanted to use the city seal somewhere on the posters, but it's so blah that I decided against it. Do you like them?"

"They look great, even in orange. I hate orange. I even hate oranges; they break me out."

"But you're a Floridian."

"Maybe my parents hadn't been natives long enough to innoculate me." He looked at Mary Lee appreciatively. She was wearing a soft green dress that clung in all the right places and enhanced her greenish eyes. "You look especially pretty today."

"Thanks." Mary Lee began to tremble.

"Uh, I was thinking that we might have dinner this weekend; what do you think?"

"Is it kosher, our being seen outside office hours? I mean, I'd love to."

"What I do on my own time is my own business, Mary Lee."

"Well, then, okay."

"Saturday night?"

"Sure."

"Good, now let's get back to unimportant things. How are you going to advertise this thing? We don't have that much money for tour–"

"Press releases. I'll mail out releases to every paper within miles, some of the larger state papers, and some of the papers up north. We're bound to attract some new blood; everyone loves to lie."

"I like that–everyone loves to lie. Okay, work up some sample press releases for the council to read. Once we get them to read something, they usually know what we're talking about for at least half an hour. And how about designing another poster with a fish motif? You know the councilmen like variety. And add the city seal to one of the posters. Maybe I'll bring up changing it as an emergency, if only to get rid of the crossed eyes on the sun. They drive me crazy. I–"

"We need to talk, Frank, right away," Odlum said urgently, as he came through the door. "Sorry, Mary Lee, I didn't mean–"

"That's okay, Oddman. Frank and I were through." She began to roll up the posters. "One thing more, Frank. Are the handbills okay?"

"Yes, Mary Lee, they're fine. See if you can come up with a new city seal while you're thinking."

Odlum laughed bitterly. "Perhaps you might design a leaking sewer pipe surrounded by–never mind."

"DEP?"

"DEP."

"Shit! How bad?"

"We've got one year to clean it all up; after that, a consent order."

"Mary Lee," Bonano said, "maybe you'd better follow Oddman's advice. A sewer pipe with–"

"A cross-eyed sun at the far end?" she asked. She smiled at Bonano and left the room. He stared after her.

"Frank, what are we going to do? There is no way on earth we can get a bond issue through in this burg in a year's time. Got any bright ideas?"

"Can you lay pipe alongside the leaky ones and tie them in to the plant?"

"Yeah, I could do that, but we still have to find the money."

"Let me talk to the mayor. I do have an emergency fund I could dig into if necessary. Let me know exactly how much pipe you're going to need."

Odlum slumped into a chair and shook his head. "You don't want to know."

"Maybe you should go to Tally and talk to the DEP, tell them the problem and see if we can't gain a little time."

"Hell, they won't listen to me. I'm just hired help. The request has to come from one of the council."

Bonano smiled inwardly. "I'll ask Lila Mae to go with you."

Strike pulled up outside Dee Slugge's house and got out of the car. The house looked unoccupied, but then, all of the homeowners on Merriweather Drive strove for the unoccupied look. The theory in the gated community was that thieves would be discouraged if it was difficult to tell whether anyone was at home.

As an insurance man, he liked that approach; it would be impossible for a thief to determine occupancy other than by ringing a doorbell, but the street lacked a sense of life. The lawns were primly manicured and without character; one longed to see a bald spot where mole crickets had damaged the grass. The shrubbery around each house was identical and trimmed to finical exactness. Of course, Merriweather Drive was the town's only gated community and every citizen who lived in the compound obeyed the Rules, carved in stone, no doubt on Mount Sinai, by a committee chaired by Joe Tyler.

Whimsically, he wondered if the occupants were stiff creatures done up by the local taxidermist. Were each of them placed by some force other than themselves in the garden at ten in the morning, propped on a weeding bench, trowel in hand, then seated by the pool in the afternoons?

He rang the doorbell and waited, whistling quietly, for Sally to respond. She had insisted that he let her accompany him on his moonlight prowl of the river mouth.

"How is Dee going to feel about your gallivanting after dark with another man?" he had asked.

"Dee doesn't even know I exist, Gavel. I'm there to get breakfast for him, and occasionally on weekends, I see him for part of Saturday afternoon. Other than those times, he's 'at work' and I'm not to disturb him."

"Sally, I'm sure you've heard the gossip that I'm having an affair with Kelsey, even though Guy is my best friend. Do you want to be subjected to the same sort of dirt?"

"Gavel, I want to help you save the mud flats, and I don't care what they say about me. At least if they gossip, someone will acknowledge that I exist!"

He had felt sorry for her then, ashamed that any living creature felt so unnoticed by its kind. His own experiences had been in the opposite direction–from his early childhood he had been subjected to merciless teasing. He was aware that he was physically unattractive; he knew that people snickered over his bottle-bottom glasses and his round head, but over the course of his life he had developed a thick armor and he no longer gave a damn. He had never loved anyone other than his parents and Mother Nature. In a state increasingly dominated by an insistence on conformity, they, almost alone recognized the worth of an individual.

He often wondered how Floridians had become so obsessed with conformity, and decided that the change was wrought by the influx of people from the north. He had come to the conclusion that many of the retirees had worked in factories or for large companies before moving to Florida. They were simply unaware of the cult of individuality that had developed in the south.

He had become accustomed to being a loner, had learned to appreciate his solitude and to make good use of it. Then he had met Guy Fawkins and found meaningful friendship. They were both guardians of Mother Earth.

The front door opened slightly and he saw Sally. "Hi. You ready to go?"

"Yes, but I'll come out the back of the house and leave the chain on the front door. See you in a sec."

He went back to his car and got in, impatient. He wanted to get down to the river mouth before full dark, and he was running late. Tonight was full moon. Yesterday, Jack Fatigay had called him earlier in the day on an insurance matter and made some crack about the Hatchacootee River and full moon tides. The senator had been laughing about how, in Sunshine, even the tide was stupid. Fatigay had piqued his curiosity.

But then he remembered his mother telling him that good boys didn't go to the river mouth on full moon because they might be spirited away. There had been a pair of young lovers, his mother said, who disappeared mysteriously from the river mouth when she was a girl. It was bosh, naturally, but he intended to find out if there was any truth in what he had heard.

Sally slipped into the car beside him. "I brought some bug repellent and a blanket to spread so we can sit down."

"There won't be any mosquitoes tonight, Sally. Too dry. But better safe than sorry, I guess. You sure Dee won't raise hell when he comes home and finds you out with me?"

"Dee is in Tallahassee for the next two or three days. And even if he were here, he wouldn't care; I'm not a legal case."

"Come on, Sally, cheer up."

"It's hard to be cheerful when your husband doesn't even know you're alive," she griped. "But to heck with him. Where are we going?"

"When I was a kid, my mother told me about two lovers disappearing from the mouth of the Hatchacootee River on full moon. I always thought it was an old wives' tale–something

Mother made up to be certain I stayed in at night, but yesterday I was talking to Jackson and he made some reference to the tide doing strange things when the moon is full."

"I'll bet Jackson has never been near the mouth of the Hatchacootee, even at midday," Sally retorted. "Wildlife doesn't hire any lobbyists to give him a handout."

Gavel laughed appreciatively. "Never thought of it that way. He said Joe Tyler told him about the strange tide."

Sally made a rude noise. "No doubt, the Lord told Joe all about it. I'm trying to remember if I ever heard anything about an abnormal tide down there, but I don't think I have. Of course, I didn't grow up right here in Sunshine, so that's probably why."

Gavel turned left on Hatchacootee Boulevard and headed west. The sky had deepened and the first stars began to glimmer.

"What time is high tide?"

"The tide was due to begin rising at three. I do hope it was on time."

"If a strange current comes along, won't it be dangerous for us to be down there?"

"No, there's a spot where we can watch what happens in perfect safety."

The moon gave them light to see their way through the small copse of scrub oaks that occupied a little peninsula of high ground. To their left and right, sedge moved gently in the night wind. They reached the end of the peninsula and looked down at the mud flat that stretched to the water's edge.

Halfway to the water, the offending sand scrawled a pale comment for a hundred yards across the mud.

"I was out here yesterday, and the birds have moved away from this area entirely. I suppose all the worms are dead below the sand, and it's probably affecting the mud around it." Strike turned to face Sally. "Can you imagine all this turned to a beach? It would be a disgrace!"

"Dee said that the mayor has already got some flack from Heart County about turning this area into a beach. Said

Englehardt threatened to bring in the EPA or something like that."

"For once, I have to agree with Heliotrope. Gawd, what a name. I wonder what her parents were thinking when they named her?"

Sally tittered. "Pretty bad thoughts, obviously. Maybe they wanted a boy." She peered at the scene before them. "How can you tell if the tide is coming in?"

"See that rip farther out? Guy told me that the only time he's ever seen a riptide out there is when the tide is coming in. I wonder why?"

Sally's eyes seemed to glow. "Have you ever studied the tides, Gavel? I mean, the way they move around the world, and how currents form and affect the climate? I've always been fascinated by tides and currents, but haven't really spent much time actually learning anything."

He looked at her with new appreciation. "We can learn together. And with the council determined to destroy the river mouth, I guess we'd better learn fast." He glanced up and stiffened. "Look how that riptide is moving in. I've never heard of that happening before. Hey, it's coming straight in to shore!"

Sally gasped. "How high will the tide come, Gavel? That rip looks mean; I sure wouldn't want it to get me!"

He instinctively put his arm around her shoulders and pulled her closer, protective. Through her cotton shirt, he could feel the delicacy of her bones. Her body was slight, frail, like a tiny bird. He wondered at this as she melted into his side. "We're safe, but look how the water is rolling up onto the mud; it's almost reached the sand."

The water roiled and advanced, relentless. They could hear a sound almost like the clapping of hands as the tide moved up the mud flat. Then it reached the sand.

Sally gently disengaged herself from his arm and spread the blanket she had brought. "Sit down, Gavel. We don't have to stand here with our mouths open; we can sit and gape just as well."

Gavel grabbed her by the shoulders and shook her, beginning to laugh. "Sally, I think Ma Nature is going to make damned sure no beach is ever put here. When that water recedes, what do you want to bet the sand will be gone?'

"No takers on that one, Gavel." She sank onto the blanket and pulled him down beside her.

An hour later, the pristine mud flat glistened in the moonlight, little pools of water still marking the area where the sand had lain.

CHAPTER TEN

Department of Environmental Protection
The State of Florida
19 March, 2—

Hon. Melba Tosti
Mayor, City of Sunshine
2344 Hatchacootee Boulevard
Sunshine, Florida 3766500

Dear Mayor Tosti:

It has been brought to my attention that the City of Sunshine is dumping sand on the mud flats at the mouth of the Hatchacootee River in a misguided effort to turn the area into a beach.

As you are aware, the estuarine lands formed by the Hatchacootee River and its delta are vital to the State of Florida. With the exception of the sewage that is leaching into the river from your ancient system, this delta is pristine, the only one of its kind in the state, and provides important feeding grounds for an enormous migratory bird population. In addition, the delta and its surrounding mud flats are home to species of tube worms, the Polychaeta, which feed the migratory birds. The addition of sand on the mud flats would destroy the worms, thereby doing great harm to our wild bird population.

I will be coming to Sunshine on 30 March to make an inspection of the flats, and would appreciate your taking time from your busy schedule to accompany me on this inspection. At that time, we can discuss ways for Sunshine to bring to an end any further damage to the estuary and its lands.

I look forward to meeting with you again.

Sincerely,

D.b. sarious
———————————————
Donald B. Sarious, Chief
Estuarine Lands Division

Melba muttered imprecations on the head of Teddy Rainmaker and reached for the telephone. He answered on the second ring.

"Know what we have on our hands, darling?" she asked nastily.

"What? Melba, you shouldn't be calling me at ho–"

"The effing DEP is on my back about a report that sand has been dumped on the mud flats at the river mouth! I told you it was a stupid idea!"

"Actually, you said you liked the plan, my dear," he reminded. "Who sent them the report, did they say?"

"No, it's a letter from Don Sarious, that prick who knows more than God. You remember the guy who came down last time we were in the frying pan over some environmental stupidity?–the same one. Now he's coming on the 30th for a field inspection. What are we going to do?"

"Keep your cool, lay low, don't panic, and all that other fatherly advice. Just remember one thing, Melba, *we don't know anything about this!* If some dastardly creature has been dumping sand on the mud flat, we'll do everything we can to find the culprit. Of course, we won't do a thing, but Sarious doesn't have to know that." Teddy was quiet for a moment. "When was full moon, do you know?"

"I have enough to keep up with, Teddy, without worrying about when the moon is full," Melba snapped.

"I would have thought, you being a woman, that you would know intuitively. Aren't women ruled by Selena?"

She snorted. "You are ruled by crap, Rainmaker. Why do you want to know?"

"I heard some tale when we first moved here, something about whatever is on the flats at full moon disappearing. Of course, I think it's an old wives' tale, but–"

"Right. Triton or Poseidon comes ashore and sweeps up the place. Or maybe they use a vacuum cleaner. So what should I do?"

"I've already told you, Melba. Nothing. Just give the guy a call and tell him how anxious you are to see him, that sort of thing. We know nothing."

She chewed her lip before replying. "I'm not that good at lying, Teddy. I mean–"

"Nonsense!" he retorted. "You're a politician; you lie to the public every day. What's a single man from the DEP compared with the entire city of Sunshine?"

"Bastard!"

"Just keep your wig on, Melba."

"You–!" She slammed the receiver into the cradle and rose, furious. Then she sat back down, flipped through her Rolodex, and dialed a number in Tallahassee. "Mr. Sarious, please. This is Mayor Tosti from Sunshine. Don, how are you? Just got your letter and I wanted you to know that I'll be able to give you a full morning or afternoon. Your choice. Morning? Okay. I really look forward to seeing you again. And I'm certain, Don, that you won't find any problems here in Sunshine. See you at eight on the 30th here at City Hall. 'Bye."

She hung up, nervously tapped her fingers on the desk, then grabbed the telephone again. "Get me Mr. Bonano, and if he's in a meeting, that's tough. I want to speak to him right now."

"Jee-sus!" Frank Bonano's right hand hurriedly went through its ritual, picked up the pen on his desk, and slammed it to the wooden surface.

His secretary looked at him with pity. "That bad, huh?"

"Worse. Her Majesty is in receipt of a letter from DEP about sand on the mud flats. She wants me to drop everything, get my ass down to the river mouth, and report to her pronto. What sand? I thought we had a sewage problem down there. Do me a favor, will you? Call Odlum and tell him I need his company for the trip. Tell him I'll stop in for him on my way to the car. Then call Licensing and tell 'em they'll have to reschedule the meeting."

He went down the hall to Odlum's offices and stuck his head in the door. "He here?"

Odlum came from his cubicle, took his jacket from a coat rack in the corner, and looked at Bonano quizzically. "Where we going?"

"River mouth."

"What the hell for? I'm working on an estimate for new pipe for the whole city and you want me to baby sit while you go for a ride?"

"Her Majesty has a burr up her ass. Got a letter from DEP about sand on the mud flats down at the river mouth. You heard anything about it?"

Odlum turned red, then looked at the floor and stammered, "Uh, yeah, I actually meant to tell you that somebody had been dumping down there, but it slipped my mind."

"Thanks, good buddy. How long ago did you see it?"

"Uh, when I took Lila Mae down there to check out the sewage leaks." Odlum blushed even harder.

"You sick, Oddman? You got that flu that's making the rounds? You're awfully red."

"Yeah, I mean, no, I'm not sick, Frank. It's hot today, don't you think?"

Bonano waved the comment aside. "You heard anything about who's behind the sand on the flats?"

"Not a peep. It doesn't make any sense to me, Frank. Why would anyone want to put sand on top of a mud flat?"

"You forget that Her Majesty wants a beach for Sunshine, Oddman. She's probably behind it, probably got one of her Yankee buddies to do it on the sly just to see what would happen. I wouldn't put any thing past her. Man, she's so tough I'll bet she ate her ex-hubby's balls at the last breakfast she made for him. Ambition like she's got isn't feminine, you know?"

They walked across the parking lot and got into Bonano's Jeep, which was parked beneath the only tree in the parking lot.

"You heard that the council are pissed at you for not planting trees at their parking spots?"

"No, but they're always pissed at me for something, so it's no big deal." Bonano laughed shortly. "I was thinking of planting palms by their parking spaces, Oddman. Serve them right."

The big man snickered. "Got a point. Make it coconut palms, and we might enjoy the next bad storm we have. How come Melba is so hot for you to drop everything and get out to the river mouth?"

"DEPuty dog is coming to town on the 30th, and she's mortally afraid they might do something to interfere with her plans."

"Personally, I think her beach idea is crazy. We never had anything remotely resembling a beach since I was a kid, and that wasn't yesterday. We always had the delta and the mud and a lot of birds."

"Politics does funny things to people's heads. They get a god complex and think that by waving a magic wand they can change the world." Bonano shook his head. "I don't look forward to the election campaigns this year. With Melba and Joe running against each other, it's going to be nasty. Fatigay is running too, and his opponents always get disemboweled." He glanced at Odlum. "Speaking of campaigns, I spoke with Lila Mae about going to Tallahassee with you to see about some help with funding. She said she'd be delighted to go; you just call and let her know when."

Odlum blushed. Bonano looked amused, then surprised. "Oh, I didn't know."

"Didn't know what?"

"I don't know." Bonano shrugged and put his foot on the accelerator.

Gavel Strike picked up his beer, held it aloft to check the level in the bottle, and finished it off. Then he looked at Guy and Kelsey, who sat across the table from him. "I'm telling you, wonders never cease. You know who called me this afternoon?"

"Anyone home?" Sally Slugge called from the side of the house.

"We're back here, Sally," Kelsey answered. "Come on back." She got up and went to get another glass.

Sally came around the end of the house, saw Gavel, and hesitated. "Am I interrupting something?"

"Certainly you are," Guy answered. "A very high level conference. Gavel was just about to amaze us with some astounding information. Take a pew. You want beer or wine?"

"Oh, I'll have wine." She pulled a chair up to the table and sat down next to Gavel. "What new miracle has occurred?"

"I got a call from Lila Mae Warner today," he announced.

"What did she want?" Kelsey asked, coming back with a wine glass and a fresh bottle.

"She wanted to know more about Polychaete worms," he said. He laughed as Guy's jaw dropped. "No kidding."

"Why would she want to know about something like that?" Sally asked.

"Said she was going to Tallahassee about the sewage leaks, and she intended to be armed and ready when the DEP jumps her."

"I don't quite follow her reasoning," Guy said.

"Is there anyone who can? She's nice, but she's not all that educated," Kelsey poured Sally's wine and handed it to her.

"I told her about Polychaeta in general, about how there are free-moving worms and sedentary ones that build tubes, but she wanted more specific information. Like what was found in the mud at the mouth of the Hatchacootee. So I explained about the Tubifex, the sludge worms, and how their presence is a sign of pollution. She wanted to know if they had any other use, outside making trouble for Sunshine, and I said that they're gathered and sold as tropical fish food. For some reason, she got really enthusiastic about that." Gavel shrugged and opened another beer. "After about half an hour on the subject, she thanked me and hung up. Strange."

Sally sipped her wine, seemed to hesitate, then grinned impishly and said, "If you were married to Henny Warner, you'd be strange too."

"Why?" Guy asked.

"Can you imagine crawling into the sack with a man like that?"

Gavel had just taken a swallow of beer and he choked.

Kelsey jumped up and pounded him on the back. "I'll bet that when he was courting her, he brought her bouquets of fried chicken legs–either that or fried mullet. Do you suppose he offered her a ham bone engagement ring?"

"I don't think Lila Mae has ever worn an engagement ring, just her wedding band," Sally answered.

"Women are the cruelest creatures on the face of the earth!" Guy exclaimed. "How can you talk about poor Henny that way? I mean, he's not a Clark Ga–"

"You can say that again," Kelsey remarked. She peered at her colleague. "You going to live, Gavel?"

Wincing, Gavel nodded. "Yes, thanks. You can quit practicing karate on me now. I–I still want to know why she was curious about the worms."

He was shocked by what Sally said; she had always seemed so retiring and delicate, so proper! He wondered, he had to wonder, if she and Kelsey had ever talked about him in that way–what would it be like to be in the sack with Gavel Strike? No, on reflection, Kelsey would never discuss a subject like that. She was so direct, she'd just ask him if he were an accomplished lover and have done with it. Of course, there were times when she was far too direct, but Kelsey was Kelsey and, hopefully, nothing would ever change her.

He was surprised to find himself thinking about such things; he had always considered himself a cold fish where women were concerned. They had long found him unattractive and he was content with that. While the mating habits of the invertebrates or the birds were riveting, the courtship rites of *Homo Sapiens* he had always found less than interesting.

He remembered the feel of Sally's tiny bones within the protection of his arm, and the way she had seemed to melt into his side, and how she looked in the moonlight, with the oaks' leafy shadows across her face. Those thoughts made him feel strange, like there were squiggles going on in his intestines.

"...had one beer too many?" Guy asked, concerned.

Gavel snapped back to reality. "No, I was just wool-gathering. I cannot imagine how Lila Mae is going to use the information she has on worms."

"We have to figure out some way to reach the city council," Kelsey said.

"I suppose I can talk with Tyler," Guy said. "He and I have had some business dealings in the past and, although he thinks I've got a wild, terrible wife, we get on fairly well. But they've got to get over this idea of a beach; it won't happen."

Gavel asked, "Who's going to tackle the gorgon?"

Sally burst out laughing. "I can see her now, wearing one of those funky snake print jerseys, with a wig of snakes to match. Think we might suggest it to her, Kelsey?"

"She'd probably think you were serious. Okay, I'll tackle Melba. Sally, you hit on Joe too; he's going to be the worst one. He's your kin and he'll have to pay you some attention. Guy, you take on Merlini, because he considers himself a great businessman, and..."

"He must have done something right," Guy retorted. "He certainly made a killing in the sausage business."

"...Gavel takes Lila Mae, because he's established himself as an advisor."

"I wouldn't go that far, Kelsey."

"If you talk further with her, she might even start asking you for advice. After all, she can't get much help from Henny."

"And who is to take on Rainmaker?" Gavel asked.

Kelsey smiled. "Sally and I will work on PooPoo and take the cowards' way out."

State/Local   The Tallahassee Crier   Page 5

News Around the State

A BILL TO FORCE THE RETURN OF SLAVERY?

Tallahassee-- A bill introduced yesterday in the Senate by Senator Jackson Fatigay of Heart County has the Capitol in an uproar. The sixth term senator's bill would end prisons as we know them.

If this bill is passed into law, a person convicted of a felony would go through a short term in a state facility to teach them The Rules. Then the convict would be sent out to serve his term as a bonded servant to people in need of an extra pair of hands.

"This is nothing more than an attempt to return to slavery," said the Attorney General, Irma Law. "With due respect, I am forced to wonder if the senator has lost his marbles. What citizen in his right mind would take on a convicted murderer, child molester, or thief to help around the house? We would have dangerous criminals at large all over the state."

Senator Fatigay has defended his bill as the only feasible way to end the hemorrhage of tax dollars into the ever-expanding penal system. "Coddling our prisoners now costs the State of Florida $14 billion a year. Under my plan, the only expense to the State would be the bullwhip supplied with each prisoner to ensure good behavior. It's time we taught these felons that the state will no longer tolerate their crimes."

Representative Henry "Sandfly" Bates, whose District overlaps part of Senator Fatigay's, said that the proposed bill was another example of how far the Right will go to infringe on the rights of citizens. "In our great nation, slavery is against the law. The citizens of Florida need to be ever vigilant against the encroachment of extremism. Whether we like it or not, felons are humans."

During the last session of the Legislature, the Senator introduced a bill requiring complete submission to her husband by every married woman in the State. The bill was defeated in the House.

Frank Bonano got out of his car and looked around curiously. He'd never been to any of the homes in this particular neighborhood, and was surprised to find how small they were. Mary Lee lived on a nice street, there were plenty of trees, and the sidewalks were still almost intact, but the residences were tiny. They reminded him of the little mill houses that were prevalent across the south around the turn of the last century:

bedrooms barely large enough for a double bed, kitchens the size of closets, and living rooms even smaller than the bedrooms.

He started up the walk to Mary Lee's, then paused to look around once more. He started. Four doors down, Melba Tosti's Lincoln was parked in the driveway, and he saw the mayor carting in a bag of groceries. He turned away, lest she look around and spot him, and hurried to the front door. Before he could ring the bell, the door opened and Mary Lee motioned him inside.

"I just saw her pull up. Come in quickly; she's as nosy as they come."

"I didn't know she lived down here."

"It's the cross she bears, Frank. She thinks that, as mayor, she should live in some grand quarters. I guess that's why she's so bitter sometimes."

"Hell, if she spent less money on wigs, she could live in a mansion. They don't come cheap, you know. When she first became mayor, she kept insisting that I come to her house whenever she had a new brainstorm. I always refused, telling her that I was worried about her reputation. I thought she'd get the message, but she keeps calling me and when I refuse, she gets nasty. I don't know what she wants most, a lover or a dog's body to kick around. I feel for her secretary; she runs her ragged and it's nothing but ego trip."

"She's not a very nice person," Mary Lee agreed. "She was really put out when she found that she lives so close to one of the city menials."

"Ignore her; there's nothing she can do."

He looked around the small living room and was pleased with what he saw. The walls were painted a neutral off-white, and the furniture, scaled to the size of the room, was cheery and looked comfortable. "Nice digs."

"Thanks. All I can afford on my salary, Mr. City Administrator. Think you can spare a raise?"

He laughed ruefully. "I could do with one myself. Haven't had a raise in the last four years."

"Why not?"

"The city doesn't have the money, and I make a lot more than some of the others who work their butts off. One of these days–"

"When hell freezes over," she said, interrupting him with a laugh. "Or later than that, even, when the city council is made up of intelligent, caring–"

"Whoa, Nelly! Don't get carried away there. Ready to go?"

"Where are we going?"

"Into Heart County, away from the prying eyes of Sunshine and the fishy smell of Southern Fried."

"Isn't it a shame we have to go somewhere else to have dinner? I mean–"

"Discretion is the better part of valor, my girl."

PooPoo drove down Hatchacootee Boulevard, occasionally turning to look at Rainmaker. "Cheer up, darling."

"I can't; I'm worried. If Don Sarious is coming on the 30th to check up on the health of the mud flats and he finds that sand, all hell will break loose. The DEP, the water management district, the county commission, and God knows who else, will be down on us. And with Her Majesty handling Sarious, who's probably never laughed in his whole life, it could get nasty."

"Suppose the old tales are true, and the flat is cleaned every full moon. If there's nothing there, Sarious can't do a thing but feel like a fool."

Rainmaker brightened a little. "True. Then he can go after whomever tipped him off. But if the sand is gone, that means we'll never have a beach."

"Not necessarily. How much did Fielding dump–six loads? That isn't very much. If the Legislature okays the project, then there's nothing the DEP can do but go along, and then we'd have enough sand, thousands of tons of the stuff. No tide could ever take that much away."

"We're going to have a tough time in Tallahassee, PooPoo. Fatigay isn't going to take this lying down."

"He might get voted out of office after this last bill he introduced. The man must be mad! Bonded servants? Shall we apply for seven or eight to help out at Rain, and perhaps one or two for the house? We'll let Jack the Ripper do the meat cutting, and put a poisoner in charge of the salads–"

"Right. A serial killer as gardener; they're good at digging holes to hide the bodies." Teddy chuckled. "The Right frighten me; they are truly corrupt. At least the Left still have some ideals."

"I don't object so much to their corruption, I just wish the Right would have an original idea once in a while. They seem doomed to mud-slinging and repetition of bad history."

"I don't think we've seen mud yet. Wait until Melba and Joe get going."

"I thought Joe was pretty straight-laced, but I have to admit–!"

"He is, but he's as crooked as they come, and as dirty a fighter as you'll ever see, outside Jackson Fatigay. Watch out for men who hide behind the facade of 'Christian;' they're dangerous as rattlers. Hell, Tyler's doings make me look like a piker, and I'm a crook. I'm certain he's worked out a deal with the lawyers on the Mosquito Row land, and I'm equally certain that whatever deal he's done will benefit me, but I don't do anything about it, do I?"

"Darling, you're no crook!" PooPoo protested.

"Of course I am, and as long as it's between friends, I'll admit it. I have no illusions about myself, PooPoo. With all the businesses we own a part of, everything I vote on is questionable because I can profit directly from my vote. The only thing that might excuse me is that it's done all over the state."

"Well, if everyone is doing it–"

"Everyone doesn't have that bitch, Melba Tosti, breathing down his neck. I have to go along with her or she'll blow the whistle. Sometimes I think I should just resign from the council and have done with it."

"Don't you dare. You're the only intelligent person Sunshine has, outside Frank Bonano."

They pulled up at the road's end and got out of the car. PooPoo took a deep breath and choked. "What is that awful smell?"

"Sunshine's old problem; our sewer pipes are leaking badly. We should have done something about the system a long time ago, but it wasn't politically expedient. I suppose we're going to be forced to fund replacement of the entire system, which means a bond issue, which means recriminations and idiocy on the council. They're so afraid that they'll lose a vote that they're frozen in time. This town will never go anywhere with that bunch."

"They probably say the same thing about you."

"More than likely, but at least I do give attention to things that need to be done. Now, where did Fielding dump the sand? I don't see a trace of it."

The Gulf sparkled, gray under the morning sun. On the horizon, two fishing boats were headed south. It was low tide and they carefully walked out on the mud to the water's edge, skirting colonies of feeding birds that paid them little attention. Above the reedy island in the center of the Hatchacootee, seagulls wheeled and cried. A gentle puff of wind from the water gave them temporary relief from the stench of sewage.

They peered left and right across the mud. There was no sign of sand anywhere.

"It's gone–I'll be damned! Maybe the old tales have something to them. Tell you what, after Sarious's visit, we'll get Fielding to put some more down, and you and I will be here on the next full moon to see what happens."

CHAPTER ELEVEN

"You don't screw where you work, Frank. I'm warning you, you see that cheap bitch again and I'll have your balls." Melba slammed her fist on the desk, glared at Bonano, then looked at the pile of mail on her desk. "You've been playing the reluctant virgin with me for as long as I've known you, and now you're banging that slut who works at City Hall? I should fire you on the spot, you know that? Run your ass right out of–" her voice was rising.

Bonano's right hand leapt to its duty, hesitated after checking the knot in his tie, clenched, and fell to his side. "Madam Mayor," he said coldly, "what I do in my private life is none of your affair, and to insinuate that I am banging Miss Mince is outrageous. I insist on your apology."

"Put your head where the sun never shines, Frank. I know screwing around when I see it. You can visit our neighborhood to carry on with a city employee, but when I ask you to come to my house, you've always got–"

Bonano's voice was ice. "If you insist on continuing this conversation, Melba, you will have my resignation on your desk before noon. You have no right to make such accusations, and you also have no right to insist that I waste what little time I have away from my duties waiting on you at your home. You're merely a mayor, Melba, not some frigging royalty. You have your options–an apology or my resignation by noon." He turned away.

"There are a lot of city managers looking for work, Frank," she snarled.

"Hire one, then–if you can find anyone stupid enough to work for you. You've got a bad reputation, Melba, in case you aren't aware of it."

"What do you mean, a bad reputation? Sunshine has never before had the leadership it has under me, and furthermore I–"

He left the room, shutting the door quietly behind him.

"She's really on a tear this morning," Melba's secretary whispered.

"Well, she can tear herself a new one," Bonano replied pleasantly. "I think she's going to want you to take a letter, and it's not going to be pleasant for you. I apologize."

The young woman rolled her eyes and sighed.

As he walked back to his office, he felt free. For years, he'd been weighed down by hefty alimony payments to his ex-wife, but she had recently remarried. During that time, he had borne Melba's arrogance, Joe Tyler's apocalyptic threats, Merlini's constant carping over matters on which he knew nothing, Rainmaker's bitchiness, and Lila Mae's warm and fuzzy ignorance. Problems with personalities teemed within the municipal government. He wondered sometimes if there was something in the water that spawned dubious eccentricity.

Time and again, he'd sworn he would just quit, disappear and live anonymously somewhere under another name. But he'd become disgusted with himself when he thought that way. The truth was, he felt sorry for poor little Sunshine.

He was certain that if he left, the whole edifice would collapse. If that happened, a lot of innocent folks would lose their jobs. The retirees who expected government to run smoothly, to give them some modicum of protection during disasters, even the old folks who attended the council meetings for their weekly outing, would have nowhere to turn if they needed help. He was the axle on which the wheel of city administration turned; it was his responsibility to make certain no one was hurt by the bumbling, self-serving decisions of the council.

Last week he'd received a fabulous offer from Ocala. They offered him almost double the salary he was making. He'd given serious consideration to taking the job, but down deep, he'd known that if he left, he would feel like a rat.

Now, thanks to Melba, there was a real possibility that he would write that resignation–he had no intention of backing down. It was time he took control of his life, put aside those who made it a misery. His Italian blood was up; he felt like a man again. He'd been a *gambero*, a crab hiding in a hole, for far too long.

He was so pleased that he'd put Melba in her place that he stopped just outside the door to his office and danced a little jig.

"I really appreciate that tip about the lots next to the Lightning Bug Bar," Ferdy O'Doole told Tyler. "Picked them up for a song from the estate; the heirs all live out west and don't have any interest in ever coming here. You got any idea yet how much the lots are going to sell for?"

"We haven't discussed that yet," Tyler said, "but Crawley is making sure we get a nice profit.

"Shit, I should have beat you to the draw, Ferdy, and bought them myself. What did you think of Jack's bill?" Tom Fellows asked. "Bet that blew 'em away in Tally."

"Those godless legislators will probably kill it, just like they did with Jack's last bill," said Brady Hack, owner of Sunshine's only liquor store. "They love coddling felons so much, you'd think the jailbirds were keeping them in office."

"Sandfly Bates must be out of his mind, saying that criminals are human too. They ain't; they're monsters!" O'Doole said.

"What else do you expect from a damned lefty?" Brady snarled.

"The Legislature had better take this seriously," Tyler rumbled. "Fourteen billion is a lot to spend feeding criminals."

"That's one thing I don't think was spelled out in the paper," O'Doole said. "Who's supposed to feed them felons, the taxpayer who uses 'em?"

"Looks that way, don't it?" Fellows remarked. "But I guess that we pay in the end anyway." He shifted uncomfortably, looked at O'Doole out of the corners of his eyes, and cleared his throat. "Uh, Joe, I–I mean, we–we got a problem we got to talk out."

Tyler was immediately on the defensive. "What?"

"Well, you're in pretty deep shit with the folks in the church, taking money from Zona's girls. Learned Speaker says he wouldn't support you for Lay Speaker because you drifted away from the God Book. When Learned Speaker says you've fallen from grace, Joe, that's damned serious."

Tyler felt himself begin to tremble inside. It was hell having one's spirituality questioned. "I didn't interpret the passage in the God Book the same way Learned Speaker did, that's all. I mean, I'd never interpret taking a campaign contribution as keeping money from a laborer. He said I was arrogant, and that ain't so! It was an honest mistake and I can always give the money back. It wasn't all that much; it won't break me." He looked at his lifelong buddies beseechingly.

"Hell, Joe, we won't throw you out of the Saved Sons Society; you're our president. But I think you ought to give the money back and sort of lie low for a while, let it all blow over. Learned Speaker is really upset over this." Brady Hack said prissily. "We all make mistakes, but as long as we can learn from them and walk upright in the world as righteous men, all will be well. You just lie low for a couple of months and see if I ain't right."

Tyler lowered his head, pretending a humility he did not feel.

It was fine for Hack to pontificate about lying low and giving back perfectly good campaign contributions, he thought bitterly. Hack was the designated Lay Speaker now. In fact, he wouldn't be at all surprised if Brady was the one who suggested the whole thing to Learned Speaker in the first place.

Sunshine was getting more and more out of his control and he had to do something startling to take the reins of leadership again. He'd have to think about what to do, what would make a really big splash, get in all the papers. He might make the *Tampa Tribune* and the *St. Petersburg Times* again.

At the next meeting of the council, he'd have that report on the illegality of breaking the law to contend with, and he was certain that Dee Slugge would come up with something good. That ought to be good for an editorial, at least. Maybe he should come up with another ordinance; the public loved ordinances.

The last ordinance they'd passed had made most of the state newspapers, television, and *All Things Considered* on public radio. Sunshine had really been put on the map. Of course, there had been those who didn't understand the importance of keeping dog doo off the streets and sidewalks, and they had made fun of the ordinance, but the council had stuck together and faced down their detractors.

Maybe he could come up with something more about dogs; he hated dogs. Yes, yes, they were man's best friend and all that rot, but they left untidy piles of excrement everywhere and they bit people. He had tried to have dogs banned from Merriweather Drive, but he'd been voted down. Several of his neighbors kept the beasts, and twice in the last month he'd found piles of dog doo on his front lawn. He'd sat up for five nights in a row until three in the morning, trying to catch the neighbor who so fouled his turf, but had failed in his efforts. Besides, when he was a kid, his dog, Piggy, had failed him.

His Pappy had kept hunting dogs, but hunting dogs were different; they were pack animals with some purpose to their lives. They lived in kennels away from the house and didn't dare bark for fear of a beating. His Pappy knew how to train animals, by God! It was a shame Pap wasn't around today to give him a little advice on how to bring both the city and his church to heel.

O'Doole took a cheap cigar from his shirt pocket, peeled off the wrapper, bit off the end, and prepared to light it.

"You going to smoke that thing in these sacred quarters, right under the cross that Jesus died on?" Hack asked.

"Ain't the same cross, and I haven't heard a complaint from it yet, Brady." O'Doole turned the cigar around and around in his mouth.

"Smoking cigars is an abomination," Hack said.

"So is drinking liquor, fornicating, polluting, and all the fun things," Fellows observed. "Let Ferdy smoke in peace, Brady."

"I hate the smell of the weed."

Sensing a change in the alignment of sentiment, Tyler pounced. "Hell, Brady, is there anything you don't hate?"

Fellows snickered. "I know why he's so pissed off at you taking Zona's girls' money, Joe."

"You just–" Hack began.

"Yeah," O'Doole joined in, "he feels like he made in involuntary contribution to you; he's one of their customers! I saw him coming out of there last week with a big grin on his face."

"Does Learned Speaker know about it?" Tyler asked gleefully.

"I was just calling on Zona to discuss—I mean—" Hack had turned purple with embarrassment.

"Hell, Brady, you get to bang the madam herself?" O'Doole teased. "I'm impressed."

"Bet she was, too," Fellows chortled. "Brady told me he ain't circumcised."

Tyler sat back and watched the exchange with great satisfaction. Maybe he could teach Brady a lesson after all, he thought savagely. Learned Speaker didn't cotton to taking laborers' money, but he despised men who used the services of the damned.

"My idea isn't silly,' Al," Merlini insisted. "You look at the museums in St. Petersburg, places like Sarasota, and you'll get the picture. Museums are important to the culture of the community. The more museums you have, the more tourists will come. Come on, where's your vision?"

"Meats, I agree that museums are an added attraction in an area, but when it's the only attraction, the draw just isn't there. And a museum dedicated to the history of meat may seem a fine idea to you, but you're only one person in a state of almost twenty million."

Merlini rose from the chair where he sat and began to pace. "You got to take a more positive attitude, Al. This paper don't do much of anything but poke fun at the city council and its members. That ain't fair. I think it's time you stopped carrying that Noessit dame's column, you know? Prolly help your circulation a lot, getting rid of that. Gossip's got no business in a newspaper."

Al McDonald leaned back in his chair, put his hands behind his head, and watched Merlini pace. He always enjoyed visits from the councilmen; they were usually the funniest part of his week. "What's really bugging you, Meats?"

"You got no respect for sausage, that's what bothers me," Merlini said. "Do you realize the whole history of man can be written in sausages?"

"Really? Like, maybe the ancient Hebrews had sausage?"

"Yeah!" Merlini cried.

"Where did their pigs come from, Meats?" He leaned forward, earnest. "Come on, admit you're full of it. The ancient Hebrews didn't eat pork, the Muslims don't eat pork, the Chinese—"

"Been eating pork since the beginning of time," Merlini interrupted. "You ever eat a Chinese sausage? They're delicious. And the—"

"Meats, I am not going to editorialize about the benefits of a meat museum to the tourism industry in Sunshine. I'm sorry, but that's where it is. I agree with the council; it's a stupid idea."

"They haven't turned it down," Merlini protested. "It's just tabled."

Al shook his head. "Meats, forget it."

"I'll never let them drop it," Merlini swore. "Never."

"What do you think about the proposal to turn Mosquito Row into a park?"

"I think it's a waste of money, myself," Merlini said seriously. "Who's going to go to a park that smells like a toilet? You ever wonder why the Hatchacootee smells so bad, Al? I wonder what they're throwing into the water upstream to make it smell so bad."

"The Hatchacootee upstream of Sunshine is pristine, Meats. It's our sewage that's causing the problem."

Merlini looked genuinely shocked. "It is? Are you sure?"

McDonald sighed with exasperation. "You all discussed the matter at the last council meeting, Meats."

Merlini snapped his fingers. "Oh, yeah, I remember now. Odlum and Bonano say we have a leaky sewer system, but I think they're full of shit. You don't believe that crap, do you?"

It was McDonald's turn to be shocked. "You think they made it up?"

"Yeah, they make up stuff all the time. Civil servants come up with crises so they can keep their jobs and make elected officials look stupid, you know that. You really expect me to believe that all the sewer pipes in the city are bad, and we're leaking all that mess into the Gulf of Mexico? The fish would die if we were doing that, and I see people catching fish all the time."

"Well, yes, Meats. To tell the truth, I did expect you to believe it because you just said there's no point in putting a park by a river that smells like a toilet."

"That don't make it our fault," Merlini said in a final tone. "You're just after the city council, is all."

"Councilman Merlini," McDonald said in his best newsman's voice, "the city has received a warning letter from the Department of Environmental Protection. E coli has been found at the mouth of the river. Your city manager and your utilities director have both told you that the sewer system is leaking badly and must be replaced, *and you don't believe it?*"

"Nah, I don't believe it, and you better not stick it to me because I said so, Al. There's libel laws."

"There's also responsibility, damn it. You are a public servant, elected to serve the people of this town, Meats, to look after their welfare."

"Jee–sus, Al, you must be losing it, I ain't a public *servant*–I am an elected official!"

Melba gave a final tweak to her new cherry red wig before the mirror in the ladies' room, then closed one eye to darken the green eye shadow she wore on her lids. That finished, she squinted the other eye shut and applied more shadow. The last time she'd been on television at the studio, they told her to wear more makeup.

She loved the new wig; it gave her such a *gamine* appearance, reminding her of her younger days, when she was married to Antonio. She wet two fingers and pulled down two wisps of synthetic, stepped back to survey her face from a distance, then took out her blusher and added more color to her cheekbones and chin. Yes, that did it. Of course, the cameraman would fume because, as usual, she wore no lipstick. She had explained over and over to him that she had always felt that pale lips made her eyes larger. This time, his argument would no doubt be that she was wearing a cherry red dress and wig, and she needed a cherry mouth.

Cherry mouth! Joe Tyler would have a cherry mouth when he found out she was kicking off her campaign in March rather than waiting until the end of summer. There were quite a few voters who were gone during the summer months, who didn't return until late October, and she intended capturing every one of them.

She had heard rumors that Joe had been slapped in the face by that idiot who called himself Learned Speaker. Served him right, the sanctimonious prick! She couldn't believe that, after being beaten in three mayoral races, he intended running against her. Apparently he just didn't know when to quit, and his attitude made her life far more difficult that it should be. Outside Joe, the Right couldn't come up with a half-decent candidate if they tried.

She had felt really badly about having to leave the Right to run for mayor, but they insisted on maintaining the old boy crap, and so she had joined the Left, who had welcomed her with open arms. She had felt funny, changing parties like that, and had thought that folks might not trust her, but she'd been wrong. Of course, the Right had resorted to the switch-over-then-switch-back tactic back in the '90's and gained a number of seats in Tally as a result, and she might have gotten away with the same thing, but she was so pissed at the old boy network that she refused to do it.

She gave a final pat to her wig, adjusted the large donkey made of red, white, and blue rhinestones that graced her lapel, and went out to face the camera.

The lights were incredibly bright and Melba tried hard not to squint. She was seated on a little stage in the center of the studio. Next to her on the platform, slumped in his chair going over a list of questions, was the local television personality, Aysure Wood. He sported a goatee that she was certain he had frosted, and insisted on wearing ascots. She considered him artsy-fartsy to the nth degree.

Wood had flatly refused to go over the questions he was going to ask before they were on the air. She didn't like going into an interview blind; she didn't think that quickly on her feet, but he said that he wanted spontaneity. Okay, she thought grimly, she'd give him spontaneity.

Suddenly Wood sat erect, beamed at her, then said to the camera, "Welcome to Sunshine Live. I'm Aysure Wood, and today, my guest is someone every person in Sunshine wants to know all about–our mayor, Melba Tosti." He nodded to her encouragingly, as if she were dead of stage fright, then continued. "Tell me, Melba, what's it like being mayor of Sunshine?"

She flashed the camera her best smile, the really toothy one, and leaned forward to show the little cleavage the suit allowed. "It's a wonderful opportunity to serve the people of the community," she gushed. "Of course, it's hard work, but worth every minute. I'm a full-time mayor, you know, Aysure, the first full-time mayor that Sunshine has ever had. None of my time is spent grubbing for money like my predecessor did. I believe in giving my all to our fair city."

"I'm sure you do, Madam Mayor," Wood murmured. "Can you tell us some of the things you've accomplished?"

The rotten son of a bitch! Her brain reeled as she tried to remember a real accomplishment. She could feel her smile becoming a grimace. "I–I–I–last year I had eight shuffleboard courts built outside our Museum of Shuffleboard, and authorized our city manager to purchase a permanent trophy, for one thing. And then there was–"

"Yes," Wood enthused, "I recall those courts, but then, Madam Mayor, I think that most of Sunshine looks upon the shuffleboard museum and anything to do with it as an accomplishment of the former mayor, Josephus Tyler."

Oho, she thought, that was the game. He was on Joe's side. Her thoughts continued to run wildly through her cranium, searching for some nugget to bring forth, but all they found were blocked synapses. "Yes, Councilman Tyler did build the museum, which I have always thought to be a complete waste of tax dollars. There are very few folks nowadays who even bother to learn the rules of shuffleboard, much less actually play. And I–"

"Well, if you consider shuffleboard a lost cause, Madam Mayor, why did you spend those precious tax dollars to build courts and add a trophy?"

"The expenditure was a small one, Aysure, nothing to compare with what the former mayor spent on the museum itself. I think that–"

"That small wastes of tax dollars are better than large ones?" he asked gently.

"Yes, yes, that's what I meant. And furthermore–"

She stopped speaking. She had to get out of this nightmare he had trapped her in, but how? There was an old trick, proven devastating to hostile media by politicians over the millennia, but she couldn't remember what it was! Something about turning something inside out, or was it upside down?

"Has the cat got your tongue?" Aysure teased, his eyes glinting evilly.

Damn the man! Then the elusive reply illuminated her mind. Yes!–she would bring him toppling from his ego perch. She smiled brilliantly, wagged her index finger before Aysure's nose in reproach, and replied in a loud voice, "That's not the question, Aysure. The *real* question is, *why does the cat have my tongue?*"

"I'm waiting breathlessly to find out, Madam Mayor," he replied, unruffled.

Why did the cat have her tongue? What had made her blurt such an idiotic question? And now she had to answer, but with what? She forced down the beginnings of panic, took a deep breath, and suddenly she felt sure of herself again. She had, somehow, slain whatever dragons had been lurking.

"This city has to develop, Aysure. We need tourist dollars to bring about an economic boom, and I am hot on the trail of those dollars we so badly need. I have a plan that will bring such a change in Sunshine that the citizens won't even be sure they live in the same town, but I can't reveal it at this time. It's top secret. If I let the cat out of the bag before the cows come home, then everything might go up in smoke, and we'll have jumped our fences before we closed the barn doors.

"But this city also has problems to face, and we'll all face them together and come through, as we always have, thick or thin. We–"

"Have a bad problem with sewer leaks, perhaps? I understand that the Department of Environmental Protection has given the city one year to clean up its act," Aysure said innocently.

"Yes, we did get a letter from the DEP and it's being answered. As a matter of fact, I dictated it this morning. As to the sewer leaks, I am looking into them. I–"

"And when you look into those sewer leaks, what do you see?"

"I see–I see, yes!–you might ask, what do I see? Well, I see that the mouth of the Hatchacootee must be cleaned up. We've got to get rid of all the mud that the place is infested with, and we have to bring in those tourist dollars so that the city can prosper under my guidance."

"I don't understand, Madam Mayor, what mud and sewage have to do with one another."

"Because that mud stinks of shi–of the wrack and ruin that has been left to Sunshine by my predecessors. It is time for us to move forward, to go hand in hand into a shining future, prosperous, peaceful, and–"

"It's been said that you look upon your mayoralty much like a beauty queen looks upon her duties. Is that so?"

"Absolutely foundationless accusation, Aysure. I have attended every public function, every classroom contest, every opening of every business in Sunshine. I held a ribbon-cutting when MacDonalds opened, and one when Taco Bell opened, and even a cornerstone-laying ceremony for the dog pound. Before I became mayor, there was virtually no public ceremony for the citizens to enjoy and take a part in. I believe in being seen before the public; I even instituted television coverage of our council meetings so that the public might be informed. Under my leadership, Sunshine has a government of the people, by the people, and for the people."

"But what have you actually accomplished?"

"I think I have been very open and frank, Aysure. No one could be more open than I am, and nothing is going to be hidden from the citizens of Sunshine, and if it ever is, it'll be over my dead body!" She relaxed somewhat and smiled at him. "It's a pretty sad frog that won't croak for its own pond, Aysure."

"Even a polluted pond, Mayor?"

"Even a polluted pond."

"I see we're running out of time, Madam Mayor. Before we go, I'd like to ask you a question, just one simple question, and I'd like a straight answer. Promise?"

"I always keep my promises, Aysure," she answered grimly.

"Are you kicking off an early campaign, by any chance?"

"Of course I am, you idio—I mean, yes, I am running again because I feel this city needs sound judgement. When the pilot at the wheel doesn't know where the compass is, it's a sad ball of wax. This town has been ruled too long by the good old boys who have become nothing more than a cliché, and if there's one thing I detest, it's a cliché."

With relief, she saw the director make the cutthroat motion. Wood nodded.

"Thank you for coming, Mayor Tosti. You have been as informative as ever."

The camera panned them once, and it was over.

A Note From The Florida Senate

Dear Learned Speaker,

I received the enclosed missive from Joe Tyler the other day, and after much soul searching, I have decided to send it on to you. I don't understand why Joe has suddenly turned against one of his oldest friends, implicating me in his scandalous behavior the way he has, and it has hurt me grievously.

But I am outraged that he has questioned your probity and morals!

As you know, I am running again for public office, and hope that you will give me your support and that of your congregation. I look forward to the end of session, so that I might again enjoy the company of my fellow Christians.

Do not turn away from Joe; he is an old and dear friend who has strayed into devilish paths.

> Your servant,
> Jackson Fatigay

CHAPTER TWELVE

Op/Ed The Sunshine Bulletin Page 6

EDITORIAL

THE INSOLENCE OF OFFICE

This writer has always looked upon our mayor, Melba Tosti, as an embarrassment. But her showing on *Sunshine Live* with Aysure Wood on Monday afternoon revealed yet another disturbing trait: insolence. Her babbling one cliché after another in answer to serious questions can only be construed as contempt for our citizens.

Our sewer system is coming apart, and the fault lies with the mayor and the City Council, who have known for years that the problem exists, but are too overcome with inertia to respond. When our so-called leaders refuse to tackle problems that pose serious threats to public health and safety in order to make certain they remain in office, they are irresponsible. Is this the kind of government we really want?

Sunshine is desperately in need of tourist dollars, Mayor Tosti said. That is true; the city lacks the natural amenities enjoyed by other areas of the state. When asked what she intends doing about the problem, we were treated to another string of meaningless phrases.

More and more, we get less and less where our government is concerned. Rainmaker and Tosti are serving their third terms, and Rainmaker is the only member of the council willing to address serious issues. Warner and Merlini are serving their second terms. Joe Tyler is on his second term and served three terms as mayor before Tosti beat him twelve years ago.

Merlini's second term should be his last. His insistence on erecting a museum celebrating the history of meat is an idea whose time has never arrived, and probably never will. Aside from that, he is convinced that the sewage problem and the ground tremors reported by citizens are figments of the city manager's imagination.

Sunshine needs a new city council and a new mayor. Yesterday, Tosti corrected Wood with that trite political turnabout, "That's not the question, the real question is..." and fell flat on her face.

The real question is, "Why is Melba Tosti the mayor of Sunshine, and will our citizens be foolish enough to elect her for another term?"

"There are times when I could almost hug Al McDonald!" Lila Mae said to Henny. "You read the editorial?"

"You know damn well I don't waste time on that crap," Henny growled. He pulled the classified section toward him, took a gulp of his coffee, and dropped the comics on the floor by his chair. "Wasn't anything funny in the funnies this morning," he griped.

"McDonald wrote that Melba shouldn't be elected for another term," Lila Mae mused. "And I know he don't like Joe Tyler, so you have to wonder who he wants."

"Stupid nonsense, politics."

"Henny, somebody has to lead the way," Lila Mae said, exasperated. "Suppose everybody felt like you?–we'd have a bunch of crooks and clowns running for public office and they'd get elected because you wouldn't know one from the other. You got to read something besides the classifieds and the comics!"

"Chicken has gone up a cent a pound," was the reply.

"Are you paying any attention to me at all?"

"What for? All you're doing is talking shit."

She took a deep breath, put down her section of the paper, and clasped her hands. "Henny, I want a divorce."

"I got a big catering to do on Saturday night, barbecue for almost two hundred people, and I'm gonna need you to help out, so if you got plans, cancel them."

"Henny, I ain't going to be here; I'll be in Tallahassee."

"Like hell you will. You expect to live under my roof, you're going to start doing like a proper wife. I was talking to our pastor the–"

"I want a divorce. I don't want to be your wife any longer, Henny."

He gaped and lay down the paper. "You *what?*"

"You heard me. I don't want to be your wife any more. I want a divorce."

"You can't do that–I got this big catering on Saturday night and I'm going to need all the help–"

"Then hire some!" she shouted. "Pay attention to me, damn you! I said I want a divorce and all you can do is talk about food?"

He scratched his head, mussing his hair even more. "Why you want to leave me, Lila Mae? I ain't ever done anything to you."

"That's right, Henny; you have never done one single, solitary thing to me or for me and I'm sick of taking second place to a chicken leg."

"Them chicken legs is what supports you, Lila Mae. There was a time when you was damned proud of them chicken legs. What's got into you?" He picked up the paper again and continued his perusal of the classifieds.

"I'm moving out today. It's the only day this week I don't have meetings."

"Suit yourself. Hey, here's some U-pick beans I didn't know about. Wonder if I can get them cheap?"

Lila Mae felt like strangling him. Granted, she hadn't expected much reaction from him, the man was incapable of real feeling, but she did expect him to ask her to stay! He really didn't care, he didn't care at all.

She should have left him long ago, she thought, back when she began pretending there was a man in her life who loved her and who could satisfy her. She felt like slapping herself when she thought of all the years wasted on listening to Henny talk about mullet and chickens when she could have been having orgasms.

She didn't even feel guilty, although she supposed that, as a good Methodist, she should; she had been committing adultery.

"That all you got to say?"

"About what?"

"About my divorcing you."

"You're full of shit, Lila Mae. You won't last five minutes on your own." He belched, scratched his chest, and rose from the breakfast table. "You want chicken or something else for lunch?"

Lila Mae sighed.

Joe Tyler licked his lips and erased what he'd just written. He always had a hard time writing speeches, but he sure didn't want to look like as big a fool as Melba had on television, so he'd get it down on paper. He brushed away the eraser bits and bit the pencil.

That would have been right sharp, what she'd tried, but she screwed up. "That's not the question–the real question is..." He really liked that. But she'd automatically stolen Wood's words and it had gone wrong for her. She was always stealing something, an idea, a piece of the action, anything she could get her greedy claws on. "The real question is, why does the cat have my tongue?" He had laughed until he cried.

He had been accused in the past of stealing others' ideas, but he was a piker compared to Melba Tosti. She would buttonhole some expert and pick his brain a little, then stand up and parrot the expert's words even though she didn't know what they meant. It had gotten her into trouble a couple of times.

Served her right, going on that abomination's show. Aysure Wood was bound to be one of *them*–look at those funny scarves he always wore. Why couldn't the man wear a bow tie like real men did? But his mind was wandering and he had to get back to the job at hand.

There was something wrong; he felt uneasy. Then he realized that the house was eerily quiet. His wife was out for the evening with the women of the church, and the television wasn't playing; that was it. He rose ponderously and crossed the room to grab the remote, switched on the television set, and then sighed as the voice of Anall Smithers filled the room. He listened for a few minutes, enthralled. Such a great televangelist! Almost as good as Learned Speaker. Then he adjusted the volume downward and returned to the desk and his chore; religion was an important part of his life, but being reelected was foremost.

He sat down, picked up his pencil again, and paused long enough to gather his thoughts.

Thummmppp!

The floor shifted slightly beneath his feet and he froze, alarmed. What had caused that? He barely breathed, but the noise and movement didn't repeat themselves, so he resumed writing. Probably a jet breaking the sound barrier, or the moon mission coming home again. Then he remembered old lady McIntyre and her earthquakes. For a moment, he wondered if she had been right about them, but everyone knew she was crazy, so he dismissed her from his mind.

His speech-writing went better than he had thought it would, so he went up to the bedroom and stood before the full-length mirror hanging on the closet door to practice. Paper in one hand, glasses perched on his nose, he struck a pose which he considered earnest, legs two feet apart, torso leaning slightly forward, neck craned toward the mirror, hands clasped at his waist. He tried to read his script with the paper at his waist, but the letters were blurred, so he unclasped his hands.

"Fellow citizens, many of you have brought to my attention in recent months the crying need for leadership in the city of Sunshine. For twelve long years, our fair city has borne the weight of inept government brought to us from the north."

No, that wouldn't do. There were a lot of voters out there who were from the same north, and he certainly didn't want to alienate them. They were the ones who put Melba Tosti in office in the first place, which showed how stupid they were, but a vote was a vote.

"For twelve long years, our fair city has borne the weight of inept government brought to us–" Maybe "brought to us" was the wrong phrase. He wandered across the room and sat on the bed, moved aside the glass of water that his wife dutifully placed on the bedside table for him each evening, and scratched out some of what he had written. Then he stared into the water, searching for inspiration.

He should probably wait until after the next meeting to announce his candidacy; that would give him time to put forth his new ordinance proposal and take again the leadership position he so richly deserved. Yes, that would be his plan. If he announced two days after Melba had made such a fool of herself, the public might lump the two of them together, and that would never do.

He muttered, "borne the weight of inept government period." Yes, that was it. He could go on from there to castigate Melba without accusing the voters of having made a terrible mistake.

Thubummmp!

What was that–what was going on? Then he saw that the water in the glass was sloshing gently. Was there someone in the house? He rose from the bed and tiptoed back downstairs, pencil and paper forgotten, to search his premises.

Then he heard the click as a key turned the lock at the front door and slumped in relief. The noise had been his wife's slamming the car door. She was home.

The morning sun seemed late, which meant that they might have some weather that day, Melba thought as she waited in her office for Donald Sarious to appear. She looked at her watch–seven forty-five. She had let herself into the building at seven fifteen, intent on reducing the pile of correspondence that seemed to be spreading across her desk like hydrilla across a lake.

For once, she looked forward to seeing Sarious. Bonano had reported that there was no sand, not even a trace of sand, on the mud flat. Until now, she had not remembered that, having been engaged in preparing for her television appearance and her speech last night at the Bella Luna Italian Club. She chuckled nastily. This time, Don Sarious, she thought, you're going to apologize to me and to the city for all the trouble you've caused.

Pain in the neck, those DEP types from Tallahassee. Just because that section of the state had not experienced the phenomenal growth that more southerly counties were going through, the bureaucrats were sour and meddled whenever they could.

She read three handwritten notes from people living just off Hatchacootee Boulevard, all complaining of ground tremors, and threw them into the waste basket. What were the old biddies drinking these days, she wondered, that had them hallucinating about earthquakes? Of course, old Mrs. McIntyre had complained of the same thing, but she could safely be ignored. She was known as a crazy and continually haunted City Hall looking for something to bitch about.

She was feeling really well this morning, having spent the evening before shopping over in Heart County. She'd purchased a really stunning apricot wig for evening wear, and a terrific dress to go with it. And she'd seen the most beautiful purple wig, but the exchequer wouldn't handle two in a month, so she'd just have to wait.

Then she picked up a handful of correspondence and sorted through it, coming across the carbon the letter of apology she'd been forced to write. Her sunny mood disintegrated and she got angry all over again. Just who did Frank Bonano think he was, God? He had been so sure that she would back down that, even though she had deliberately waited until twelve fifteen to send her secretary over with the apology, he hadn't bothered to hand in his resignation. And if he had, she'd have been forced to beg him to stay. He was popular with the citizens of Sunshine, almost a hero, in fact. She found such adulation silly—all he had done was to take over the reins of municipal government a week after the councilmen and mayor had gone to jail some years back, and made sense of the mare's nest that city government had become. That was no big deal; anyone with a modicum of sense could have done it. But he'd dared her and she had capitulated. He had to go. She would replace him after reelection.

And she'd get rid of that little slut, Mary Lee Mince. Simpering fool! She should have suspected something when Frank hired her. Every time Mince got near Frank, she started trembling. Lust like that wasn't normal; she must be a nympho. He said he wasn't banging her? Ha!–let him tell that to the Marines.

You had hoped to snare him for yourself, an inner voice reminded.

"Nonsense!" She looked out the window and saw Sarious getting out of a taxi. Hurriedly putting the shameful apology into one of her desk drawers, she grabbed her purse and went to meet him.

A gray haze had smeared across the horizon, giving the water in the gulf the look of beaten pewter. The wind was from the west when they got out of Melba's Lincoln at the end of Hatchacootee Boulevard, the damp air filled with the reek of raw sewage. The smell seemed to engulf them in waves as the wind forced the marsh grass into submission.

"That fact that you've let this go on for so long is almost a criminal act, Madam Mayor," Sarious said. "Twelve years have gone by since you had the first sewage leaks, and you still haven't done anything about repairing the system? I recommended that we put you under consent order immediately, but I was overruled."

"I thought you were here to look for sand, Mr. Sarious," she replied icily.

"I'm here to talk with you about compliance with the law, Mayor. During your term, state law has been completely ignored."

"That's not true!" she said hotly. "Every time you people have told us to clean up our mess, we've done it."

"You've continually put bandaids on a potentially deadly problem, Mayor. *E coli* is nothing to toy with. It mutates."

So did you, you humorless jerk, she said to herself. If there was ever a mutant, it was Donald B. Sarious. He never smiled, he never joked, and she wondered if he even ate or slept. He was nothing more than a dictating machine in human form, spewing letter after letter on minor matters. When she pulled the file this morning, she had found seventy-two letters from him on the subject of Sunshine's environmental lapses. Didn't the man have anything else to do? Why did he pick on her?

Was her city the only place in the state with problems? Look at Miami, or Jacksonville. For that matter, look at that abomination, the city of Dunwurkin in Heart County. Over a million retirees jammed together in the middle of the county. No proper highways, just paths for their golf carts, some houses, and dinky "lanai" apartments with no room to breathe. Was Sarious going to tell her that Dunwurkin didn't have sewage problems? Of course they did; she knew how much sewage a million people generated. Until recently, they had injected all the gunk into the limestone aquifer beneath the county, saying it had been contaminated years before by some crap or the other. But finally the state had come down on them.

"The photographs I was sent clearly showed sand right where we're standing, Mayor." He sounded disappointed.

"I'm standing on mud, Mr. Sarious, and it isn't doing my shoes any good. Do you see any sand?"

"No, I don't. How did you clean it up?" He stooped and dug out a handful of the mud, then examined it carefully. "There are particles of beach sand here, Mayor."

"I sent Mr. Bonano down here the morning I received your letter and he reported that the mud flat was perfectly normal. I think you've been hoaxed, Mr. Sarious. Some of your greenie friends have been playing tricks."

"Then why is this sand mixed in with the mud?"

"I'm sure I don't know. Where dirt is concerned, I'm not the purist you are."

He gave her a baleful glance and got to his feet, staring west over the gulf. He maintained the pose for several minutes, craning his neck and ignoring her while her heels sank further and further into the muck. They were going to be ruined and she'd have to replace them. Then he walked quickly to the water's edge, calling back to her, "Do you see that?"

"What?"

"The color of that water out there; it looks milky."

"I don't see anything strange."

"I need to see Bonano, Mayor. Let's get back to the City Hall. You're free for the rest of the day."

Bonano slowed down as they approached the river mouth. He and Sarious had rented an outboard motor boat at the marina where the fishing boats tied up, and headed to where Sarious swore he had seen white water.

"This about the right spot?"

"No, a little more offshore. You know where those springs empty into the gulf?–in that neighborhood."

"Oh, okay." He pointed the bow west and increased the throttle. "You sure it wasn't a cloud shadow or something?"

"Frank, there isn't a cloud around today. Looks like we're in for some weather later, from that haze out there, but the water was white, I tell you, in stark contrast against the sky." He stood up in the boat and moved toward the bow. "Yeah, there it is, see?"

Bonano stood up as well and, shielding his eyes against the overhead glare, looked where Sarious pointed.

The water was milk white.

He cut the engine and they drifted into the strange water. It had no clarity at all, unlike the water usually found in the gulf. He put his hand into it and rubbed it between his fingers. He could almost swear he felt grit. "What could be causing this, Don?"

"I don't know, but I'm going to find out. I'll get some of the geologists at the water management district to come out here and check it out. There are only two things I can think of that might be causing this–some weird alga or dissolution of the limestone somewhere ashore. We'll just have to see what it is. Then we'll know what to do about it."

Bonano unscrewed the cap on a clean mayonnaise jar that he'd taken from his tool shed, filled it with the milky fluid, and put the cap back on. "Okay, there's a sample. It sure is white, isn't it?"

"Yeah. Let's get on back inshore. I want the district to get on this right away." Then Sarious smiled grimly. "I'm certain it isn't the sand that someone photographed on the mud flat."

Bonano nodded. "The sand was there, Don; Odlum saw it. But he's been preoccupied lately with his sewer replacement report that's due this week."

"You think they'll finally float a bond issue?"

"Only if they're forced to, Don. It's election year."

The telephone rang just as Bonano and Sarious reached his office. He grabbed the receiver and barked a hello, then listened intently.

Sarious picked up his water jar and briefcase and waved.

"Hold on a minute," Bonano said. "Don, wait. This might be of interest."

Sarious stopped in the door and lounged against the frame. "What is it?" he asked as Bonano hung up.

"A sinkhole has just opened up two blocks west of here, at the corner of Florida Avenue and Hatchacootee Boulevard. A car drove right into it."

"How big?"

"Big enough to eat a car."

"Maybe all that rain we had last fall was more acid than we knew and we've got some serious aquifer dissolution. Or perhaps the sewer leaks have damaged the limestone. It will, you know." Sarious stood erect. "Hell, Frank, you might lose the whole city of Sunshine if you're not careful."

Bonano shuddered. "Don't even think the thought. See you."

"Right. Go pump some concrete into your sinkhole and make everybody happy. I'll let you know what gives."

Bonano smiled hollowly. It was beginning to be a very long day.

CHAPTER THIRTEEN

Gavel Strike hung up the telephone and covered his face with his hands. The news he had just heard from Mel Bath at the water management district frightened him badly. When he had called Mel about an Audubon Society meeting, Mel told him that limestone somewhere in the aquifer was dissolving at an alarming rate.

The water management district had sent divers to check the output from the springs in the Gulf two miles off the mouth of the Hatchacootee as soon as they had received the water sample from Sarious. The divers collected water that showed 496,000 parts per million of dissolved lime. What could cause dissolution like that?

And where was it happening?

He shivered uncontrollably, then reached for the phone and dialed Guy's office number. "Hi, it's me. I just got terrible news from the District. Mel Bath says the water samples they took from the underwater springs off the mouth of the river showed a dissolved lime count of 496,000 ppm."

"Oh, my God!" Guy exclaimed. "Do they have any idea where this is happening?"

"None at all."

"Why not call Frank Bonano and see if you can find out what he knows."

"Okay, I'll give it a try. Should we let Al McDonald in on this?"

"I guess you could tell him."

"I'll call Frank. Talk to you later." He hung up and dialed Bonano's number.

"Bonano."

"Frank, have you heard anything from the District on the water sample you and Sarious took?"

"No, haven't heard a word, but I've been out and my secretary is sick. What's the word?"

"496,000 parts per million of dissolved lime."

"Jee–sus, that's half solid!"

"Yes. Do you have any idea where this dissolution could be taking place? Anything unusual happening around Sunshine? Bath said that this is so sudden that something catastrophic is bound to happen."

"We've had a couple of minor sinkholes open up within the last couple of days, but nothing else that I know of."

"Where?"

"One at the corner of Florida Avenue and Hatchacootee, and one a couple of blocks closer to the City Hall."

"If we lost Melba's monument to herself, I'd celebrate. Why she couldn't be satisfied with the old city hall is beyond me."

Budumpphhh!

"Shit! Did you feel that?" Bonano sounded squeaky.

"Yeah, I did. What happened?"

Bonano's voice was filled with awe. "A frigging sinkhole just opened up in the next block, Gavel. Another piece of Hatchacootee Boulevard just fell in. Let me get off the phone and get hold of Odlum. This is bound to have something to do with these sewer leaks."

"I think it's something worse, Frank. If we can do anything–" He hung up, then grabbed the receiver again and dialed the newspaper office. "Let me speak to Al McDonald, pronto."

Melba irritably looked at her watch. She had gone out of her way to be on time and Joe Tyler was late. He had promised to meet her here at the La Plata at twelve sharp, and it was already twenty minutes past.

She looked around the restaurant with interest. The place was relatively new and she had not eaten here before. The word was that the food was rather commonplace, if expensive, but the decor was fabulous. The walls were covered in antiqued mirrors, with formal swags of silvered cloth falling at intervals from the mirrored ceiling. The tables were made of some substance that looked like beaten silver, as were the chairs, which were covered in silver lamé. The floor was silvery gray carpet. In contrast, the potted ferns perched on silvery pedestals were startling.

She studied her reflection in the mirrored wall. Dressed in the same cherry red suit and wig that she had worn for her television interview, she looked positively brilliant. She turned and surveyed the other diners, noting with satisfaction that none of them stood out the way she did.

She felt sorry for those poor, colorless people who paid truly outrageous taxes to live in Heart County and its one remaining municipality, Dunwurkin. As much as she loved the thousands of shops in which to browse, she detested the whole idea of Heart County. It was known as a "strong county," unlike poor Hillsborough, which had died under the mad annexations that Tampa foisted upon it during the '90's. Heart County had forced virtually all of its municipalities out of business. Dunwurkin was the only city that had survived its voracious appetite, and they fought a long and arduous court battle to prove their right to exist.

It had been hard for her to deal with the arrogance of the Heart County Commission. They kept the bureaucracy in Tallahassee stirred up about the lack of response from Sunshine on issues which they considered important. Englehardt's constant carping about the dangers of *E coli* had actually driven the DEP to harass her. Look at Sarious's behavior–a prime example of harassment if there ever was one.

Her reverie was interrupted by Joe Tyler. "I saw you the moment I came into the room, Melba. You certainly know how to stand out in a crowd."

She was pleased. "Thanks, Joe. You're late."

"Traffic this time of the year would make the Second Coming late. And having to detour around Dunwurkin takes time. I don't know why the county doesn't just condemn some land, drive a road right through that abomination, and get it over with. Damned shame, wasting everyone's time by going around that place just because they don't allow automobiles within their city limits."

She signaled the waiter, took one last look at herself in the mirrored wall, and turned to her colleague. It was time for business.

"You ever eaten here before?" he asked sourly.

"No, so I can't recommend a thing."

"Hate places like this. Looks like a grave or something."

"Joe, it is gorgeous!"

"Women and perverts might like this, but I don't. No decent Christian would be caught dead in such a place. Now, what did you want to talk with me about?" His tone was guarded.

"About what we're going to do when we condemn the land at Mosquito Row, naturally. I know damned well that you've made a deal with Crawley to take care of you price-wise, Joe, so there's no use denying it. I don't object to your making a killing on the land, even if it does come from our long-suffering taxpayers, but I want in on the deal or I'm going to blow you out of the water."

"That's extortion!"

"What you're setting up is criminal."

His face was mottled with rage, but he kept his voice down. "I have never seen anything like you, Melba. You are the most crooked, sneaky—"

"You mean I'm almost as bad as you are?" she interrupted. "No point fighting over this, Joe. I'm serious."

Then it hit her: the way to get rid of him once and for all. She would stop this conversation now, talk about the park or something else, tell him to think it over. And when they next met to discuss just how much it was going to cost him, she would be wearing a wire. She would triumph in the end, yes!—and he would go to jail.

"I need some time to think," he began.

"Take all the time you want, Joe. I know you need to think it out. We can meet again in a couple of weeks and work out the details, but you just make sure you've got some details ready to work out."

"Okay. That'll be better. I didn't really think you were serious. So I can leave?"

"Oh, stay and have lunch; I'll even buy. We need to talk about what we're going to do with Merlini's little idea, for one thing." The waiter came to take their order. "I'll have the paté, a small salad, and frogs' legs. What'll you have, Joe?"

"A shrimp cocktail and the small New York strip," he answered. "With french fries and a tossed salad." He asked her curiously, "How can you eat frog legs? They're cold-blooded animals, and Learned Speaker says—"

"Screw Learned Speaker. How are you going to vote on the museum issue?"

He glared. "I can't imagine why you even ask; it's the dumbest thing I ever heard of, a museum on the history of meat. Merlini's mad. I trust you're going to do away with it at our next meeting?"

"No, not yet, Joe. We got to have his vote on the Mosquito Row condemnation, and on a couple more things before we make him angry. And he will be angry. Like you said, he's nuts."

"Oh, so we're going to table it."

"Yeah."

"We get Slugge's report, too," he said. "I want that ordinance passed."

"First we have to hear Slugge; he's the expert on the law. What else is coming up?"

"Sewers."

"We have to do something. Sarious was really nasty. They couldn't wait until after elections, oh no, not those bastards." She smiled sweetly as the waiter placed her paté in front of her, and gave Joe his shrimp. "You got any idea how much it cost to fill that damned sinkhole?"

He was glum. "I tried to get hold of Bonano to find out, but he wasn't in his office. I meant to tell you, another one has opened up. Happened just before I left to come down here."

"Jesus! Where?"

"Half a block away from City Hall."

"This could get serious," she said.

"Yep. We haven't had three sinkholes in Banter County in the last forty years, and now we have three in Sunshine in two days. What did Sarious say?"

"Oh, he was miffed when he found no sand down there on the flats, and he had photographs of the stuff, so I know it was down there. Tide must have been extra high. Then he said the water looked funny and wanted to hotfoot it back to find Frank. I dropped him off and went to a meeting. I still don't know what excited him, but he's so strange—"

"You say there was no sand??"

"The mud was clean as a whistle."

Joe smiled hugely. "If the tide takes sand away, Melba, I guess you're going to have to forget your beach idea."

"Never. If we put enough sand there, the tide will just have to lump it."

"Sometimes, Mother Nature don't agree with what we try to do, Melba."

She was puzzled. He looked almost as if he were happy. "Joe, the town needs a tourist attraction and you know it. You going to go along with the beach, or try to stop me?"

"Melba," he said solemnly, "I would never try to stop you when you've got a brainstorm. You go right ahead with your plans."

Odlum looked glumly at Bonano, shaking his head. "There is no way that our sewer problems could cause those sinkholes, Frank. The only sewer lines near those holes are the small connecting lines, and they're in good shape. It's the big ones that are failing."

"You certain about that, Oddman? I mean, suppose that over the years some sort of acid had built up, something that would cause the limestone to dissolve faster than it normally would because of rain? What would happen then?"

"Godamighty, Frank! You just said it and don't even know it. What was located in town back in the '50's? Just four blocks from the Stop N' Shop, there was a chemical plant. My daddy worked there. They were making some kind of acid, I know that, because he damaged his lungs breathing the fumes. That's what killed him."

Bonano stared at Odlum, then nodded. "I believe you've hit it, Oddman. I'll give the District a call and see what they have to say about your idea. So this could just be aquifer dissolution in one confined area, is that your thinking?"

"Yes. Let's see, Daddy said it was about four blocks to the left of the department store. That would place it about—"

Bonano paled. "Under this building. Holy shit!" He buzzed his secretary. "Get me the police, tell Rufus I want him in this office *now!* Get me Records and tell her to get up here quick. See if you can locate the mayor. I want Emergency Services and Disaster Preparedness in my office ASAP. Get moving, honey. We have a real problem."

Odlum snapped to attention. "What do you want me to do?"

"Stand by for a disaster, Oddman. I don't know that anything is going to happen, but with our luck, it will. You know of any old plats from around that time? See if you can dig up something so we can find out exactly where the plant was located."

"I've got all the old city maps right down the hall. Be right back."

Bonano's secretary came in, looking frightened. "What's wrong?"

"You able to get hold of anyone yet?"

"Yes, sir. Chief Hicks is on his way over, the Disaster Preparedness chief is out of town, but I told them to send someone, Emergency Services is on the way, and I can't find the mayor."

"What about Records?"

"She said, could you please call her because she's almost finished with microfiching all the old records and doesn't want to stop."

"Good. Call her and tell her to get all the microfiche to the old city hall before the day is out. And any other vital records. Got it?"

"Yes, but—"

"GIT!"

His secretary fled and Bonano took a deep breath, then buzzed Mary Lee Mince.

"Can you come to my office right away? I need another pair of hands badly."

"You wanted to see me, Frank?" Rufus Hicks asked as he sauntered into the office. "I was busy, and we—"

"Rufus, these sinkholes we've been having–it looks like there is some serious aquifer dissolution going on under us, and I want this part of town evacuated until further notice. Got it?"

"You crazy? The Council will have our balls if we do something like that."

"There's no time to do a snow job on them, Rufus. I just have a gut feeling that something awful is going to happen, and I don't want any lives lost. I also don't want any argument. I am responsible for the entire thing and you don't have to worry about taking any flack. But if you don–"

"All right, all right, don't get your bowels in an uproar." Hicks eased into a chair and took off his hat. "Where are we going to put all the evacuees, and what do I tell the businesses when they have to shut down?"

"Tell them I think this part of town might cave in, and I just want to make sure they don't cave in with it."

"This is crazy, Frank! You going to shut down the whole center of town because you got a hunch? How long you going to keep this up?"

"Until we do some investigations, Rufus. I want to get some ground-penetrating radar in here and it won't take more than a day or two. Now, the homeowners can be billeted in the old city hall–at least it's got a lot of toilets. You get 'em in there, and Disaster Preparedness will take care of them. Just get cracking, okay?"

Hicks stood up and scratched his head, examined his fingernails, then replaced his cap. "Where do you want me to begin?"

"By getting your molasses ass in gear!" Bonano roared. "NOW!"

Joe Tyler got out of his car and carefully locked the doors. He was in an excellent mood; Melba was determined to pursue her beach and when the full moon tide took away those millions of dollars' worth of sand, she could kiss any future in politics goodbye.

He chuckled and strolled toward the back entrance of the Stop N' Shop Department Store, then stopped as he heard a hollow boom from beneath his feet. The ground trembled slightly and his smile disappeared as he wondered if another sinkhole was opening up. This nonsense could cost the city a fortune in concrete.

He went through his back door and immediately was accosted by the assistant manager. "What is it, Selma? I'm busy."

"I need to see you, Mr. Tyler. It's serious."

"What is it, woman?"

"We've been ordered to close the department store for a day or two, and the premises are to be evacuated immediately. Since you weren't here, I didn't know just what to do." She dithered, uncertain.

He could feel his blood pressure rising astronomically. Who would dare order him to do anything? "Who told you this?"

"Chief Hicks, Mr. Tyler."

"On whose say-so?"

"Mr. Bonano's," the woman said miserably. "Mr. Tyler, I guess it would be better if you spoke with Mr. Bonano and let him explain," she answered.

"I most certainly will!" he almost shouted. "Get him on the phone for me right now. No, wait, and I'll call him myself from my office. Tell the clerks to get right back to work. This business will close when I say it will close, and not one minute before!" He hurried upstairs to his desk.

Was the whole city going mad? First, Madam Mayor wanted a beach, then Merlini wanted a museum, the Pervert wanted palm trees, and now Bonano was manufacturing emergencies? What emergency could possibly be serious enough to warrant the loss of revenue by the city's entrepreneurs?

"Bonano."

"Have you lost your mind?? Tyler bellowed. "How dare you order my business closed?"

"Mr. Tyler, all I can ask is that you trust me for a day or so. It looks as if we might have some serious sinkhole activity starting up in this area and I want to make sure no one is hurt. The District is getting ground penetrating radar stuff together right now, so we know what's going on under us."

"You will call a halt to this nonsense right now, Frank, if you know what's good for you."

"Sir, I am doing what my best judgement tells me is right for the safety of our citizens. That's what I was hired to take care of, and I'm doing my job."

"You either stop right now or you'll be fired tomorrow morning."

"So fire me."

"Let me–" Tyler snapped his mouth shut and stared at the receiver as if it were an alien. Frank Bonano had hung up on him!

SINKHOLES PLAGUE SUNSHINE
Special to the Tampa Tribune

Sunshine: During the last forty-eight hours, three sinkholes have opened up in downtown Sunshine, located at the mouth of the Hatchacootee River in Banter County. The first one was small and damaged a ten foot section of a residential street, said City Manager Frank Bonano, but the second swallowed a car. That sinkhole, now filled with concrete, measured fifteen feet in width and twenty feet deep.

A third sinkhole opened today, only half a block from the new City Hall, completed four years ago. The City Manager has ordered a ten block area around the new City Hall evacuated, and asked businesses to close for a day or two so that scientific evaluations of the situation might be done.

Mrs. Rosa McIntyre, whose house faced the first sinkhole, was understandably worried about the future of her neighborhood. "I told the commissioners just last week that we been having earthquakes, and they just ignored me. This keeps up, we're going to have a lot of lakefront property in Sunshine."

The West Coastal Water Management District is looking into the cause of the sudden rash of sinkholes in Sunshine. "We're very concerned about this matter," said Georgia Pelham, the public information coordinator for the District. "Sinkholes are not a common occurrence in the area, and we're moving ahead rapidly to investigate the root cause."

Mayor Melba Tosti could not be reached for comment, but one of her colleagues, Councilman Gianni Merlini, brushed aside any idea that the council was worried about the little city's future. "We're fine in Sunshine," he commented. "Sinkholes happen. In Florida, they're a fact of life, and if we do get more, we'll just plant trees around them."

CHAPTER FOURTEEN

Mayor Melba Tosti fluffed her cherry red wig, adjusted the lapels of her red and black print blazer, cleared her throat, then banged her gavel. "The meeting of the City Council of the City of Sunshine will now come to order." She then looked upward and intoned, "All rise for the Invocation and the Pledge of Allegiance." After a quick glance to make certain the camera beamed her image, she rose.

Josephus Tyler, prominent businessman, a member of the Living Witness Holy Confederation, and president of the Saved Sons Society, shook himself in preparation for the prayer. He closed his red-rimmed eyes and clasped hands beneath his layered chin. "Lord God, Maker of all things, Knower of all sins, we humbly beseech Thee to lead us to do Thy will while we attend the business of the City of Sunshine." His voice assumed the cadence of the pulpit and he squeezed his eyes tighter shut. "Help us, Lord, to avoid the terrible pitfalls of power! Guide our thoughts, Lord, to Thy ways, that we might prosper. There are those in this city, Lord, who wilfully exceed their power and we ask that You use Your mighty fist to bring them down, Lord. We also have those who wallow in iniquity and sloth. They have backslidden until there is no hope! Stamp them out, Lord–" He grunted as Melba's foot made contact with the back of his leg. "Huh..?"

"Cut it short, Joe," the mayor whispered. "We got a very long agenda."

"...and let us walk in Thy path all the days of our lives, Amen." He opened his eyes, glared at Melba, spun to face the flag, clapped his hand to his heart, and began the pledge. The voices of citizens who regularly attended their meetings rang in faltering echo to his own.

Opening rites concluded, Melba got down to business. "I need a motion to accept last week's minutes."

"Got it." Merlini smirked at Lila Mae.

"Second." Tyler's voice was filled with suppressed excitement.

"All in favor?" Ayes all round. "Motion passed."

"Any outstanding financial matters?"

"Well, there is the matter of the sewers, Madam Chairman," Lila Mae reminded.

"That doesn't belong under financial matters," the mayor snapped. "No financial matters."

Lila Mae treated Merlini to her new smile, moved her microphone aside, and whispered, "When she finds out what the new sewers will cost, she's going to die."

Merlini snorted. "I'd like that; I'd even send flowers."

"Councilman Merlini, we are in session," Melba said sharply.

"Yeah, yeah, Mzzzz. Mayor, that's why I'm here."

"Are there any items to be withdrawn from the consent agenda? No? Okay, I need a motion on the consent agenda."

"Got it." Rainmaker glared at DeLeon Slugge, who sat just below him.

"Second."

"We're moving right along," Melba said. "Councilmen's items. District A?"

Lila Mae readjusted her microphone. "I got three sinkholes in my district, Madam Mayor, and only one of them has been filled. The one that opened yesterday down the street is a doozy, and it's really screwing up traffic." She frowned, then favored Merlini with another smile. "Oh, and I've had a bunch of calls from citizens complaining about the ground shaking. Must be something in the water. That's all, except for the sewer problem."

"We will address the sewer problem under old business," the mayor almost shouted. "Can't you think of anything nice, for Pete's sake? District B?"

Merlini grabbed his microphone and snarled, "I'd like to know who ordered all the city records that are on microfiche moved to the old city hall. It's stupid, dividing government like that. Remember what George Washington said, is all I can say—a divided government can't stand on its own two feet. We got paper records here in the new place, and microfiche moved over to the old place—a man won't know where to go if he needs his death certificate or something." He scowled as Lila Mae giggled. "Some of my folks have been evacuated, too. What's the idea behind all this, spring cleaning?"

"Ah, that will be taken up later in the meeting, Councilman," the mayor said. "Anything else?"

"Hell yes, I ain't finished. I also got a lot of calls about the ground shaking. Prolly due to watching that new TV series, Earthquake. Hollywood ought to be ashamed, putting these weird ideas into peoples' heads. And I hope you got my museum on the agenda."

"Of course, Councilman Merlini." Melba's voice was silky. "District C?"

"I've had a number of calls about tremors, Madam Chairman, and in view of the continuing disturbances, and the sinkholes that have developed, I'd like to commend our city manager for his quick response to the possibility of danger. Looking after the health and safety of our citizens is our job, and Mr. Bonano has exhibited–"

"That's our job!" Tyler said hotly. "And Frank is out in left field, Pervert."

"Madam Chairman, I have the floor," Rainmaker said loudly. "Can you restrain God's ape here, so that I might finish my report?"

Someone in the back of the chamber began to laugh.

"Order!" Melba screeched, banging her gavel. She glared at Tyler, who glared back and folded his arms across his chest.

Mollified, Rainmaker continued. "As I was saying, Frank, I want to commend you."

"Thanks, Teddy," Bonano murmured, "I appreciate the support."

"Thank you, Councilman. District D?"

"I want to know when we're going to hear Slugge's report on whether breaking the law can be considered a crime," Tyler said stubbornly.

"We are taking up that item under old business," the mayor responded between clenched teeth.

"And I want to object to Pervert praising Frank Bonano for making probably the dumbest, lousiest mistake I ever came across. Just goes to show you. This man has closed down perfectly good business so he can play at being hero, and I want his neck." Tyler began to pound on the desk. "He has scared a bunch of old women out of their wits; my wife had nightmares last night about the ground giving way and her house falling into a hole! He's deliberately made rattlesnake hash out of the city records, wasted Lord knows how much money having Rufus Hicks run from place to place–gas costs money, Bonano, and Hicks has a budget to meet. Emergency Services and Disaster Preparedness were pulled lock, stock, and barrel out of their holes and put to work. For what? For nothing. I want to make a motion that we fire Bonano right now!"

"You may make that motion under new business," the mayor said. "My secretary reported twenty calls about the earth shaking. I want to recommend that we consider asking the county health people to look into this, this–mass hysteria that seems to be going around. Now," she looked meaningfully at the cameraman and was pleased to see that he adjusted his zoom and focused on her, "I want to assure our citizens that there is no problem, and never will be a problem as long as I am mayor of this town. These sinkholes are a silly nuisance, that's all. Sinkholes happen in Florida because of the landscape–it's called a farce terrain–I looked it up."

She tried on a frown, found it didn't fit too well, and so she smiled again. "I must agree, however, with Councilman Tyler that your actions, Mr. Bonano, will require a lot of explaining. It is unconscionable for you to close downtown on a whim, and you have frightened a number of people." She tidied her papers, then looked at the camera again. "Councilmen's Issues concluded, we'll go on to old business. Mr. Slugge, will you be kind enough to give us your report?"

Slugge rose and went to the lectern, adjusted the microphone, then smiled at the council. "Good morning. I am here to report on whether it is necessary for the City of Sunshine to pass an ordinance making it illegal to break the law." He looked apologetically at Tyler. "We did a search of case law and found only one. In Platz vs. the State of Florida, such an ordinance was considered unconstitutional as it would place the felon in double jeopardy. Judge Heimlich also wrote, and I quote, "...ordinances of this nature are void for vagueness. The public would never understand such a law, and laws that are misunderstood are laws that are meaningless." I might add, as my personal opinion that, given today's society, we can never have too many laws, but I am afraid that such an ordinance would never stand up in court. However, should the Council wish to pass such an ordinance, my firm would be most willing to represent the City of Sunshine when the ordinance is challenged, which it is certain to be because of what I have previously said. Are there any questions?" He smiled politely.

Tyler half-rose in his seat, his face mottled. "You mean we can't pass the ordinance?" he thundered.

"I didn't say that, Councilman. I said that case law finds such an ordinance unconstitutional, but that doesn't mean that you can't pass such an ordinance. It merely means that you'll have to defend the ordinance in court if there is a challenge, and I feel that it will be challenged. You see, Councilman, ordinances are subordinate legislation under the statutes of the State, and—"

"When I pass an ordinance, it sure as hell ain't subordinate!" Tyler yelled. "You lost your mind?"

The gavel crashed. "Order!"

"Order, hell! What do we pay them for if they don't find out what we want?" Tyler growled. "Sit down, Slugge. Well, Madam Mayor, shall we have that ordinance drawn up?"

"The man just told you that all it will do is take us into court to defend it!" Rainmaker said loudly. "Don't you understand plain English?"

"You shut up, Pervert. He also said that we could pass it if we want, and they will defend it."

"But we'll lose, Joe," Lila Mae burst out. "Teddy's got a point; ain't no sense passing a law that'll be thrown out of court. It will be a waste of tax dollars."

"What do you know?" Tyler sneered. "You just barely finished high school."

"You shut up," Lila Mae retorted. "You only had a year of college yourself."

"Order!" Melba banged the gavel so hard that her wig slipped to one side. She hurriedly pulled it straight and glared at each of the council in turn. "If we may proceed? What is the council's wish on this matter?"

"Table the frigging thing and let's get on with serious work," Merlini suggested.

"Councilman Merlini, we are in session," Lila Mae said, shocked. "You shouldn't use language like that where people can hear you!"

Merlini colored. "Sorry, Lila Mae, I didn't mean to–"

"May we have order?" Melba roared.

"Jee–sus! I move that we table the matter for further discussion."

"I second," Rainmaker said hurriedly.

"All in favor?"

Four ayes, one nay. Tyler sulked.

"Our next business is the report on sewer replacement for the city. Mr. Odlum, would you please address us?"

Odlum gathered a sheaf of papers, rose, and strode to the lectern. He adjusted the microphone to accommodate his exceptional height, then beamed at the Council. "Hold on to your hats, please; this report will come as a serious shock."

He slowly and carefully explained that the entire gravity flow sewage system was damaged and in need of replacement. The leachate from the broken mains was contaminating the soil and the river, thereby contaminating the estuarine areas and the water in the Gulf. The council listened attentively, as they had heard this explanation many times before and actually understood part of what Odlum was talking bout.

Bonano sat watching the utility director. He had expected to be fired for doing his job, and he had not been disappointed. Much to his surprise, he didn't feel bitter. The council really didn't give a damn about anything more than remaining in office, and by reacting to prevent a possible catastrophe, he had stolen the limelight, an unforgivable thing to do when dealing with politicians. He smiled as Mary Lee caught his eye, then switched his attention back to Odlum.

Odlum's expression was grim. "This would have been cheaper eight years ago, but you chose not to address the issue. How much is the replacement going to cost us today? Approximately two hundred and fifty million. Any questions?"

The council sat, stunned by the enormity of the amount he had named.

"Are you certain of your figures?" Rainmaker asked.

"They're pretty accurate, Councilman. Of course, I haven't put out bids, but we're in the ball park."

"Two hundred and fifty million dollars for *pipe!* I don't think we even want to hear more of this," Tyler snarled. "You're wasting our time, Odlum."

"He ain't, Joe. We got to do this or we'll be under a consent order. And even if it costs me some votes, I'm going to vote for it because I care about the public," Lila Mae said hotly. "We got to think about their health and safety."

"What's got into you, Lila Mae?" Tyler said indignantly. "You touched in the head?"

"Order!" The gavel crashed. "Is there a cheaper alternative to what you've given us so far, Mr. Odlum? This is an ill omen that's blowing bad wind."

The others stared at her, trying to make sense of her latest pronouncement.

"Well, yes, there is. We could put in an innovative low pressure system that would require retrofitting our customers with individual pumps. This would be considerably cheaper up front, but down the road, operations and maintenance costs would eat you alive."

"How much money would we save?" Rainmaker asked.

"About a hundred million up front, as I explained."

"That's quite a savings," Melba muttered.

"Yes, it would be, Madam Mayor," Rainmaker said, "but what about the future operations and maintenance costs? Aren't we better off biting the bullet and getting this bond issue passed, rather than placing the future citizens of Sunshine in financial jeopardy?"

"You getting ready to lecture about the public purse again?" Tyler snapped. "You don't think we've heard enough about–"

"I am attempting to address a very serious subject, Councilman Tyler," Rainmaker said. "If you will keep your fat mouth shut, I just might be able to finish my thought."

"Please!" Melba flashed a smile at the camera, then tented her fingers. "Do we have to vote on this today, Mr. Odlum?"

"No, ma'am, but we have to make a decision soon."

"Let's table the matter," Merlini said hurriedly. "We got some pretty important fish to fry."

"Speaking of fish," Lila Mae whispered to him, "I'm getting a divorce."

Merlini's jaw dropped. "Why? I mean, won't it hurt your chances of reelection?"

"They'll forget about it before I run again, Meats. You don't worry."

"Councilman Merlini, will you and Councilman Warner please pay attention."

"We going to table this?" he asked rudely.

"Hell, yes!" Tyler growled. "I so move."

"Second," said Merlini.

The vote was four to one, Rainmaker dissenting.

The purchase of palm trees passed without discussion, even though the site for planting them had not been decided.

"Now," chirped Mayor Tosti, "more old business. Last week, Councilman Tyler suggested that the city condemn Mosquito Row, raze the buildings, and turn the area into a park. Do we need a study on this matter?"

"Why?" Tyler asked. "It would just be a waste of money, and if we're going to have to shell out all those millions for treating sewage, we need to save every dime we can. We can condemn the land and do what we got to do without Fyndar and Ramirez saying it's okay."

Rainmaker smiled nastily. "I must concur with my colleague, Madam Mayor. Such an action on the part of the city would be a silly waste of public funds, under the circumstances. In fact, the condemnation of the land and subsequent purchase by the city would not benefit the taxpayers in Sunshine."

"Oh, no you don't!" Tyler warned, shaking his finger under Rainmaker's nose. "We're going ahead with this and you can't stop us."

Rainmaker went pale. "I wasn't aware it was a done deal, Councilman. If it is, then you have dealt with the matter out of the Sunshine and have broken the–"

"You shut up!" Tyler bellowed.

"Do I have a motion?" Melba asked loudly.

"I so move," Merlini responded.

"Second," snapped Tyler.

"Could someone please tell me what motion we're voting on?" Rainmaker asked. "Or is this too much trouble?"

"What do you mean, what are we voting on?" Melba demanded.

"I mean, I have heard no motion, Madam Mayor, so I don't know why we're voting."

The councilmen looked confused. "Teddy, you think we don't know what we're doing?" Lila Mae asked.

"Did you hear a motion?"

She peered into the chamber, then back at Rainmaker. "I think you're right."

"What are you two talking about?" Melba almost screamed.

"I thought we was voting on whether or not to give Fyndar and Ramirez a job," Merlini said.

The mayor went pale. "No, indeed, Councilman Merlini! We must put out bids; you know the procedure."

"Oh, okay. Then I move that we put out bids for the study on condemning the land at Mosquito Row."

Melba sighed with relief. "Do I hear a second?"

"Got it," Joe Tyler said.

"Thank you, Madam Mayor," Rainmaker said. "I am so glad we have a motion to vote on."

She glared at him. "All in favor?"

The motion passed, three yeas and two nays.

Melba looked at her watch and shook her head. The meeting was going on far, far longer than she had anticipated. "May we postpone our presentation on the Liar's Festival–don't you just love the name?–until next week? We have a good deal more business to cover, and time is getting short." She favored Mary Lee Mince with a nasty look.

"Suits me," Merlini said, beaming. He had voted with Joe, now Joe would have to vote for the museum. Of course, he'd also have to support Melba's beach, but that was no big deal; it would make a nice setting for the museum. "What about the museum?"

Melba's voice was pure honey. "Would you mind terribly if we put that discussion off a week, Councilman Merlini?"

"Not at all," he said expansively.

"Fine, that bring us to new business. I have decided that we need to redesign the City Seal. If we're going to have palm trees, they need to be reflected on our escutcheon."

Lila Mae leaned forward to look at the Mayor. "Reflect on our what?"

"Escutcheon."

"I didn't know we had one. Does it bite?" Merlini sniggered and she grinned at him. "That'll keep her going for a while," she whispered.

"Madam Mayor, don't you think, in view of the serious business we have ahead, that we might table such a matter until next week?" Rainmaker asked.

"I don't see why we have to postpone it," Melba snapped.

"Because we have had three sinkholes in this part of town in the last two days, because our people are complaining of the earth trembling beneath their feet, because you are going to consider firing the one person in this whole damned city that is responsible to the citizens, and because, at this time, it is trifling and unworthy of our consideration." Rainmaker's voice was rising and he was flushed with anger.

"I think that the Pervert is right," Tyler growled. "We got a lot more important stuff on our plate than a new city seal."

"Very well, we'll table the matter until next week," Melba said in a tight voice. "Do I hear a motion?"

"Got it," Rainmaker snapped.

"Second."

The motion to table passed with the mayor dissenting.

"Madam Mayor, I would like to bring an emergency," Bonano said.

"Very well, Bonano, we'll hear the emergency, and it will probably be your last one."

He shrugged. "Two days ago, Donald Sarious of the DEP and I went out to the springs that empty into the Gulf a couple of miles offshore of the river mouth. The water was white, like milk. It felt gritty. We took a sample and Mr. Sarious dropped it off at the District for analysis. They found an abundance of dissolved lime.

"The District sent divers down yesterday morning to the underwater springs. They took samples from the spring and found 496,000 parts per million of dissolved lime. That's half solid, in case any of you aren't familiar with the terminology. Their feeling is that there is something catastrophic about to happen in the aquifer, and they don't know where it will happen.

"For the last two weeks, citizens have been complaining about ground tremors in this neighborhood. Some of the tremors have been felt as far away as Merriweather Drive. Mr. Slugge's wife experienced two." He leaned forward, intent, staring at Melba. "Mr. Odlum pulled all the old maps, and reminded me that, back in the '50's, there was a chemical plant just about where this building sits. The plant produced hydrochloric acid. I went back in the old records and there were reports that one of the big acid vats had split and there was a spill of some hundred thousand gallons of the stuff. Nobody was particularly worried because the acid just soaked into the ground, but it may, and I want to emphasize *may*, have been eating at the limestone that holds up this city, especially in this area. If it has, we may be in trouble.

"The District has scoured the state and located ground-penetrating radar equipment, the very latest, to investigate this area. They're due to begin tomorrow. I felt that, until we know for certain that there is no cavity beneath this part of Sunshine, we'd better play it safe. If any of you have questions, I'll try to answer them."

"You took it on yourself to close down businesses?" Tyler almost shouted.

"I did, Councilman Tyler. I don't want any loss of life if there is a catastrophe."

"Sounds like a crock of sh–sounds stupid to me, to worry about something that happened over fifty years ago," Merlini opined. "You should of waited until today and got our permission," he added.

"I think you both are full of it," Lila Mae said. "Frank was hired to do a job, and when he does his job, you jump on him. If there's anything stupid, it's us."

"How dare you insinuate that we don't know what we're doing?" Tyler bellowed. "You sit back and shut up. I heard from Henny what you're planning, Jezebel."

"Joe, you could bore God to death," Lila Mae shot back. "Why don't you shut up for a change?"

"Heresy!"

The gavel crashed. "Are we going to discuss this emergency or not?"

Merlini stared at Lila Mae. Jezebel? What had she done?

"I got calls from over a dozen businesses complaining about Bonano's high-handedness," Melba said. "That's bad business, to alienate our chamber members like that. You should have located me before you went to the press, before you did anything at all–"

"You could not be reached, Madam Mayor," Bonano said coldly. "However, in order to save you and the council further embarrassment, I will resign as of this moment."

"Like hell you will!" Tyler screamed. "You're fired."

Bonano began to gather his papers.

"This is a disgrace!" shouted Sally Slugge from the rear of the chamber. She jumped to her feet and ran down the aisle, pale with anger. She grabbed the microphone at the lectern. "How dare you, *how dare you* spit on this man? He has saved your sorry asses so many times I can't count them. I'm sick and tired of being ashamed of where I live, damned sick of having people snicker when I tell them I'm from Sunshine. I demand responsible government, and if you cannot be responsible, then resign your offices and we'll put jackasses in your places. They'll do a better job!"

The entire council sat as if turned to stone.

Dee Slugge shook off his inertia, jumped to his feet and, grabbing Sally's arm and twisting it horribly, tried to wrest the microphone from his wife, but she slapped him in the face, kicked his shin for good measure, and strode back to the seat she had vacated.

The mayor's comments were drowned in applause.

CHAPTER FIFTEEN

The moon, riding low in the western sky, cast its waning light on the green and white of electric fires that sparked across the far side of the chasm as one utility pole after another dropped into oblivion.

Chief Rufus Hicks stood ten yards from the edge of the abyss, staring at the ravening monster that had devoured his car, the buildings in front of him, the trees, the utility poles–everything. It still gnawed its way westward and to the north, biting off great chunks of sidewalk and street, gulping the few automobiles in sight, chewing up one house after another. The buildings shrieked and grated as they were ripped apart and fell into the chasm.

"Oh, God, make it stop!" he moaned, riven with fear.

He had been driving west along Hatchacootee, about three blocks from the new City Hall. Suddenly, his car had begun to shake violently. He rammed the gear lever into neutral, flung open the door, and scrambled out. It was then that he felt the heaving of the pavement beneath his feet. Panicked, he ran back the way he had come. He'd been knocked flat by what sounded and felt like an explosion. Groggy, he lunged to his feet and looked back. Everything behind him had disappeared!

Unable to move, he stared across the ravenous maw toward the city hall and the station, his one refuge in this madness. His mind struggled to make sense of the scene before him. Another rumbling roar blotted out reason, slamming him to the ground. The city hall and its surrounds began to topple into the hole. He could make out a desk dropping into the abyss, which sounded as if it was filling with water. Electricity crackled and snaked through the darkness.

He scrabbled to his feet, shaking with fear. He wanted to look into that awful depth, but was afraid to go any nearer; he had barely missed being buried in that horror.

Blocks away, he could hear the fire engines begin to scream. Naturally, the boys would respond to the noise, figuring that the gas mains had exploded. But they'd be rushing in the wrong direction; the mains were laid in the right-of-way to U. S. Highway 15-B. That thought brought him some comfort; at least they wouldn't lose their fire engines. But all his patrol cars were gone except the two he had just dispatched to make another fake raid on Mosquito Row and the Lightning Bug Bar.

When the third section caved in, he was buffeted by the shock wave, but it didn't knock him down. Then he realized that his nose was bleeding and his head was pounding. Dazed, he collapsed on the sidewalk, then sat up, put his feet in the gutter, and pulled out his handkerchief to stanch the flow of blood from his nose.

Was his family safe? He didn't know, didn't have a car, couldn't check on the damage, couldn't even tell how much of a town was left beyond that eerie, gaping maw.

Then the odor hit him--the reek of wrenched earth, of ancient rot, and the stench of raw sewage. He rolled over onto his side and vomited into the gutter, then lay back on the concrete, sobbing raggedly. The unthinkable had happened; Sunshine was dead!

Rainmaker was thrown from his bed to the floor. He opened his eyes, groggy from sleep, the physical blow he had received, and the awful noise that seemed to engulf the world. PooPoo! Was he–? He struggled to his feet, then was knocked to the floor as another blow hit the house. The sliding glass doors shattered and seemed to blow across the carpet. What was going on?

From the other side of the bed came a moan. He rose shakily, lit a candle he kept by the bed, and crept to where PooPoo lay, tangled in the sheet. His lover's face was covered with blood. He grabbed a corner of the sheet and wiped away some of the gore. There was an ugly gash on his forehead.

Rainmaker knelt and touched PooPoo's cheek. "Are you conscious, Hon?"

Moaning, PooPoo struggled to sit up. He looked around the room, dazed, then touched his forehead. "Teddy, I'm bleeding! Could you bring me a towel?"

Once again the house was shaken by a shock, but the force had lessened. Rainmaker started for the bathroom, but PooPoo cried out and he ducked as the windows shattered, turning the ruined carpet into a sea of glass. "What the hell is happening?" he shouted.

PooPoo rose and touched his forehead. An ugly knot was rising above the gash. "I don't know what I hit, but I think we need to go to the emergency room. This cut will need stitches. Give me some light." He began to pick his way gingerly across the room, trying to avoid cutting himself.

"Put on your slippers," Rainmaker said automatically. "I'll get dressed."

Through the shattered window they could hear sirens in the distance. Then they heard frightened screams from homes in their neighborhood.

He hurriedly drew on a polo shirt and a pair of khakis while PooPoo donned a dressing gown and slippers, still holding the towel to his forehead. "You're not applying enough pressure, Hon."

"I can't stop the bleeding. Come on, let's get over to the hospital."

"And leave the house wide open like this?"

"Can't be helped. Do you suppose one of the gas lines has exploded?"

Rainmaker shivered. "Sounded like they all went up. God help Sunshine."

Odlum rolled out of his bed and hit the floor running when the first shock hit. Frank had been right on the button, by God!

The second wave sent him reeling, but he stayed on his feet and made the closet as the third shock hit. Then he heard some glass tinkle downstairs, but most of his windows seemed to have survived the shockwaves.

He lived a couple of miles from the city center, out past the posh Merriweather Drive community, on five acres filled with old oaks, maples, and sweetgums. It was quiet where he lived, peaceful, and shockwaves didn't belong in this place of serenity.

Outside, he could hear the birds complaining of the intrusion into their domain. He agreed with them; chaos had no business in his yard.

He threw on some clothes, then grabbed the telephone and dialed Frank's number, going over in his mind what would need to be done immediately. The sewer lines would be ruptured, pouring waste into the sinkhole. Those had to be sealed off, and new lines rerouted around the damage to serve the city's residents whose homes would be affected. There would be a lot of homes affected, of that he was sure.

He wondered if Lila Mae had escaped, and an enormous knot rose in his chest with the thought. She had moved out of the home she had shared with Henny, and put herself in harm's way for his sake. When Frank answered the telephone, he was hoarse from emotion.

Bonano was slumped in his easy chair, reading a detective novel. He had given up on sleeping at 3 A.M.. The events of the day had left him jittery, so he had risen and made some hot tea, then picked up his book. Reading for a while always made him drowsy. And besides, it took his mind off the spectacle at his last meeting with the City Council.

Joe Tyler had leaped to his feet and begun to call down the wrath of God on Sally Slugge, while Dee scrambled to recover his dignity, which had been sorely bruised by his wife's unprecedented attack. Melba had started banging the gavel and yelling at Tyler, then she turned on Merlini, who was shouting something unintelligible. Rainmaker and Lila Mae had simply sat, staring at the others and probably wondering if they had gone mad. He had picked up his papers and gone to his office, emptied his desk, and come home. To hell with them all.

Suddenly, he was flying across the room in a shower of diamonds. He wondered at this, then realized that all his windows had shattered. He slammed into the wall and dropped to the floor, where he lay fighting to inhale for what seemed like an eternity. He was horrified. He knew what had caused that knock-out blow to his house. The only thing he did not know was how bad it was.

He struggled to his feet, which were snatched from under him again as another shock wave hit. He found himself flat on the floor. "Shit!" Then a third blow hit, but a lesser one.

His telephone began to ring. He got up again, hobbled to the telephone, listening to the eerie sound of the glass shards dropping to the floor, and grabbed the receiver. "Bonano."

"God help us," Odlum whispered. "I wonder if there's much left."

He groaned. "No way to find out but to look. I'll meet you on Hatchacootee, as close to City Hall as we can get. Then we'd better set up emergency quarters in the old city hall. It's going to disturb some of the folks camping in the shelter, but that's too bad." He skipped a few beats, then said, "You heard anything from Lila Mae?"

"No, I called you first."

"Give her a holler, see if she's all right." He could almost feel the relief pouring through the telephone. "We're going to need some extra hands, so see if you can get her to come down."

"Right. See you in about fifteen minutes." Odlum rang off.

Bonano shook his head, then wearily felt his way to the bedroom to dress. Poor son of a bitch, he thought. He must be worried half to death about Lila Mae.

Thank God for Frank Bonano! When she surveyed the scene, it was the first thing that came into Lila Mae's mind. Lord, if he hadn't moved all those old folks who lived on the streets off Hatchacootee, how many people would have died? She shuddered and turned to Rainmaker. "This is beyond horrible, Teddy."

"Yeah," he said gruffly.

She had rented a small house on Kennedy and Fifth Avenue, not more than a couple of blocks from the hospital. The first thing she had done, after getting all the glass out of her hair, was to dress and rush to the hospital to see how many people had died in the gas mains explosion. In the emergency room, she had found Rainmaker and PooPoo. And no one else.

"What happened?" she had asked Rainmaker.

"Frank Bonano was right."

"Jesus, you mean—?"

"We had to detour all over the place to get here. There's an enormous sinkhole. PooPoo was bleeding like a stuck pig, so I brought him straight over here, but we need to find out what's happened, and see what we can do about it."

"You go ahead with Lila Mae, Teddy, and I'll get myself back to the house when they're through here," PooPoo had said. "If I can do anything, just call me."

They had headed south on Fourth Avenue, turned east on Hatchacootee, and headed for the city hall. But Hatchacootee Boulevard ended a few feet beyond the Stop N' Shop Department Store. Most of "new downtown" was gone.

"What's that awful smell?"

"I think it's called Eau de Sewage, Lila Mae."

She gasped. 'Where is Oddman? I need to find him."

"Get back in the car, Lila Mae, and let's see just how big this thing is. I think we've lost a damned big chunk of Sunshine this morning. God help us all."

"I got to find Oddman." She looked back at the chasm and shuddered. "If you were Frank Bonano, where would you set up base?"

"Old city hall. It's only used for storage, but the phones are still there."

"Let's go over there."

His wife was screaming for mercy, her voice thin with panic. He bolted upright in his bed, disoriented. He was covered with jewels, so why was his wife screaming? Then Tyler snapped awake. "What's wrong, why are you carrying on like that?"

She was on her knees in the middle of the room, surrounded by glass shards, begging hysterically for forgiveness. He stumbled across the glass-strewn carpet and shook her. "Sarah, calm down. What's the matter?"

A blast of air buffeted the house and he staggered.

"The end is come!" Sarah screamed. "It's because you took money from those women and made Learned Speaker angry." She began crossing herself.

"You stop that!" he ordered. "Only Catholics and other heathens cross themselves!"

Face drowned in tears, she glared at him, slit-eyed. "You have put our mortal souls in danger, Joe Tyler. Don't you yell at me."

He stared at her as if she had come unhinged. "It ain't the end of the world, Sarah; it's all right. Sounds as if a gas main has blown sky high. I'll go down and see what the trouble is, and you have some breakfast ready for me when I get back." He patted her awkwardly on the head, and she seemed to calm a little. "I promise you, Sarah, it ain't the end of the world."

He glanced at his watch. It was 3:45. Frowning, he tiptoed through the glass shards to the closet. It must have been one hell of an explosion, he thought. It would disrupt traffic for a week. Last time something like that had happened near 15-B, they had five accidents. He just hoped that the phone company and the electric company were standing by.

He decided to drive down Gulf Gambol, then east on Hatchacootee. That way, he could avoid any heavy traffic that was bound to have accumulated at the explosion site, see what he wanted to see, and get back home for some coffee and breakfast. Being waked so early made him hungry.

He wasn't alarmed in the least; Sunshine did have a good fire department. And now their Disaster Preparedness department was increased to four people because of a state mandate.

He was sick and tired of getting orders from Tallahassee. Why didn't they mind their own damned business? But no, the council had been forced to waste money on people who probably would never do an honest day's work for the city, folks who spent all their time drawing up complicated plans that they were very pleased with. He was proud to have been on the losing side on that vote, by God!

He whistled a hymn as he drove along Gulf Gambol. He liked using the road that meandered about a quarter-mile inland from the marsh that fringed their infamous mud flats. It was the only road built to specs that he had ever seen done by a developer. Since it was never used, it had held up well, even though the developer had gamboled straight into bankruptcy when he tried to put in a really posh sub-division twenty years too early. The land between the marsh and No-Name Road, which ran parallel to First Avenue, was pretty. At present it was filled with trailer parks, but he had plans for that space in the future.

He reached Hatchacootee and turned east, then slowed in confusion. There was nothing going on at Highway 15-B at all. It was only three blocks from where he was, and he could see the odd car and a number of trucks whizzing by on the overpass, unimpeded. What had caused those awful blasts, then?

He continued along Hatchacootee to Fifth Avenue, where he was stopped by a roadblock. Instantly angry, he parked, got out of the car, and hastened to where he saw Odlum and that damned Bonano standing with Rufus Hicks. He grabbed Bonano by the shoulder and yanked him around.

"What are you doing here? You're fired, and you got no right—"

"Go to hell, Joe," Bonano said tiredly. "Shut your mouth, open your eyes, and take a look. In another couple of hours, you are going to be out of business."

"What do you mean? Rufus, what's going on?"

"The whole damn thing's caved in, Joe. All the land from Adams down to Bog Walk, and from 6th Avenue up to O'Doole, is down there. And the sides are still falling in. I think it's over a hundred feet deep—could be deeper. Stop N' Shop is sitting right on the edge of the biggest damned sinkhole I ever heard of, and the building is beginning to break up. We got a hell of a mess, Joe. A hell of a mess."

"Jesus!"

"He ain't going to be any help, Joe. Not any help at all," Odlum drawled.

"He's got to help," Tyler retorted. "Let me through; I got to see about the store."

"Sorry, Joe," Rufus answered, "but no one goes beyond this point. You might get killed. We got to wait until it stabilizes, then you can go in."

Tyler opened his mouth to argue, then noticed Odlum staring past him, his mouth agape. He turned and gasped. At the end of the block, part of Stop n' Shop was tilting toward the abyss. They heard a nasty crack followed by lesser noises, and a quarter of his department store toppled into oblivion. He went down on his knees, howling with anger and grief.

Melba stumbled around in the dark, cursing and hunting for a light switch that would work. Then she realized that the power was off. How dare Hatchacootee Power and Light fail when something terrible had obviously happened? Didn't they realize that she could get cut with all that mess on the floor?

Her windows had broken and the glass lay helter-skelter across her bedroom. She felt her way back to the bedside table, opened the drawer, and groped for a box of matches, then inched her way to the chest of drawers and the candle she kept there. Shakily, she lit the thing, only to have it gutter and die from the early morning breeze that drifted through her defenseless windows.

"Damn it, how am I supposed to get dressed?" she asked the darkness.

She opened her closet, pulled out a dress, and hauled it over her head, then grabbed a wig and jammed in atop her hair, hoping they wouldn't clash with one another. She slipped on a pair of heels, then felt her way into the kitchen where she'd left her purse. Opening the back door, she stepped on the porch and drew a deep breath, then gagged on the horrible stink that pervaded her yard. Senses scrambling for a resemblance, she decided that it was a graveyard smell.

As she hesitantly went down the back steps, every cell in her being screamed for her to turn back. She wondered if she was going crazy, then decided that perhaps it was some kind of instinct that clamored, so she went back up the steps to get a flashlight. Maybe there was an intruder lurking; mayors did make enemies even when they did no wrong.

Armed with her flash, she went back outside and played the light around her yard, but she could see nothing, not even the tree that shaded the back porch. Puzzled, she inched down the steps, stepped onto one of the stepping stones she had planted, and realized that, after the next stone, there were no others. She aimed the flash for where the third stone should have been and saw that, four feet from her steps, the world ended. She was looking into a deep hole. Looking up, she peered through the gloom and realized that the house that backed onto hers was gone. Disoriented and frightened beyond measure, she ran back up the steps, through her little home, and out the front door. She murmured a fervent thanks to God that the sidewalk greeted her, and her newly planted elm tree stood where it belonged.

It was then that she realized her car, her baby blue Lincoln, must be in that awful hole. Beginning to cry, Melba walked hurriedly to where Mary Lee Mince lived. Mary Lee parked her car on the street, so she still had transportation.

She arrived just in time. Mary Lee was leaving her house.

"Where are you going?" Melba asked.

"Old city hall. You want a ride?"

"Yes, my car is in the hole," Melba said, a sob catching in her throat. "What's wrong? Have you looked out back?"

"Yes, I have. Frank was right, Madam Mayor. The city hall has fallen into the hole, and a good part of downtown Sunshine with it."

"How do you know?"

"Frank called and asked me to come in to help him."

"Help him do what?" Melba felt stupid. "He can't give you orders; he's fired."

"He's working, Madam Mayor," Mary Lee said coldly, "for the people who live here."

Merlini lived above his sausage factory at the corner of No-Name Road and Hatchacootee. He believed a man should be close to his work, and he had lived in an apartment above his factory in Brooklyn before he retired. His father had always said it was important for a man to keep his work close to him, as work was man's lot in life.

He got up to go to the bathroom, had been halfway across the bedroom, when the first blast hit, blowing out all his second floor windows. He had hit the floor, convinced that someone was shooting at him, when the second shockwave slammed into the building. He sat, stunned, as the third and final shock destroyed his big shop windows downstairs. The sound had been both terrible and beautiful, like the tinkling of a million chimes in the midst of hell.

"Jee-sus, what is going on?" he asked the night.

Bathroom forgotten, he hurried downstairs to check on the damage. He still had power, thank God, so his stock was safe, but now all those thieves and welfare types who lived on Mosquito Row could just walk right in and steal all the sausage they could carry away.

He'd just board up the front windows, he thought. There was plenty of plywood in the back room, kept there in case of a hurricane. He went back upstairs, pulled on some old pants and a shirt, then went down to put the coffee pot on. Grumbling, he then went through the shop to the back room and began to haul out plywood for his repairs. He'd just finished stacking the fourth sheet of ply against the door, and was pouring himself a cuppa, when the telephone rang.

What the hell?–it was 4:30 A.M., for chrissake! He grabbed the receiver. "Yeah?"

"Frank Bonano here, Meats. We got an emergency and you probably need to come down to the old city hall."

"What?"

"Sinkhole. Enormous. The new city hall is gone, Tyler's department store in teetering on the edge and will probably fall in–it's horrible. I need all the help I can get."

"You handle it, Frankie boy. I got problems here at the plant. See you later."

He rang off, then slurped some of the coffee, and eased his back.

What was Bonano thinking of, for chrissake–why wake up the whole city council over a hole in the ground?

By the time Melba and Mary Lee found a way to get around the sinkhole, it was daylight. Their way was blocked by the curious citizens who had not been evacuated. They stood in frightened little knots, gaping at the remains of the city center. Some were half dressed.

"Blow your horn, Mary Lee, and get those idiots to move out of the way."

"I suspect that a lot of them are in a state of shock," Mary Lee answered. "Can't say I blame them. Where do you want me to take you?"

"Hell, I don't know. I don't have a–I mean, I suppose I have to go in and take charge. Take me to the old city hall."

They moved slowly along Tyler, then cut west on Monroe. Melba pulled the mirror from her purse and began to try to repair the way she looked, but she looked pretty bad. She had yanked a sunny yellow dress from the closet, and put on her new cherry red wig. She was horrified, but it was too late to do anything about it. She'd just have to tough it out until she could commandeer a car, sneak home, and dress properly. There were bound to be television interviews later in the day, and she wanted to look her best.

She caught Mary Lee sneaking a look at her. "You don't look too smart yourself, Mary Lee," she said nastily. "You might at least comb your hair before you come to work."

Mary Lee bit her lip and said nothing. She wondered if the mayor had noticed that her dress was on wrong-side-out.

As they approached the old city hall, Mary Lee allowed herself a tight smile. The place was surrounded by television vans and she wondered fleetingly how they managed to find out what was going on before Heart County was awake. As they pulled up between two vans, Melba hopped out of the car, smiling brilliantly at the cameras that were aimed at them.

CHAPTER SIXTEEN

Frank Bonano thankfully took the cup of coffee that Odlum handed him, then got back on the telephone. It seemed impossible to get the county government to respond at dawn. He dialed another number and smiled briefly as the Chief of Disaster Preparedness over in Flag City finally answered. He hoped Blake had enjoyed his night's rest; he was about to have a bomb dropped on him.

"Bonano here. I was beginning to think Flag City was down a hole too. You need to get your people over here fast, John. The whole city center has dropped into a sinkhole that looks like it covers about two hundred acres. No, I'm sober; it's too early for anything but coffee. You really sleep soundly; the impact must have been felt for miles around. Deaths?–I don't think so; I evacuated a ten block area around City Hall day before yesterday, got fired for doing it, but to the best of my knowledge, no one went back." He moved the receiver from his ear and looked at it, then up at Odlum. "John is upset."

Odlum nodded mournfully, then walked to the window and looked out at the chaos in the parking lot behind the building. "Lila Mae and Teddy have arrived," he said. The relief in his voice was obvious.

"Good. Yes, John, get them over here pronto. And how about calling Fred Baron. Tell him that I'm calling in the Governor and he'll have to coordinate the visit; I don't have the time. Yeah, I know it's his prerogative, but this is a real emergency and I can't get him to answer the damned telephone. Tell him it's pure chaos over here; I've lost most of my resources. I need Public Health, too. We have broken sewer mains out the kazoo. Yeah? Okay." He hung up and looked at Odlum, then began dialing again. "Any sign of the mayor?"

"Yeah, she's out there with the television cameras. All I can say is, at least she knows there's been a disaster because she had to drive all around it to get here. I wonder how close it came to her neighborhood?"

"Not close enough," Bonano answered shortly. "Hello, Marge, this is Frank Bonano from Sunshine. Sorry to wake you so early. Would you please inform the Governor that we have a major disaster here? Yeah, you better disturb him; this is for real. He needs to get down here and take a look, because we're going to need a presidential disaster declaration. Look, I know I'm going above his head, but I've lost a good chunk of my city to a sinkhole and I can't rouse him. Okay." He gave the Governor's personal assistant his phone number and hung up as Rainmaker hurried through the door with Lila Mae in his wake.

"Anybody dead?" Rainmaker asked.

"Not that I know of," Bonano said. "We did a complete evacuation. Of course, the only thing we can do is wait and see if anyone is reported missing; there's no way we can send a team down into that hole to search for bodies; the sides are still falling in."

"Has Rufus showed up yet?" Lila Mae asked. "He could drive around, sort of check things over. I think every window in town is broken, so you better call in the National Guard to prevent looting. I don't think that any of our people would loot, but you never know."

"Rufus was almost a casualty, Lila Mae," Odlum explained. "He was right on the edge of the damned thing, and his car went into the hole."

"Oh, my God! Is he all right?"

"Only the good die young," Rainmaker said tightly. To Bonano he said, "You called the county?"

"Yes, and the Governor. Told Marge that he needs to get down here this morning if he can." Bonano sighed. "We need to set up some teams to prevent crime, that sort of thing, but half the telephones are out and I can't reach city personnel. I—"

"You tell me where to go, and I'll get them," Lila Mae volunteered. "I'm not much use around here, and my car's outside."

Bonano nodded and began to write down names and addresses. He was thankful then that he managed a small city. He knew everyone and where they lived.

"Should you have called the Governor?" Rainmaker asked. "Won't that tread on Baron's toes?"

Bonano shrugged. "Probably, but by the time we go through all the explanations, and Baron is convinced that we have a problem, then figures out his logistics, how to deploy his troops– you know how he is. Military idiot."

"Yes, I suppose you're right, but he's going to give you some flak."

"I've been shot at before."

Fred Baron, Administrator to Banter County, one-time military man, Bonano thought. Referred to the county employees as his troops. He'd heard that Baron actually used to inspect the county employees daily to see if they were dressed to his code, but a lawsuit fifteen years before had put an end to that. Baron was barely five and a half feet tall, sported a crew-cut, spoke in clipped military jargon, walked like he had a spike up his ass, and wore epaulets on his shirts.

Wondering why he had to deal with such people, he sighed and dialed another number.

Mary Lee Mince pushed through the throng of media people on the steps of the old brick building. The shocks had damaged one corner, she noticed, and some of the bricks had fallen into an untidy heap on the weeds that had overtaken the lawn. It was a shame, she thought, that the building had been abandoned in the first place; it had character. But there had been no stopping Mayor Tosti when she made up her mind that they would have a new city hall. Her excuse for the expenditure had been that a new city hall would allow the government to function more efficiently. And the taxpayers bought it.

A lot of the people in town thought that Melba was a good mayor because she was always running from pillar to post for photo ops, but the fact was that she paid little attention to Sunshine's problems. Everything Melba did seemed to focus on being reelected.

She shuddered, still frightened by how close the sinkhole had come to swallowing her house. Who would have thought that the ground could cave in over so large an area? She'd seen sinkholes, lots of them. A great many lakes in the area began as sinkholes, because Florida was karst terrain, a landscape of limestone eaten away over the millennia by water. The whole aquifer was like a giant sponge, and the only thing that supported it was the same water that had made the limestone full of holes.

Over the past couple of years she had heard talk about how the aquifer was being overpumped in their area to supply the phenomenal growth of Heart County, but who paid attention to talk like that? Water was there for people to use; it certainly wasn't anything to worry about–or was it? She ran her tongue over her teeth and cringed inwardly; there had been no way to brush this morning. Then she pictured the entire city with "morning mouth," wandering in dressing gowns through the shattered landscape, politely avoiding one another with apologetic smiles. She grinned. That's what advertising did to your head, she thought.

"Boy, am I glad to see you!" Bonano exclaimed as she walked through the door. "There's a phone in the next room. Get hold of Marge Daley in the Governor's office again–here's her number, and ask her to get the Governor to call in the National Guard. Every window in town is out, and the place will be a sitting duck for looters. And later, see if you can notify the Corps of Engineers. Odlum is going to need help; that hole is gathering a lot of sewage at this point, and I don't want it to become a health hazard. "

"You think any of our people would loot when the whole city is hurting?" she asked, incredulous.

"Honey, people will stoop to anything; all we need to do is slacken the reins a little. And you forget those low-lifes who prey on the retirees in Heart County; all they have to do is cross the bridge." Then Bonano yelped. "Jee–sus! I forgot about the bridge. Is it safe?"

"Judging from the number of television vans outside," she answered drily, "I'd say it was in mint condition."

"What are you doing here?" Melba snarled as she came through the door. "Get out right now! I'm here, and I'll take over."

Bonano looked up at her. "Madam Mayor, I have no intention of leaving while there's work to be done. I'd suggest that you just stay out of the way and leave this to professionals. We have a major disaster."

The truth of his statement stung her. "I am well aware that there has been a disaster. My own car is down in that awful hole and—"

"If you want to help out, Teddy is in the next room. We need to go over the tax rolls and see just how much property has actually been destroyed. In order to get FEMA assistance, we have to prove that more than a hundred homes and businesses have gone down that hole. I've sent someone to locate the microfiche you'll need."

"The records went down with the city hall," she sneered.

"No, I had all the microfiche transferred over here, along with some of the other records. If you recall, Meats objected to my moving it," Bonano explained.

"You had no right to order those records moved," she answered hotly. "I am the mayor of—"

"Either go to work or get out of the way!" Bonano roared.

Tyler stumbled through the door, looking lost. He flinched when Bonano yelled at Melba, then awkwardly patted her shoulder.

She spun around . "What the hell do you want?

"You better clean yourself up a little, Melba. Your clothes ain't on right, and it's not fitting that a woman in your position look so—"

"You go to hell, Joe. I—"

"I have gone to hell," he snapped. "My entire life is down in that hole. I'm only insured for about five million. I'm a ruined man!" He sagged against Bonano's desk and put his face in his hands.

Bonano grimaced. "Joe, how about helping Teddy?"

Tyler shook his head. "No," he said darkly, "the Pervert is probably one of the reasons God has visited this plague on the city. You get a city employee to do that; that's what they're paid for, and their labor will not anger the Almighty, for the laborer is worthy of his hire. I'm going home for my breakfast. Then I'm going to pray. And I got to tell Sarah she's a poor woman." He shoved himself away from the desk and staggered out into the hall.

"Useless ass!" Melba snarled. "All he can think about is himself. Has anyone figured out what I'm supposed to use as an office?" Her mouth snapped shut as she caught the expression on Bonano's face.

"Get the phone company. I don't care what you have to do to get a response; we need more lines in here, today. And you'd better clean up, as Joe said. The Governor's coming."

"I don't have electricity. Do you realize that my whole neighborhood is out? And we don't have water."

Bonano rolled his eyes and sighed with exasperation. "Tell you what, Melba. Just go home and I'll call you when the next wave of media arrives."

"You bastard!"

"God give me strength," Bonano muttered.

Then Melba's face suffused with spite. "God had better give you a job, Bonano. You sure as hell won't ever have one in this town again."

Bonano shook his head as she flounced from the room. Melba would come through just fine, he thought, but he wondered if Tyler was losing it. *The laborer was worthy of his hire?* Just what thought process had turned that up?

By nine o'clock, the news of Sunshine's disaster had spread to the major networks. The circuits into the area were hopelessly clogged with calls from families seeking assurance that their kin were still alive. Bonano assigned three volunteers to field the calls, then sent Guy Fawkins, who had arrived with a gaggle of his friends, to gather the City Council. The Governor would be flying into Flag City at ten, and would be in Sunshine by ten-thirty. They had to be on hand to greet him and accompany him on his tour of the city.

The old city hall was besieged by citizens from the eastern side of town, who drove around the enormous sinkhole to complain that they lacked water and electricity. A desk for complaints was set up outside, manned by Kelsey Fawkins and Gavel Strike, who plotted outages on a utilities map of the city provided by Odlum's office.

The Disaster Preparedness team came in from Flag City and began working to move those who had no amenities and were afraid or unable to stay in their homes into shelters. Blake brought with him several police as well, to assist the officers of the law, who were hopelessly swamped. Down at Mosquito Row, some fool had started the rumor that The End Had Come!, and the streets were jammed with praying women and children clamoring for a miracle.

By nine thirty, hundreds of sightseers from Heart County had driven across the bridge and were clogging Hatchacootee Boulevard. Rufus Hicks pulled in all his deputies to try and control the gawkers, who surged forward, arguing among themselves, trying to get close enough to the sinkhole to look over the edge.

"What're we going to do with all these damned people?" the police chief wailed when Bonano happened to run into him. "At the rate they're going, we'll have half the population of Heart County at the bottom of the hole!"

"Well, see if you can't get some help from Heart County to keep 'em away. We don't want to be sued for stealing their tourists," was the short reply.

Fred Baron arrived in a patrol car ten minutes ahead of the Governor. He jumped from the car almost before it had halted, and marched briskly into the old city hall and the room occupied by Bonano and his aides. He stopped, clicked his heels, and glared at Bonano.

"You have broken protocol!" he snapped.

"Off with my head," Bonano said tiredly. "I tried to reach you, tried to get Fowler Dayes, and none of you would answer your damned telephones, so don't get on my case, Fred, I'm warning you." He rose and went to the window to look out on the parking lot, which was still covered with media vehicles. "He here yet?"

"*The Governor* will be here at–" he looked at his watch, then back at Bonano, "at ten hundred hours plus four minutes. Where are the councilmen? I want them on the lawn in front of the building to greet him."

"Any particular way you want them to line up?" Bonano asked sarcastically.

"You're not funny! Why isn't that grass mowed, sold–I mean, Frank? Damned bad show to have the place a mess, when the Governor is coming."

"Tell you the truth, Fred, all the city's mowers are about a hundred feet down in a sinkhole, and I just couldn't be bothered to go round them up in time for your visit. And if you think the lawn is a mess, wait until you see what Ma Nature has done for us. The councilmen and the mayor are in the room two doors down the hall to the right. They're waiting for you, and they probably won't pass inspection." He snorted as the county's administrator growled an obscenity and stalked from the room without a backward glance.

"You've pissed him off," Odlum said.

"Good. Why isn't the lawn mowed, for chrissake!" Bonano slumped in his chair, then jumped up again and grabbed his jacket. "Come on, let's go meet the big man. At least he's got some sense."

Governor Slate was a giant of a man, over seven feet, with a small goatee and mustache of snowy white. Had he not been so tall, he might have passed for Colonel Sanders, as he usually affected the "southern gentleman's" look of the century past, with rumpled white linen suit, string tie, and a floppy Panama hat.

As he unfolded from the car, he caught Bonano's eye and winked, then favored Fred Baron with a frown. "Why didn't you call me about this, Fred? Ain't that your job, calling me about disasters?"

Baron snapped to attention, almost saluting. "Yes, sir, it is, but I was superseded by a subordinate, and I–"

"Better watch that being superseded, Fred. Might get sandspurs." His eyes lit up as Lila Mae burst out laughing. "Madam Mayor, councilmen, I hear y'all have one of the largest problems in Florida. Shall we go and see the damage?"

"Oh, Governor, we meet again," Melba simpered. She held out her hand, which the governor shook, then turned to introduce her colleagues. "This is—"

"Hell, Melba, I know who they are," the jovial giant said. "Come on, let's get cracking; I have a cabinet meeting this afternoon and have to get back. Where is this thing that's swallowed your new city hall?" He charged off on foot, leaving the councilmen, the mayor, and his entire entourage to scramble after him.

"I love that man," Bonano said softly as he hurried after the others.

"Why?" Melba demanded of Mary Lee Mince. "This is an emergency meeting and it doesn't have to be recorded."

"Sorry, Madam Mayor," Mary Lee said quietly. "The law mandates that all your deliberations be done in the sunshine."

"Screw the law!" Melba said nastily. She adjusted her cherry red wig and turned to the others, who were sitting around a scarred table in the middle of the room. "Will the meeting come to order? Thank you. I've called this emergency meeting because we have—"

"An emergency?" Rainmaker asked.

"Very funny," Tyler snarled. "My entire life is down in that hole, and you start making jokes about—"

"Shut up!" Melba shouted. "Damn it, can't I even finish a sentence? Where's Dee Slugge? I want to find out what he can be charged with."

"What who can be charged with?" Lila Mae asked. "If you'd tell us what you're talking about, Madam Mayor, maybe we could help."

"I hardly need *your* help," Melba said.

Merlini chuckled, then said to Lila Mae, "She's prolly upset because her wig don't match her dress, and the governor told her she looked like hell."

"If you don't mind, Councilman Merlini, we are having a meeting," the Mayor almost screamed.

"Yeah, yeah, Mzzzz. Mayor, that's why I'm here. Who you want to charge?"

"That son of a bitch, Bonano!" she exploded.

Tyler stopped mumbling prayers and his mouth dropped open. "Why?"

"Because he's fired and he's got no right to be down there running the show," she explained.

"You want to refire him, maybe?" Rainmaker asked.

"I want him in jail."

"Madam Mayor," Lila Mae began, "you seem to forget that if it weren't for Frank, a whole bunch of people would probably be walking around dead."

"Lila Mae is right," Tyler thundered. "God has punished us for our transgressions, but yours is the worst. You want to punish the man who has saved us all. Remember what Jesus said, Madam Mayor, and do not sling the first arrow. Ungrateful wretch, you–"

Shut the fu–shut up!" Melba yelled. She looked around for something to use as a gavel, but could find nothing, so she yanked off one of her shoes and crashed it onto the table. "How are we to conduct serious business when all you can do is shout about archery, for chrissake? This man is guilty of insubordination and I want him punished."

Merlini raised a finger and said, "Madam Mayor, I move that we rehire Mr. Bonano as of yesterday. In fact, since the record of yesterday's meeting is down in that hole, I suggest we pretend we never voted to fire him. I'm ashamed that I voted with you."

"How dare–!"

"I second the motion," Rainmaker said.

"I won't call for a vote," Melba snarled.

"You will or we'll take legal action, you whore of Babylon," Tyler threatened.

Melba went livid. "That's libel, you bastard!" Then she leaned across the table, glaring at each of them in turn. "How many of you support me on this?"

Stony silence.

"Then damn you all, you'll be sorry for this!" She savagely chewed her lips, grabbed her purse, and stormed from the room before they could see that she was weeping with fury.

Tyler threatened her with legal action, called her a whore? That crooked son of a bitch? They were set to meet next week, and by God, she'd get evidence to send him to jail if it killed her. She stamped into her makeshift office, threw her purse across the room, grabbed the telephone directory, and looked up Detective Agencies. Running her finger down the list of offerings, she found what she was looking for. "Daily Dirt Agency, Expert electronic surveillance," she read. "Not a word escapes us."

Smiling grimly, she began to dial.

Ousted City Manager Rehired by Grateful Council

Special to the Tribune
"It's a miracle," says former mayor.

Sunshine: When two hundred acres of your city falls in and there is no loss of life because the city manager has heard the citizens' complaints and taken them seriously, he's got to be a hero–right? Not in Sunshine. When City Manager Frank Bonano evacuated ten blocks around the new city center three days ago, he was summarily fired by the Council for acting without their authorization. Even though the vote was three to two, Bonano went.

The next morning at 4 A.M., some two hundred acres, including the new city center, rested in a crater estimated to be almost one hundred and fifty feet deep. There were no casualties. "This is miraculous," said Councilman Joe Tyler, who the day before had voted to fire Bonano. "The Almighty has spoken to Bonano! I've ordered prayer meetings at the edge of the abyss, so that we sinners who have looked into the depths of darkness can give thanks to God and walk again into the Light."

Governor Slate has declared Banter County a disaster area, and personally called the President to ask for federal assistance.

This disaster is a blessing in disguise for the City of Sunshine, which has been in hot water for years because of their leaking sewer system. "Most of the sewer system is a shambles," Sunshine's utility director, Dreyfus Odlum, explained. FEMA will most likely replace the whole thing."

The public is asked to refrain from visiting the enormous sinkhole until it has stabilized. The sides of the enormous hole are still falling in, and several buildings have been swallowed up since the first three shocks shattered windows over three square miles. The latest casualty is the remainder of the Stop N' Shop Department Store, which toppled into the abyss as a crowd on onlookers scrambled to get out of the way. There are still power lines down in the area.

Councilwoman Lila Mae Warner praised Bonano. "Frank should get a medal for this, except the city never had one struck. If it wasn't for him, a lot of folks would be walking around dead."

Mayor Tosti could not be reached for comment.

CHAPTER SEVENTEEN

Kelsey Fawkins hung up the telephone and sighed with exasperation. She had been trying for three days to raise Sally Slugge, and there had been no answer. When she called Dee at his office to ask if Sally was out of town, he had replied coldly that his wife was at home where she belonged, and if she chose not to answer the telephone, it was her business. He then proceeded to hang up on her, which rankled more than she cared to admit.

She was worried. It just wasn't like Sally not to pick up the telephone; now that she had become involved with Gavel and his mission, she hated to miss anything that was going on. And she had become quite fond of Sally, even though she had thought at the beginning that they would have nothing in common.

Dee's behavior had been decidedly strange. Yes, he was a cold fish, but he generally tried to maintain some semblance of civility; after all, Guy had been a client on one or two occasions. Had he killed Sally? Her attack on him had damaged more than his dignity. She'd been startled by the look on his face the day the Council fired Frank Bonano; it went far beyond rage. She shook her head; she was being silly and letting her imagination run wild, as it often did. Sally was fine.

She switched on the vacuum cleaner and went over the living room once again–it didn't seem as if she would ever get rid of all the glass from the shattered windows and doors. The glazier was due this afternoon, and she could take down the plywood that they had nailed up to keep unwanted visitors out. When she and Guy had returned to the house the day of the disaster, they'd caught a man from Heart County sneaking out the back door with Guy's computer. Luckily, Guy carried a pistol in the car, and he had stopped the fellow.

Guiding the vacuum into the dining room, she lifted up the rug to make certain she'd gotten all the glass and found more. Did the darned stuff have feet? After moving the chairs and rolling back the rug, she went over the floor again, hoping it was the last time it had to be done. She didn't dare walk around barefooted until she was sure it was gone.

As she put the chairs back in place, she sighed. She would be so glad when things got back to normal, or abnormal, as was actually the case. The town was crawling with strangers–county people, federal people, the military.

FEMA had moved in and their staff were in the process of assessing the damage to homes, infrastructure, the city buildings that had survived the sinkhole–everything. It was quite apparent that they were leaving no stone or leaf unturned in their search for damage. The Corps of Engineers was in Sunshine, as were the Seabees, personnel from the water management district, the National Guard, and some county people who were still involved in Sunshine's rescue.

Both motels were filled to bursting, and every spare bedroom in town was occupied. Even Zona Flores had gotten into the act–she'd doubled up her girls and opened the Sunshine Gentlemen's Club to help house the visitors. She and Guy had laughed hugely over that, wondering how the men who stayed there liked billeting in a whorehouse.

The sinkhole had certainly changed her quiet little city. For the past three nights, Joe Tyler held prayer meetings at the edge of the cavity. It was the talk of Sunshine, and she had to give him credit–he certainly had been in the news. She wondered if it was real piety that drove him to make a spectacle of himself, or if he was preparing for yet another campaign to unseat Mayor Tosti. It was a given that he'd run again; he and his clique had not rested easy with the changes that had taken place in the last twelve years.

She smiled ruefully at her cynicism, thinking that it had come quite late in life. Switching off the vacuum cleaner, she checked her appearance in the mirror above the sideboard, grabbed her purse, and headed for the door. She had three hours before the glazier was due, and she was going to find Sally Slugge.

PooPoo erased the line he had just made and sighed. He had thought it would be so easy, designing two long stained glass windows to replace the two opaque windows on either side of the front door of the restaurant, but it was a lot more involved than he had thought. The artisan who would make the windows for him had offered his own design, but he hadn't liked it. Herons silhouetted against moonlight definitely did not fit into the decor of Rain, even though the guy said he could change them to macaws. Who ever heard of a macaw standing on one leg in the moonlight?

"Having a hard time with that?" Rainmaker asked sympathetically.

"Worse than that. I can see what I want the glass to look like, I just don't know quite how to put it on paper."

"Why not just draw it freehand and let him worry about transforming it into a usable pattern?"

"Darling, you're making sense again." PooPoo threw down his pencil and leaned back. "I want the windows to cast leafy shadows across the front desk and the rocks. Won't that be gorgeous?"

"Sounds like it. Speaking of gorgeous, did you see Melba's latest wig?–magenta, already."

"Yes, she was on television again last night, railing against Joe Tyler's prayer meetings. Maybe the two of them will eat each other alive and do the world a favor."

"She thinks he's doing the prayer meeting stuff to upstage her," Rainmaker said, laughing shortly. "You'd think that, with all the other problems we have facing the city, she could forget running long enough to take care of urgent business."

"Anything from FEMA yet on the sewer system?"

"Nope. All I know is, when the final tally is in, they'll pay seventy-five percent of the damages, the state will pay twelve and a half percent, and the city of Sunshine is stuck with the rest. Another bond issue or two, I'm certain, and we still have to pay off the issue for the building in the hole." Rainmaker rose and went into the kitchen, then came back with a soda in his hand. "Of course, the insurance will take care of a large portion of it, but you know damned well she's going to want to rebuild somewhere."

PooPoo picked up the pencil again, nibbled the eraser, then drew a few tentative lines. "Where?" He lay the pencil down and squinted to see the effect he had gotten.

"As Melba told Aysure, that's not the question; the real question is, why?"

"The why is easy when you're dealing with the Gorgon. The answer is 'because.' Because she is the mayor, because she is all-powerful, in her mind, at least, because it's another damned thing to stick her name on; she's put plaques everywhere." Rising from the desk, PooPoo walked across the room and opened the storm shutters to look outside. Beyond the lawn, the river flowed quietly to the Gulf. "I'll be so glad when these doors are repaired so we can get rid of these shutters. But at least we can be thankful that the river smells a little better since that hole opened."

Rainmaker followed him across the room and went out on the terrace to sniff. "There is some improvement, isn't there? I suppose there should be, when you think about it, because we now have the world's largest septic tank right in the middle of town. But the air isn't all that good, Hon. Let's close back up, shall we? It's almost time to go back to the restaurant."

PooPoo snapped his fingers and grinned. "I have it!" He turned and walked quickly back to his desk, grabbed the pencil, and began sketching. "Wait and see; it's going to be beautiful."

Rainmaker locked the storm shutters and went back to his easy chair. He'd be so glad, he thought, when things calmed down. Maybe he was getting too old for all the confusion, or maybe he just didn't find the circus that Sunshine had suddenly become all that amusing.

He wondered why Melba was acting so badly towards Frank Bonano. All Frank had done was his job, and he'd done that damned well. Maybe it was a personal thing, because the mayor certainly had it in for the city manager. Did she have a crush on him, maybe? Nonsense–she was bound to know how unattractive she was; the woman did have eyes in her head. Besides, she was about fifteen years Bonano's senior. And she was really nasty to Mary Lee Mince, who certainly had done nothing to cause anyone grief. Then he remembered intercepting a quick look between Frank and Mary Lee. It wasn't a look that lovers would exchange, but the kind of look that people who were fast reaching an understanding exchanged. Maybe they had something going. Why not? Frank needed a woman; he'd been miserable since he and his wife split. He grinned. Just for the fun of it, maybe he'd dig at Melba a little and watch the bitch squirm.

She was uncomfortable in the neighborhood; it was one of those areas of Tampa that had once been respectable but was now sliding rapidly downhill. Across the street was a topless bar that stayed open twenty-four hours a day, and next to that was a "lingerie parlor." In the strip mall where the Daily Dirt Detective Agency was located, there were six empty storefronts and a place that touted the cheapest linens in all of Tampa Bay. Melba got out of her rented Lincoln, locked it carefully, checked both ways to make certain no muggers were coming her way, then quickly crossed the potholed macadam and opened the smoked glass door. A bell tinkled somewhere in the nether regions of the detective agency and she heard footsteps coming toward the front. She quickly adjusted her navy wig and stood up straighter, a frigid smile on her face.

"Help you?" The man was short and pot-bellied, with a shiny bald head. His tiny eyes slid over her from head to foot, then crawled past her to check the door.

Melba's smile shattered. "Are you in charge?"

"Yeah, this is my place. What do you want? Come on in the office and sit down, lady. Make yourself at home." He led the way down a short hall, past a room that looked as if it belonged in a space craft, and into his tiny office.

She sat gingerly on the edge of the upholstered chair and looked around. The office was tidy and spotlessly clean. She was somewhat reassured.

He stared at her, waiting for her to speak. "Well."

"I want to be fitted with a–I think you people refer to them as 'wires'."

"That can be arranged. When do you need it?"

"Is it possible for me to get all this done today? I live in Sunshine, and it's quite a drive."

"Yeah, yeah, we can get it done today. How long you want it for?"

"A week."

"That'll be okay. Just a minute, and we'll fix you up." He rose from his desk and left the room.

"It'll be completely invisible, won't it?" she called after him. She wondered what she could wear when she met Joe that would completely conceal such a device. There had to be absolutely no inkling that she was recording their conversation. Then she shuddered. Would this greasy man have to put his hands on her– take measurements or anything like that? She would never allow him to touch her; he was most unattractive. She started as he came back into the office.

"Take your pick, lady." He held out two brooches, one of them a cameo, and one a dazzling rhinestone spray. "Which one?"

"You don't understand; I need a recording device."

"You never watched any of them old James Bond movies, did you?" He chuckled and turned over the cameo so that she might see the back. "This one will record up to three hours of conversation. The spray is only good for about an hour and a half. See?" He popped out a tiny thing that resembled a battery and handed it to her for inspection. "This does it all."

She examined the little recorder. "It looks like a watch battery, doesn't it? I had thought–I'll take the spray. I won't need much more than an hour. But how will I–I mean, there's no way I could play such a tiny–" She dropped the recorder back into the detective's hand.

"When you bring it back, I transfer it to a tape for you. A regular tape that you can play in any cassette. That okay?"

She brightened. "Yes, that'll be fine."

"Okay, let's get all the paperwork out of the way, and you're off to ruin somebody's entire week!"

"Yes!" Melba breathed. She certainly would ruin Tyler's week, she thought. And the rest of his life as well. She could see him in her mind's eye, handcuffed and being led to a police car. His fat face would be red and mottled, his eyes accusing. She would not gloat, not in public. She would be shocked by his dishonesty, absolutely horrified! There would be lots of media coverage; she'd get statewide publicity as the feisty little mayor who brought down a thieving politician. That would assure her a seat in the Senate, at least. She might even run for Secretary of State.

As she signed the contract and wrote the check, she favored the man with her biggest smile.

Ferdy O'Doole levered himself from his van and looked curiously at the car in the slot next to him. It was Tank Tower's rental Lincoln, the pink one with the roses spray-painted on the driver's door. Wasn't another Lincoln like that in the whole state of Florida. What was it doing in this neighborhood, for chrissake? Tank said he'd rented it to the mayor. What would Melba Tosti be doing in this part of town? He checked the shops in the strip mall. Nothing there but the linen outlet and the Daily Dirt Detective Agency. Maybe she was buying linen; she sure as hell wouldn't be in the dives across the street.

He went into the linen outlet and stood peering out the door, indecisive, watching the Lincoln. Had it been stolen? Then he saw Melba coming from the detective agency. Daily Dirt specialized in wires, didn't they? What would she need a wire for, unless it was to trap some poor, unsuspecting sucker? He wondered who she was after. He'd think about it.

He turned into the store and sighed. All his new customers were bitching about the quality of his linens. Said they were paying top dollar for the rooms and they wanted towels that didn't have holes in them. Stood to reason that the bureaucratic types wanted something fancy. They couldn't rough it like his fishing customers, oh no, they had to have new stuff.

Even his wife had argued that it was time to get new linens for the motel–said that Fisherman's Paradise was going to be the next Holiday Inn if that sinkhole brought in the tourists, and he'd better prepare for it. Of course, she didn't know what she was talking about, but he'd come down to the linen outlet just to keep her happy. No sense arguing with the little woman over something like that, even if all the profits did go down the drain. A sinkhole as a tourist attraction? She had to be puling his leg.

When he left the linen outlet, the pink Lincoln was gone. He'd have to tell Joe he'd seen the mayor here; maybe he could use it against her in the campaign. Humming, he dumped his purchases into the back seat and climbed into the van, changed his mind, got back out and locked it. Hell, as long as he was here, he might as well have a little fun.

Still humming, he ambled across the street to the topless bar.

Kelsey parked in the drive of Sally's house on Merriweather Drive, went to the front door, and rang the bell. She could hear the chimes inside. She waited for a couple of minutes, then rang the bell again, listening carefully. Still no response. She knocked, listened again, then went around the side of the house to the back entrance.

"Sally, it's Kelsey. Are you there?" She could see through the glass curtain that Sally had at her back door. There was someone silhouetted against the light at the other side of the kitchen, so she knocked again.

"You're wasting your time," the Slugge's neighbor called across the hedge. "I haven't seen her in several days. Maybe she's out of town."

"No," Kelsey answered. "Dee said she was home."

The neighbor shrugged, nodded, and went about her business.

Kelsey then leaned on the doorbell, determined to force Sally to open up. Finally, she saw someone approaching the back door. The lock clicked and Sally opened the door a crack. "I'm sick, Kelsey, so don't come in."

"Sick how?"

"Just–sick." Sally's voice caught and Kelsey wondered if she were crying.

"I won't catch it. Let me in."

A sigh. "Oh, all right, but you have to promise you won't say anything."

The door swung open and Kelsey gasped, then hurried inside and shut the door. "My God, are you all right? What happened?"

Sally was wearing a dressing gown. Both her eyes were swollen almost shut. Her face was a mass of bruises and contusions, her lower lip badly split. She was bent almost double. Kelsey led her to a chair at the kitchen table and made her sit.

"Who did this—Dee?"

"He—he was mad because I slapped him. I didn't know he'd do this, though. I never thought he'd be so mean, Kelsey. He was wrong, trying to grab that microphone. He kept calling me a bitch under his breath, and telling me he'd kill me, but I never thought he'd do something so mean."

"This isn't mean, it's criminal! Have you seen a doctor?"

"I don't want anyone to see me like this, Kelsey. It would be awful if folks knew about this; I'd be the laughingstock of Sunshine."

"I don't know anyone who would find Dee's almost killing you funny," Kelsey said. "I want you to put on some clothes, and I'm calling Doc Smithers. I'll get him to see you right away." Sally shook her head stubbornly. "You need medical attention. That lip looks like it's getting infected, and you—can you stand up straight?"

Sally shook her head. "No, he kicked me in the stomach three or four times. I don't know if he's broken something."

"You could just be bruised, but you're going to a doctor. Where's the phone?"

"Kelsey, if I go to the doctor, Dee will find out and he'll probably do even worse. I'm afraid, Kelsey."

"You're coming with me, Sally. After you've seen the doctor, we're going to the police, then you'll stay with us. Dee's a lawyer; the son of a bitch knows better."

Kelsey left Sally at the doctor's office, promising she'd be back in a short time, and drove to the old city hall, where Rufus Hicks had set up temporary quarters. Brushing past several officers who were in the process of changing shift, she went to the desk and asked if Hicks were in.

"He's real busy, Mrs. Fawkins," the woman at the desk explained. "Anything I can do?"

"No, thanks. Where's his office?" The woman pointed to a door down the hall, then jumped to her feet as Kelsey turned and hurried down the hall.

"You can't do that!"

As she entered the door, she heard Hicks apologizing. "I'm sorry, Joe, I just didn't understand exactly what you wanted." He said yes a couple of times, then shuffled his feet. "Yeah, Joe, I understand." He hung up, then looked up and saw her. He was obviously startled.

Kelsey closed the door behind her. "Sorry to barge in like this, Rufus, but—"

"It's okay, Kelsey. You been standing there long?"

"No, I just came in."

"You must be all hot and bothered, Kelsey, busting in like this," Hicks said. "Take a pew. What's the problem?"

"Dee Slugge has beaten the hell out of Sally. She's been hiding out at home for the past three days, afraid someone will see her and start gossip. I left her at the doctor; she's in pretty bad shape. I told her she should bring charges against Dee, and she wants to know what she has to do."

"Mmmm." Hicks chewed his lower lip for a moment, then moved a couple of objects around on his desk. "That's real bad news. I never thought Dee would have that much of a temper."

"You know how tiny Sally is, Rufus. He could have killed her."

Hicks put his hands flat on the desk, studied them with interest, then looked beyond her to the door. "That would be bad, Kelsey."

"So what should she do?"

"Well, I don't rightly know. You're putting me in a bad spot, Kelsey. I mean, Dee is the city attorney. It would look bad if his name got in the paper, you know what I mean?"

"What procedure does she have to follow?" Kelsey demanded.

"I got to look after the city's interests, Kelsey. You know that. And with that sinkhole, and all the troubles we got right now, I don't have time to mess with a fight between a man and his wife. And besides, I understand she slapped him up side the face right in public. Probably got what was coming to her."

"Got what was coming to her? She's half dead, for crying out loud. Does she have to come in here, make a report, or what?"

"Well, yeah, I guess she'd have to do that, Kelsey. Come down here, see an officer, make a report. Then we could–" His voice dwindled to nothing and he studied his hands again.

"Thanks. I'll make certain she gets here first thing in the morning."

Hicks nodded, still avoiding her eyes. "You do that, honey. If you want it to get in the paper, that is. You know Al McDonald likes to check things out down here, see what's going on."

Kelsey rolled her eyes and stalked out of Hick's office.

Even though the barriers on Hatchacootee Boulevard bore warnings about going close to the edge of the sinkhole, Tyler ignored them and held his prayer meetings right on the brink, courting disaster. When Rufus Hicks had spoken with him about ignoring the dangers, Tyler replied that the only thing in danger was Hicks' employment.

As evening approached, those who were convinced that The End was near filed into the area that Tyler had marked off with sawhorses borrowed from the city's utility shed near Mosquito Row. He had also borrowed folding chairs from the Living Witness Holy Confederation's recreation hall and set them up for the faithful to perch on.

He made a point of greeting each person who came, shaking hands, passing out "God bless you's" over and over. He was in his element; for the fourth night in a row, there was television coverage of his meeting. If this didn't bring him votes, he thought, nothing ever would.

In the background, giant earth movers and backhoes roared back and forth in the dusk, digging trenches in which to place new sewer pipe and housing for the new electric lines. The noise was deafening, and the clash and shriek of the metallic monsters hurt the ears.

When the last supplicant had been seated, Tyler went to stand with his back to the gaping hole, which reeked of raw sewage, but his years of living on the Hatchacootee had enured him to the odor and he paid it no mind.

"God be with us," he intoned.

"And with our spirits," came the ragged reply.

"We have sinned grievously and the Lord has given us a grievous burden as a result. Let us give thanks to Him for sparing our worthless hides," Tyler shouted. "Do we give thanks?"

"Yea, we give thanks!" the people cried.

"Are we sinners?"

"Yea, we are sinners!"

"Will we repent of our sins and walk in righteousness?"

"Yea, we will repent and walk in righteousness."

"Are we sick to our stomachs yet?" Bonano asked Mary Lee. They stood back from the crowd, watching the scene before them.

"He's shameless, isn't he?"

"No, honey, he suffers from an almost fatal case of televisionitis. He's been pissed ever since Melba started going on the tube to explain how much she does for the folks in Sunshine. He demanded equal time and the station wouldn't buy it; said he isn't the mayor."

"Good thing for the station manager that he lives in Flag City," Mary Lee said. "I wouldn't put it past the Saved Sons Society to visit harm on the guy."

"He's really testing the Lord's patience, standing that near to the edge. If he got a dizzy spell, he'd topple right in."

"Come on, Frank, you know he's in no danger," Rainmaker said as he joined them. "Didn't you know that God's ape can walk on water? PooPoo saw this act on the boob tube last night, and told me about it. I had to come and see for myself. How long does this go on?"

"About an hour, Mr. Rainmaker," Mary Lee said.

"Everything under control, Frank?"

"Yes, Teddy, I think so. They've run some temporary lines and tomorrow the sewage will be rerouted around the hole. That's progress, I can tell you."

"What has FEMA said about that problem?"

"Hallelujah, we're getting the whole thing replaced with a system that is up to code. It won't cost us nearly what Oddman estimated. They even offered to help move the treatment plant, if we thought it was necessary. But Oddman says that's in good shape. We can replace the lines and that'll take care of the situation."

Rainmaker chuckled. "Maybe Joe's prayers are doing some good after all." He stared at Tyler and his group for a few moments more, then slapped Bonano on the back. "You've done a hell of a job, Frank, and don't think most of us don't appreciate it."

"I wish the mayor felt that way," Bonano said.

"Screw the bitch. Why don't you and Mary Lee go have dinner at the restaurant? Tell PooPoo it's on the house."

"That's not necessary, Teddy, but thanks."

"I consider it necessary. You may consider it an order from the city council."

CHAPTER EIGHTEEN

Lila Mae Warner sighed. She did wish Melba wouldn't wear that cherry red wig; she looked like a clown, especially when she wore too much blusher. Even the governor had said she looked like hell in that wig.

She peered around the council chamber in the old city hall. It wasn't fancy like the one they had lost, in fact, some of the plaster had fallen during the sinkhole shocks, and the room didn't have the city seal that Melba had insisted on, but it was as familiar as bedroom slippers. She shoved the microphone aside and said to Merlini, "Well, we're back where we started."

Merlini looked at her appreciatively. She seemed to get better looking every day. Maybe being separated from Henny was a good thing. "Yeah, and we'll prolly be here for a long time. Got a lot to do before we rebuild any city hall."

Mayor Melba Tosti fluffed her wig, cleared her throat, then banged her new gavel. "The meeting of the City Council of the City of Sunshine will now come to order." She then looked upward and intoned, "All rise for the Invocation and the Pledge of Allegiance." After a quick glance to make certain the camera beamed her image, she rose.

Josephus Tyler shook himself in preparation for the prayer. He closed his red-rimmed eyes and clasped hands beneath his layered chin. "Lord God, Maker of all things, Knower of all sins, we humbly beseech Thee to lead us to do Thy will while we attend the business of the City of Sunshine." His voice assumed the cadence of the pulpit and he squeezed his eyes tighter shut. "Help us, Lord, to avoid the terrible pitfalls of power! Guide our thoughts, Lord, to Thy ways, that we might prosper. We have heard Your terrible voice, Lord, and witnessed Your awful might. Be kind to us sinners, God, and keep the rest of our little city safe from harm. We know there are those who wallow in iniquity and sloth in our city, Lord. They have backslidden until there is no hope! Stamp them out, Lord–" He grunted as Melba's foot made contact with the back of his leg. "Huh..?"

"Cut it short, Joe," the mayor whispered. "We got a very, very long agenda."

"...and let us walk in Thy path all the days of our lives, Amen." He opened his eyes, glared at Melba, spun to face the flag, clapped his hand to his heart, and froze. "Where the hell is the flag? Who took the flag?" His hand dropped to his side and he turned to Bonano. "Where's the flag, Frank? You know we can't open a meeting without the Pledge of Allegiance."

Bonano's right hand stayed on the desk. "We lost every one of the city's flags down the hole, Councilman Tyler. I have ordered another for this chamber, but it will take several weeks to be delivered. I apologize."

"You don't need the flag to say the pledge, for chrissake!" Merlini said. "Just go on, say it, and let's get on with business. We got a long agenda."

"Oh, all right." Tyler sounded uncertain, but he placed his hand over his heart, stared hard at the opposite wall, and began. The voices of the citizens in the chamber followed in a ragged echo of his own.

Melba tidied her papers and gave the technical people in the chamber her special smile. "Everyone here? Fine. Now, I need a motion to adopt the minutes of the last meeting."

"Got it."

"Second."

"All in favor?" Ayes all around. "Motion carries. Are there any financial matters before us?"

Bonano raised a finger. "Madam Mayor, if you wish to take up the preliminary reports on the damages here, we could do so."

She glared at him. "I asked if there are any financial matters before us. Mr. Odlum, do you have a report?"

Odlum rose and walked to the lectern, adjusted the microphone, and said, "I've got bad news and good news, Madam Mayor. Which do you want first?"

"This is hardly the time and place for levity, Mr. Odlum," Melba scolded. "But if you insist, give us the bad news first."

Odlum glanced briefly toward Lila Mae. "FEMA will pay seventy-five percent of what is needed to replace the sewer system, Madam Mayor. This replacement will bring it to present code and end the problems we've been having. The—"

"Who's supposed to pick up the tab for the other twenty-five percent?" Merlini interrupted.

"I was just going to sa—"

"Councilman Merlini, please don't interrupt," the mayor said sharply. "We are having a very important meeting."

"Yeah, yeah, Mzzzz. Mayor, that's why I'm here."

Odlum cleared his throat. "In answer to your question, Councilman Merlini, the state will pick up the tab for half of the remainder, and the city is responsible for the other half. That's the bad news."

"Do you have any hard figures yet?" Rainmaker asked.

"Not yet, Councilman, we're still working on them. I hope to have a full report in about two weeks."

"Fine." Rainmaker beamed upon Odlum, causing Tyler to glare at him.

'Why don't you have that report today, Odlum?" Tyler demanded.

"Because we haven't finished assessing the damage, Councilman, and because the gentleman from FEMA was called back to Washington for a few days' consultation. This is a large project."

"Just call Washington and tell them we don't have time for their shilly-shallying," Tyler snapped.

"I'm afraid it isn't that sim—"

"You don't pay any attention to Joe, Oddman," Lila Mae interrupted. "He's just in a foul mood."

Tyler almost rose from his seat. "I am sick and tired of dealing with an inefficient leftist bureaucracy," he said loudly.

"Joe, why don't you be quiet?" Lila Mae asked. "My God, the folks from all over will think we're a bunch of dummies if you keep that up."

Odlum stifled a smile. "Shall I continue, Madam Mayor?"

"Yes, please do," Melba gushed.

"I want to know why we have to pay so much money for something that ain't our fault!" Tyler almost shouted.

"Because it's our responsibility, Ape," Rainmaker snapped. "Sinkholes are a natural occurrence, or an act of God, if you will. If you don't like the setup, why don't you address God during one of those prayer meetings you're holding and see if you can't do a deal?"

"Blasphemy!" Tyler bellowed.

The gavel crashed. And broke. "I want order!" Melba screeched. "I need a new gavel."

"I'm sorry, Madam Mayor, but that's the last gavel I have. I've ordered new ones, but–"

"Then why the hell didn't you order them sooner?" she said nastily. "Been too busy?"

"Mr. Bonano has his priorities straight, Madam Mayor," Rainmaker said. "Gavels aren't tops on the list."

"What's he doing, Teddy, giving you a portion of his salary?" she snarled. "I want a new gavel by the next meeting, understand?"

"Yes, Madam Mayor. I'll see to it." Bonano made a note on the pad before him and looked at the council attentively, which he knew well would drive Melba mad.

"Any other financial matters?" Melba asked.

"If you would like, Madam Mayor, I can give you a tentative assessment of the city's losses in the catastrophe," Bonano said.

The mayor ignored him. "Fine, as there are no more financial matters, we will move on to the consent agenda."

"Madam Mayor," Rainmaker said, "the city has lost all but two of its police cars, some other vehicles, its police department, streetlights, roads, city buildings, private homes, businesses, and I could go on. Are you really going to ignore this because you're sore at Frank? Doesn't this reek of fiscal irresponsibility? It is your dut–"

"Why didn't someone tell me that all that stuff had been lost?" Merlini demanded. "That's serious!"

"How dare you accuse me of fiscal irres–" Melba snarled.

"Meats, where did you think it all went to?" Lila Mae interrupted. "Everything that was on top of that hole is now in the hole."

"Oh. I didn't see it like that."

Melba's shoe crashed. "Order! Bonano, give the damned report."

"Thank you, Madam Mayor. As I said, we don't have hard figures yet, but FEMA will give individual assistance to uninsured people who have lost their homes, pay the difference in replacement of homes if insurance is inadequate, and give assistance to individuals who have lost their businesses. Substandard housing will be brought up to code under this assistance, which will mean a great deal to our citizens who have suffered so badly in this disaster.

"The city will receive remuneration on the costs of evacuation, the costs to repair or replace buildings, and hazard mitigation, which is a quarter of the total figures on individual assistance and municipal assistance.

"If you wish, I can present the Council with the complete figures at some later–"

"That will do, thank you, Mr. Bonano. I don't think we have any interest in the final figures. Now, let's move on to the consent agenda. I need a motion."

"Got it."

"I second."

"All in favor." Ayes all around. "Motion passed."

"Madam Mayor–"

"What do you want now?" she snapped.

"If any of the council members would like to see the final figures, they will be available in my office," Bonano said.

Melba ignored him. "Councilmen's items next. District A?"

"I expect we all have damage to report, Madam Mayor. Some of my folks are really hurting. That's all." Lila Mae leaned over to Merlini. "What does she expect us to report, snow?"

"Prolly doing this to crap on Frank. She's really pissed about us rehiring him."

"Councilman Merlini, I am trying to conduct a meeting!"

"Go right ahead, Mzzzz. Mayor, I don't mind at all."

"District B?" Melba grated.

"I don't really have all that much damage in my district, Mzzzz. Mayor. It's all east of the sinkhole. But I can tell you, folks over there are really pis–anxious about us restoring the power and stuff. That's all I got to report."

"They'll have to wait their turn," the mayor snapped. "District C?"

"I have extensive damage in what is left of my district," Rainmaker said. "And I would like to commend Mr. Bonano on his superb handling of a terrible situation."

"District D?"

"God has seen fit to swallow part of my district, as well as my business," Tyler said sadly. "But I am speaking with the All High, and He has assured me that our little city will now be safe from harm."

Merlini shoved his microphone aside. "Now he's talking to God? He's lost more than his store."

Lila Mae grinned and whispered, "I sure wish I could talk to the Lord, think how much we could get done."

"If you two don't mind!" the mayor snapped. Then she said brightly, "All in all, the damage wasn't too bad, but that does not excuse the city's employees for their–"

"We lost the whole downtown and you say it ain't bad?" Lila Mae said wonderingly.

"The city employees have shone in this, Madam Mayor, and you have not," Rainmaker said hotly. "Cool the crap and let's get on with business. I thought we had a long agenda."

"How dare yo–!"

"Move along, Melba," Tyler shouted. "Or hand over the gav–uh–"

Someone in the back of the auditorium laughed.

"Is there any old business?" the mayor asked coldly.

Rainmaker grabbed his microphone. "I want to again express my appreciation for the way Mr. Bonano has done his job, and to reiterate my vote to rehire him."

"Yeah, me too," Tyler rumbled.

"Even though we ain't voting on this, I vote yes," Merlini affirmed.

Lila Mae smiled. "You did a wonderful job, Frank, and so did all the city employees. Melba, I guess you lost out, didn't you?"

The mayor looked as if she might burst.

Bonano raised a finger again, infuriating the mayor. "Madam Mayor, if I might suggest that we..."

"No one asked you one damned thing," she snarled.

"...postpone the Liars' Festival until things in the city are stable again?"

The mayor tidied her papers, then pretended to write.

Tyler reached over and grabbed her shoe.

"What are you doing?"

"Taking control of the meeting, Melba, since you don't have sense enough to pay attention." He banged her shoe on the desk. "Order. We need a motion on postponing the Liars' Festival."

"Point of order!" Merlini shouted. "You don't have any right to use Melba's shoe; it's personal property."

"Oh, for God's sake," Bonano muttered.

"What did you say, Frank?" Tyler asked, still gripping the shoe.

"I was praying for guidance, Councilman."

"I so move," Rainmaker said quickly.

"Second," Lila Mae cooed.

"All in favor?" Four ayes, one nay. "The motion passes." Tyler positively glowed with victory.

The mayor extended her hand and he reluctantly returned her shoe. "Thank you, Councilman. Any further old business?" Her voice would have cut stone.

"What about the museum?" Merlini asked.

Rainmaker rolled his eyes. "I move that we table this item until the emergency has passed," he said.

"This would be a good time to discuss it," Merlini insisted. "We got to plan a new city center at some point, and we could—"

"I agree with Councilman Rainmaker," Lila Mae said softly. "I'm sorry, Meats, but we got more pressing matters right now."

Merlini sulked.

"I have a motion; is there a second?"

"Second," Lila Mae said. She patted Merlini's hand apologetically.

"All in favor?" Four ayes, one nay. "Motion passes. Next item?"

"The city seal–" Bonano began.

"Move to table the issue until later," Rainmaker said.

"Second."

"All in favor?" Ayes all around. "Motion passes." Melba smiled at the camera, adjusted her wig, and called on DeLeon Slugge.

Slugge went to the lectern and favored the council with a chilly smile. "I have drawn up the contract for Fyndar and Ramirez. They are to recommend the procedures the city will follow in the condemnation of the land at Mosquito Row, and the subsequent development of a park. Are there any questions?"

"I have a serious question, Slugge," Rainmaker said. "I am not aware that we put out bids on this proposal, and I'd like to know just how you have drawn up a contract when no bids have been received?"

Slugge blinked twice. "I was instructed to put Fyndar and Ramirez on retainer, Councilman, so as to save the city the expense of putting out bids on small items such as this one."

"Instructed by whom?" Rainmaker's voice was acid.

"My instructions came from Mayor Tosti and from Councilman Tyler. I naturally assumed that the council concurred and went ahead as instructed."

"This matter has not been discussed in a meeting, and it is illegal," Rainmaker insisted. "I demand that this contract not be considered, and that proper bids be tendered. And I want that retainer for Fyndar and Ramirez canceled."

"I was under the impression, Councilman, that your primary concern has always been the public purse. This will save the taxpa–" Melba was all business.

"This procedure is *illegal!*" Rainmaker insisted.

"It ain't illegal if we make it legal, Teddy," Merlini said. "We can vote on it now. I so move."

"You so move what, you fool?" Rainmaker roared. "What is transpiring here is illegal, don't you understand that? Slugge, what is the penalty for this sort of nonsense, or do you deal only with the shadier aspects of the law?"

"I will ignore your libelous remarks, Councilman, out of respect for the rest of the members of the council. Madam

Mayor, when you wish the contract, my firm has it prepared." Slugge went back to his seat.

Melba glared in the direction of Al McDonald, whose tigerish expression bode ill for the council. "Mr. Slugge, I apologize for my colleague's lack of propriety. Do I have a motion to accept this contract?"

Lila Mae cleared her throat, looked questioningly towards Merlini. "Madam Mayor, I move we table this matter for further discussion."

"Second," Rainmaker snapped.

"We have a motion. All in favor?" Three ayes, two nays. "Motion tabled."

In the back of the auditorium, several newcomers arrived. The mayor waited until they were seated, frowning. What were denizens of Mosquito Row doing at a council meeting? Most of them were aliens, illegal, more than likely, and they had absolutely no right to participate in any deliberations of the governing body.

Then she saw that the television camera had moved to pan them, then come back to her face. She smiled brightly. "No more old business? Fine, we'll move on to new business."

Tyler almost jumped to his feet. "I want to propose a new ordinance, Madam Mayor. In view of the discombobulation that our fair city is now experiencing, I propose that we ban dog-walking. As you know, we have already passed an ordinance against dogs poo—leaving their—I mean you are all familiar with the ordinance, and we further need to restrict these pests in view of the recent tragedy. I would like us to discuss this matter."

"Lord," sighed Lila Mae, "now we really are going to be the laughingstock of the state."

"This is not a matter for frivolous comment, Lila Mae," Tyler said ponderously.

"Personally, I don't think it's a matter worthy of any comment at all," Rainmaker said. "We have lost a major portion of our downtown and you want to worry about whether dogs can walk in the city? Get a life, Tyler!"

"I don't think that's a good idea, Joe," Merlini ventured. "You want to build condos, you got to let in dogs, because all these old ladies who live in condos have little dogs that have to have somewhere to poop."

"We already have made an ordinance against that," Tyler reminded him. "I want to keep them off the street."

"But then, how're they going to poo–"

"You're absolutely right, Councilman Merlini," Rainmaker said. "We need to consult with our utilities director on this matter; he is the resident expert on handling such things." Rainmaker leaned forward, intent. "Please, I beg you, let us not consider this ridiculosity; we manage to look like idiots as it is."

In the back of the room, the citizens burst into laughter and applause.

Lila Mae sent them a big smile. "I think you're right, Teddy," she said. "Oddman, what do you think about this?"

Odlum colored and went to the lectern. "I have no opinion in this matter, Councilman Warner. However, I think that if we pass such an ordinance, we might be cited on constitutional grounds. But I'm not a lawyer." He sat down.

"What constitutional grounds?" Tyler demanded. "There ain't anything in the constitution about walking dogs."

"Mr. Slugge, would you care to comment on this?" the mayor asked.

Smiling, Slugge approached the lectern. "I believe that such an ordinance might infringe on our citizens' first amendment rights. I understand that dog ownership is considered a part of free speech."

Tyler gaped. "Could you tell me how a dog is a part of speech?"

"He don't mean nouns and verbs, things like that, Joe," Lila Mae said. "He means we all got a right to own dogs."

"I know what he meant, you idiot," Tyler snapped. "But I disagree with anyone's right to walk their dogs on a public sidewalk."

Rainmaker hid his face in his hands. "God give me strength."

Tyler looked at him approvingly. "I am glad to see you learning to pray, Pervert."

"I would have to disagree with you, Councilman Tyler," Slugge said. "I believe that the only sidewalks that could be protected under such an ordinance would be private sidewalks."

"Then we can make all of 'em private," Tyler shot back.

"I don't believe this conversation," the mayor said. "Councilman, were we to declare all the public sidewalks private–"

"Enough of this!" Rainmaker roared. "I move we table this matter for further discussion."

Merlini let out a sigh of relief. "Second."

"We have a motion. All in favor?" Four ayes, one nay. "Motion passes."

Al McDonald jumped from his seat and started up the aisle, saw the folks from Mosquito Row, then turned around and sat back down. He looked expectant.

Melba cleared her throat, adjusted her wig, and smiled at the camera. "Any further new business? Very well, it's time for public comment." She frowned toward the back of the chamber. "In order to comment to this council, you must be a citizen of the United States, able to speak English, and you are limited to three minutes. Anyone wish to address this august body?"

Bonano covered a smile and winked at Mary Lee, who was looking suspiciously solemn. She shot him a warning look.

Kelsey Fawkins came down the aisle to face the glares of the council. "Kelsey Fawkins, Sunshine. I simply wanted to stress how grateful the citizens of this town are to Frank Bonano, Dreyfus Odlum, and the rest of the employees who have worked so diligently in our time of need. We are fortunate indeed to have such dedicated public servants. I'd also like to thank Councilmen Warner and Rainmaker, who worked right along with the staff. Thank you." She turned away.

"And what about the rest of us?" Tyler demanded.

Kelsey kept walking.

Two Hispanic men rose in the back of the room, hesitated, spoke to Kelsey, then came forward to the lectern. The shorter touched his forehead in greeting, then adjusted the microphone. "Councilmen, Mrs. Mayor, I am Jorge Granita from Mosquito Row. I–"

"Are you a citizen?" Melba snapped.

The man nodded. "I get my citizenship five years ago. I own land on Mosquito Row. My family worked hard to pay for the land, it is free and clear. We think you have no right to spoil people's lives so you can make a park. The river smells, all you rich people don't want to live there, but we do. We have our little gardens, our little homes. And I–" The buzzer went off.

"Your time is up, Senyore Whatever," the mayor said coldly.

The man tapped his watch. "I set my watch, lady, and you can't fool me. I don't speak three minutes. All you sit there and make fool of yourself for hours, we have to sit and listen. Now you listen to me. You don't condemn our land. If you do, I take you to court. Thank you." He smiled for the first time, then made way for the other gentleman.

"Thank you for letting me talk to you. My name is Pedro Gonzales, I live on Mosquito Row. All the time we see police, they come to the door and yell at my wife. We do nothing wrong. We are citizens of this country; we have rights too. Yes, we are poor, but we go to church, we send our children to school, we are good citizens. Now you want to run us away and plant stupid palm trees. They do not pay taxes, those palm trees. I pay taxes. And I will vote. Thank you."

"The nerve of those people!" Tyler said under his breath.

"Did you say something?" the mayor asked.

"Yes, I said, is that the end of public comment?"

"Is there any further comment from our citizens?" Tosti asked sweetly.

"Yes, there is," Kelsey Fawkins called out. "Do the people have any rights in this town?"

"If there is no further comment, the meeting is adjourned. Do I hear a motion?"

"Got it."

"Second?"

"You have it."

The meeting was adjourned.

CHAPTER NINETEEN

Op/Ed   The Sunshine Bulletin   Page 6

EDITORIAL

Madam Mayor, the real question is, do citizens have any rights at all? The arrogance of some members of our city council became shockingly evident yesterday when citizens from Mosquito Row requested that the proposed condemnation planned by the council be terminated. Mayor Tosti treated Messrs. Jorge Granita and Pedro Gonzales with the utmost contempt, with rude interruptions and even an attempt to shut up Granita by buzzing long before his three minutes were up. Is this the kind of government Sunshine needs? With elections coming up in November, we must be certain that we replace the incumbent rot. This means getting rid of almost everyone on the city council. And Sunshine badly needs a new mayor.

From this writer's place in the wilderness, I cry, "Isn't there anyone in this city who is willing to challenge incumbent Melba Tosti and her old enemy, Josephus Tyler? Neither of them is fit to govern this community."

Sadly, politics has become an arena where only fools rush in. We have seen in the last quarter century a government on autopilot: no incumbent will take responsibility for his actions. Politics has plumbed depths never dreamed of by our founding fathers. Issues are never the issue; mudslinging is all. The ballots are covered with the names of liars, scoundrels, con men, or convicted felons. Is this government of the people, by the people, for the people?

Wake up, Sunshine. The sinkhole isn't the only disaster we have to face.

Sally Slugge hesitantly went into the old city hall and through the door marked, "Police headquarters." She wore enormous dark glasses, bright red lipstick that was supposed to hide the stitches.

"Help you?" the receptionist asked.

"I'd like to file a report, please," Sally said. She did wish Kelsey would hurry up and get the car parked so she could give her some backup. She'd never done anything like this before, and wasn't really sure how to go about it. But then, she reflected, most of the folks who lived in the city would be in the same predicament.

"What about?"

"I need to speak with an officer," she said.

"There is no one around but me. Our whole department went down in that hole, you know. You're lucky to have any protection at all."

"I wish to see an officer; I need to file a report," Sally said stubbornly.

"Look, dearie, the whole police force is turned upside-down. You want to file a report, you talk to me. Come over here and sit down; tell me all about it."

Kelsey came breezing through the door, spotted Sally, and joined her.

The receptionist reacted immediately. "Are you also the offended party?"

"No, I am with Sally and I'll stay with Sally. If you recall, I spoke with Rufus day before yesterday."

"I know," the woman growled. "I almost lost my job for letting you in."

Kelsey laughed shortly. "Honey, do you really think you could have stopped me?" To Sally she said, "Are you okay?"

"I guess so. I just want to get this over with and go back to lie down. I really feel rotten."

"Okay, so let's get the report done," the receptionist said. "Name?"

"Sally Slugge."

The woman's eyebrows shot up. "Husband?"

"DeLeon Slugge."

"Okay, what happened?"

"He beat me." Sally sank onto the wooden chair and sighed. "I think he tried to kill me."

"You seen a doctor?"

"How do you think she got sutures in her lip?" Kelsey said.

"I didn't ask you. You seen a doctor?" the woman repeated impatiently.

"Yes, I saw Dr. Smithers. He said I have mild internal injuries not requiring surgery, a split lip requiring sutures, two black eyes, and the good sense to get the hell out of Dee's way," Sally replied. "He said Dee should be in jail."

"Doctors don't know beans about the law," was the sour reply.

"Is that all?" Sally asked.

"Yeah," the woman said. "You'll be hearing from us."

"When?" Kelsey demanded.

A shrug. "How should I know? I told your friend here, everything is upside-down."

Kelsey took Sally's arm. "Come on, Sally. Sign the thing and let's get you home."

"You aren't going to press charges, are you?" the receptionist asked.

"I probably will, yes."

"But he's the city's attorney, Mrs. Slugge."

"If he had committed murder, lady, would that have exonerated him?" Kelsey said sarcastically. "I thought the law applied to everyone."

The woman shrugged again. The Chief had told her what to do with the report. As soon as the two young women left, she balled up the sheet of paper and tossed it into the wastebasket, then went back to her serious work.

Joe Tyler dropped onto the hard wooden chair at the Saved Sons Society meeting room and sighed. It had been a hard day; his head was reeling with the questions asked by the insurance adjusters, the tax men, his accountants. Hell, wasn't losing the business enough of a burden?

But he had finally been able to make an appointment with Learned Speaker for tomorrow, and that made him feel a little better. The more he thought about Brady Hack going to Zona's place for a little piece of action, the angrier he got. Damned hypocrite!

He had heard through the grapevine that Hack had been the one to remind Learned Speaker about the laborer being worth of his hire. No wonder the son of a bitch was so familiar with the God Book passage; he hired those laborers regularly!

He looked up as Ferdy O'Doole came through the door.

"You're a mite early, ain't you, Joe?"

"Yeah, I was looking for a place of refuge, Ferdy. If I go home, Sarah gives me hell about bringing down the sinkhole on Sunshine by accepting donations from Zona's girls. She's been playing that infernal record for weeks now; it's time she got over it. I explained to her that if I'm going to beat Melba this time, I got to have a bunch of support, but she doesn't understand."

"Maybe you should take her a little present, something like that. The sinkhole scared the hell out of my wife, and I bet it did the same for Sarah."

"So what did you give yours? A cigar?"

"Nope, she was nagging about new linens for the motel, so I give her about three hundred dollars' worth. Tickled her to death. You should do the same for Sarah." O'Doole laughed. "My wife thinks the sinkhole is going to bring in thousands of tourists. Talking about us becoming the next Holiday Inn. You ever hear such crap in your life? Women kill me."

Tyler snorted in agreement as O'Doole took a cigar from his shirt pocket and unwrapped it. "If I took Sarah a bunch of new linens, she'd use them to hang me. But you're right. I'll make a donation to the church in her name."

O'Doole bit off the end of his cigar and shook his head. "Joe, you got a lot to learn about women. Get her something *personal.*" He licked his cigar reflectively. "Speaking of linens, I saw something downright bothersome in Tampa the other day. Melba Tosti was coming out of Daily Dirt Detective Agency."

"What the hell were you doing there. You ain't going to those topless places, are you?"

"No, there's a good linen outlet in the same strip mall. Who you think she's planning to use a wire on?"

Tyler's antennae were already fully erect and humming. His meeting with Melba to work out an acceptable deal was scheduled for the end of the week. So that was what the bitch had in mind, was it? Well, he could use wires as well. He'd give his cousin in St. Pete a call first thing in the morning, drive down there, and get fixed up himself. When he and Madam Mayor talked, he would say nothing that could possibly incriminate him; he'd even pretend that the meeting was a chance one to avoid any appearance of breaking the Sunshine law, and he'd make rattlesnake hash of her. He gave O'Doole an unaccustomed grin. "You know Melba, Ferdy. She's always plotting, plotting, plotting. Maybe she'll catch herself in her own net."

"We got to get something good on her, Joe. Can't let her win this coming election; if she does, we won't have any voice in government, because you'll be out like you were the first time she beat you."

"I know," Tyler said glumly. Then he brightened. "But I don't think we have to worry about her any more, Ferdy. I think I know just how to trip her up."

"What we going to do about that Mosquito Row thing? Al was really getting on in the paper this morning. Hell, the way he was ranting, you'd think them greaseballs got rights."

"Yeah, I guess it's time we drove over to Flag City, talked to the publisher, and let him know that if he don't get rid of Al, we'll boycott the newspaper. If we can get everyone in the church to work with us, we can put a hurting on him."

O'Doole stopped turning the cigar in his mouth and struck a match to light it. His forehead creased with a frown. "I don't know if I'd go as far as a boycott, Joe. Hell, I'd miss Margie Noessit. We wouldn't have any idea what was going on in town."

"Ferdy, we can always ask folks what's going on," Tyler said impatiently.

"It wouldn't be the same."

"Anyway, the condemnation will go through. We just got to put out bids, to shut up the Pervert. You think Al was ranting? You should have heard him about giving Fyndar and Ramirez a retainer is illegal. Just sit back, we're going to make some good money yet."

The next morning, the St. Pete Times' beloved columnist, Harmon Tacks, waxed poetic on the previous meeting of the city council. Melba was furious and put in a call to the editors.

"Mayor Tosti," one of the senior editors explained, "when one takes public office, one must expect to be skewered at times."

"I'll sue!" she threatened.

"Please, Mayor Tosti, take criticism in the spirit in which it is given. You have to remember that if we don't jolt you once in a while, the rightist papers in the area will be after you, and they won't be nearly so kind. After all, you did change parties to win the election, and that went out back in the '90's in west central Florida."

She slammed the receiver into the cradle and read the infamous doggerel once more.

Little Melba Sunshine
by Harmon Tacks
(With apologies to James Whitcomb Riley)

Little Mayor Melba's come to our house to stay,
To run the city government and chase the bats away,
The citizens should teach her, since they don't have her clout,
That arrogance will git you if you don't watch out.

Mayor Melba has her buddy, Sunshine's Holy Joe,
To say the prayers and catch the dogs that wander to and fro,
Never mind the sinkhole and the problems that it's brouwt,
Arrogance will git you if you don't watch out.

Look at the disaster that has come upon the town,

> While Melba shopped for funny wigs that make her look a clown.
> Does the council have a single clue that Sunshine's in a rout,
> And that arrogance will git you if you don't watch out?

She grabbed the telephone again and dialed the number for Slugge, Crawley, and Schyte. "This is Melba Tosti. Put me through to DeLeon right away."

Tapping her foot impatiently, she waited for Slugge to answer his telephone. She wanted to talk to him about the possibility of suing the St. Petersburg Times and that son of a bitch, Harmon Tacks. If he thought for one moment that he could make fun of her wearing wigs, he had another thought coming.

"Melba? Dee here. Can I help?"

"Did you see that trash in the *Times* today?" she asked.

"Er, yes, I did."

She could have sworn he had swallowed a laugh. "I want to sue them."

"Melba, suing the *Times* can be a very expensive business. They have legal eagles advising them all the time as to whether something they're going to print is liable to bring down trouble on them. I would not advise you to take them on single-handedly. Not even if you had the entire budget of Sunshine at your disposal."

"Then I need to make some money fast, because if those bastards think they're going to make sport of me–"

"I have some free time in about an hour, Madam Mayor. Why don't you come over then?"

Melba smiled. An idea had suddenly leaped into her brain fully formed, and it was a brilliant one. If things went her way, she'd have all the money she'd ever need. "I'll see you in an hour, Dee," she said happily. "I've got something else to talk over with you."

Why had she not thought of this before? With two hundred acres down the spout, Sunshine's citizens would need homes, wouldn't they? The only land available within the city limits was an older area of town that had gone to seed–rundown trailer parks and the like–a very depressing place indeed.

But north and east of Sunshine was good land, inhabited by a couple of cattle ranches that could be picked up for a song. If she and a couple more folks bought that land, annexed it into the city, and built a nice development or two, they could really clean up.

All she had to do was work out a deal with Dee. He had plenty of money and he would be aware of others who were willing to go along. There was an even better reason than money-making to consider. The city had lost a whopping lot of its tax base with that sinkhole; if they planned carefully, she could take care of that problem too.

Humming happily, she left her office and went down the block to the deli that some New Yorkers had opened. Though she didn't often eat lunch there, she felt like a sandwich before she met Dee.

Teddy Rainmaker opened the door for her, and she could tell from the aroma rising from the bag he held that he had purchased hot pastrami sandwiches and pickles. "Melba, what a pleasant surprise. I didn't realize that you frequented places of this ilk."

"You forget I'm a New Yorker, Teddy, darling," she replied. "As a confirmed damned Yankee, I hanker for hot pastrami once in a while." Still affable, she nodded toward the package in his hand. "I see you do too."

"You're right. I adore pastrami on rye. Melba, a word, if you don't mind."

"Out of the Sunshine, dear?"

"Hardly. I want to caution you on your behavior with Frank Bonano; it's the talk of the town."

She was instantly on guard. "What do you mean?"

"Hell hath no fury like a mayor scorned," he said. "Your covetousness is showing."

"I don't know what you're talking about!" she objected.

He wagged his finger under her nose. "Naughty, naughty. It's bad policy to screw where you work, especially with a younger man." Seeing that he had drawn blood, he laughed, waved two fingers in farewell, and left the store.

Guy Fawkins carefully loaded the film in the camera, then put it aside. "You gals want to come with me, just in case I fall out of the tree and break my neck?"

Sally smiled, then gasped as her lip stung. "I'd love to go, just to get out of town for a while. Pretty bad when you're willing to smell sewage for a change of scenery, isn't it?"

"Gavel said it's not as bad down there since the sinkhole opened. Of course, we have the world's largest septic tank at this point, but it is filling with water, so maybe that'll help. Have you looked down into that thing?" Guy asked. "It's really strange to see the remains of a city sort of tumbled about like so much tossed salad, with cars and trucks here and there like radish slices. I wish I'd taken my camera down there when it first fell in, but who was in any condition to think straight right then. You coming, Kelsey?"

"Absolutely. I figure two of us can handle Dee if he comes after Sally, but I sure won't face him alone."

"Dee would never go after you, Kelsey. That would be actionable. He may be a shit, but he's a smart lawyer."

"Maybe not as smart as he thinks," Kelsey replied. "I can't wait to see his face when a deputy goes to call on him."

They drove west on Hatchacootee until they reached the turnabout, then parked. Guy walked out on the small peninsula where Gavel and Sally had set up watch. Kelsey and Sally brought up the rear.

"Where are you going to hide it?" Sally asked.

"Up a tree. I can tie the whole business, battery and all, to a limb with a bungee cord, set it, and when anything moves on the mud flat, the camera will record automatically." He walked among the stunted, wind-twisted oaks until he found one he thought strong enough to bear his weight, and began to climb.

"Be careful," Kelsey cautioned.

"If I fall from this height," her husband said, "I'll probably get bruised, if that," he said. "Okay, hand me the camera and I'll make it fast, then you can pass me the battery pack."

After giving him the battery pack, the two women wandered through the marsh grass to the beginning of the mud flat, which was inhabited by a large number of feeding birds, who regarded them casually and then continued their quest for food.

"I'd hate to have to eat those worms Gavel's always talking about," Sally remarked.

"Come on, they couldn't be any worse than snails," Kelsey retorted. They both shuddered with revulsion.

"I've been thinking, Kelsey, that I should probably see Dee in his office and make some arrangements. I can't live with you and Guy forever."

"You can stay with us as long as you like."

"I know that, but I can't go on this way forever; it's not fair. I would never go through a beating like that again for anything. Only thing is, I'm afraid of him now. I'm not sure just what I should try to do. I don't think I can talk with him in private."

"I know what you mean, and talking about a split certainly cannot be done in front of others. Why not get a lawyer to contact him? He certainly won't try to beat up on another man."

Sally brightened. "That's a good idea." She looked around at all the birds. "You know, all the years that Sunshine has sought a tourist attraction, it's a wonder they've never looked down here. This area would be the Audubon Society's dream."

"Except for the smell."

"But after the water is cleaned up, don't you think this would make a grand magnet for birdwatchers?"

"Bring it up at a meeting and see what the council says," Kelsey advised. "But wait until they've forgotten that you wanted to replace them with jackasses."

Sally smiled ruefully. "How long do you think it will take them to forget?"

"About two weeks," Kelsey replied, laughing. "Their memories are very short. Look at how they've managed to forget the sewage problem for the last twelve years."

CHAPTER TWENTY

Melba cursed and slammed down the receiver, then dialed Frank Bonano's number. "What do those asses mean, I have to move within forty-eight hours? Do you realize how this inconveniences me? My condo isn't quite ready and–"

"Madam Mayor, the geologists and the engineers are worried about that part of the rim falling into the hole, and your house and belongings will be lost. They consider such sloughing to be imminent, and you are not to spend another night in the place. If you want my advice–"

"I hardly need your advice, Bonano."

"Then why did you call?" he asked politely. "I was going to say that you should probably get a moving firm in there right away and have them take out everything. They can contact the Corps of Engineers people, who will warn them of what to be on the lookout for, so they can get out if they need to. But you'd better get moving if you want to save your things."

"Why wasn't I notified earlier of this?"

"We have been trying to reach you since early morning, Madam Mayor, but you haven't been available. I'm sorry. And you have not been singled out; everyone in the neighborhood is already on the move."

Melba hung up on him and chewed her lips savagely. Bastards, all they could think about was making it as rough as possible on everyone. What the hell did they know about how the earth was going to move?

Ever since the sinkhole, she had lost control of what was going on in the city and that son of a bitch Bonano was everyone's hero. The place was crawling with all kinds of important people, all those men from the Corps on Engineers, the FEMA people, who should rightly be consulting with her rather than city staff–everyone in the frigging place was kissing Bonano's ass. And what for? He had saved a few lives. Big deal!

This sloughing of the rim or whatever was all Bonano's doing, of that she was sure. She could almost hear him telling the boys to make it bad for the mayor, since she was such a bitch. There were times when she hated men!

Her thoughts were interrupted by a soft knock on her doorframe. She looked up and scowled as Mary Lee Mince came in. "What do you want?"

"I got Bastion Movers to go in for my things, Madam Mayor, and I wondered if you'd like for them to take your stuff as well? They're the only ones I could find who're free, and they want to get finished and get out of that area as quickly as possible."

Melba hesitated, not really knowing how to accept the gift of assistance gracefully. "Yes, yes, tell them to go ahead and do my place. Here are the keys. Wait, do they know how to handle delicate things?"

"They have a good reputation, Madam Mayor," Mary Lee said. "I've got a lot antique cut glass and I'm not concerned."

She fumbled in her purse and pulled out her house keys. "Well, all right. Can you take care of it for me? And how much is it going to cost?"

"Yes, ma'am, I can give them your keys. They're going to store the things until we've all found a place to live. I understand insurance is paying for the move; it's a lot cheaper for them than your losing everything. I'll let you know as soon as I find out."

"I am hardly old enough for you to address that way," Melba snapped. But she was too late; the baggage had already left. *Ma'am!* She grabbed the telephone again and dialed Fielding's number, which was busy, as usual. Really angry now, she took her purse and left the office. Where the hell was she supposed to live?

Op/Ed   The Sunshine Bulletin   Page 4

There is Something New Under the Sunshine
By Margie Noessit

Well, dear readers, your Margie has seen it all. Josephus (Holy!Holy!Holy!) Tyler has brought a suit for malice of intent against this writer, whose identity he does not know.

Tyler alleges that your Margie meant him grievous harm when I wrote that he had extorted campaign contributions from Zona Flores. His attorney, Michael Crawley, doesn't quibble with the truth of what was written, he merely asks the court to agree that I was motivated by intent to do harm.

I have two questions to ask of Mr. Crawley and Councilman Tyler. The first is, how do you sue someone whose identity you don't know? And the second is, and this is the most interesting question–why was the case brought before Judge Hiram Meekins in Traffic Court? Do either of these three prominent gentlemen think that the public is not aware that Meekins and Tyler are related? And they are cronies as well.

Do you suppose Judge Meekins will find me guilty of a traffic violation? Let's wait and see.

More news of interest to those who watch the political circus in Sunshine. Councilman Lila Mae Warner has filed for divorce from her husband, Henry Warner. Is she, perhaps, tired of southern fried chicken and mullet, or is she onto something more interesting? Only time will tell. And who will get the restaurant, Southern Fried, which is a landmark in Sunshine? Although Lila Mae inherited Southern Fried from her family, Henny has operated it for the past fifteen years.

Good luck, Lila Mae, but please keep Henny cooking.

More kitchen news. Seems like DeLeon Slugge, prominent attorney, is doing his own cooking these days. Sally has moved out after filing a complaint against him for beating her. The most interesting aspect of this is that Chief Rufus Hicks has somehow lost the report and has never investigated the occurrence.

Must be nice to be one of the top dogs in Sunshine. Apparently the law doesn't apply if you help the councilmen with their skulduggery.

Merlini pushed back his chair and belched loudly. He had just finished an enormous lunch of hot Italian sausages cooked in good olive oil with peppers and onions. It had tasted exactly like the sausages his mother used to make when he was a kid. Pity that he had never learned just how to duplicate the sauce she had made; it was heaven.

Things weren't going his way at all. It was clear, after his museum idea being tabled so many times, that the rest of the council were quite willing to table the matter into infinity, until he either lost an election or died of old age. Creeps!

No imagination–that was the trouble with the other council members. Give 'em a perfectly wonderful idea, and if they couldn't take credit for it, *strrcch!*–they cut its throat.

Look at the way Teddy had brought up the idea of Sunshine having a beach, and the next thing he heard, Melba was galloping all over hell and back claiming it was her idea.

He had to do some serious thinking about where his idea was going. Of course, he could always build the museum himself; it would still put Sunshine on the map, but it would take a lot more money than he had set aside for his retirement. Yeah, his little sausage business here in Sunshine took care of all his living expenses, but suppose when he got older, something happened to him? He was only sixty-three now, in the prime of life.

He took a sip of the chianti in his glass and smacked his lips appreciatively. He was so glad he was Italian; Italians knew how to eat. They knew how to drink. They knew how to create things. They were the best people on the whole frigging earth. Look at him, all he had to do was let his Italian mind do its homework and the way to raise money to build his museum would come to him from the air, just like that!

He smacked his lips again, patted his belly. *O fame*–he hungered still, but not for food. He wanted something that would give his life meaning. Of course, there were always the sausages, his companions, his passion. Each day he created masterpieces with his own two hands, and each night he devoured that art. His sausage creations were far too good for the people who lived in town. They were satisfied with breakfast links, for chrissake!

What would Sunshine need that he might supply that could make him a pile of money? He chewed a thumbnail, stared at the wall where the framed photos of his old business in Brooklyn were hanging. Good old Brooklyn. He remembered, when he was a kid, that his mother and father once took him for a drive out to the end of Long Island, to where they grew potatoes and vegetables to supply the towns that were strung out along the coast. He had sniffed with delight; there was a strange perfume in the air, and his father, God rest his soul, had explained that the smell came from potato blossoms. He would never forget that. *That was it!*

There was land outside Sunshine—of course it didn't smell of potato blossoms, more like cow flop—but there were a couple of old cattle ranches that barely broke even. If he could get a consortium going, they could buy up that land, develop it, and build homes for all those poor creeps in Sunshine who had lost theirs to the sinkhole. If they had the right builder, someone who knew how to build cheap and make a good-looking product, they could make a real killing.

Who could he get to engineer a deal with him? Teddy?—no. He'd give Dee Slugge a call first thing in the morning, talk to him about it. Prolly make Dee's day, with his wife leaving him and all that shit. Yeah, if they could do a deal, he could make enough to build his museum, even if it did have to be smaller than the one he had planned.

Grinning, he lumbered across the room, rummaged in the liquor cabinet, and poured himself a glass of anisette. Catching sight of himself in the mirror across the room, he raised the glass. *"Buon giorno, Maestro."*

Good old Italian minds; they came through every time.

4 Op/Ed _ The Tampa Tribune

EDITORIAL

Is corruption becoming idiotic?

Ludicrous, infamous, unethical, downright stupid–all of these apply. Small cities in Florida are noted for their wacky politics. The antics of some city politicians are often amusing. But the finding by Judge Hiram Meekins that a gossip columnist, Margie Noessit, is guilty of malice of intent goes beyond ridiculous. The Florida Bar must intervene in this downright stupid instance of abuse.

Miss Noessit, whose identity has remained a mystery for almost ten years, reported that Councilman Josephus Tyler forced the town madam to contribute to his campaign. The truth of the story is not in doubt; there was hard evidence supplied by the madam, who rightly felt she was being shaken down by some members of the city council. But Tyler was angry that his position as the city's leading righteousness guru was in question. So his attorney sued someone who remains unidentified. This is ludicrous.

Even more infamous, the suit was not brought in the proper venue. It was brought before Judge Meekins, who is cousin to Councilman Tyler and runs the Traffic Court. That the judge had the audacity to pronounce on such a matter should raise grave concerns in Tallahassee. His action was unethical and he should be removed from the bench immediately.

This is a classic example of the rot that sets in when cretins seize the reins of power and hang on by hook or by crook, mostly by crook, judging from the disgraceful events that have taken place.

Joe Tyler pried himself from his Cadillac and looked around the parking lot of the church. Not a car in sight. He felt relieved, as all the press coverage he'd gotten had put him even deeper in trouble with his wife and the other women of the church.

"You had to sue, didn't you, Joe?–had to give them a chance to drag your name through the mud all over again? I'll never be able to hold up my head again with the women of the Living Witness Holiness Confederation." She had begun to weep, and that really made him feel bad. "You can dirty your reputation;

it's your right–but do you have to do something so stupid that they write editorials about it?"

He'd have to call the editorial staff at the *Tribune*; they were getting far too liberal. The *Trib* was a rightist paper, damn it, and they had no business writing such left-wing trash. Talk about yellow journalism! He' have to remind them that the sainted Ronald Reagan said that those on the right should never speak ill of one another. Great man, Reagan, even if he had left the economy back then in a shambles. Star Wars!

He strode across the parking lot and into the back entrance to the sanctuary, took a deep breath of the incensed air–Learned Speaker had a special fondness for balsam– and knocked on the great man's door.

It opened immediately. "Come in, my son," said Learned Speaker. "I was glad to get your telephone call; I've been thinking much about you."

"I'm glad you could see me, Learned Speaker. I want to talk to you about one of our brothers, who has fallen on bad times and is in need of solace."

Learned Speaker indicated a chair and went behind his desk to sit. "Who are you concerned about, Joe?"

"Brady Hack," Tyler began. "He is damned."

"Why?" Learned Speaker leaned back in his chair and tented his hands. His eyes bored into Tyler's.

"He has been consorting with whores."

An eyebrow rose gently. "You have witnesses of this offense against the Lord?"

"Ferdy O'Doole saw him coming out of the Sunshine Gentlemen's Club on several occasions," Tyler said in an outraged voice. "Smiling."

"That is a serious offense, consorting with the damned. But I find your offense worse, my son. You have, to put it bluntly, become a tattletale. At your age, it is unfortunate."

Tyler felt his blood pressure shooting heavenward. "I am no tale-bearer; I am concerned about this indiscretion because he is the Lay Speaker and he is tainted."

Learned Speaker shook his head sadly. "Joe, Joe, you are the tainted one and you cannot see it. Lay aside this curtain of dubious piety which you hide behind and look at what you have become. Your arrogance has become such that you are headed for a fall, my son. You have forgotten humility and what it means.

"I will speak sharply to Brady Hack, have no fear of that. But his sin is small compared with yours. I think you need to go to a place of solitude and pray for guidance."

"I pray daily!" Tyler snapped.

"Really? Or do you inform the Lord as to your intentions? There is a difference."

"I am beginning to wonder if you are failing, Learned Speaker," Tyler said coldly.

His opponent nodded affably. "I have been doubted before," he said. He rose to indicate that the interview was at an end. When Tyler didn't move, he said, "When you can get on your knees before the entire congregation and ask forgiveness, we will accept you back into the fold. Until then, you are shunned."

Tyler shot to his feet. "You won't get away with this," he thundered.

Learned Speaker smiled.

Even though the power to streetlights had not been restored, the dark around the old city hall was dissected by myriad bands of light from a couple of hundred flashlights that illuminated placards which read, "Poor people have rights," "Down with the City Council," "Joe Tyler stinks!," "Mosquito Row Won't Go," "¡Ni Pensarlo!," "¡No nosotros vamanos!"

The local television station and another from Heart County covered the protest from the citizens of Mosquito Row.

"What do you intend doing if the city council tries to condemn the area?" a reporter asked Jorge Granita. "We will call in the ACLU and sue the pants off them!" Granita replied hotly. "We come to this country to make a better life, we work hard, we look after their houses and their children, and they want to be rid of us? When people who don't know this council going to stand up for rights too, eh? When all the poor are go from Sunshine, nobody be able to go to work. They have to stay home, look after their *niños*, and everything go bang."

"How do you know the ACLU will help you, Jorge?"

"I talk to them already, they send a lawyer next week. They say poor have rights, rich have rights in this country."

Behind them, the crowd roared and they turned to see what had happened.

"The mayor has just driven up in a pink Lincoln and the crowd is going wild. Will she address this angry mob, or will she–she's coming over now. Good evening, Mayor Tosti. We didn't expect to see you here."

"I'll bet you didn't. What's all this about?"

Jorge Granita pushed his way to her side. "We here to protest that you condemn Mosquito Row, Mrs. Mayor. All the people in Mosquito Row damn mad about this."

"Now, now, Mr. Granita, calm down," Melba said soothingly. "We have not even signed a contract on a study about the issue, so there's no need to get all hot and bothered."

"When you sign contract, they say what you want to hear. You think, because we poor people, that we don't know how Sunshine work?"

In the background, the crowd began to chant, "Mosquito Row won't go! Mosquito Row won't go! Mosquito Row won't go! To hell with city council!"

"What's your reaction to this, Madam Mayor?" a reporter from Heart County asked. He held out his microphone for Melba's reply.

She realized she was on camera and smiled brilliantly. "You know that government of the people, by the people, for the people has always been my main concern. But demonstrations like this do no good; these folks should stay at home and mind their business. We know what's best for Sunshine and its citizens, and we'll do our jobs like we always have." She winced as someone flashed a light into her eyes.

"Mosquito Row won't go! Mosquito Row won't go!" the crowd bellowed.

"Noisy, aren't they?" Melba asked a bystander. Then she realized that she was talking to Zona Flores. She hesitated, then turned to try and regain the safety of her car.

"Where are you going, Melba?" Rainmaker asked. He had left the restaurant and hurried down as soon as he heard there was a ruckus.

"Out of here," she snapped. "Listen to those damned people, will you? Did you know that they've called in the ACLU?"

Rainmaker threw back his head and laughed. "Good for them! I guess you'll just have to table Joe's brilliant idea, leave the hotbed of pregnancy alone, and get on with putting the city back together."

"Not likely, friend," she snarled. "These greaseballs think they can pull this and get away with it? Where is Rufus Hicks?"

"I told him to get over to the sinkhole and put his men there to make certain that no one falls in." Rainmaker was grinning broadly.

"Whose side are you on, Councilman?" she asked.

"I'm with them, Melba; they're in the minority. We have some citizens who refuse to be bullied, and I love them for it." Then he sobered. "I never liked the idea to begin with. If Joe thinks he can run everyone he doesn't like out of town, it's a sick scene. What are we, fascists? And if we continue and they do bring in the ACLU, we're going to be forced to defend our actions in court. I think we'll lose. I don't think we have any right at all to force people from their homes to satisfy some bigot who happens to sit on the council. Think about it, because we have a lot of problems to deal with now, and we need all our resources to put this city back together."

"You never did fit in," she began. But he had walked on and she was talking to the night air.

As she went toward her car, she noticed a very disturbing thing. Even though it was obvious that several people recognized her, they ignored her. How dare they? She was a champion of the people!

CHAPTER TWENTY ONE

Joe Tyler felt like a complete fool sitting alone at La Plata. That Melba would love the place was a given; he considered it arty-farty. She had gone on and on about the, what was it?– *decor d'argent interior*. Sounded like a disease more than anything else. The whole place looked very, very sick to him.

He glanced at his watch, sipped some water, checked the tiny pin on his lapel, and smiled. Yes, today was the day! On the other side of the lapel was a tape recorder, and he'd only to encourage her to incriminate herself.

Then he remembered that she would be wearing a wire as well. Bitch! But she'd never get him to say a word, not one word during the entire meal, that could possibly incriminate him.

In a way, he was glad she was late. Gave him some time to think. There were far too many things going wrong recently, the latest of which really hurt. His own wife was shunning him. He had never realized what power Learned Speaker wielded, had always thought of the man as his protegé, and now look what had happened!

Yesterday he had gone home after leaving the church and Sarah refused to look at him. How did word of his shunning spread so fast? When suppertime came, there was no food on the table. She had moved into one of the guest rooms to sleep, and this morning he'd had to go to that Yankee delicatessen for breakfast. Damn Learned Speaker!

Grumpy, he looked again at the entrance to the silver cave. Melba still wasn't in sight. He grabbed Al McDonald's paper, which he'd brought with him, and opened it, hoping to pass the time learning of misfortunes other than his own.

Op/Ed The Sunshine Bulletin Page 6

EDITORIAL

THEY WON'T GO!

The dark was sliced into thousands of ribbons as flashlight-wielding citizens from Mosquito Row protested on Thursday night. The reason for their anger is simple; the City Council has plans to condemn the area, destroy all the housing there, and turn Mosquito Row into a city park.

The reason for this latest nonsense from the council is quite simple: Joe Tyler doesn't want those he considers beneath him to live in the same city he occupies.

The idea is a bad one for several reasons, the least of which is Councilman Tyler's overriding arrogance. This is a free country, and in a free country, one man cannot tell five hundred citizens to get out because he doesn't wish to be near them. He's not near them; Merriweather Drive, Sunshine's only gated community, is a very long way, financially and physically, from the banks of the Hatchacootee River and its sewer stink.

Another reason for dropping this bad idea is that the city government doesn't have the right to destroy folks' homes and properties for no good reason. Tyler's objections to Mosquito Row seem to focus on the place being "a hotbed of pregnancy." Does he mean to imply that only white, wealthy folks are allowed to have children? Didn't Adolph Hitler have the same idea? Does the fact that these people live normal lives give him the right to raze their homes?

The main reason the council should drop this idea is financial; the city faces an uphill battle to rebuild its downtown around a crater of stupendous proportions. Even with assistance from the federal government and the state, there will be an astounding amount of money required to rebuild the city center. Any funds available should be put to this use.

For many years, this city has been run by a clique of good old boys and their hangers-on. This has to stop. The city council once had a chairman. The Mayor did not chair the Council. Joe Tyler changed all that, disregarded the city charter, and ran things as he wished. His successor, Melba Tosti, has continued in the same vein.

The Council has advertised for bids to study this proposal. The proposal doesn't need a study, it needs to be stuffed in the wastebasket and forgotten.

He choked and rapidly folded the paper, then lay it on an extra chair. He and the boys needed to get over to Flag City to see the publisher right away. Al McDonald had gone much too far this time. To accuse him of being a Hitler was almost a sin.

His reverie was interrupted by Melba's arrival. She bustled across the intervening space, a riot of color. He shuddered; she was wearing a perfectly hideous bright purple wig and her black, purple, and blue-green dress, which was apparently a favorite. On her shoulder she wore a rhinestone spray pin. He assumed it was the recording device. Against the *decor d'argent* of La Plata, she looked like some hellish bird. Watching her approach, he really appreciated his wife, even if she was shunning him.

"Joe, what a surprise to see you here," she greeted him.

He smiled inwardly. "Well, hello, Melba, I just happened to be sitting here in the restaurant and you walked in. What a coincidence."

She sat down and smiled around her at the diners who stared at her head gear. "I had no idea that you dined in places like this. What can you recommend?"

"I've eaten here only once before, and I had the New York strip. It wasn't too bad."

Her smile faltered. "Isn't that a coincidence! I've eaten here only once before, myself. I had frog's legs and paté. I think I'll try the strip this time; I didn't have time for breakfast."

"I was going to have lunch at home, but Sarah is busy today and so I decided to come down here for a change of scenery." Did she know he was wearing a wire? Why didn't the idiot come right out and say why she was here? Then the reason hit him in the face; he could not think why it had not occurred to him before. She was wearing one too, and would never say anything that might incriminate her. She was going to be as cagey as he was. But he'd be damned if he'd be the first one to call a halt to this silliness.

"The editorial in the paper wasn't very kind to you, was it?

"No, it wasn't, but what do you expect from a liberal like Al McDonald? He'll regret it in the end."

"How is Sarah?"

"Fine."

"Things going well at the sinkhole?"

"As far as I know, Melba. I leave those matters to Bonano."

"Yes, Frank has done a wonderful job, hasn't he? I'm so glad that he works for us, rather than somewhere else. Think what might have happened if he had not been so resourceful."

"I had nightmares about our people losing their lives," Tyler said piously.

"You know that I was forced to move myself, even though the condo isn't ready for occupancy."

"Really? Oh, I meant to tell you, just before I left town, I got a call from Bonano. Your house went into the hole, along with all the rest of them along that street. They hope this is the last of the cave-ins."

Melba went white. "That's terrible! When is that damned hole going to stop growing?"

"Soon, I hope, or we won't have much of a city left."

"Oh, let's not talk about serious things, Joe. Let's be gay."

"Be what?" He stiffened. "I don't even consider that funny."

Shaking her head and chuckling, Melba said, "I meant, let's be carefree. Sorry about my choice of words."

Somewhat mollified, Joe nodded. "Yes, no point talking about matters we'll probably have to vote on. Have to remember the Sunshine Law."

"Oh, yes, indeed," Melba agreed enthusiastically. "I am so glad we live in a state that requires open government, aren't you?"

He had had enough. "I know you're wearing a wire, Melba. I'm wearing one myself. Do you really think we should carry on with this nonsense?"

She looked as if she might faint, which made him feel immensely better. "How—I didn't—who told you?" Her voice was pure acid.

"A friend of mine saw you coming out of the detective agency, and no one goes to Daily Dirt for any reason other than a wire. Frankly, you never wear jewelry other than that damned rhinestone donkey, so the spray was a dead giveaway." He gave her a triumphant smile.

She chewed her lips. "Where'd you get yours?"

"Friend of mine in St. Pete. A cousin."

"That dinky little thing in your lapel?"

"Yep."

"Congratulate your cousin for me; the damned thing is very convincing. American Red Cross pin?"

"Yes. I'll pass on your message."

The waiter came to take their order.

"You buying this time, Joe?" Melba asked.

"Yeah," he said ungraciously. All he wanted to do was leave and go to a place where he could get some real food, like fried chicken, mashed potatoes, and a big plate of greens. But he would see this through if it killed him.

"I'll have oysters on the half-shell and a New York strip," she told the waiter. "Medium rare. And I'd like a double vodka on the rocks with the oysters."

He might have known, he thought, disgusted. A drunkard! "Make mine the same," he said testily. "Without the vodka."

The waiter nodded and vanished.

"Are you a teetotaler?" she asked curiously.

"Never in my life has a drop of demon rum touched my lips," he said.

"Maybe you ought to tie one on, Joe." She was serious. "Really do it up right and get all that piety out of your system. You'd be a better man."

Over the vodka and oysters, Melba grew a little warmer. "You know what we need, both of us?"

"I can't imagine either of us needing the same thing, Melba," he said stiffly.

She colored. "I wasn't talking about sex or anything like that, Joe."

It was his turn to redden. "I certainly didn't have such a thing in mind!"

"How much of a loss did you take on the store?"

It was none of her business. How dare she ask such a personal question of an enemy? He had actually done quite well, but she would never know it. In fact, he had made a small profit because he was over-insured.

Never in his wildest dreams did he envision losing the entire building to a hole in the ground. The building itself was barely able to pass the new safety codes, and he had been loath to spend money to make repairs. And a lot of his stock was old; people were running into Heart County to shop at the fancy new malls. He had been losing more business with every passing month.

"I took a real bath, Melba." He cleared his throat. "It looks as if we might get a lot of opposition from the greaseballs. If they bring in that ACLU–"

"The city would have to spend a bundle to defend its position. I see your point." Her voice was silky. "But that doesn't mean that we can't make money another way, does it?"

"What do you mean?" His antennae began to twitch.

"I mean, the folks who lost their homes are going to need some place to live. If we buy up those cattle ranches, then annex the land into the city, we can develop it–on the Q.T., of course, and make a killing. I know a couple of builders who would be more than willing to build really cheap housing that looks good. And we'd kill another bird with the same stone. We'd build back the tax base. That took a shellacking with the sinkhole."

Tyler was a natural for the scheme, she thought. He'd have all that insurance money to invest. She'd have to borrow her portion, but it would be a quick payback and the interest wouldn't kill her; she'd still make a fat profit.

"Who would front for us?"

"Dee Slugge, who else? I'm sure he's interested; I've already spoken with him, and he's never turned down a buck yet, no matter how it's made."

Tyler finished the last of his oysters and regarded Melba with hard eyes. "You can't use this against me, you know. I'm recording it too."

"Oh, for God's sake, Joe, forget the wires." She removed the spray from her shoulder and tossed it into her purse. "Are you in or out?"

He thought rapidly. He could probably double whatever money he put into the venture, and it certainly would help to solve the city's present problems. Housing was an absolute necessity. Most of those who had lost their homes were living in old portable classrooms that the county had dumped on them. "Count me in. You call Dee and make an appointment for us to see him, and we'll meet at his house rather than his office. Have to maintain the appearance of propriety, you know."

"I know all about that, Joe. I'll call Dee tomorrow."

Frank Bonano sighed and made a note, then looked up at the Corps engineer. "You think it's finally stabilized?"

"Yes, it would seem so. We've checked the whole perimeter and that looked like the last really weak spot. So now we have to decide what to do."

"What do you mean?"

"Will the city attempt to fill it?" The Corps man consulted his notes, nodded grimly, and looked at Frank for an answer.

"I don't even have to consult the council on that one. The answer is no. I got out my trusty calculator, and figured that I'd need about half a million cubic yards of concrete to fill a hole of that size, and came to the conclusion that there's no need to bankrupt the state for what is essentially a landscaping problem. We will have Lake Sun N' Fun or something equally ridiculous by the time the council finishes naming the thing, and that will be that."

"Mmmm," said the environmental engineer from the Department of Environmental Protection. "Lake No-name will pose a serious public health and safety threat until all that sewage dies a natural death."

Bonano laughed. "For Pete's sake, man, don't use that name around the councilmen. We already have No Name Road just east of Gulf Gambol, and I don't need another piece of silliness just now."

The engineer grinned. "How did No Name Road get its name?"

"Back when Joe Tyler was mayor, the road was cut, and some wag wanted to name it Delilah Way or something like that; maybe it was Salome's Slink–who knows? The mayor, being a rigid fundamentalist when he's not a total hypocrite, rejected every name submitted out of hand. He decreed that the road would have no name at all. So the Works Department folks had a sign made, and it's been No Name Road ever since."

The DEP man suppressed a smile. "How do you stand it, Frank?"

"It ain't easy, my man. Now, what can we do to control this threat to public health and safety until all the critters in the water are dead?"

The Corps engineer scratched his head, did a quick calculation, then grimaced. "I was going to suggest putting in lime to raise the pH to something like eight or nine, but the amount of lime required would be almost as ruinous as the concrete. You'd need tons of the stuff."

"Then what can we do?"

"Frank, I think the best thing for now would be to fence the thing off, let Ma Nature take her course, then, like you said, turn it into a lake. But I'd sure never open it for swimming." The DEP man shook his head. "Can you imagine what's down at the bottom of that hole? You've got rotting metals, volatiles, the whole shebang, in addition to all that macadam."

Bonano nodded. "Actually, I've given it a lot of thought and I'm appalled." He leaned forward. "Would you believe that I've already had about six telephone calls from salvage firms who want to plumb those depths? I think they're under the impression that everyone who lived in downtown Sunshine was loaded with family jewels. Man, what people won't do for moola!"

The Corps man shuddered. "You couldn't pay me to dive in such a place, even if the water were pristine. That jumble is a death trap."

"Yeah, one guy said he'd been diving in sinkholes since he was a young man, but this one is really special." Bonano drew a deep breath. "Okay, so all I need to do now is buy a lot of chain-link fencing and a few hundred rolls of barbed wire. I'll get on it right away."

"Don't you have to get an okay from the council?" the DEP man asked.

"No, FEMA is going to pay for it; part of the hazard mitigation money. And it's got to be done now; the council doesn't meet until early next week. I have nightmares about some kid wandering too close to the edge and falling in; I want this problem out of my hair."

Teddy Rainmaker hung up the telephone and grimaced. "Fielding is putting down more sand at the river mouth tonight. Says he's going to take about twenty loads, maybe thirty, if he can get it done without being seen. He thinks that the reason the last sand disappeared is because he simply didn't put down enough."

PooPoo was studying the effect of his new wet-look vinyl that had transformed the restaurant interior. "I think it's gorgeous, don't you?"

Rainmaker nodded. "It is, and you were right, as usual. I almost expect to see a jaguar come out of the bush."

"Darling, jaguars don't inhabit south sea islands, they live in South America. Why is Fielding so hell-bent to put down more sand? Didn't you explain what you'd heard about the currents down there?"

"Yes, I did, but he see's himself really making a killing building beachfront houses. I tried to tell him that he still won't be able to build because of the marsh, but he doesn't listen."

"I wish you'd distance yourself from him a little, Teddy. He's like Joe Tyler in some ways, and he's getting too big for his britches."

"I have already, Hon. Told him the other day he can buy me out if the price is right, and he seemed downright happy to accommodate me. Said he'd talk to his accountant, get in touch with my lawyer, and settle up. With everything going on around here, I'd rather make less money and be a little cleaner."

"Teddy, I told you before, you're not a crook."

Rainmaker looked at his watch. Five o'clock. Almost time for the dinner crowd to begin arriving. He walked to the bar, poured himself a hefty scotch and water, and stared into the restaurant, liking what he saw. He gazed at his partner, then took a long swallow of his drink.

"PooPoo, if there were an investigation of the council tomorrow—say someone did something to bring the eyes of the Attorney General or the Feds to bear on us—I'd go to jail. I've been playing fast and loose with the public trust for quite a while now, and you know it.

"Public office is a drug; we get hooked and can't shake the habit of thinking we're better than everyone else because they voted us into office. We forget that, in reality, we're elected to *serve*. We get the idea that we're the great leaders of the populace, and we're not. We're the same greedy fools that we were when elected."

"I didn't realize it was beginning to affect you this way. Greedy for what?" PooPoo poured himself a glass of white wine and sipped it.

"Fame? Our names in the paper? Shoving staff around? Hell, I don't know. I only know that damned few people in politics are there because they're concerned about the public weal."

"Do you want out?"

"Not particularly, and that's the disgusting part of it. How many times have you heard some politician swear that he'll only serve for two terms, and then he'll step down to make way for someone with new ideas? Two terms pass, and if the pol could do it without getting caught, he'd kill to stay in office."

Rainmaker slumped onto a bar stool and shook his head. "When my term is up, I'll probably run again for the reasons I've just outlined, but I am going to clean up my way of doing the public's business. I have actually become disillusioned with myself, and it's not a happy state."

PooPoo hugged him and rumpled his hair. "What brought this on?"

"A lot of things, starting with what Frank Bonano went through to save the people in this stinking little place. I am humbled. He didn't give a damn that he was fired–didn't care what we thought–he just went ahead and did what he had to do to keep things together. And this condemnation of Mosquito Row that Joe keeps ranting about–it's wrong. Those people are poor immigrants for the most part, but they have a right, damn it, to their lives and their property. That's what they came to this country for. At this point, I think it's my duty to help make sure they get a fair shake."

PooPoo raised his glass in salute. "You look ten years younger, Teddy. Maybe a mission is what you've needed all along."

Kelsey tossed the salad and sprinkled it generously with freshly grated Parmesan cheese, the tossed it again. She set it on the table, then turned the wine glasses right side up, uncorked the wine so it could breathe, then hurried to the microwave to check the potatoes.

"You move around a kitchen like you were born in one," Sally said admiringly. "I never can get everything going so that it's ready at the same time."

"The woman is a pro," Gavel said. "She once even managed to fish and cut bait simultaneously."

"Go to hell," Kelsey said cheerfully. "Gavel, make yourself useful and see if Guy has the meat ready. The potatoes are almost done."

"What's the occasion?" Sally asked curiously. "Or do you do this every weekend?"

"We are celebrating the fact that both your eyes are now sufficiently open that you don't need a guide dog, if you want to know the truth."

Sally laughed. "Thanks. I've taken the big step, Kelsey, and I don't feel right. I just hope I'm not doing the wrong thing."

"What have you done, committed a crime?"

"No, I've filed for a divorce. I don't think I could ever live with Dee again, or trust him any more. I'd always be looking over my shoulder, afraid that he'd lose his temper and kill me."

Kelsey gave her guest a brief hug. "Can't say I blame you. Does your lawyer think Dee will agree?"

"Yes, he does. Said that Dee doesn't really seem to care much one way or the other, just so long as he doesn't get taken to the cleaners."

"You should hit the son of a gun for everything he's got," Gavel said, coming back into the kitchen. "What he did to you should send him to prison." He put out his hands to stop Sally's protestations. "No, don't say that you provoked him by slapping his face in public, don't go into that place where you start making excuses for that shit. No man, no real man, would ever treat a woman in the way he treated you." He brought himself up short and laughed. "Besides, isn't hitting men in the wallet the way women fight?"

Kelsey threw a piece of lettuce at him. "You don't want any food, do you?" But she was amused by the adoration in Sally's eyes.

"I'm sorry, ma'am, please forgive me," Gavel said in mock contrition. Then he changed the subject. "I wonder if Guy's camera will ever record anything but birds and that pair who were making out on the mud flat?"

"You don't really think they'd try it again, do you? There's bound to be a better place to make love!"

CHAPTER TWENTY TWO

Florida House of Representatives

Representative Henry Bates

Councilman Gianni Merlini
1923 Hatchacootee Boulevard
Sunshine, Florida 3766580

Dear Mr. Merlini:Meats

I am sorry to tell you that the bill to obtain funds for your museum failed to pass the Civic Affairs subcommittee. The general opinion of the committee members was that an art museum or something of that nature might be more appropriate.

The fact is that the pressure brought to bear on the Legislature by the animal rights lobbyists has made most of the members loath to expose themselves to ridicule in the home press. This year, there are some forty registered animal rights lobbyists in Tallahassee and, judging from the intensity of their passion, I would guess that most of them are rabid. What a shame we can't innoculate people against silly ideas.

I would appreciate a call from you to let me know how things are going in Sunshine. I've tried calling each of the council members and the mayor numerous times, but I get nothing but busy signals, so things must really be hopping. I can't even get through on SunCom.

Again, I am distressed to send you such bad news. Perhaps we might try again next year, when the vegetable rights folks might possibly invade Tallahassee to save the carrot from extinction and make meat popular again.

I hope that the council will not go on with the condemnation of Mosquito Row. It would certainly harm Sunshine's reputation in the state press, and might even be picked up by the national press. Since Sunshine is trying to develop a tourist industry, destroying the homes and businesses in a poor section of town will do much more harm than good.

Please give my congratulations to Frank Bonano on a job well done.

          Warmest regards,
          Sandfly

Merlini grunted and put down the letter. What was wrong with people these days, he wondered. All those crazies trying to pass laws that would allow a cow to sue over being eaten–what good did it do to sue after you were dead, especially if you were a cow? And since when did cows have lawyers?

Then he remembered the old lady in Brooklyn who had driven everyone wild with her insistence that unclothed animals were lewd. She wanted all the squirrels in Brooklyn put into panties, for chrissake! She had so much press coverage that she got into hot water with the local politicians for stealing their limelight.

Ever since man rose from wherever he rose from, Merlini told himself, man had eaten meat. Nature back then had not grown carrots, for chrissake! Lila Mae was right when she said they had eaten tigers–hell, they ate everything in sight. Even Sandfly Bates knew about the cavemen making sausage from elephants. That was the problem today; too many crazies. Prolly came from eating all that grass. Everyone knew that if you didn't eat meat, you'd go nuts.

Okay, Legislature, he said to himself, if that's the way you want it, that's the way it's going to be. I'll make myself a little pile, build the museum myself, and shame all of the gutless jerks who're scared to fight the nut cases. He could see the headlines now, "Merlini Rescues Sunshine from Oblivion!" He'd be a hero.

He shuffled across the office of his factory and looked up the number for Slugge, Crawley, and Schyte, Attorneys at Law.

Melba parked her car in the drive and got out, wondering who the third car belonged to. Was Dee having a party, or what? This was supposed to be a private business meeting. She made her way past the shrubbery to check out the extra auto, then recognized it as belonging to Meats Merlini. What was he doing here?

She shrugged and went to the front door. It opened immediately and Meats greeted her.

"You're late. Come on in before somebody sees you."

"How can anyone see me in the dark, Meats?"

"You know what I mean. We're really out of the Sunshine here, Melba. Gotta keep this private as hell."

"Is Joe here?"

"Yeah–just the three of us and Dee."

"Is anybody else in on this?"

"You crazy? Teddy and Lila Mae won't go for this at all." He led her through the entrance hall and into Dee's study.

"Good evening, Melba," Dee Slugge said. He was seated at a desk littered with papers. Behind him, bookcases rose to the ceiling, their contents bound in tan leather.

She looked around curiously. The whole room was done in brown, black, and tan. And not done very well. She hated places that lacked color; they made her uneasy. She seated herself gingerly in a dull brown leather chair, then nodded to Tyler.

Dee was all business. God, he was a cold fish! With all the gossip about his beating the hell out of his wife–she understood that he'd almost killed Sally–he still maintained his cool. Sally had been right to slap him the way she did. Even though she'd been yelling at the council, the way Dee had twisted her arm to get the microphone had been sadistic; he had meant to hurt her.

"...I said, Melba, are you ready to begin?" Slugge's voice stabbed into her thoughts like an icepick.

"Yes, gentlemen, any time."

"So, as I understand it, the three of you wish to form a consortium to purchase those two cattle ranches and develop them so that the people of Sunshine who have lost their homes will have places available to them as quickly as possible."

"Yes, yes," Tyler said. "And we plan to annex the property into Sunshine to shore up our tax base."

Slugge made a note. "Very well. How are we going to capitalize this venture? Joe?"

"I–I'll have some insurance funds to use," he said. "And I can always borrow more if we need it."

"Melba?"

"I'll have to borrow," she said simply. "But I shouldn't have to put in as much as you all do, because it was my idea."

"Like hell!" Merlini objected. "I called Dee myself with the idea."

"Actually, Melba, you and Meats called me within four minutes of each other. I made a note on my calendar because of the coincidence."

She licked her lips. "Okay. If you say so."

"You can always take a lesser interest in the endeavor," Slugge suggested.

"No way. I'll talk to the bank tomorrow."

"Meats?"

"I got some savings and I'll borrow money too."

Slugge nodded and made some notes. "I've located a builder who can put up a house that looks like it's worth about two hundred grand for just over seventy-five thousand. He's a real master at camouflage." He looked each of them in the eye, then continued. "Unless, of course, you intend making less profit and want to give quality for the money."

"Are you crazy?" Tyler rumbled. "What's the point of going into this thing if we cut our profits from the very beginning?"

"Yes, the object of this endeavor is money," Melba concurred. "We're taking a big chance, doing this." She leaned forward, intense. "You realize, Dee, that this consortium must remain totally anonymous."

"Of course, Madam Mayor," he murmured. "When I release the news to the press, no names will be mentioned. I'll say that the developer is a large, out of state firm that doesn't want its competitors to know it's moving into the area."

"Good idea," Merlini chortled. "If we make enough of a killing, we could prolly do this again."

"Let's not count our bridges before we burn them," Melba cautioned. "You have any idea what they're going to want for that land, Dee?"

"I have called both the owners and made appointments to see them. One of the ranches hasn't paid county taxes for about eight years, so they're anxious to sell for any amount that will give them a way out. I think that one will go for about two thousand an acre. The other one will take some negotiation."

"How long will it take you, before we can start?" Tyler asked.

"I think we can go ahead and make arrangements with the developer," Slugge said. "After all, there are so many folks who're in need of housing that the bank will fall over itself to lend money. The deal can't fail."

"You going to see Pruitt at the Sunshine TrustBank, I assume," Tyler said.

"Who else? He'll probably want a piece of the action," Merlini answered.

"Nobody, but nobody gets a piece of this action outside us," Melba said firmly. "Dee, it's important to get the land fast because we need to go through annexing it in the council."

Slugge nodded.

"Now, what will we call this place?" Melba asked.

"I already thought up a good name," Merlini volunteered. "'Shangri-la'. How do you like it?"

"Meats, there are about five trailer parks named Shangri-la in Heart County," Slugge said. "We need something different."

"Oh, I didn't know. I don't go over there much. Anybody else got an idea?"

"What about 'Last Horizon'?" Tyler asked. "Most of the folks who lived in the downtown area are old, and this will be their last home."

"Joe, that's like naming a nursing home One Foot in the Grave Manor," Melba retorted. "It would kill sales. And we don't want just old folks in the place, we want the young ones as well. But what about 'Lost Horizon'? That has a nice ring to it."

"Hey, that's a good idea, Melba," Merlini said. "Then you could have a street named Shangri-la."

Slugge nodded. "Yes, we could." He looked at the three of them. There was no point in going into serious detail with the fools; he'd just keep them busy with extraneous things and that way, they'd stay out of his hair. He began writing busily. "We have to get the place surveyed and platted before anything else, but do you have any other street names? They're very important, you know."

"Tibet Place, Madagascar Circle, Timbuktu Drive," Melba counted on her fingers.

"What about Paris Place?" Tyler asked.

"Paris isn't exotic, Joe," Melba explained. "We want exotic names."

"Maybe we should get the Pervert in on this," he responded sourly. "If anything was ever exotic, it's that thing he lives with."

"Now, Joe, let's not get started on Teddy and PooPoo," Slugge cautioned. "If you do, we'll be here all night. And I must remind you that you are paying me by the hour on this, and the clock started ticking when this meeting began."

Merlini guffawed. "Good old Dee! Wouldn't give his mother a free minute if she asked him to dinner."

Slugge nodded in agreement. "Lawyering is about making money," he explained cooly. "Time is money. Are we going to have only three streets?"

"Morocco Road, Casablanca Circle–"

"Utopia Lane," Tyler added. "Shanghai Street."

"Now you're getting into the spirit of things!" Merlini chortled. "Tangier Road, how's that?"

"Beautiful," Melba enthused. "I believe we have a winner!"

Slugge slid contracts across the desk to the three of them. "If you'll sign these, I can get started in the morning."

The sky to the west of them was alive with fiery light as the setting sun colored Hatchacootee Boulevard orange. Except for the heavy equipment and its constant roar and clank, the center of town was quiet and deserted. Most of the retirees liked to eat early and the restaurants at this hour were filled to overflowing. The clouds above them were soft and looked as if they might melt; a sure sign of warm weather approaching.

Lila Mae, walking with Oddman as he checked the perimeter of the sinkhole, slipped her hand into his and smiled up at him. He grinned and leaned down to kiss her quickly.

The giant hole was still surrounded by the concrete traffic barriers that had been hastily assembled from all over the county. Those areas that lacked the barriers were roped off, and warning signs had been placed every ten yards. But in spite of the warning signs and the very real danger, folks still tried to test their luck by getting to the water, which had rapidly risen to fill the hundred foot depth that remained after the town center had filled up the bottom. The geologists figured the hole had been about a hundred and fifty feet deep originally.

"If it didn't stink, it would be all right," Lila Mae remarked.

"Well, once we get the new lines laid and don't have any more sewage going into the hole, it will clean itself up. But it will take a while. Frank's ordered fencing for the whole thing; it's the only way we can keep people from trying to kill themselves." He stiffened, then dropped Lila Mae's hand and sprinted ahead to where two young boys were climbing the barriers. "Stop right where you are, boys!" he yelled.

They jumped down and stood looking guilty. "We wasn't doing anything," one of them protested.

"Yes, you were. You were disobeying your parents, for one thing," Odlum warned. "Bobby, if you got in there and drowned, how do you think your mother would feel?"

The boy looked at his shoes and scuffled his feet. "She'd feel pretty bad, I guess."

Lila Mae caught up with them. "Evening, boys."

"Evening, Mrs. Warner," they piped.

"You know what will happen if you get into that water?" she asked.

"No, ma'am."

"Well, you'd get typhoid scarlet cholera, and that's deadly; there isn't any way to cure anyone of that. So you'd die. Does that make any sense?"

"My dad says that antibiotics will cure anything, even the crud," the other lad piped up.

"Well, your dad is wrong about this." Odlum smiled. "You get typhoid scarlet cholera, you're a dead duck. I won't call your parents this time, but the next time I catch you trying to climb those barriers, you're out of luck. Now go on home. You're too young to be out after dark."

The youngsters climbed on their bicycles and took off.

Lila Mae shook her head. "Boy, talk about an attractive nuisance! What if people climb the fence after it's up?"

"Frank ordered that really wicked barbed wire to top it. I don't think anyone will try to get past it. If they do, they belong in an insane asylum."

"You reckon the sides will ever look natural? I mean, like a lake?"

Odlum looked down at her. "That can be done with equipment, Lila Mae. What do you have in mind?"

"Well, I was thinking that when the water is cleaner and doesn't smell so awful, we could really turn this into a nice park in the middle of town. Plant the palm trees that we voted to buy, buy out a little more space and grass it over, make a tourist attraction out of the hole. I suppose it's one of the biggest sinkholes in the state; that ought to be worth something."

"What about funds to buy the land you'll need?" Odlum leaned down to pick up a warning sign that had been knocked down and leaned it against the barrier.

"I guess I could talk to the ladies in the garden club, get them to help out with fund-raisers. And maybe the women in Joe's church would give a hand. If they can raise the money, so much the better. It'll give them a sense of accomplishment." She sighed.

"What's wrong?"

"Nothing. I just got to meet with Henny day after tomorrow and work out a settlement. I'm going to keep him on at the restaurant; the customers just love his cooking. And I have to find a real place to live. I like having my own place, not a rented house."

Odlum cleared his throat. "You could stay out at my place permanently, after your divorce is final."

"Oh, I couldn't do that, sugar, because it would look bad. Not that I wouldn't love to," she added hastily.

"Well, it wouldn't look bad if you were Mrs. Dreyfus Odlum, would it?"

She smiled at him. "You been waiting a long time to say that, haven't you?"

"Sure have, Lila Mae."

"Well, then, I guess I have something to look forward to," she said.

"The bastards have done it again!" Gavel Strike exclaimed as he burst into the kitchen at the Fawkins residence.

"Done what?" Sally cried, alarmed.

"Dumped sand on the flats down at the river mouth. An enormous amount of it, this time. Looks like about thirty truckloads."

Kelsey grinned and wiped her hands. "That is great!"

"What's great about it?" he asked. He opened a cupboard, took out a glass, and went to the refrigerator to get cold water.

"You forget the camera, Gavel," Sally said.

"I had," he admitted.

Kelsey went into the hallway and called Guy at his office. "We've got more sand on the flat. Shall we collect the equipment?"

"Yes!" Guy exclaimed. "Take the whole lot over to Photomania and get them to develop the film. Tell 'em we need it yesterday. I want to find out who the jerk is, really badly."

"Okay. We're off. I'll see you after work." She hung up and went back into the kitchen. "Come on, guys, we're off to the races."

The turnabout at the end of Hatchacootee Boulevard was deserted. Kelsey led the way onto the little peninsula of high ground. When they reached the tree where the camera and battery pack were hidden, she pointed upward. "You have to climb up, Gavel. Tree climbing is not one of my talents, and Sally is under doctor's orders to play it cool for a while. Up you go."

"Okay," he said. He started up the tree. "I haven't done this since I was a kid," he told them. "What if I fall?"

"From that height? We'll just move aside so you don't smash us," Kelsey said. "It must be all of ten feet."

"Yeah, but I'm delicate," he rejoined. He leaned down and handed her the camera. "Now I'll get the battery pack," he said.

A few minutes later he was down the tree again. "Look out there at all that sand. I can't wait to find out who's dumping it. Come on, let's go. The sooner we get the film to Photomania, the sooner we'll have our perp."

"Our what?" Sally asked.

"Perpetrator," Kelsey said, laughing. "I forgot to warn you, Sally, that Gavel loves detective novels."

CHAPTER TWENTY THREE

Mayor Melba Tosti pulled her bright purple wig tighter to her head, cleared her throat, gave her new gavel a tentative tap, and then banged it. "The meeting of the City Council of the City of Sunshine will now come to order." She then looked upward and intoned, "All rise for the Invocation and the Pledge of Allegiance." After a quick glance to make certain the camera beamed her image, she rose.

Josephus Tyler shook himself in preparation for the prayer. He closed his red-rimmed eyes and clasped hands beneath his layered chin. "Lord God, Maker of all things, Knower of all sins, we humbly beseech Thee to lead us to do Thy will while we attend the business of the City of Sunshine." His voice assumed the cadence of the pulpit and he squeezed his eyes tighter shut. "Help us, Lord, to avoid the terrible pitfalls of power! Guide our thoughts, Lord, to Thy ways, that we might prosper. We have been humbled by Thy might, Lord, and we are heartily sorry for our transgressions. Lead us into the path of riches, Lo–I mean, lead us into the path of righteousness, for there are those among us who wallow in iniquity, Lord." He opened one eye to see if Melba was going to kick him as usual, but her foot stayed where it belonged. His voice rose. "They have backslidden until there is no hope! Help us to walk in Thy path all the days of our lives, Amen." He opened his eyes, smiled at Melba, spun to face the flag, clapped his hand to his heart, and froze again. "Why don't we have a flag yet, Frank?"

Bonano's right hand stayed on the desk. "We are supposed to get delivery of the new flags in about three weeks' time, Councilman Tyler. I apologize."

"You don't need the flag to say the pledge, for chrissake!" Merlini said. "Just go on and say it. We got a long agenda."

"Oh, all right." Tyler placed his hand over his heart and began. The voices of the citizens in the chamber followed in faltering cadence.

Melba tidied her papers and gave the technical people in the chamber a nod. "Everyone here? Fine. Now, I need a motion to adopt the minutes of the last meeting."

"Got it."

"Second."

"All in favor?" Ayes all around. "Motion passes."

Lila Mae pushed her microphone aside and said to Merlini, "Do you think she tries to look like a freak, or that she's color blind?"

Merlini snorted. "One thing she ain't, and that's colorless. For chrissake, what's she coming up with next–polka dots?"

The mayor shot him a warning look. "We are in session, Councilman Merlini. Would you mind awfully if we went on with business?"

"Not at all, Mzzzz. Mayor. Go right ahead."

Bonano's eyebrows shot up. Something was wrong.

"No, a Black Watch plaid to match that suit she has," Lila Mae whispered.

"Councilman Warner, do you mind paying attention?"

"If you quit fussing and get on with the business, I'll be glad to pay attention," Lila Mae shot back. "You're the chairman, not my mother."

Several of the onlookers laughed.

Mayor Tosti pulled her wig tighter to her head and frowned. "Are there any financial matters?"

Bonano raised a finger. "Would you like a report on what's been done so far, Madam Mayor?"

"I would not. When everything is taken care of, then you can compile one report and send it to us by courier so that we can inspect it at our leisure. We are very busy peo–"

"Might I ask why we cannot hear an update on the ongoing repairs?" Rainmaker asked nastily. "Is it your dislike for our city manager, or sheer stupidity, that presses you to ignore this very serious matter?"

"Point of order!" Tyler rumbled. "You quit insulting Melba, Pervert."

"I would like to have an update on what is happening," Rainmaker said stubbornly. "Madam Mayor, I ask that we vote on this."

Melba glared at him. "Very well. We have a motion on the floor to hear an update. Do I hear a second?"

"I second," Lila Mae said quickly.

"All in favor?" Two ayes, three nays. "Motion defeated." She smirked at Rainmaker, who rolled his eyes.

"Before you leap to your feet and do your victory dance, are we going to hear an update on the sewer problem, or are you pissed off with Mr. Odlum as well?"

The mayor chewed her lips savagely, then smiled brightly as the camera's eye swung toward her. "We will hear that, certainly, Councilman, but under old business."

"Thank you, Madam Mayor."

"Are there any items to be removed from the consent agenda?"

"None, Madam Mayor," Bonano said.

"Do I hear a motion to adopt the consent agenda?"

"Got it."

"Second."

"All in favor?" Ayes all around. "The motion passes."

Merlini leered at Lila Mae, who had come to the meeting dressed in a long skirt slit halfway up the thigh, and a tailored silk blouse. "You sure are wearing some different clothes."

"Yes, I am, Meats. Do you like this blouse?"

"Yeah, but I like the skirt more. I never knew you had legs that went up so high."

"Meats, you really are a dirty old man."

"Councilman Merlini, please pay attention."

Merlini tore his eyes away from Lila Mae's equipage. "Certainly, Mzzzz. Mayor. My apologies."

"Next on the agenda are the councilmen's items and—"

"Madam Mayor," Rainmaker said, "we have people here from the DEP who need to get on with their jobs, and folks from the water management district who have reports to give us. Can't we hear them before this next item so they don't have to sit through the entire meeting?"

Mayor Tosti smiled brightly at the visitors. "Of course, Councilman Rainmaker. A grand suggestion. Who wants to report first?"

Frank Bonano raised a finger. "Madam Mayor, we have Ralph Frink from the DEP to give us a report on the water in the sinkhole. With your permission, I'll ask him to go first."

"Mr. Frink, we would love to hear from you."

Frink rose and went to the lectern. "Madam Mayor, Councilmen, I am Ralph Frink with the Department of Environmental Protection. Without any preamble, I want to tell you that we have a serious threat to public health in that new lake of yours. The water is fouled beyond belief with sewage, and the lake must be fenced off to keep people away until the health threat is gone.

"There are a couple of ways you can address the problem other than fencing, but I think you'll find that they're mighty expensive. Lime could be brought in and dumped into the water, which would raise the pH level and destroy the bacteria. The problem is how much lime you'd have to dump in there to do the job. The cost would be astronomical." He nodded as Rainmaker raised his hand. "Yes, Councilman Rainmaker?"

"Can this problem be left to take care of itself? Will the water eventually clear?"

"Yes, sir, it can be left alone, and that's what we're recommending. Fence off the lake, keep the public away from the water, and we'll check it again in six months' time and see what we have. Mr. Odlum has told me that they'll have the new sewer lines operational in about a month, and once there's no more fresh sewage going into the water, gradual bacteria death will occur. Are there any questions?"

"Why can't we fill the hole with concrete and dirt?" Tyler asked. "I don't like the looks of that hole in the ground. It certainly doesn't add anything to the city."

Bonano signaled the mayor. She ignored him. He cleared his throat and rose, but she still refused to acknowledge him.

"Give me strength," Rainmaker muttered. "Frank, you want to say something?"

"Point of order!" Tyler thundered. "He hasn't been recognized."

"Joe, quit trying to start a fight," Lila Mae warned. "I don't see how we're going to get through this meeting if Madam Mayor keeps acting like an idiot."

The gavel crashed. "Order! Speak, Bonano," Tosti ground out.

"I did some calculations, Councilman Tyler," Bonano said. "We would need about a half million cubic yards of concrete or dirt to fill that hole, and then we'd have a flood. The water is so contaminated that we can't pump it into the river, so there's nowhere for it to go."

"Half a million cubic yards!" Merlini cried. "Holy sh— moley."

"Mr. Frink," Mayor Tosti said, "might we use that water for public supply? It would certainly save us a bundle. We presently buy water from the county."

"No, Madam Mayor, that is not possible. Of course, you could install a reverse osmosis plant and clean it up with really good filters, but it would cost millions, and you'd run out of water."

"How could we run out of water?" the mayor asked. "It rains all the time, and there's water down in the aquifer, I believe."

"Do you mind if we refer to Mr. Pavlov from the water management district on this matter?"

The mayor nodded to the young man, who rose and went to the lectern. "Good morning, Madam Mayor, Councilmen. I am Nick Pavlov from the West Coastal Water Management District. You would not be allowed to pump either the lake or the aquifer in this area, because of salt water intrusion.

"First, the water in the lake is too dirty to clean up, in my opinion. It will foul the aquifer as it is, but fortunately, the lateral movement is toward the river, and so the nutrients will eventually end up in the Gulf, as they do now."

"Why is the salt water coming in?" Merlini asked.

"Heart County is guilty there, I'm afraid, Councilman. They have over-pumped for years to fuel their growth, and it has taken its toll."

"I think we ought to sue them," Merlini said to the council. "Sue the bastards right now."

"Meats!" Lila Mae cautioned. "You're on television."

He shoved the microphone aside. "It don't matter; they got a bleeper. I can say what I want."

"What's lateral movement?" Mayor Tosti asked.

"The way the water moves underground," Mr. Pavlov explained.

"It moves sideways, Melba," Lila Mae explained. "Like a crab."

"I am impressed with your scientific mind, Councilman Warner," the mayor sneered. "Thank you for your dissertation."

"I never touch dessert, Melba, and I wish you'd stick to one subject. I thought we were talking about water, not about food." She whispered to Merlini, "That'll pay her back for that purple wig."

"So we're stuck with the hole in the ground, no matter how we cut it," the mayor summed up.

"Yes, Madam Mayor, I'm afraid you are. Are there any further questions?"

"No, thank you, Mr. Pavlov. Did you have anything further to add? I mean, since you're standing there, you might as well give us your report."

"Nothing more than to tell you that you have a very contaminated brackish lake of two hundred thirty point three acres. I believe it's one of the largest sinkholes in the state. Thank you." He returned to his seat.

"Mr. Frink, I apologize for keeping you there. Is there anything further you wish to say?"

"Yes, Madam Mayor, there is. Sunshine is very lucky in that the sinkhole has made it necessary for the DEP to accept a certain amount of contamination in the Hatchacootee River for some time to come. The state is fortunate in that FEMA has come in and helped you to replace a decrepit sewer system with one that conforms to code."

"Why is the state so lucky?" Merlini interrupted rudely.

"Because we won't have to waste public funds to take you to court, Councilman."

The mayor smiled brightly; the camera was focused on the dais again. "Next on the agenda is Councilmen's items. District A?"

Lila Mae Warner pulled her microphone close. Her touch sent an eerie squeal through the room. She winced. "That's about how I feel. Sorry. Madam Mayor, I don't have anything to report except that citizens are complaining that everything's moving too slow. I just keep telling them that Rome wasn't rebuilt in a day. Thank you."

"District B?"

"Ditto."

"That is hardly a report, Councilman," the mayor chided gently.

"Ain't any sense in repeating what Lila Mae said, Mzzzz. Mayor."

"Thank you. District C?"

"Yes, Madam Mayor, I have something to report. Some of our citizens protested last week in front of City Hall because of our discussion about razing Mosquito–"

"They got no right to protest, Pervert," Tyler said loudly. "When their betters make a deci–"

"I do not consider you one of their betters, Councilman Tyler," Rainmaker snapped.

"Go to hell!" Tyler snarled. "And it ain't your district, so it's none of your business."

"Weren't you compared to Hitler in the press? Doesn't that tell you something about your attitude?" Rainmaker asked.

"You–!"

"Order!" The gavel crashed.

"Madam Mayor, I have the floor," Rainmaker said. "Can you control God's ape so that I might continue my report?"

"Joe, let him finish so we can get this over," the mayor said.

"I've met with some of the folks in Mosquito Row," Rainmaker continued, "and they want some help from the city to improve conditions their area. Mr. Granita said that the only city personnel they ever see are the meter readers and the cops, who harass them continually for no good reason. That doesn't speak well for the way we treat our citizens."

"They don't pay enough taxes for us to look after them! And they are hardened criminals. You look how often our valiant police have to go down there," Tyler howled. "They deserve the slum they live in, that's what I say."

"If every citizen had to shell out for his individual protection, Tyler, we wouldn't have a society at all." Rainmaker bored his behind into his chair. "You are supposed to be a leader in this community, so lead for a change. Make changes. Do something besides looking out for your own good!"

"I'm afraid that such assistance in Mosquito Row is out of the question, Councilman Rainmaker. We would tear out the bottom of the public purse, and as you have said many times before, we must be fiscally conservative. Render unto Caesar what it takes to call the tune." The mayor's tone was final.

Rainmaker covered his face and moaned. "That is all I have, Madam Mayor."

The mayor gave him a triumphant smile. "District D?"

"The Pervert has already given my report," Tyler rumbled. "Let's get on with the meeting."

"Next on the agenda is old business. Any old business?"

"Yes!" Tyler said quickly. "The ordinance to ban dog walking."

"Joe, I don't see how we can pass that ordinance," Lila Mae said. "You ever try to train a dog to use the toilet? Or to get into a litter box? They got to get out to do their duty."

"It is up to dog owners to teach their pets responsibility." Tyler replied in a cold voice.

"Fiscal responsibility too?" Lila Mae asked.

Merlini stared at her. What was going on? They had never talked about dogs being fiscally responsible, had they? He was confused. He leaned across Lila Mae's fabulous bosom. "Melba, what's going on?"

The mayor moved her microphone aside. "I don't know." Then she spotted a reporter from the *Tampa Tribune* in the back of the auditorium and twiddled her fingers at him. "Do I hear a motion on this item?" she asked briskly.

"I move that we pass the ordinance," Tyler thundered.

"Second," Merlini said.

"All in favor?" Three ayes, two nays. "The motion passes. Mr. Slugge, would you be kind enough to draw up the ordinance for us?"

Slugge nodded and made a note.

"Next under old business is the Liars' Festival," the mayor said. "I want a motion to cancel it. We have pressing matters to attend."

"You got it," Merlini said.

"Second."

"All in favor?"

"Madam Mayor, point of order. We have had no chance to discuss the matter."

Rainmaker sounded tired.

"There's nothing to discuss, Pervert."

"All in favor?" Three ayes, two nays. "The motion passes. Bonano, I understand that you made unauthorized expenditures on this matter–posters and the like. In the future, you must get permission from this council before wasting the peoples' hard-earned dollars. Is that clear?"

"Madam Mayor, under the city charter, I am not required to consult the council on day-to-day matters, and I will continue to operate as I am empowered to do by the charter. In any event, Madam Mayor, permit me to remind you that this council did authorize the expenditure in memorandum number eight of April 6. This memo came over your signature."

"Are you going to argue with me?" Melba screeched.

Bonano said nothing.

"Answer me, you–!" Then she remembered the reporter in the back of the room. "Thank you, Mr. Bonano." She adjusted her wig and smiled at the camera. "And now we're going to take up new business, and I have some simply fabulous new business to discuss. We are going to expand! Isn't that exciting?"

"Are we pregnant, Madam Mayor," Lila Mae asked.

The audience began laughing.

Melba frowned. "Very funny, Councilman Warner. A secret consortium is going to develop those two ranches just outside town, and build homes for our poor citizens who lost theirs in our recent tragedy. Isn't that grand?"

"I fail to see how this perfectly wonderful news is going to affect Sunshine," Rainmaker said. "Those ranches are not within city limits."

"Well, they will be," Mayor Tosti snapped.

"Are you proposing annexation?" Rainmaker's eyebrows were almost at his hairline.

"I am."

"You mean that you intend starting a war with the county?"

"Screw the county!" the mayor snarled.

"Sounds like that's just what you intend to do," Rainmaker said. "After all the help they've given us, I don't think it's a very nice gesture. But I can see your point–we have to bring our tax base back to normal. I just hope the county understands."

"I want a motion to annex those ranches as soon as the land deal is approved."

"What land deal?" Rainmaker asked.

"Yes, what deal are you talking abut, and how are we going to know when that's done?" Lila Mae asked.

"I believe our attorney is handling the matter," the mayor said brightly. "Aren't you, Mr. Slugge?"

He gave her a warning look. "Yes, Madam Mayor, our firm has been chosen by the consortium to handle their end of the matter."

"And just where is this consortium from?" Rainmaker asked.

"They wish to remain totally anonymous, Councilman Rainmaker," Slugge said smoothly. "Naturally, I will accommodate their wishes."

"Why?"

"Why would I accommo–?"

"Why would they wish to remain totally anonymous? Usually developers come to the council or the commission, whatever the case, and brag about how much their efforts will enhance the lives of–blah blah blah. This group piques my curiosity."

"They are very high profile, and don't wish their competitors to know of their interest in the area," Slugge replied.

"You built them a Chinese wall?" McGinnis yelled from the back of the chamber.

"Order! You may only speak during public comment." The mayor looked hard at Merlini and Tyler. "I want a motion to annex that property."

"You got it," Merlini said.

"Second."

"All in favor?" Four ayes, one nay. "Motion passes."

"I think we've just been had," Lila Mae muttered. She was surprised that Merlini didn't agree with her. He usually did.

"Now, we're ready for public comment," the mayor said. "Anyone wishing to speak may have three minutes." She frowned as Jorge Granita came forward.

"Please state your name and address."

"My name is Jorge Granita. I live in Mosquito Row and—"

"Do you pay taxes?" Tyler growled.

"Mr. Tyler, I remember you from last week; why you cannot remember me? I pay taxes, I am a citizen. Councilmen, all we want is for the sides of the roads to be cleaned and fixed so they empty when it rains. All the rain comes into the houses there because there are no drains. We have no drug problem down there, but the police go to the houses and threaten people. They tear up property. Just last night they wake up an old woman and tell her she will go to jail. What we ask don't cost a lot of money. If the police leave us alone, the city will save money."

Lila Mae pushed her microphone aside. "Why would the cops go down there if there's no problem?" she asked Merlini.

Merlini snorted.

"You said something?" the mayor asked politely.

"Yeah, Mzzzz. Mayor, I said that it is low down there; my plant is close to the area. We could use some drainage."

"Thank you, Councilman Merlini," Granita said. He went back to his seat.

"Hey, you're welcome," Merlini shouted after him.

The mayor glared at him. "Next?"

Old McGinnis hobbled forward. "Harold McGinnis, 2244 Flowerpetal Drive, Sunshine. I want to know when we're going to have power and water over at our place. It's high time that you people get the finger out; we've been inconvenienced long enough."

Stony silence.

"Y'all can sit there like bumps on a log, but I think we should get some answers," he said stubbornly. He turned to face Odlum. "Oddman, can you tell me what I want to know?"

"Certainly. We're expecting to hook you back up in about three days. That's for electricity and water. Sewer doesn't matter because you're on septic tanks out there. Anything happens, I'll let you know."

"Thanks." McGinnis turned back to the council. "He should be sitting where you are. At least he knows his butt from a hole in the ground." Grumbling, the old man returned to his seat.

"Any further public comment?" the mayor said icily.

Gavel Strike strode down the aisle.

Lila Mae sighed. "Worms again, I'll bet."

Strike smiled at her and gave his name and address. "You're right, Councilman Warner. Worms again. More sand has been dumped at the mouth of the river, and I'm asking that the city make some effort to stop the person who is doing it. I ask this for two good reasons: it's against the law, and it is the duty of the city government to enforce the law, and it is damaging the feeding ground for our wild bird population.

"Most places would give anything to have the diversity of wild birds that flock to our delta, but this city continues to ignore what could become a viable incentive for tourists to flock to Sunshine. Maybe the only way to get you people to respond is by pointing out some way you can make a buck from it. Folks love birds. Do something with that idea."

"You're very cordial today, Mr. Strike," the mayor said.

"I am always cordial, Madam Mayor, when I'm not dealing with fools."

"Does this mean that you no longer consider us fools?" Melba asked.

"No, it does not. I am merely containing my contempt by wielding an incredible amount of willpower."

Merlini snorted.

"You have no right to criticize your betters," Tyler snapped.

"I have one further matter to bring to your attention. A friend of mine was recently beaten badly. Although she made a report to the police, Rufus Hicks has flatly refused to investigate. I think you need to take a close look at how your police department operates, and who gives Hicks order. And this is a job for the council, not for Frank Bonano. There's something pretty rotten in this city, and it's time the rot was cleared out. Thank you."

He stalked to the back of the chamber and resumed his seat.

"What on earth is he talking about?" Lila Mae asked. "Is Rufus here?"

"No, he's not here to defend himself," Tyler said hotly. "But then, bug-smoochers only pounce when there's no one around to stop them."

"Oh." Lila Mae sighed. "I do wish you'd talk some sense, Joe. I never saw anybody kiss a bug yet, especially Gavel Strike."

Someone in the back of the room snickered.

"Any further public comment?"

A stony silence from the back of the room.

The mayor shrugged. "I need a motion to adjourn."

The meeting was adjourned.

CHAPTER TWENTY FOUR

6 Florida/State _ The Tampa Tribune

SUNSHINE TO ANNEX PART OF BANTER COUNTY

Sunshine: At the regular meeting of City Council, Mayor Melba Tosti announced the council's intention to annex almost a thousand acres of Banter County. The annexation will bring into the city limits a new development, Lost Horizon.

This move on Mayor Tosti's part took some of the members of the council by surprise. "First word I've heard of it," Councilman Lila Mae Warner said. "But then, the mayor is always springing things on us. It's almost as if we don't exist."

Theodore Rainmaker, another council member, was chagrined by the announcement. "We have to rebuild the tax base, so I voted for it. But we have always had a good relationship with the county and recently, they helped the city deal with the sinkhole that swallowed a good portion of downtown Sunshine. I don't think this back-stabbing is the way to go, but we don't seem to have much choice."

Fred Baron, Banter County's administrator, was outspoken in his opposition to the plan. "They want to steal a part of the county? I'll send them a bill for the services we've rendered so far. Can't allow insubordination in the ranks, you know."

But this latest move by Sunshine's council was offset by business as usual. At the same meeting, the council voted, three to two, to ban dogs walking out of doors in Sunshine. Councilmen Warner, citing the difficulty in training dogs to use litter boxes and toilets, voted against the ordinance, as did Councilman Rainmaker.

The council heard a report by a representative of the Department of Environmental Protection. The city will be required to fence off the two hundred thirty acre sinkhole that swallowed the new city center several weeks ago. Broken sewer mains have leaked into the water that has risen in the sinkhole, giving rise to concerns about public health and safety.

For more information on the sinkhole, go to our Web site http://www.tribune.fla.tda.sinkhole

---

16 April, 2

Frank Bonano, City Manager
The City of Sunshine
436 Monroe Street
Sunshine, Florida 3766580

Dear Frank:

I read with interest the article in the Tampa Tribune regarding Sunshine's plans to annex the Folder and Hyman ranches. As you are no doubt aware, this will remove some thousand acres of county land from the tax rolls.

In view of the recent expense that the county has borne because of the sinkhole in Sunshine, we consider this annexation as an act of aggression. It will be dealt with summarily. We will not tolerate raids across our border.

I realize that you must get your tax rolls back to there they were, but this annexation is not the way to do it. There is plenty of land in Sunshine that can be better utilized. I would suggest that you encourage the developers to look at the land north and east of what was the new city center. The run down homes in those areas should be bought out and razed to clean up your camp.

Sunshine is not the only municipality in Banter County. Were the other towns and cities to follow your example, there would be no Banter County left. We will defend our integrity, have no doubt of that.

I must warn you that if the council continues with this annexation, you will bring down the wrath of the county. We are mustering the troops.

Warm regards.

Fred

Page 2–The Flag City Gazette–

Flag City: Fowler Dayes, Chairman of the Banter County Commission, said at a press conference today that if the City of Sunshine thinks it can get away with what Tampa did at the end of the '90's, they're sadly mistaken. Banter County, he stressed, is here to stay.

"They think they had trouble when their new city hall dropped into a deep hole? They haven't seen trouble yet. We will fight any attempt to take over Banter County in Tallahassee. We will go to Washington, if necessary, to keep their greedy hands off our territory. Pretty soon there'll be no Banter County, no county commission, nothing but Sunshine silliness. We will not take this matter lying down. I see Mayor Tosti's plan very clearly," Dayes warned. "Let her beware."

County Commission member Christine Suggs warned that if Sunshine tries to annex any part of the county, she will recommend that the county funding for the library in Sunshine be discontinued. She also said that Sunshine would be billed for every cent the county had spent assisting the city, and that assistance to schools within the city be abandoned.

Commissioner Marlowe Fips suggested that the county discontinue its assistance to the roads jointly financed with the City of Sunshine. He asked the County Administrator, Fred Baron, to total everything the county spends on Sunshine. "We'll cut off every red cent," Fips said. "And if they don't like it, let 'em eat cake."

Mayor Tosti could not be reached for comment.

Florida House of Representatives
Representative Henry Bates

Frank Bonano, City Manager
The City of Sunshine
436 Monroe Street
Sunshine, Florida 3766580

<u>Private and Confidential</u>

Dear Frank:

I have received a number of calls from citizens who live outside the city limits about Sunshine's annexation of the two ranches. These people are concerned that the city administration might have plans to annex a larger portion of unincorporated Banter, thereby raising their taxes.

Can you let me know what's taking place? I realize that it's hard to know what goes on under Melba's hairpieces, but could you make some tentative forays and find out her plans? (I use the term, 'foray' because Fred Baron blind copied to me the letter he sent to you)– mustering the troops, indeed!

Councilman Merlini called me yesterday and assured me that he had found the means to build the museum on the history of meat. He will build it himself. His conversation was somewhat garbled, but it usually is. Either he's more confused than ever, or they use very strange syntax in Brooklyn. I thought you should be warned ahead of time. He spoke of locating the museum in some lost place!

Sorry to add to your already full plate, old friend. I think of you daily, and you are in my prayers.

Warm regards.

                                          High fives,
                                          Sandfly

Guy opened the envelope containing the prints. He spread them on the kitchen table and then went into his study to get a magnifying glass.

Kelsey called Sally to come downstairs. "We've got the prints, so come on. Now we'll know who the perp is, as Gavel would say."

Sally came hurrying down, grinning. "Should we call Gavel?"

"Guy called him from Photomania. He's on the way."

"I can't wait to see who it is."

Both of them went into the kitchen and watched impatiently as Guy carefully checked the photos with his magnifying glass. Aware of their curiosity, Guy slowed down his perusal to frustrate them. Finally Kelsey could stand it no longer.

"What do you see, for crying out loud!"

"I see a truck out on the flats, but its taillights are to the camera, so I can't see what's printed on the side panels. Damn it! I was sure this would work."

"Didn't you get them to blow up the prints?" Sally asked.

"Yes, but the blowups aren't going to show anything more." Disgusted, Guy tossed the magnifying glass on the photograph and sighed.

Sally grabbed the magnifying glass and leaned over the table. Then she smiled and looked up at Kelsey. "Men are so dumb!"

Guy shrugged and went to the refrigerator. "I need a Coke. Anyone want one?"

"What do you see?" Kelsey asked. "Yes, Guy, please get one for me. Sally?"

"No thanks. I see a license plate, and if we can run it through a scanner and enlarge it, we'll have the perp."

Guy set down his glass and hurried to the table. "Let me see that!" He peered at the photograph, then straightened up and grabbed his car keys from the counter. "I'll be right back; keep Gavel here. I'll run to the office and follow our sleuth's suggestion."

After he had gone, Sally sat at the kitchen table. "I found an apartment. It was hard, with so many people having to camp out until there are houses built, but I found one."

"Where?"

"Over a garage out on Merriweather Drive. The folks that built the place had a relative living up there, but now it's unused. They're cleaning it up and repainting, so I'll be out of your hair pretty soon."

"Any word from Dee to your lawyer on a settlement?"

"Not a peep. Suits me. I'll just continue using my credit cards and the bank account until everything's settled. But I need some things from the house, so I'm going in there tonight. He'll be working late, and then he'll go somewhere for dinner, so I won't run into him."

"Want me to come with you?"

"Kelsey, you and Guy have done enough. I'll be perfectly all right. It'll take me an hour or so, so you all can have some privacy."

Kelsey's brow furrowed. "I don't like you going there alone."

"He won't touch me again; I won't give him any reason."

"Sally, you're defying him; can't you see that? He's a control freak, that's pretty obvious. You're taking an awful chance."

Sally hugged her. "I'll be fine; don't worry."

"It's because I'm short, ain't it?" Sitting hunched over the table, Henny scowled, reminding Lila Mae more than ever of an armadillo.

"What, Henny?"

"I hear you're seeing somebody, somebody tall and thin." He picked up the morning paper he had discarded earlier in the day and began looking through it for the comics page.

"Tall and thin must mean Oddman, and I do see him every day, Henny. He's the director of utilities."

"That ain't what I mean. Are you having an affair with him?"

"That's not your business."

"Hell it ain't! You're my wife until we're divorced, and it don't look right, your running around when you're still married."

"You jealous?" she asked, incredulous. He had not touched her in three years.

"Hell no, I ain't jealous. But I got a call from the Saved Sons Society telling me I should straighten you out good and proper. Makes me look like a fool, that's all. And if I look like a fool, it'll hurt business. The Saved Sons are calling you a Jezebel, Lila Mae, ain't you ashamed? They said I should beat the devil out of you." He half rose, then thought better of it and sat back down.

"You tell your holy buddies that if you ever laid a hand on me, you'd wake up dead," she said flatly, "and then I might go after them. Now, we got together to talk about how to settle the property, so let's get on with it. I want you to keep the house; you worked hard enough to pay for it. And I want you to run the restaurant. You can pay me rent on the property, and a quarter of the profits–after all, it was my family's restaurant. So you'll be in business for yourself."

"I want fifty percent!" he demanded.

"Fifty percent of what?"

"Of everything. I was reading in the paper this morning about some movie star having to shell out fifty percent for palimony, and I think I got a right to the same thing."

Lila Mae shook her head. "Henny, you have never been a pal in your whole life, or a companion, or a husband, for that matter. You're just a cook; food is the only thing you're interested in."

"What's wrong with that? Everybody has to eat or they'll die, and if you can make money out of it, fine. And food don't want fancy dresses to keep up with the mayor."

"See what I mean?"

"What about your salary that you make as a councilman? I should get a cut of that, too."

"You want half a string of poofs?" she asked coldly.

"A what?"

"That's what you said, isn't it?–that my salary as councilman didn't amount to a string of poofs."

He scratched his head, confused. "No, I said 'a string of farts,' but what's farting got to do with this?"

"I never could figure that out myself–thought it was just you being you again."

"What?"

"Never mind," Lila Mae said tiredly. "Let's finish this; I got other fish to fry."

"Speaking of fish, I got some really pretty catfish yesterday," Henny said with enthusiasm. "They're frying up nice and crisp."

"Henny, you okay with what I laid out?"

"You mean, I pay you rent and a piece of the profit, and keep the house?"

"Yeah."

He wiggled his shoulders, glanced at the comics page with obvious longing, and shrugged. "I suppose so. I need to get a lawyer?"

"No, not if you agree. My lawyer can take care of the papers." She was so happy to be escaping the deadly boredom of marriage with Henny that she felt guilty, really guilty about the way she was treating him. But on the other hand, she thought he deserved it.

There had never been any real affection between them. What she first perceived as love had merely been lust, and that short-lived. And after her unfulfilled lust there had been years of drudging sameness: the same thing for breakfast, day after day, the same offer of fish or chicken for lunch, Henny's same free-fall into bed at night, snoring the moment his head touched the pillow, the same armadillo at the breakfast table the next morning.

Were all marriages so boring?–she wondered. Did men turn into zombies the moment they wed? Oddman was upset over her reluctance to marry again. She would have to explain how she felt, try to make him understand that she could not spend the rest of her life facing the crushing sameness she had known with Henny.

How would it be with Oddman? He was so sweet, so considerate, and amazingly, a passionate lover. He was wonderful, but would marriage change all that? After a while, would he grow to look like an armadillo at breakfast too? She hadn't been out to his house yet, but he had suggested that she come out this weekend and she was thinking hard about it. No one in her new neighborhood paid much attention to her, and they would assume, if they saw she was gone overnight, that she was out of town on city business. Councilmen did travel from time to time.

Of course, she had driven by Oddman's home on numerous occasions on her way to Tallahassee, but she had seen only trees; the house wasn't visible from the road. If it was that private, maybe they could make love in the grass. She had always fantasized about making love outdoors, under the sky. But such fantasies stayed fantasy on Florida's west coast. If you lay in the grass to make love, fire ants would eat you alive.

He had talked about his home with obvious enthusiasm–how he waked each morning to a chorus of birdsong, and sat on his back porch watching the sun make its slow way through the leaves above. He sounded almost like a poet when he talked like that.

"...do when you come to the restaurant for dinner?"

"Huh?"

"I said, do I charge you regular price when you come to the restaurant for dinner?"

She laughed shortly. "Of course, Henny. You'll be in business for yourself, and you got to share some of the profits with me, so you'll have to charge me like everyone else." But she wondered if she would ever eat in Southern Fried again. She had eaten enough fried fish, barbecue, fried chicken, and the like, to last her all her days.

Guy came in through the back door, an expression of triumph on his face. "We got the bastard!"

"Who is he?" Gavel asked.

"Fielding."

Sally pulled out a chair and sat at the kitchen table. "Come on, Guy, sit down and tell us how you found out."

They all sat but Kelsey, who went to get the two men beer. "You want a glass of wine, Sally?"

"Yes, let's celebrate."

When Kelsey came back to sit, Guy grinned. "I ran the photo through the scanner, then blew up that piece of it until I could read it, called the police department and told them I had just dented the truck and wanted to leave a note so the owner could contact me. They were cooperative as they could be. The woman asked my name and I made up something to satisfy her. But it's Fielding's truck, and he really dumped the sand down there this time."

"When did he do it? That's what I want to know," Sally said.

"Probably just after dark. The place smells so bad that it's usually deserted anyway, but after dark, there wouldn't be anyone to see what went on. Haven't you heard the rumor going around that the whole Hatchacootee is going to sink and form something akin to the Grand Canyon?" Gavel laughed. "The Grand Canyon, yet!"

"Well, it would be interesting," Sally said. "Think what a field day the press would have with something like that."

"It boggles the mind," Kelsey said. "So now what do we do?"

"I'm going to get the DEP involved again. We've got a name for them, the night photographs, the digitalization, everything. I'll get hold of Don Sarious in Tallahassee first thing tomorrow and see what they'll do about it." Guy gathered the photos and put them in an envelope, along with everything else.

"When is next full moon?" Gavel asked.

Sally looked at the calendar on the wall. "Three days from now."

"Well," he drawled, "Mr. Sarious had better shake a leg if he wants to see it personally. What I don't understand is why he keeps on dumping sand down there. If the first lot washed away, the second will too, but in the meantime, he's destroying a lot of the Polychaeta."

"Who knows what motivates developers?" Kelsey said.
"I do," her husband answered promptly. "The green stuff."

CHAPTER TWENTY FIVE

Just after dark, Sally parked in the drive of the neighboring house and went quickly across the lawn to the hedge that separated the two properties. She and her neighbor, Marge, had made a little gap in the hedge so they could slip back and forth for morning coffee and, amazingly, the landscaping committee on Merriweather Drive had never discovered it.

There was a light in Dee's study, but his car wasn't in the drive where he always parked it, so she dismissed the glow from the window as she glided silently to the back door. Cautious, she let herself into the kitchen entrance, left the door slightly ajar, and started through the kitchen. Then she froze. He was home; she could hear the drone of his voice in the study.

Was he on the telephone, or was he dictating? He quite often brought work home for dictation, and would sit until the wee hours droning into his recorder before he finally went up to bed.

She tiptoed down the hallway to the door of the study and, barely breathing, listened to Dee's voice. She knew she was being foolish, but there was something about his tone, an avid nastiness, that would not let her move.

"Lost Horizon file, confidential, for my ears only. Mayor Melba Tosti and two councilmen, Josephus Tyler and Gianni Merlini, have instructed me to begin negotiations with the Folders and the Hymans on the purchase of their ranches. The purpose of these acquisitions on the part of the Lost Horizon Partnership is to build a subdivision to provide housing for those who have lost their homes to the sinkhole, to attract younger families into the city of Sunshine, to restore the lost tax revenues by this means, and to enrich themselves greatly.

"I have finished the negotiations, and made arrangements to purchase the Hyman ranch for two thousand an acre. The Folder property will be bought at three thousand five hundred dollars an acre.

"I met this afternoon with Farley Pruitt at the Sunshine TrustBank to discuss the financing of this package. He has spoken with Mayor Tosti, Gianni Merlini, and Josephus Tyler, and has made arrangements to take care of the money end of the deal for ten percentage points. He feels, as I do, that this is a win-win situation, as the three investors are empowered to annex the property into the city limits, which will make the housing more attractive."

Dee was talking about the city council members breaking the law, Sally thought. And he was helping them, even though, as an officer of the court, he was sworn to uphold that same law. She didn't dare look around the doorframe; he might be a little hard of hearing, but his eyes were like those of a ferret.

"Crest Development has agreed to my proposal if he gets a high density break from the county comp plan, which is one housing unit per acre. The annexation will give us an end run around the comp plan, even though the county is going to threaten, and I have authorized him to put in one unit per one-tenth acre.

"Crest has contracted with the firm of Ringum and Smutz to handle all the contracting for the job. They are to build two bedroom homes for forty thousand dollars, three bedroom homes with three car garages for sixty-five thousand dollars, and villas of one and two bedrooms for twenty-five thousand dollars. The villas will sell, ninety thousand for the one bedroom, a hundred and twenty thousand for the two bedroom, and the houses will be priced accordingly. This should bring in a substantial profit for the investors.

"My fee is hourly. I am charging them three hundred fifty an hour, which is considerably higher than my normal fees, but then, they are breaking the law. This file is to be updated weekly."

Sally heard him put down the microphone and take the tape from the cassette, the toss it into his desk drawer as he had done so many times before. She then heard him rise, sending a thrill of terror through her. She tiptoed hurriedly to the hall closet and hid herself among the rain wear hanging there, and just in time. Dee came through the study door, stretched, looked at his watch, and went upstairs.

She stayed in the closet, unable to think of any safer place to hide. There was no hint of rain; it was the dry season, and the only things kept in the hall closet were raincoats and ponchos. She could hear him overhead, ranging over the master bedroom.

Surely he wouldn't be going to bed at this hour, she thought. It was about eight thirty, and he never went to bed before midnight. Maybe he was changing his clothes to go out to dinner; that was a lot more likely. It had sometimes seemed to her that Dee hated going to bed, hated the hours that his body and brain required for rest, simply because they're hours stolen from his preoccupation with making money.

She remembered the countless hours he had sat in his study, poring over the statutes, examining case law, trying to figure out how the law could be bent. Bent, but never broken. Dee had been quite casual about his tortuous approach; it was healthy, he said, to take a law and twist it until it became a parody of itself. After all, look who wrote the laws–the politicians–and what did they know? He had explained, rather condescendingly, that when the lawmakers happened to be lawyers, they worked diligently with lobbyists to mangle the very laws they had produced–all this after swearing to defend the State. It was part of the *practice*–and he had voiced that word with love, as though he were talking about something holy. It was, he said, how the system functioned.

She considered such a perception of the law a disgrace; the law was meant to protect people, wasn't it? When she voiced this thought to Gavel, he had laughed hugely.

"The law meant to protect citizens?" he said mockingly. "Of course not, Sally. The law in Florida is meant to protect those who can manipulate it. That means lawyers, politicians, and big business. The common-garden citizen doesn't stand a chance."

She was pretty certain that Dee could be disbarred for his activities unless he had some very powerful friends at state level, and she didn't think that was the case. Wondering if he could go to jail, she made up her mind to wait until he was gone, then take the tape he had just made and leave the house. He would never hit her again

Her bruises were clearing, but there were still smudges on her face that she hid with makeup, and each evening when she washed her face, she remembered the expression on her husband's face that night. It had been a gentle expression, as though he were going to make love to her.

He had come into the kitchen through the back door, set his briefcase on the floor, and walked to the sink where she was rinsing a glass. "Sally?" he had said nicely.

She turned to him, surprised, because she had expected anger. "Yes, Dee?"

"I am going to kill you." Softly, sweetly. And then he struck the first blow, and the second, and all the time he beat her, he smiled. She went down on her knees, and he began to kick her. She didn't remember anything after that.

She heard him leave the bedroom and start downstairs. She held her breath, cursing herself for a fool. She could have pretended to come in while he was upstairs, called out that she had come for some things, and he would have probably been okay. But if he found her hiding in the closet he'd know she had overheard him, and that would be very dangerous; he might really kill her.

He went into the study, opened the closet door, shut it with a curse, then came back into the hall. He rummaged on the hall table, muttering to himself. Then she heard him coming closer. The closet doorknob turned.

"Where did I--?" he said to himself. "I came in, put them— oh yes, on the kitchen chair."

The door swung wide open with its usual squeaky protest. She closed her eyes so that he might not feel their panic. A heart-stopping time, and then his footsteps retreated down the hallway. She felt as if she might faint.

Then she heard his exclamation of surprise. "Must be losing it, leaving the back door wide open."

The back door closed. She heard the key in the lock and slumped, spent with tension, against the closet wall. Even though she heard him backing his car down the drive, she didn't venture from her hiding place for half an hour.

When she left the house, she scurried through the gap in the hedge and then crept, mouse-quiet, along Marge's drive to her car, praying that he was really gone, that he would not leap on her from the cover of the dark.

After she had locked herself in her car, she was still shaking.

"I have been frantic with worry!" Kelsey exclaimed as Sally came in through the back door. "You've been gone for hours."

"He was home, Kelsey, dictating. I hid when he–I waited until he went out for dinner, then I–look what I have." Sally was so excited that she fell over her words. She scrambled in her purse and brought out a cassette. "This will probably hurt him badly. He's doing something really dishonest."

"What are you talking about?" Kelsey snatched up the cassette and examined it closely, as though she could read its contents by peering through the plastic case. "What's this?"

Guy came into the kitchen and looked at the two of them. "What's going on? Sally, I was almost ready to go over there and call him out of the house to see if you were still alive."

Kelsey held out the cassette. "She nipped this from Dee's study–heard him dictating. Want to hear it?"

"Damn right, I do. What's it about, Sally?"

"A deal he's doing with the mayor, Cousin Joe, and Meats Merlini."

"A deal? That's illegal!"

They hurried into the den and Guy stuck the tape into the player, then they settled back to listen. Halfway through the tape, Guy rose and went to the telephone.

"Who are you calling?" Kelsey asked her husband.

"Al McDonald. I want him to come over and hear this, give me some advice as to how to use it. This is much too big to be botched by inept handling, and so I don't dare go to Rufus Hicks. He'd sweep it under the rug, like he did with Sally's complaint." He stopped dialing and listened, then smiled. "Al, Guy Fawkiins. Can you get your butt over here right away? I have something that will blow this town apart." He nodded, grunted, and hung up. "He'll be here in fifteen."

"Could we give it to the Feds?" Sally asked.

"I don't think so," Guy said. "They're breaking state law, as far as I can make out. I mean, there's nothing wrong with the three of them going into business together. You've heard that politics makes strange bedfellows, and if that old saw was ever proven, they've done it. But as I understand the Sunshine Law, if they're going to annex the property into the city limits, they'll have to vote on it, and I believe that will hang them."

"You mean they won't go to jail?" Kelsey asked.

"I don't know; I just hope so," her husband replied.

There were two roads leading into Mosquito Row: Luna Avenue, which was occupied by a tatty strip mall on the east side, and the trailer park where McGinnis lived on the west, and Mosquito Road, which Rainmaker followed. He was on his way to the Lightning Bug Bar to meet Jorge Granita.

He had been surprised when Granita spoke to the city council; he had no idea that there were immigrants in Mosquito Row who actually owned the land they occupied. Although he and Fielding leased land from Tyler and collected rents from the hovels that Fielding had erected years before Teddy became involved with him, he had never actually been down to the area to see exactly what it was like.

He parked his car on the weed-infested verge of the road and got out, checked the door to make certain it was locked, then looked at the building that was home to the Lightning Bug Bar and Grill. It was a discarded portable schoolroom set on cinder blocks to raise it above the hard-packed earth. The windows had long been broken out and replaced with external shutters to keep out the weather and iron bars to keep out thieves. There was no sign of an air conditioner in the windows, and he wondered how the owner or the customers who frequented the place bore the humid summers that plagued the west coast of the state.

There were two partially rusted metal tables set on the hardpan outside the entrance, with lopsided chairs ranged sloppily around them, for customers who preferred to drink their beer or rum *al fresco*. But Rainmaker could not imagine anyone deliberately sitting outside; the air was foul with the smell of briny mud and sewage.

The tide had to be low, he thought, for it to stink so, otherwise people could never inhabit this place, never stand for twenty-four hours a day that nose-numbing reek.

A drunk staggered around the corner of the building, where he had obviously gone to relieve himself as his fly was still unzipped. *"¡Hola, amigo!"* the man cried joyfully. *"¿Que tal?"*

"¿Conoce Usted Jorge Granita?" Rainmaker asked.

"Sí, sí," the drunk answered gravely.

"¿El senor esta en el bar?"

"Sí, sí, y espere un hombre muy importante."

Rainmaker smiled at the man's face, whose expression reflected his faith in the absolute gravity of Jorge Granita. *"Muchas gracias, muy amable."*

The drunk gave him a lopsided grin. *"De nada."* He collapsed into one of the chairs, which sagged dangerously to one side, and stared blankly at his open fly.

Rainmaker went up the two block steps and into the bar proper. It was dimly lit; bright paper shades covered the bulbs that hung on electrical wire from the ceiling. On the walls were several paintings that, in the dim light, looked quite good, and in a corner stood a wood carving that almost seemed alive. At the far end of the room was a crudely built counter with stools before it, and scattered here and there around the perimeter of the room were tables and chairs. They were all occupied, and as he entered, all eyes turned to watch him warily.

He spotted Granita at a table close to the bar and went toward him, wondering if the center of the room was used as a dance floor. *"Buenos tardes, senor Granita,"* he said gravely.

"Everyone here speak English, Mr. Rainmaker. We thank you for coming. Please to have a seat."

"Thank you." Rainmaker sat, looked at each person in the room, then leaned back in his chair and called to the barman, *"Traigame una cerveza, por favor."*

He would not offend them by buying a round at this point, he thought. He did not want to be thought of as an arrogant *gringo* who tried to buy popularity, because he knew well that the people of Mosquito Row had little reason to like him, or anyone on the city council, for that matter. It was just as well, he reflected, that they did not know how long he had profited from their misery, and he felt cleaner for having broken his connection with Fielding. He smiled briefly as the barman brought him a beer, then looked questioningly at Granita.

"We ask you to come here, Mr. Rainmaker, because what the council is planned is a bad thing for our people."

"Mr. Granita, I am sure that this matter will be forgotten. Most of the council members were not aware that there were landowners here other than Mr. Tyler and Zona Flores. I own one lot myself, but it is a small thing. Your talking to us the other day, and the demonstration that you and your people had at the city hall brought the truth to light. I will make certain that the matter is killed."

"For this I thank you, Mr. Rainmaker. There are other things—"

"When we get drainage here?" one of the men across the room asked in a hoarse voice. "When it rain, my ni–children walk in the mud. It is terrible, how my children live. I try to dig a ditch, the management district say no. They say we ruin water flowing, or some such thing."

"I will see that Public Works comes down here and does what is necessary to help the area with the draining problem," Rainmaker said. "I will work with you to make Mosquito Row a decent place to live."

"We have no one who sell drugs here," another man said. "The police come at all hours, and when we say there is nothing, they laugh."

"Yes," another agreed. "All the time they come to my house when I am at work. They tell my wife they will arrest her. Why do they keep threatening us, Mr. Rainmaker? Why they bother people who have done nothing?"

Rainmaker looked grim. "I wasn't aware that this was happening, and I can assure you that such harassment will stop. Does Chief Hicks come here?"

"No, he always send the tall one. This man is terrible."

"I'll take care of it." Rainmaker looked at his watch, then at Granita. "I really had no idea that you were being harassed by the police. I don't know who has given them orders to do so, but I have a good idea." He looked around the room, then focused on the carving in the corner. "Mr. Granita, who did that carving?"

"One of our young men. He works on the garbage truck to live, but he is a great carver."

Rainmaker pulled out a business card from his wallet and extended it to Granita. "Ask him to call and speak with Mr. Pickles. He's opening an interior decorating shop and may have some work for him." Then he leaned forward and addressed the men in the room. "I would appreciate it if more of you would attend our meetings. Government cannot respond to problems it doesn't know about, and you need to bring your troubles to our attention."

"What for?" an aggressive young man called out. "I heard how they treated Jorge."

"We're not all like that," Rainmaker protested. "Your being there and speaking out will make a difference."

"We will do it," Granita said.

The men gathered around Rainmaker and began to voice their complaints. Comfortable that he could do so without seeming to condescend, he ordered a round for the company.

Lila Mae sighed and leaned back against the tree. It was so peaceful out here, she thought, so quiet and clean. The air didn't have even the slightest tinge of sewer smell; it was like wine. She just wished that Oddman would get back. He'd been called back into town on some emergency–a piece of heavy equipment had broken down.

The whole of downtown was a mess, she thought. Oddman had every piece of machinery he could find working around the clock to get the city back to normal. If you went to the city center at three in the morning, you were deafened by the roar of earth-moving equipment as men worked to lay pipe to replace the city's sewer system. Right alongside the sewer system, pipe was being laid to carry the electric lines that fed Sunshine power. It was probably a good thing that no one could live there anymore, she thought. They'd be kept awake every night by the din.

She laughed quietly. Sunshine was having all its veins and arteries replaced, and it had a new heart, that was for sure! It was being turned into a bionic city, and would never be the same. Then the thought occurred that all cities were bionic in that sense, and this made her look again at just what it was she had responsibility for. "Lord, lord," she muttered, chuckling. But she sobered when she remembered the quiet, peaceful little village that her mother had described to her, and the small town in which she had grown up.

Before the influx of the northerners into west central Florida, the Hatchacootee had been a beautiful river–mud bottomed, yes, but clean. She and her brother went crabbing when they were little. Down where the marina now stood, there had been an old, rickety dock that went out over the water for about twenty feet. They would take chicken gizzards and necks, tie them together in little bundles, and drop them into the water, then lie flat on the dock and peer intently into the water. In the shadow of the dock, they could watch as the crab sidled along the river bottom, then swam up to grab the meat. Then she would gently pull the string upward–she had to be really careful not to disturb the feeding shellfish–and her brother would lower the crab net and catch the thing. Her brother always said she was the best "stringer" he had ever seen.

She didn't think often of Howard; he had been killed in the Grenada war back in 1981, and was a piece of history. But at moments like this, when the evening breeze rustled overhead among the leaves, and the moss hanging in the oaks drifted gently from side to side when nosed by the breeze, she missed him.

Maybe that was why Oddman appealed to her, she mused. Because, like Howard, he was extremely tall and gangly. Howard had shot up like a weed, Mama always said–just like a piece of dog fennel–short one day and seventy-leven feet tall the next. Of course, she and Howard fought like a pair of wildcats when they didn't get along, but most brothers and sisters did.

That thought brought her to the city council and the constant infighting among its members. Why on earth did they get on that way? Of course, she was probably as guilty as the rest, but somehow she didn't think so. She wasn't a plotter like the others were; she was content to go along with the herd as long as they didn't go leaping over a cliff, like those things called lemmings.

She mulled over her idea of getting Tallahassee to allow them to collect those Tubifex worms that Gavel Strike was always going on about. Could that possibly generate some jobs in Sunshine? She hadn't mentioned it to anyone yet, because of the sinkhole and all the problems it had brought them, but there was bound to be some way they could capitalize on all those worms just lying around in the mud waiting to be eaten. Gavel said they were sold other places as fish food. What would happen if she brought it up at the next meeting? Would anyone back her up?

At the last meeting, she had the feeling that something had changed. Why would Melba be nice to Joe Tyler? She hated him. They were probably the most bitter rivals she had ever seen. But then, maybe they had something on each other. That would be more true to form for the two of them. And how come Meats Merlini was suddenly taking Joe Tyler's side? And Melba's? He had always sided with her so he could try to peer down her neckline while he talked. And he thought she didn't know what he was doing.

Maybe she'd give Jackson Fatigay a call, as much as she despised the man. Of course, if she did, she could expect a long lecture about being a Jezebel. He would go on and on about how she was supposed to stand by Henny, because Henny was a member of the Saved Sons Society. But Jackson Fatigay might have heard something.

"Lila Mae, are you out there in the dark?" Odlum called from the back porch.

"Yeah, honey, I sure am. Didn't even notice it had gone dark, to tell the truth."

She saw the flashlight playing across the lawn as he approached her, and suddenly she realized that she'd been sitting there for what seemed like hours and no fire ants had bitten her. Rising, she decided that she was going to fulfill that fantasy; she was going to get laid in the grass. Languidly, she began to strip off her clothing, smiling in anticipation.

CHAPTER TWENTY SIX

Al McDonald played the tape over again. Was it a hoax? He wouldn't put it past Dee Slugge to put serious pressure on the councilmen and mayor if he thought he could get away with it, but what would his reason be? He had the city business tied up; he usually took Sunshine for at least half a million a year, and the council paid it like the dunderheads they were instead of hiring a hardworking youngster who needed to learn lawyering. The city usually managed to stay out of serious trouble, thanks to Frank Bonano, so having a powerhouse to work within the city structure wasn't a necessity.

Try as he would, he could find no motive for Dee Slugge's making the tape. And if it was true, then what would the mayor and her cohorts be guilty of? Nothing more than breaking the Sunshine Law, and that was what really galled him.

Here they were, the so-called leaders of the city, working their bums off in an effort to fleece the citizens of the city who had lost their homes. All they were after, Tosti and her Lost Hurrah, were the FEMA and insurance dollars that were pouring into the place.

"The Lost Hurrah." Yes, he liked that and would probably use it when and if he broke the story. No, there was no "if," no real "if," because Sally swore that she heard Dee dictating, had hidden from him, and then nicked the tape and skedaddled after Dee had left the house. And he could never doubt that Tosti and the other two would try such a thing; it was common knowledge that Tyler would do anything to make a profit, and that Melba was as greedy as they came. The one thing that made him wonder was Merlini–the guy had enough money to keep him until the end of time–so why would he consort with the others on this venture? Of course, their little partnership did explain their politesse at the last meeting. They were usually at one another's throats.

In a way, he was glad to find that Teddy Rainmaker and Lila Mae were relatively clean. It certainly didn't look as if they had an inkling of this plot.

He swivelled back to his figures–he'd been working with a calculator trying to figure out just how much money they'd all make if Lost Horizon sold out, and it was a nice packet. Melba would be able to have every wig in Christendom and shoes to match, but what was driving Merlini?

Then it hit him; *the guy wanted to build his meat museum!* He slapped his forehead, trying to knock some sense into his head. Of course, that was the answer. Merlini was a mental case, had always been one. He thought his sausages had personalities, thought they were genuine art. There was no guile in Merlini; he actually believed the crap he spouted. He wanted money to pay for that thirty foot bronze sausage-in-the-sky. Poor, deluded Merlini. He would spend some time in jail just because his head wasn't on right.

McDonald swivelled again to face his computer, rested his wrists on the edge of the keyboard tray, and paused again. He'd wait a while, see what happened. Maybe he'd get a prize out of this one day if he was a little patient.

Then he changed his mind. If this was for real, he needed legal advice. If he blew it open and they tried to cover their tracks, they might accuse him of breaking and entering Dee's house, no matter what anyone else said. He reached across his desk and pulled his Rolodex toward him. Flipping through the A's, he found the number he wanted, picked up the receiver, and punched in the number of the Attorney General's office in Tallahassee. On something like this, he figured he was safe going straight to the top.

Rufus Hicks parked his car in front of the Fawkins residence and motioned for the three police who were with him to spread out and cover the back of the house. The officers nodded and split to make certain there was no avenue of escape.

Guy Fawkins was on the point of leaving for his office when Kelsey shrieked and pointed to the shadow of a man pressing his face against their back door. "Guy, who is that?"

Guy snatched open the door and stepped back quickly as the officer of the law stumbled forward; he had been trying to see through the curtain, and he almost fell flat on his face. "Can I help you, officer?"

Just at that moment, the front doorbell rang. Kelsey said that she'd answer, and hurried through the kitchen and into the hallway. Sally appeared on the stairs, her forehead creased in a frown.

"There are cop cars outside, Kelsey."

"Yes, I know. Guy has one of them in the kitchen. Looked almost as if he was trying to break in, for crying out loud!" The doorbell pealed again. "I'm coming, I'm coming!"

"It's Rufus," Sally whispered. "I saw him coming up the walk."

"What do you suppose they want?" Kelsey asked her.

"I'll bet Dee sent them," Sally said. "He found the back door open, and now that he's discovered the tape is missing, he'll assume I have it here at your house."

"Then we're home free, aren't we? We'll be sweet and innocent as lambs." Kelsey opened the door, looked startled, then smiled. "Well, good morning, Rufus. What on earth are you doing here?"

"I got a search warrant, Kelsey. We have reason to believe that you are harboring stolen goods."

"I thought people harbored criminals," Sally said.

"You better hope we don't find anything, Mrs. Slugge," Rufus shot back. "If we do, you'll be in jail. Breaking and entering Dee's house is a serious criminal offense."

Guy came into the hallway. "Morning, Rufus. I heard you, and I'd like to see the search warrant, if I may."

Rufus held out the warrant and Guy took it. "Signed by Meekins. Stands to reason," Guy remarked.

"Could you tell me what I am supposed to have stolen when I broke into my own residence?" Sally asked sharply. "This had better be good, Rufus."

"You stole a tape when you broke into your house."

"I did not!"

"Well, Mrs. Slugge, I intend taking this house apart to find out." Rufus shoved past them and into the living room, where he proceeded to dump all the sofa cushions on the floor.

Guy smiled grimly. "His goon is in the kitchen emptying all the drawers onto the kitchen table." To Rufus he said, "If you damage anything, Rufus, I'm suing the city, so you and your boys had better be damned careful."

"You talk big for someone who's harboring stolen goods," Rufus snarled. He was carefully feeling each sofa cushion, squeezing every inch, to see if he could locate the contraband.

Kelsey couldn't help herself; she burst out laughing. "Rufus, you look so silly doing that. You look at too much television. If you think I'm going to cut open a sofa cushion to hide a tape, you're crazy. That couch cost me over two thousand dollars."

Hicks stopped what he was doing and frowned. "People like you would do anything."

Sally stepped forward. "Rufus, could you please tell me what makes you think that I stole something from my own house?"

"I found your fingerprints all over that place, Mrs. Slugge."

"Of course you did; I've lived there for almost ten years." She took his arm. "Come upstairs with me, Rufus, and search the room where I've been staying since Dee tried to kill me. If I've stolen anything from my own home, which is ridiculous in the first place because I own what is in my home and therefore can't steal it, I certainly wouldn't implicate my friends who have been good enough to put me up by hiding something on the premises that *they* inhabit, would I?" She started to lead him up the stairs, but he pulled away.

Guy whispered to Kelsey, "Sally is the one who should have gone into law."

"Don't you try that, Sally Slugge," Hicks warned. "I ain't going upstairs without a witness. You ain't going to claim that I tried to rape you."

"Oh, for–Officer," Kelsey called, going to the back of the hall. "Will you please come and babysit with the chief while he's upstairs with the suspect, or whatever? He's afraid Mrs. Slugge might rape him."

"I'll get you for that, Kelsey Fawkins," Hicks warned.

"I'm taping this whole conversation," Guy said casually. "Wait until the press gets their hands on this!"

The doorbell rang. Guy dodged the officer who was trying to grab the little recorder he carried with him to take notes, and opened the door. Al McDonald stood there, looking thoroughly perplexed. "What in the hell?"

"Rufus is searching the house. He thinks Sally stole something from her home, and has accused her of breaking and entering her own premises."

McDonald came into the hallway. "Rufus, have you lost your mind? What on earth has sent you on this wild goose chase?"

"Dee Slugge is missing some stuff from his house," the chief said unwillingly.

"What?"

"A tape."

"Simon and Garfunkel or what?"

"How the hell would I know. He said he's sure his wife stole it."

McDonald pocketed the tape that Guy removed from his recorder and handed to him and retreated out the door. "Thanks, Guy, and when you get a chance, give me a call. I want to ask you a couple of questions about the sand." He hurried down the walk and jumped into his car. If Rufus realized he was going, he'd probably try to stop him. As he drove off, he grinned. Judging from the look on Rufus's face, Margie Noessit was going to have some real fun.

"Bonano here." When he died and went to his just reward, whatever that might be, he thought, he'd ask the Lord to give him a telephone to glue to his ear so he'd feel normal. "Yes, oh, hi, Don. No, I've been far too busy to go to the mud flats. By the way, thanks. I think your sharp eyes saved a lot of lives. You've got more photos and know who the guy is? That's great. Yeah, but if you want to actually see the sand, you'd better get down here either today or tomorrow. Full moon on Wednesday night, and it'll all be gone again. Okay, call me back."

He hung up and turned back to the estimates he'd been going over. Looked like someone in the Office of Budget Management was using a lunatic adding machine. Biting his pencil, he began punching figures into his calculator. A knock sounded on his doorframe. He looked up, saw Gavel Strike, and sighed. "Come on in, you'll save my life."

"From what?"

"I hate doing numbers. Rather go to hell. What's up?"

"I just stopped by to tell you that Rufus Hicks and three of his officers raided the Fawkins house this morning and tore the place apart. Guy had an appointment with a new client over in Heart County, and asked me to talk to you. Apparently Dee Slugge is missing a tape or something from his house, and sent Rufus after Sally. Two questions: since when does Slugge order the police around, and since when does Rufus go in for this strong-arm stuff? First, he refuses to investigate a claim by Sally that Dee beat the hell out of her, and now this.

"I went by there to drop off some papers, and the place was a complete wreck. They hadn't actually destroyed anything, but every drawer in the house has been dumped on the floor, the mattresses thrown off the beds, the closets emptied into the floor–you can imagine how angry Guy and Kelsey are. Can you do something?"

"I sure can." Bonano reached for his telephone and dialed. "Chief Hicks, please. Rufus, you send out a couple of people to put the Fawkins house back together as it was or you're fired. I don't want any argument, I don't want any guff, you just get your ass in gear and do what I say. And I hope to hell you found whatever you were looking for." His eyebrows rose. "You didn't find anything incriminating? What the hell did you expect, you asshole! Get cracking now, and," he added ominously, "I want to see you this afternoon." He hung up and grinned at Strike. "Thanks, Gavel. I got a chance to blow off some steam, and I take particular pleasure in venting at Rufus."

Strike sat down. "You get the feeling that there's something drastically wrong in this town?"

"Yes, I do, and I can't quite put my finger on what it is. Maybe the loss of his equipment sent Rufus around the bend, but there's something else–Melba and Joe are being polite to each other, and that bothers me. I've only seen them polite once before, and they were cooking something then. I'll wager they're cooking something now."

"That's against the law."

"Since when do pols in this state pay attention to the law, unless they're forced to? I guess whatever they're planning will come to light–it always does." He shook his head. "By the way, Don Sarious is coming down to view the sand with his own two eyes. I told him he'd better get here before day after tomorrow."

Gavel nodded agreement. "He'd better; because once that rip comes in, it's gone for good. Well, I'm off to work."

"Why haven't you submitted a bid for insuring all the new equipment, Gavel?"

"I didn't know anything about it. I've been running my butt off."

"Okay, I'll have one of the staff fax the stuff to your office later in the day."

"Thanks."

"Don't mention it. We advertised in the *Tampa Tribune*, and I didn't know if you had seen it."

Strike grinned. "Busy with more than insurance these days, Frank."

Bonano laughed shortly. "I know, I know!"

After Strike left, he leaned back in his chair, stared at the ceiling, then punched his intercom. "Call Chief Hicks and set up an appointment for this afternoon, and stress that he'd better be on time. Then get me Dee Slugge, and after that, Mayor Tosti."

He'd do a little sleuthing on his own.

Farley Pruitt reared back in his padded leather chair and stared at Tyler. "I shouldn't be talking to you at all; you're shunned. What do you want?"

"I want to know how much mortgage there is left on the church."

"Why, Joe?"

"Well, I been thinking of paying it off."

"That won't do you any good. I don't know what you did, but Learned Speaker is really angry with you. He said that until you get on your knees before the congregation and ask forgiveness, you're to be shunned."

"I know all that, but I think that a gesture of true humility like this will please him."

Pruitt chuckled. "I think that Learned Speaker would consider such a gesture arrogant, Joe, but I will ask him, and if he wants you to know, I'll tell you. But where are you going to get all this money, with this new business you're getting into?"

"You mean the housing development? I should clear enough out of that to more than cover the church mortgage."

"Suppose things don't go as you plan, and the thing backfires? You're going to owe the bank a packet, and I have to think of our liquidity."

"You never gave a thought to the bank's liquidity before; we've been doing deals for years."

"We live in changed times, Joe. Your store is gone, your wife is living with her sister so she doesn't offend Learned Speaker, and you're in a venture that is, at the very least, against the law. You better hold on to what cash you have until all this blows over. That is the advice from your banker."

"Damn it, Farley, if I get on my knees, I'll lose a lot of respect."

"Humility is a virtue that each of us should acquire." He swivelled to face the window and stayed in that posture until he heard his office door shut. Then he smiled briefly and returned to the paperwork on his desk. Perhaps, he mused, he should have insisted on fifteen percentage points for himself, but a good Christian was never greedy. And envy was a sin. But he still wished he had been in on the ground floor of the Lost Horizon deal; it was a sweet one.

"What do you mean, you couldn't find the tape? It is there, I tell you! No one but Sally could have come in the back door; she has keys still." Slugge bounced his paper knife against the blotter on his desk, staring with icy eyes at the figure of the police chief.

"I mean it ain't in the house, Dee. I looked everywhere. If Sally did take it, and you don't really have any proof that she did, what would she do with it? I mean, so you're missing a tape, so what? What was on the damned thing, something that would incriminate you?"

"Don't be ridiculous. I know she was there because I have special locks on the back and front doors, and it's impossible to get in without a key. I locked the back door when I got home, then went to work. When I left the house, the back door was open."

"Well, why didn't you look for her then?"

"I wasn't thinking about it; I slipped up."

"So now you want me to risk my job and hound your wife. That don't make any sense, Dee. If you're so sure she's got the thing, then call her and ask her for it."

"We are not speaking."

"I guess not, after what you did to her. She really filed for divorce?"

"That is none of your business. Your business is to find that tape, if you know what's good for you."

"I got an appointment with Frank Bonano at three this afternoon. He's really pissed and threatening to fire me. I ain't going to lose my job over this, Dee, and that's my final word."

Slugge stabbed the paper knife through his blotter as he rose. "Get out! You incompetent bag of shit, get out of my office!"

Rufus Hicks, seeing for the first time the fury in DeLeon Slugge's eyes, turned and almost ran from the room.

Just as Bonano began to pull his office door shut, the telephone rang again. The sound of it had a particular urgency, so he sighed and crossed the room to his desk. "Bonano."

"You had better lay off Rufus Hicks or you're going to be sorry," a voice whispered.

"Oh, yeah? Says who?"

"I am warning you that if you threaten him again, something terrible will happen to someone you love."

Bonano snorted. "And I am warning you, Dee, that if you pull this sort of shit again, I am going to the Bar. You think I don't recognize your voice? You're mistaken. I've heard you whisper many times, remember?" Then he sat down at his desk again. "You'd better watch out, Dee, you sound as if you're losing control, and that isn't good."

His caller hung up.

"Kee–rist! What is going on in this town?" He started to rise and the telephone rang. He snatched up the receiver. "Bonano."

"The time has come."

His face relaxed and he grinned. "Yeah?"

"Yes, the time has come. I'm making chicken in lemon sauce, with chilled wine, luscious fruits, and I am naked. Come and get it."

"You or the chicken?" he asked.

"Both, you jerk. But since I am naked and the chicken can wait, the order in which you get it is set in stone." Mary Lee giggled. "I've never done anything like this before."

Bonano rose from his desk. "There's always a first time. I'll be right over."

As he began to close his office door, the telephone rang. This time, he ignored it.

Dear Editor,

I am seventy-three years old and a widow. If the City Council is serious about this stupid dog-walking ordinance they've just come up with, I don't know what I'll do.

My dog, Puffy, weighs a hundred and twenty pounds, and I weigh ninety-eight. Am I supposed to put this large animal on my toilet so he can go to the bathroom, or what?

My neighbor is even older than I am and she has three dogs. Can you imagine what a mess her house is going to be in if these dogs can't get outside? This is an outrage.

Is Joe Tyler crazy? If that so-and-so thinks he's going to get the vote of dog owners, he's got another think coming. I think it's time we hounded (ha!ha!) them out of office if they can't come up with better ordinances than that.

What about people who have cats? Are the cats going to be allowed to wander around the neighborhood still walking on people's cars and leaving pawprints and other unmentionables everywhere? If dogs have to use the toilet, then I think that cats should have to use the toilet too, and I hope they all fall in and drown.

Your faithful reader,
Florence Snyder

CHAPTER TWENTY SEVEN

Op/Ed   The Sunshine Bulletin   Page 6

Long Arm of the Law, Duh!
By Margie Noessit

I suppose that we should be grateful that our Long Arm of The Law, Rufus Hicks, isn't noted for his brutality. Police are usually noted for brutality when they're not beloved neighborhood fixtures, lauded as heroes, or as Josephus (Holy!Holy!Holy!) Tyler once described them, "God's warrior angels."(?)(question mark mine).

I was never sure that Chief Hicks had any notable qualities at all, until the other day when he and three of his warrior angels descended on the home of Kelsey and Guy Fawkins in search of a cassette. After listening to a tape given to Alvin McDonald, I've come to the conclusion that Rufus Hicks, Chief of Police of the City of Sunshine, Florida, has one notable quality. Stupidity. I mean <u>DUH!</u>

It appears that DeLeon Slugge is missing a cassette from his home, and naturally, he has accused his wife, Sally, who is suing him for divorce, of absconding with the celluloid. Can't you find your Grateful Dead, DeeDee? Or are you missing Mussorgsky?

Chief Warrior Angel and his Demons trashed the Fawkins residence, then left empty-handed. But in the process of this intense investigation, Hicks assured Sally Slugge that he knew she was guilty because <u>he found her fingerprints all over her house!</u> And he refused to search her room unless accompanied by another officer. Hicks felt that Sally would accuse him of rape!!!!

Come on, Rufus (Warrior Angel) Hicks! Rape??? If you can't figure out that Sally's fingerprints would naturally be all over her own home (she has lived there for ten years), could you even find your zipper if you had to whiz?

Al McDonald sat in the anteroom of the Attorney General's office in the Capitol, watching idly as the odd person passed by in the marble floored hallway outside. He liked the Capitol; it was a real zoo at this time of the year, and he enjoyed watching wild animals.

The Legislature was in session, and the city of Tallahassee awash with lobbyists, earnest protestors of one kind or another, and bright young aides with circles under their eyes from the too-long hours demanded by the lawmakers. In their quest to accommodate their big campaign contributors, they worked the socks off everyone. The Legislature met in session only two months each year. The other ten months, he reflected, must be for catching up on sleep.

He had caught Henry Bates in his office between committee meetings, and had enjoyed a nice chat with him. Briefly touching on his reason for being in Tallahassee, he was reassured that Sandfly thought his action the right one.

"It's better that this be handled from high up," Sandfly had explained. "Give it to the local public prosecutor, and it'll get all mixed up in politics. If he's a lefty, he won't want to touch the others, and if he's a rightist, the same thing applies. They always look after their own. Who're you seeing in the A.G.'s office?"

"Someone named Peter Grant."

"Stands to reason; you're the press and he's a P.R. person, but once he finds out what this is about, he'll put you onto someone who can give you some help. If you need me, I'll be in the Finance Committee meeting over in the House Office Building. Just signal my aide—I'll let her know you might show up—and she can call me out."

He started as a muscular young man touched his shoulder. "Excuse me, are you Alvin McDonald?"

"Yes, I am. You Peter Grant?"

"Yes, come into my office, please." He led the way through a small maze of offices and finally into a small cubicle. "We're somewhat short of space. Have a seat."

"I thought the A.G. had all sorts of attorneys working under her."

"She does, but they're in another building. Government is spread all over this town. Now, how can I help you?"

"I have in my possession a tape made by the city attorney in Sunshine, outlining a venture between three partners who happen to be the mayor and two councilmen. Their plan is to purchase two failing ranches outside the city, annex the land, and build a big housing development that's really shoddy, but looks good. This is to avail themselves of all the FEMA and insurance money that's floating around since that sinkhole ate the city center. As distasteful as their venture is, it isn't illegal that I know of, but I think that since they have voted on annexing the land, they've broken the Sunshine law. Am I right?"

Peter Grant's eyes lit up. "You mean the mayor and councilmen are conspiring to gyp their own citizens?"

"Yes."

"I'm not the person you need to see, Mr. McDonald, I'm just P.R.. Let me make a call or two, and steer you to someone who can really be of assistance." Grant busied himself at the telephone for a few minutes, then grinned. "Come on, I'm taking you to a super-hot attorney who specializes in Sunshine Law. She's great, and your city is her pet peeve."

They left the Capitol by the front doors and turned right, crossed the brick courtyard between the old and new Capitols, and skirted the Senate Office Building, then went two blocks south on Monroe to the Collins Building.

In the elevator, Grant laughed and said, "Be prepared for something of a shock."

McDonald nodded. He had yet to meet a Tallahassee type who could shock him; bureaucrats were bureaucrats.

They left the elevator on the third floor and went down a hallway, then turned in at an open door. A receptionist smiled at them, and nodded at Grant to go ahead to the inner sanctum.

Grant stepped through the doorway, then stood back to let McDonald get a good view. He grinned again. "Al McDonald, this is Janice Madison, our Sunshine specialist. She'll help you out, and if I can do anything further for you, just give me a holler."

Before McDonald had a chance to thank him, Grant waved vaguely and left the room to go back to his office.

"Call me Jan, and I'll call you Al," said Ms. Madison, rising from her desk. And she just kept on rising.

"My God, how tall are you?" McDonald burst out. Then he began to stammer, trying to apologize.

"Cool it, friend, I'm accustomed to having to pick up folk's teeth. I am six seven in my naked feet, and I love high heels, so it gets worse. Of course, being black helps; I absolutely loom. It's all that Ashanti blood, you know." She waved her long, elegant hand. "Take a seat. What do you have?"

McDonald pulled the tape cassette from his pocket and handed it to the woman without a word, then sat studying her while she listened to it.

Eggplant skin, dark, lustrous, and an exquisitely shaped head on a long, slender neck. She was wearing a pale lavender sweater and a string of pearls. She was gorgeous, absolutely gorgeous, he thought. This was probably what the Queen of Sheba looked like, only maybe the Queen of Sheba was not quite so tall. He felt as if he were in the presence of a royal skyscraper.

She leaned back in her chair and tented her long fingers, staring into space through slitted eyes. When the tape came to an end, she looked at him, whistling softly. "How did you come by this, Al?"

"Slugge and his wife are in the process of getting a divorce; he lost his temper and could have killed her, he beat her so badly. She's staying with friends, and has recently found an apartment, which are in damned short supply in Sunshine now. She went back to the house the other night to get some things. Figured she was safe because her husband usually works late, but he was in his study dictating this tape. When she realized what he was saying, she hid in a closet until he left for dinner, and then nicked it and ran.

"They called me that same evening and I went over and took the tape for safekeeping. I was pretty sure there would be a hullalballoo and I was right. Since that time, Slugge got the police to search the place where Sally is staying, the Fawkins' house. They trashed the house, and Frank Bonano, our city manager, made them go back and clean up their mess.

"I started to expose it in my paper, then figured that if I did, it might get swept under the rug. Sunshine has a way of doing things differently."

Jan laughed shortly. "That's the understatement of the year. I've never seen a place stay in so much hot water, and it's all brought about by the city council. What's wrong with the folks there, the ones who elect those yo-yo's?"

"What's wrong with all of us, Jan? We get caught up in our own lives, forget there's a world out there to which we owe some responsibility, and these fools stay in office."

"I don't think the average Joe Blow would ever acknowledge that he has some responsibility for the world around him, Al. That's a little idealistic."

"No, it's not. As John Donne said, 'No man is an island, entire of itself.' I was brought up to believe that if we don't assume some personal responsibility for what goes on in the world around us, we surrender, to some extent, our claim to being part of the human family. And it's so easy to do today, Jan. We drive, alone, to work. Most of us work in cubicles. We drive home, alone. The kids are watching the boob tube. The wife is on the computer because she works at home, alone. So you've got very little family interaction, and there is no interaction between citizens unless they're pissed over a zoning ordinance or something trivial. It's a damned shame, but it's the truth."

"I never realized you newsmen were so philosophical."

"I don't think I'm the only philosopher around, Jan, although some of the media frenzies we go through would make you wonder. At any rate, that's how our councilmen and mayor stay in office. Through apathy."

"One of these days, I'm going to drive down to Sunshine just to see what kind of town it is," Jan said reflectively. "Poor little place; it's like God's dogsbody."

"Amen. So, what do you think about the tape?"

"Oh, you've got probable cause to go in and clean the place up, but I'd like a couple of affidavits, maybe one from Sally Slugge, and one from a corroborating witness, that they saw Sally give you the tape, that sort of thing. Then I can proceed, and I can tell you right now, I'll bring in the governor's counsel and probably the gov himself. He's not going to be amused about this. You know what a stickler he is for proper form. You fax me those affidavits, I'll consult with those on high, and let you know what to do." She rose again to her exceptional height and looked down on him with a warm smile. "It's not often a newsman will hold back on a scoop to bring closure on breaking the law. Thanks."

"Aw, shucks," he said, grinning, "next thing, you'll be calling me a warrior angel."

"What is that?"

"What Joe Tyler calls our police chief."

"He must be out of his head."

PooPoo pegged Don Sarious as homophobic as soon as he came in the front entrance. After introducing himself, Sarious had looked around as if he expected to be jumped by a pack of queens and ravished on the spot.

"Come this way, please, Mr. Sarious," PooPoo said as he led him toward the table nearest the pool at the back of the restaurant. He was worried; Bonano had called him and told him that Sarious was coming over to talk to Teddy, and he hoped that didn't bode ill for them. He had called Teddy to come into the restaurant, thinking that if things got serious, he could intervene somehow.

Still wary, Sarious remembered that he was in Rain on the business of protecting the environment, and realized that he had fallen into a well of silence. "I notice that your front windows are still boarded up. Did you lose the glass to the sinkhole?"

"Yes, it blew them in. We were lucky, those are the only two windows in the place except for a couple of small ones in the kitchen. They didn't get done in."

"Why haven't you had them replaced?"

"I'm having stained glass done to take the place of what was there, and the fellow hasn't finished it."

"I don't like stained glass; it's static."

"So is most glass, darling," PooPoo retorted. "Unless it's flying." He had heard that Sarious was somewhat obsessive, but really! He seated Sarious at the table. "Something to drink?"

"Yes, I'd like a Coke." Now Sarious looked at him with covert hostility. "Are you a, well, a–"

"Of course, Mr. Sarious. Open and above board."

"I don't approve of your type."

He wasn't being deliberately offensive, exactly, but what was wrong with the man? "Mr. Sarious, bigotry is the coin with which the inept and small-minded purchase self-esteem," PooPoo said coldly. "I'll get your Coke."

"I am neither inept nor small-minded," Sarious began to protest, "I simply don't li–where is Councilman Rainmaker?"

"Teddy is on his way, Donald, so don't get antsy." PooPoo flitted across the room with a Coke in one hand and a glass of ice in the other. "Here you are, just as you ordered. Now, can I get you something else?"

"We're not allowed to–" Sarious looked decidedly uneasy.

"It would never occur to me to attempt a bribe of any sort. I am merely extending simple courtesy." He looked at the kitchen door with relief, having just heard Teddy in the back. "He's here."

Rainmaker came bustling through the kitchen door, carrying a mug of coffee. "Mr. Sarious, I'm Ted Rainmaker. How do you do?" He set the coffee down, shook hands with Sarious, who winced slightly, and sat down. "Frank Bonano said that Sunshine is in your debt. Said that if it hadn't been for your sharp eyes, we might have lost a lot of lives."

"I think that Frank is exaggerating somewhat, Mr. Rainmaker. With all the ground tremors that were going on, and the smaller sinkholes, I'm certain he would have ordered the evacuation anyway. The one thing that bothers me is that you all fired him for doing his job."

"I voted against the motion, Mr. Sarious. I happen to be on Frank's side. Now, you asked that we meet to discuss something. What is it?"

"I understand that you are a partner of Fielding in a number of enterprises."

"'Was' is the correct term. I have broken off my business relations with Fielding; he bought me out, and I have nothing to do with him. He was getting a little too far afield for my taste."

"How long were you affiliated with him?"

"Why do you want to know?"

"I am trying to determine if you are in some way responsible for that sand down there on the mud flat at the mouth of the river."

"What sand?"

"Please, Mr. Rainmaker, don't try to prete–"

"Oh, yes, I did hear that someone had dumped quite a bit down there, come to think of it. But I had nothing to do with it." Rainmaker sipped his coffee and watched his opponent warily.

"Did you have anything to do with the first loads that were dumped there?"

"You mean last month?"

"Yes."

"As a matter of fact, I did. The council was discussing the possibility of putting a beach in down there to increase tourism, and I had heard old tales about some current taking away a pair of lovers–something like that. So I decided to put it to a test. And the old wives tales are true; whatever is on that flat at full moon gets taken into the Gulf."

"You realize that what you did was illegal?" Sarious looked as if he was enjoying himself.

"At the time, I was unaware of the possible damage that might be brought about."

"Ignorance of the law is no excuse."

PooPoo rose from the table. "I'm going into the kitchen for a minute, darlings, so don't get into a fight in my absence."

Rainmaker held out his coffee cup. "Mind freshening that for me, Hon?" Then he smiled at Sarious. "The sand is gone, Mr. Sarious, and you would be hard put to prove it was ever there. Are you secretly recording this conversation, by any chance?"

Sarious glared, insulted. "I am not!"

"Good. I was hoping that I dealt with an honest man."

"As you were in business with a man that brought business before the Council, and as you never recused yourself from voting, it is quite obvious that I am *not* dealing with an honest man," Sarious retorted. His voice was tight.

"Ah, but you must forgive, as I have repented. I say that seriously, Mr. Sarious. I began to review my life, and found that certain areas of it had become distasteful to me, and so I brought them to an end. True, that's not repentance, but I have reformed to some extent."

"To some extent?"

"Yes, I am still a homosexual, and judging from your body language, you find that really repulsive. I'm sorry."

"You're right, Mr. Rainmaker, I do not approve of your lifestyle at all. In fact, I find it abhorrent."

"That's your right. Now, will you stop being an ass? I can assure you, Mr. Sarious, that neither of us will make any attempt to seduce you. You're certainly not my type, and I suspect that PooPoo finds you somewhat—never mind. Does the Department of Environmental Protection plan to take action against Fielding on this matter?"

"Absolutely."

"Can you prove he dumped the sand? I must admit that I warned him not to do it, and I assumed that he was smart enough to follow my advice."

"Obviously, he didn't. Yes, I have evidence: photographs."

Rainmaker's eyebrows rose. "Photos? How?"

"One of the activists planted an infrared camera in the trees on that little spit of land. We were able to identify Fielding by his license plate number, which was quite clear when the picture was blown up." Sarious looked up as PooPoo came through the door with a plate of small sandwiches on a tray with Rainmaker's cup and a glass of wine. "I told you—"

"Teddy and I normally lunch at this time, Mr. Sarious. Don't get your dandruff up." He set down the tray, lay out two lunch plates and napkins, then set the cup beside Rainmaker's plate. "There, darling. Eat up."

"Then Fielding has had it." Rainmaker took a bite of the sandwich. "Unless he claims that someone had stolen his truck, and I wouldn't put it past him."

"I hardly think the police would cooperate with an environmental criminal," Sarious protested.

"Of course Rufus would cooperate, Mr. Sarious," PooPoo responded. "Fielding is his brother-in-law." He sat down and took a sandwich, then looked brightly at their guest. "One of the big problems in Sunshine is 'relativity,' as Lila Mae Warner has said many times. Everyone is related to everyone else."

The lights in the church were low, and for that, Joe Tyler was grateful. This entire Rite of Repentance was humiliating, he thought. Even if one did feel contrite, even if one sincerely repented, which he did not, this ceremony was designed to take the last vestige of dignity from a man. He had to crawl the full length of the center aisle before the entire congregation. And it was the entire congregation; attendance at the Rite of Repentance was mandatory.

He should have recognized Learned Speaker's arrogance long before this, he berated himself–should have seen, in the insistence on mandatory attendance for the Rite, that it was a psychological twist used to cow the people of the church. A very smart tactic, too; not one member of the congregation had ever missed the Rite in the past, and there had been some twenty over the years.

His enormous belly fought the sackcloth robe he had been forced to wear. Ridiculous to go to these extremes, absolutely ridiculous. Then he remembered that he was the one who had insisted, years before, that sackcloth be worn to further reduce the penitent to ignominy.

Ten miserable days of no breakfast within his own home. Ten nights alone in the bed, without the comfort of Sarah's broad backside to butt up against. In his somnambulant search for the familiar, he had butted himself backward right out of the bed, and had wakened with a start when he hit the floor. It was demeaning, such instinctive behavior; it diminished a man.

It was Sarah's refusal to come back to their home until he had repented that had brought him to the realization that Learned Speaker had won. All his money couldn't make any difference; the man wanted blood and guts, sweat and agony. And it would be agony to crawl down that aisle, physical agony. His knees hurt him a lot lately, and Doc Smithers had told him that he was wearing them out with a combination of arthritis and overweight. He didn't even want to imagine how they'd feel when he rose at the end of the aisle. If he could get up. He'd probably gained another ten pounds since the shunning began, eating in restaurants all the time. It was all Learned Speaker's fault!

Grunting, he got to his knees and began to crawl. He looked stolidly at the floor, at the blue carpet emblazoned with tiny orange crosses, and not at his goal, the skirted Cross of Redemption. He concentrated on thinking about that Cross of Redemption, but true repentance would not come into his heart; all he could think about was why anyone would ever put a white eyelet skirt on a cross!

Suppose you had a Cross of Whatever for each sin, for each act of man? Would each cross have to wear a skirt? Would Learned Speaker pick a different fabric for each cross, assigning some arcane meaning to satin, toile, or polyester? Why had he chosen white eyelet for the Cross of Redemption? Were the holes in the fabric to allow the sinner to cross through into glory, or were they there to tempt the sinner to go to the other side and begin sinning all over again?

He glanced to one side as he recognized his wife's plump leg and her black shoe, stuck out in the aisle as usual. She always insisted on an aisle seat, explaining that she had to keep herself aired out. He had never been certain what she referred to, but because he pictured himself as a true Christian gentleman, he had never asked. There were some things he just didn't want to know.

He concentrated on the blue and orange carpet again. But he spied the black and tan wingtips that Brady Hack always wore and his blood pressure soared. Damnable plotter–a real Judas!

Seeing Hack's shoes made him suddenly aware of the congregation and their hypocritical glee. Behind all those solemn faces, those overfed or skinny faces that had been wiped clean of any expression, *they were laughing at him!* Him–Josephus Tyler, who had been so respected, so revered.

God, he prayed, strike them all dead! They have backslidden until there is no health in them. Bring down Thy mighty fist and smite all these sinners. Raise Thy servant, O Lord. Give me succor.

He quickly glanced up, hoping to find destruction–except for his wife, of course. But the people were still there, staring ahead, lips turned downward at the corners to avoid the appearance of lust. Yes, lust, because he could recall the intense pleasure, almost sexual heat, that he had experienced each time he had witnessed a penitent crawling down the aisle. He hated the people in the congregation at that moment, but most of all, he hated Learned Speaker.

Lord, what was a man to do–there were Ferdy O'Doole's legs, with the ankles crossed–when his wife refused to serve him? Divorce was unthinkable; he loved Sarah. Not so with Ferdy O'Doole and the boys; they had taken up the shunning and he had been banned from the Saved Sons Society. He wasn't even allowed into the meeting room; they had changed the lock. That was unfair because he had risked his life to fish that cross-shaped piece of driftwood from the Hatchacootee, and he had donated his old navy blue sofa from his den.

He passed the highly polished shoes of Jackson Fatigay, who had canceled two appointments in the capital to attend the mandatory Rite. Jackson Fatigay, who was guilty of taking money from whores, who had forgotten that the laborer is worthy of his hire. Pharisee! Deceiver! How dare he sit there in the pew with his face pulled into a solemn frown, when he was worse than most of them in the congregation? Unworthy fraud!

He was almost there. He raised his head a little bit and saw the feet of Learned Speaker standing next to the Cross of Redemption. He began to think sad thoughts so that he would have tears in his eyes when he arose, so that Learned Speaker would think he had won this battle. He thought of his mother, but that didn't help. He tried thinking of dear, departed Pappy, but that didn't help either. Then he remembered his dog, Piggy. He pictured himself as a carefree lad running through the marsh grass with his companion racing ahead, barking joyfully. He could feel the wind in his hair, and smell the salt marsh and the stink of saline mud at low tide.

He had raised Piggy from a puppy and Piggy had died when he was eleven beneath the wheels of a car. Piggy had gone from him; the only dog he had ever really loved.

Piggy had betrayed him, had left him alone and forlorn and friendless. Poor Piggy, but even worse, poor Joe.

When he was helped to his feet at the end of his ordeal, his eyes were brimming with unshed tears.

"O sinner, you are saved!" Learned Speaker intoned. "Praise be to the Lord!"

CHAPTER TWENTY EIGHT

Lila Mae Warner leaned back in her chair, crossed her nylon-covered legs, and surveyed the crowded chamber. She moved her microphone aside and whispered to Merlini, "Why are there so many folks here today, Meats?"

"I don't know. Prolly come to bitch about something. Those old farts are always bitching about one thing or another."

"Meats," she chided, "I asked you to use the word 'poof.'"

"What for? They're a bunch of farts!"

"It's time you learned to talk like a southerner."

Merlini snorted loudly.

"Mr. Merlini, if you don't mind, I'd like to begin the meeting."

"Not at all, Mzzzz. Mayor, go right ahead." He winked at Lila Mae.

Mayor Melba Tosti pulled her chartreuse wig tighter to her head, adjusted the neckline on her black, purple, and blue-green dress, cleared her throat, and banged her gavel . "The meeting of the City Council of the City of Sunshine will now come to order." She then looked upward and intoned, "All rise for the Invocation and the Pledge of Allegiance." After a quick glance to make certain the camera beamed her image, she rose.

Josephus Tyler shook himself in preparation for the prayer. He closed his red-rimmed eyes and clasped hands beneath his layered chin. "Lord God, Maker of all things, Knower of all sins, we humbly beseech Thee to lead us to do Thy will while we attend the business of the City of Sunshine." His voice assumed the cadence of the pulpit and he squeezed his eyes tighter shut. "Help us, Lord, to avoid the terrible pitfalls of power! Lead us not into arrogance. Guide our thoughts, Lord, to Thy ways, that we might prosper. We have been humbled by Thy might, Lord, and we are heartily sorry for our transgressions. Lead us into the path of righteousness, for there are those among us who wallow in iniquity, Lord." He opened one eye to see if Melba was going to kick her new partner and she nodded to him approvingly. He smiled with satisfaction and his voice rose. "They have backslidden until there is no hope! Help us to walk in Thy path all the days of our lives, Amen." He opened his eyes, smiled at Melba, spun to face the flag, clapped his hand to his heart, and froze again. "Where did that flag come from, Frank?"

Bonano smiled. "Mrs. Lucius Rinestor has graciously loaned us the flag until our new ones are delivered, Councilman Tyler. I have drafted a formal note of appreciation and sent it for the mayor's signature."

"That was real nice of Mrs. Rhinestone," Merlini said. "You be sure you sign that note, Mzzzz. Mayor. It's nice to have citizens who care about Old Glory."

Tyler placed his hand over his heart and began the Pledge of Allegiance. The voices of the crowd in the chamber rang in faltering echo behind his own.

Melba tidied her papers and gave the citizens in the chamber a nod. "Time for roll call. Everyone here? Fine. Now, I need a motion to adopt the minutes of the last meeting."

"Got it."

"Second."

"All in favor?" Ayes all around. "Motion passes. Are there any financial matters?"

"Only those on the consent agenda, Madam Mayor," Bonano said.

"Let's move on to the consent agenda. Are there any items to be removed?" She frowned as the camera lens moved to view the room full of people. What the hell did he want to pan the citizens for? she wondered. They weren't important.

"Madam Mayor, I would like to have Item 6-b, the dog-walking ban ordinance, taken from the consent agenda so that we might discuss it," Rainmaker said.

"What for?" Tyler blurted. "It passed; we voted on it at the last meeting. This is nothing more than a formality."

"It is a formality that I wish to discuss formally," Rainmaker snapped. "If that meets with your approval."

"Well, it don't!"

"Order! Mr. Bonano, remove the item from the consent agenda." The mayor's voice was impatient. "Any further items to be removed? Very well, I need a motion to pass the consent agenda."

"Got it."

"Second."

"All in favor?" Ayes all around. "Motion passes. Now, we will discuss Item 6-b. The floor is yours, Councilman Rainmaker."

"I have had over two hundred calls against the passage of this ordinance. The bulk of those citizens feel that the city is burdening them with unnecessary nonsense. They claim, and I have to agree with them, that we have no right to deny them access to the out-of-doors if they wish to stroll with their pets. Most of them feel that their rights under the First Amendment have been violated, and six of those with whom I spoke have threatened lawsuits over this."

Merlini waved his arm to get the Mayor's attention. "Mzzzz. Mayor, could I ask a question?"

"I cede the floor to Councilman Merlini," Rainmaker said.

"Are you learning some manners, Pervert?" Tyler asked.

"Shut up, Joe, you heard Teddy. I got the floor," Merlini said. "I just want to know, and maybe Mr. Slugge can give me the answer, how walking a dog is freedom of speech?"

"How is burning the flag freedom of speech?" Tyler sneered.

Lila Mae sighed. "Meats, it's really simple. When people walk their dogs, they talk to them. I hear them all the time, saying stuff like, 'Come on, Queenie, get a move on; I ain't got all night.' Stuff like that. I mean, Queenie's owner might want to get back to watch television. But if folks can't talk to their dogs, then you're violating their freedom of speech."

"That ain't what we're talking about!" Tyler almost shouted.

"Order! Mr. Slugge, can you answer Councilman Merlini's question?" The mayor's voice was silky.

Slugge rose and went to the lectern, smiling at the councilmen. "Madam Mayor, Councilman Merlini, I am no expert on the First Amendment, but it would seem that Councilman Warner has some valid points."

Merlini rolled his eyes. "I'm getting confused. Of course her–uh, points are valid, but we were talking about dogs and poop."

Lila Mae patted his hand and made soothing noises.

"Madam Mayor, I take back the floor," Rainmaker said. "I think that we should find out if this ordinance will hold up in court before we pass such a thing. I voted against it before, and I'll do so again. What will we do next, ban birds crapping from on high?"

"Order!" The gavel banged.

"I am in order, Madam Mayor. This council voted last week to pass a ridiculous ordinance, and I am asking that we investigate the validity of such an ordinan–"

"But such an investigation will cost money, Councilman Rainmaker, and that would put a strain on the public pur–" Tyler tried hard to mimic PooPoo's voice.

"Don't you dare fling my words back at me, you ass!" Rainmaker snarled. "For once in your ignorant life, try to see someone else's side. We are putting an intolerable burden on our citizens. You are going to force feeble elderly ladies to clean up dog poop in their homes simply because you don't like dogs. *Is there anything you do like, Tyler?* For God's sake, man, think about what you are proposing. It is an abomination."

"You are the abomination, you–you–!"

"Order! Councilman Tyler, please control yourself." The mayor glared at him.

"I object to this pervert playing to the crowd," Tyler said hotly. "He has no right whatever to question what I do, and the word 'abomination' does not belong in his mouth. He is a–"

"I said order!" Mayor Tosti shouted. The gavel crashed. Its head flew off and landed with a clatter on Frank Bonano's desk. "For chrissake, can't you even order a decent gavel, Bonano?" she almost screamed.

"I will place an order for another gavel today, Madam Mayor." He favored her with an icy smile. "Or would you prefer a sledge hammer?"

The citizens in the chamber broke into laughter and began applauding.

The mayor smiled uncertainly, and then positively beamed as the camera turned her way. Let the fools think it was a joke, she fumed. She would have Bonano's head for this; how dare he make fun of her? If he had to control people like Tyler and Rainmaker, he'd need something more powerful than a sledge hammer, by God!

"I have the floor, Madam Mayor," Rainmaker continued. "I move that we table this ordinance until its validity has been established."

"I second the motion," Lila Mae Warner said. She poked Merlini in the side with her elbow and whispered, "You vote with me on this, Meats. Joe's wrong."

Merlini nodded.

"I have a motion to table the dog walking ban ordinance. All in fav–"

"You have no right to do this!" Tyler shouted.

"Aw, shut up," Merlini snarled. "You're outnumbered."

"All in favor!" the mayor repeated forcefully. Three ayes, two nays. "Motion passed."

Mayor Tosti adjusted her yellow-green headgear and smiled at the camera. "Are there any progress reports, Mr. Bonano?"

Bonano cleared his throat. "As you instructed, we are at present compiling a complete report on progress throughout the city, Madam Mayor, so that you and the councilmen might read it and reflect upon it at leisure."

"I asked you if there is a progress report, Bonano!" Melba's voice was nasty.

"Last week, you asked for precisely what Frank just told you he is preparing, Madam Mayor," Rainmaker said. "Do you change your mind when you change wigs, pray tell?"

"You bast–you are out of order, Rainmaker!" Melba shouted.

Rainmaker bored his bony backside into the chair. "When you give staff orders to compile a complete report during one meeting, and then demand an oral report at the next meeting, you're wasting tax dollars. It ties up a lot of staff, compiling a report like that, and a lot of time. And in case you don't know it, time is money."

"Are we going to have yet another lecture on fiscal responsibility?" the mayor sneered.

"If necessary. Melba, it is well documented that you are pissed off with Frank Bonano. I don't know the reason for it, and I don't care to know. But I do know this; you are mayor of this city, and you should behave as a mayor instead of some frustrated harridan."

Tyler leaped to his feet, his face flaming with anger. "How dare you call her a pervert, you abomination?"

Rainmaker looked up at the enormous belly looming in his face and grinned. "You have increased your vocabulary—congratulations! And harridans aren't perverts."

Tyler looked confused. "Then what are they?"

"For chrissake, can we get on with the meeting?" Merlini demanded. "I don't want to listen to you all day."

Through slitted eyes, Melba asked for an update on the sewer repair.

Odlum rose and towered over the lectern. "I'll make this very short, Madam Mayor, as you will have the full report in writing. We presently have the new system completed as far east as Sixth Avenue. In other words, about half the city is done. We're laying pipe around the sinkhole now, and I figure that we'll be ready to hook up that part of the city within the next three weeks. Any questions?"

"Yeah, I have a question," Merlini said. "When you going to get around to fixing the drainage around my place?"

"As soon as the equipment is freed up, Councilman Merlini."

"Well, make it quick, because it ain't long until rainy season and I'm sick of dealing with mud."

Odlum nodded and went back to his seat. Lila Mae smiled at him and pursed her lips just the tiniest bit in a kiss.

"Any old business?" the mayor asked.

"I have several letters from citizens in the county against the annexation of the land, Madam Mayor," Bonano said. "I'll pass them out so that you may read them. I also have a letter from the county administrator, Fred Baron, protesting the annexation. He threatens to bill Sunshine for all the work the county did after the—"

"I don't care if they bill us until they drop dead," the mayor snapped, "they aren't getting one cent from us. Looking after us in time of trouble is their duty. Even Heart County looks after Dunwurkin when they run into snags." She snatched the proffered letters from his hand and glanced through them, then passed them on to Merlini. "You read this crap."

"What do you think about inviting the county commissioners over here to see the damage and talk about the problem?" Lila Mae asked.

"Don't be ridiculous!" Tyler snapped. "What we do is none of their business."

"Well, Joe, I think it is," Lila Mae said. "We are a part of Banter County, whether you like it or not, and it's our duty as councilmen to keep the peace."

Tyler glared at her. "You are a native of this city, woman, and you owe it your loyalty. I don't want to hear another word of that liberal gibberish you're spouting these days. You been hanging out with the Pervert and other sinners too long."

"Oh, be quiet, Joe. You ain't in the pulpit, and from what I hear, hell will freeze over before you ever get up there again," she retorted. "I just wish I could have seen you down on your knees. And I am being loyal; picking fights is stupid."

"You–!"

The mayoral shoe banged on the desk. "Order."

"Madam Mayor, I move that we ask the county commissioners to meet with us to discuss the annexation and lay to rest any fears they might have. We need to reassure them that no further encroachment on their turf will take place. It's the only sensible thing to do." Rainmaker settled back in his chair and watched the people in the chamber.

"I second the motion," Lila Mae said.

"We have a motion. All in favor?" Two ayes, three nays. "Motion not passed. Is there any further business before we go on to new business? Good. New business."

Bonano cleared his throat. "I have had several complaints about the behavior of our local police recently, Madam Mayor, and so I have asked Chief Hicks to report on his raid and trashing of the Fawkins house, and..."

"Served them right, damned bug-smoochers!" Tyler burst out.

"...and why he took no action when one of our citizens was seriously beaten."

"I want to hear that report," Rainmaker snapped. "So far, we've never had any trouble between the police and our law-abiding citizens, and I certainly don't want to start now."

"Point of order, Madam Mayor. The Pervert has no right to interfere before you approve of this report." Tyler glared at Rainmaker, then leaned back in his chair and sourly regarded the citizens in the room.

"Joe, I think Teddy has a right to speak his mind whenever he wants to," Lila Mae said. "You going after his First Amendment rights too?"

"Order!" The shoe banged on the desk.

Lila Mae pushed her microphone aside. "I hope she breaks the damned heel off, Meats. Then she'll have to limp out."

Merlini snorted.

"We are in session, Councilman Merlini. Do you mind?"

"Not at all, Mzzzz. Mayor, you go right ahead." He waved his arm expansively.

"Chief Hicks, will you please come to the lectern and tell us about these matters?" the mayor said graciously.

Hicks rose, scratched his head, jerked on his belt to pull up his pants, then eased forward to the lectern. "Madam Mayor, Councilmen, I got a report on a beating and I plumb lost the thing, so it slipped my mind." He smiled ingratiatingly.

"How many beating reports do you get every week?" Rainmaker asked.

"Can't rightly recall getting one since the sinkhole ate the city hall, Mr. Rainmaker."

"Then your oversight was not due to an avalanche of beating complaints?"

"No, sir, it wasn't. But Dee–"

"I want no names mentioned," the mayor warned. "This is about–uh–procedure, not personalities. So you lost the report and what happened?"

"Got my ass chewed out by the city manager," Hicks said.

Someone in the audience tittered.

"Order! Is there something else you wish to report?"

"Well, I got a complaint about a tape missing from a person's house, and this person is the city att–"

"I said I want no names mentioned!" the mayor warned.

"Well, this person is someone who I was told to take care of, so I took care of him."

"By raiding the home of a law abiding citizen and trashing their house?" Rainmaker asked.

"Yeah, Mr. Rainmaker. You have to be careful when people are harboring stolen goods."

"But they weren't 'harboring stolen goods' at all, were they?"

"Well, I didn't find nothing."

"What is the purpose of pillorying this warrior angel?" Tyler thundered.

Lila Mae burst out laughing. Tyler glared at her. "Joe, Rufus ain't a warrior angel, he's a cop. Why don't you call a spade a spade?"

The mayor looked at the ceiling and rolled her eyes, then she looked at Hicks. "Rufus, don't do it again."

"Oh, I won't, Madam Mayor. Frank said he'd have my job if I did."

She turned her furious eyes on Bonano. "I will not have you interfering with the police department, Bonano."

"I have no intention of interfering with the law, Madam Mayor. I only interfere when the law picks on innocent people for no good reason. If I was out of line, I apologize. But, under the city charter, the police department is my responsibility, and I take those responsibilities very seriously."

Several people in the audience applauded.

The shoe banged. "Order!" There were times, Melba thought, when she would love to pull a gun and blow his effing head off!

"If we don't pay attention to the little things that are wrong, Madam Mayor, they will grow to big things, and we wouldn't want our warrior angels accused of brutality, would we?" Rainmaker asked.

But Melba didn't hear him. Suddenly she noticed that Al McDonald was watching the proceedings without writing down a word. He just sat there with a satisfied smile on his face. What was the bastard up to now? She put her microphone aside and turned to Tyler. "Look at McDonald; he's not scribbling. Has he been like this during the whole meeting?"

"Yes, come to think of it. Maybe he's using a recorder. Let's get this Hicks thing over with and go on, Melba. I don't want to give the Pervert any more preaching time."

She nodded, pulled the microphone before her again, and said, "Thank you, Chief Hicks. Any further new business?"

"I have one item, Madam Mayor," Rainmaker said. "We still need something other than our recent disaster to bring tourists to Sunshine. I want to propose that we enlist the help of our Latino citizens and try to put together a combination of Latin color and exotic birds. If you recall, Mr. Strike suggested at the last meeting that we consider using our wild bird population to attract visitors, and—"

Tyler rose from his seat, astounded. "You want to use those lowlifes in Mosquito Row to bring in tourists? That's the most asinine thing I have ever heard."

"Sit down, you pathetic lump of lard, and listen to a good idea," Rainmaker said.

"If you think that's a good idea, Pervert, then you've lost your mind."

"Well, at least I had one to lose," Rainmaker said pleasantly.

"I think your idea is a great one, Frank," Lila Mae enthused. "We could have papilomas and all those things."

"What?" Merlini asked.

"You know, those paper and clay things that are filled with gifts."

"Oh," Merlini said, "I didn't know they was called paperlomas. Yeah, Madam Mayor, I think it's a good idea."

"Isn't 'papiloma' a medical term?" the mayor asked, her voice pure acid.

"If it is, I hope you don't die of it," Lila Mae answered placidly. "You know what I mean."

"I move that we table this discussion until a later date," Tyler boomed.

"Second," Merlini said.

"We have a motion. All in favor?" Two ayes, three nays. "The motion didn't pass." Melba shot Bonano a look of triumph. "Any further new business? None? Very well, we're ready for public comment. You may speak, but you are limited to three minutes, and as there are so many people here today, if you're talking about the same thing, please appoint a deputy. Our time is valuable."

Jorge Granita rose and came forward. "My name is Jorge Granita, and I live in Mosquito Row. My neighbors and I are willing to make a festival for Sunshine, but we have no money. In this country, people love Latin festivals. So we will work with Mr. Bonano when he is ready."

"There ain't going to be any Latin festivals as long as I live and breathe," Tyler snarled. His eyes roamed over the room and he noticed, again, that Al McDonald simply sat there, smiling. What was wrong with the idiot?

"Then you do not serve the people of this city, Mr. Tyler," Granita said. He turned on his heel and went back to his seat.

Tyler leaned over and whispered to the mayor, "Who the hell does he think he is?"

Melba shrugged. "Any further public comment?"

There was an air in the room, she thought, an air of expectation. What was going on? It was Bonano, of that she was certain. The son of a bitch was cooking something with his welfare friends and his cheap slut lover. They were out to make her appear a fool, and for what? So that Tyler could be mayor again? So that ignorance would reign?

Joe was so friendly since they had become partners that she almost wanted to throw up. Did the idiot think that she was a friend simply because she had gone into a deal with him to make money? Did he think the rivalry was over, that they would share the mayoralty every four years, on and off? What a fool! She glanced at him with slitted eyes and found him staring at her.

"What is it?" she whispered.

"There's something badly wrong, Melba. Can't you feel it? I got a sick feeling in the pit of my stomach."

"Maybe you ate something bad at breakfast," she retorted.

"Not hardly. Sarah is very careful of my food."

She should have poisoned you years ago, she thought. And buried your fat carcass in the back yard. The only thing you're good for is pushing up daisies.

"As there is no further public comment, I want a motion to adjourn."

"Got it."

The meeting was adjourned.

CHAPTER TWENTY NINE

Al McDonald was working on Margie Noessit's column when the telephone rang. "Sunshine Sentinel. McDonald speaking."

He hated being interrupted when writing, but it was inevitable. His publisher liked to keep newsrooms understaffed. Said it made for more creative news.

"Alvin McDonald, please," a prim voice enunciated.

"This is Alvin McDonald. How may I help you?"

"Hold for Governor Slate, please."

The governor? Why would the governor be calling him, he wondered. Quickly, he pulled a pad toward him and a couple of pencils, just in case the great man uttered words of undying wisdom.

"Al, you there?" Slate's voice boomed.

"Yes, sir. How can I help you?"

"I want to thank you for taking the time to bring this cassette to Tallahassee, Al. Most journalists would have run the story first and thought afterwards, and that would have ruined everything."

"Does this mean that you're going to act, sir?"

"It sure as hell does. I'm coming down today with the Attorney General, and I'm having the three of them arrested and charged."

McDonald froze, so exhilarated that he could barely breathe. "They met yesterday, sir, so they'll be around."

"I know it; I notified Bonano that I'm coming so he can round them up. There's so much illegal stuff going on in the state of Florida that I mean to make an example of them so I can scare the pants off some of the other scofflaws who hold public office. What do you think of my plan?"

"I think it's great, sir, but what'll you do to replace them?"

"You don't worry about that; I'll replace them. Holding an election would take too long, and would just make it possible for other fools who want to sit in high places to rush in. I think it's time Sunshine had a responsible government."

"It sure is, sir."

"You know Gavel Strike?"

"Yes, I do."

"Well enough to comment on him?"

"Depends on what you want to know, sir."

"I mean to put him on the council if you think he's honest and will do a good job."

"He'd be an excellent choice, sir. If he has one fault, it's that he's too particular about details, and around here, that would be a relief."

"I'm also having the Bar look into DeLeon Slugge's activities. What do you think?"

"I think that lawyers generally find other lawyers not guilty of any offense, sir, because they work on the principle that they're going to do it next."

"I'll keep that in mind and go even higher. Well, thanks again, and tomorrow, you can put out a special edition. You can start writing now; I'll get into town around three this afternoon. Have a photographer handy, and you can tip off one television station if you think they can keep a lid on it. And tell your publisher I said he should give you a raise, a big raise." The governor rang off.

McDonald dropped into his chair, limp with surprise. "Well, I'll be damned!" Then he grabbed his telephone to call his publisher. After that, he'd call the local television station. Hell, might as well give them the breaking news for a change; they had faithfully photographed Melba Tosti long enough to deserve it.

Joe Tyler sat in the meeting room of the Saved Sons Society with Ferdy O'Doole and Tom Fellows, sipping coffee and reading the papers. He felt warm and safe again, here amid his old friends, who, even though forced to shun him, had left him as president of the Society. That kind of loyalty touched his heart, made him downright glad that he had crawled down that aisle.

He even felt grateful to that hypocrite, Farley Pruitt, for not allowing him to pay off the mortgage on the church. He had explained his intentions to Ferdy and Tom, and they had agreed with Farley, but for different reasons.

"Hell, Joe, if you pay off the mortgage you're going to make Learned Speaker look like even more of a hero than he usually does. Folks'll think he really changed your heart, and that wouldn't be good for business when you finally decide what you want to do. Noise it around that you're giving away money, every Tom, Dick, and Harry will be after you to donate to their cause. You keep hold of your cash, Joe," O'Doole had advised.

"Ferdy's right, Joe. Never get the reputation for being generous. You'll get taken to the cleaners. I've always worked to keep my reputation as a tight-fisted son of a bitch intact. Even my donations to the church are anonymous."

Now he glanced up as O'Doole pulled out one of his cigars and began to unwrap it.

At the sound of crinkling cellophane, Fellows looked up too, and made a grimace of distaste. "Didn't you read in the paper the other day that smoking cigars is dangerous to your taste buds, or something?"

"Yeah." O'Doole continued his ritual, biting off one end of the cigar, then putting it in his mouth and turning it around. "Everything's bad for your health nowadays, even living," he opined around the stogie. "Got so a man can't do anything any more. Can't get drunk because it'll hurt your liver, can't have sex because you're too old, can't eat much or you'll get fat–they have spoiled everything. Can't even die any more, at least, that's what I think."

Fellows laughed. "Why can't you die, Ferdy?"

"Damned government'll get you for non-payment of taxes."

They all laughed, nodding their heads in agreement.

"Hey, Joe," Fellows asked, "you know who's putting up that development just outside town? I mean, you voted to annex the land into the city, but do you know who you're inviting in?"

He was tempted to tell them that he had a part of it, but remembered that he had been sworn to secrecy. As long as no one knew he and the others were involved, they were safe. He was certain that if he told Ferdy and Tom, even though he could trust them with his life, the news would begin to circulate that

Joe Tyler, Melba Tosti, and Gianni Merlini were in a plot together to rip off the poor citizens who had lost their homes to the sinkhole.

He had to admit that it was a strange partnership, the three of them. Now Melba was so kittenish, so friendly–the two-faced bitch. She thought that the partnership would end the animosity between them, but she was wrong. He intended trouncing her in the fall. He had to figure out just how to use her participation in the partnership against her in a way that would play down his own part in the plan. He had to come out looking as if he'd done the deed for a good reason, while casting doubt on her. So far, his brain had refused to cooperate.

She had told him yesterday that she was moving into her new condominium today. She'd been so thrilled. Of course, he couldn't blame her; she'd been staying in a dump ever since the little house she rented had been swallowed by the hole in the ground.

"Joe's in a quiet mood today, Tom," O'Doole said.

"No, no, I was just thinking that I don't have a clue who's putting up the development. Slugge said it's a big development company that wants to stay anonymous because they don't want competition to move in."

"Sounds fishy to me," Fellows said.

"Probably some greedyguts who wants to make a killing while all the insurance money is around," O'Doole mused. "And I can't blame him, or them; there's a lot of cash floating around in the city."

Tyler's antennae perked up. Did they know something they weren't telling him? "It could be a development company, too. I guess we can't rule that out."

"No, but I got a gut feeling about this," O'Doole said. He looked down at his belly and grinned. "And you got to admit, I got a lot of gut to feel things with."

Frank Bonano hung up his telephone and scratched his head. What would bring Governor Slate back to Sunshine so quickly, and on such short notice? Of course, he was glad of the notice, because he was expected to have all the council together in the meeting chamber at three thirty.

He had asked if the governor wanted to be met at the airport, and had received a negative reply. That was strange, but then, there were so many strange things going on at the moment that one more wouldn't matter.

His secretary buzzed him. "I have that report on rebuilding Sunshine roughly put together. You want to read it now?"

"No, I have other fish to fry; Governor Slate is coming again this afternoon. Call Mary Lee and ask her to come in, please, as well as Oddman. I need them both as soon as possible. If Oddman is out of the office, tell his girl to send someone to find him. Pronto." He released the 'speak' button, bit his lip, and then picked up his telephone and dialed Al McDonald's number. "Al, I just got a call from the governor's office, and he's coming in this afternoon around three. What do you mean, you know it? Sure, I can come over, but it would be better if you could come here. I have to gather the loonies for the great man." He listened to McDonald and sighed. "All right, I'll be over in an hour. Better yet, let's have lunch. You order in. I want pastrami on rye and a large Coke. Diet Coke. I've put on at least five pounds in the last couple of weeks." He hung up and grinned. Mary Lee was looking after him very well.

Melba Tosti moved her sofa covered in lavender and orange print against the long wall of the 'grand salon' in her new condo and stood back to look at it. Should it go there, or should she angle it into the room? If she did, she could put the new end table where it would be very visible.

She had attended the gala opening of PooPoo's new interiors shop yesterday after the meeting, and had immediately regretted her decision to take a look at his latest endeavor. She had spent right up to her credit card limit, purchasing the end table, an Oriental lamp, and a carved chest with mother-of-pearl and cinnabar inlay.

Maybe she should put the chest at the end of the sofa, and use the end table next to the easy chair. She moved the chest into place and found, much to her dismay, that the cinnabar and mother-of-pearl clashed horribly with the orange in the print. Damn! She had been certain that the two would absolutely love each other, and when she mentioned it to PooPoo, he had warned her that cinnabar was quite particular about what it sat next to. What did he know? She could return the chest, which would be admitting defeat, or she could just keep company away until she recovered the sofa. It wouldn't be long before she was swimming in money.

She shoved it out of the way and put the end table in its place. The table was much more at home. That done, she placed the easy chair at an angle to the couch and put the chest against the long wall.

The real problem, she told herself, was that the room was too large for the furniture. When the money started coming in, maybe she'd just hire PooPoo to do the damned room for her. It ground her that none of her purchases belonged there, but she had bought, as she usually did, on the spur of the moment.

Her new telephone shrilled and she started, then rushed to the kitchen to answer it. "Yes?"

"Bonano here. The governor will be here at three thirty and would like to address all of you in the council chamber. Can you make it?"

"Why is he coming?"

"He didn't see fit to confide in me, Madam Mayor."

She sighed. "Okay, I'll be there. Three thirty?"

"Yes. Thank you." He rang off.

She looked at her watch. Twelve twenty-five. She would unpack a little more, then take a luxurious bath in her new tub, and dress before her full length mirrors. For just a little while, she could wallow in luxury, and then she'd go and listen to what that damned beanpole had to say. After his last visit, when he had told her she looked like hell, she detested the man. She just hoped that he wouldn't go on for hours; she wanted to get back to her new abode.

Merlini sliced another onion and added it to the pan. First he would soften the peppers and onions, then remove them from the olive oil and add his hot Italian sausages. They would simmer until perfectly done, and then he'd carefully smother them in the vegetables. Once they were warm, he'd eat them with good Italian bread and a glass or two of chianti. Mama Mia!–no one but Italians knew how to eat.

He had spent the morning making mortadella and he had even made a little kielbasa. Once in a while, he got away from Italian sausages just so he could appreciate all over again the genius of his people. It wasn't that he didn't like Polish sausage, or even German sausages–he did, but when you got right down to the facts, Italian sausage was the best in the world.

On occasion, he would make some bratwurst and cook it tenderly with small potatoes and onions, then serve himself some green peas to go with them. Yes, that was what he considered his sweet meal, bratwurst and green peas. And in the spring, he liked to make knockwurst cooked up with navy beans. Then there were Chinese sausages. Once in a very long while, he made himself Chinese sausage and cooked it with a nice bit of cabbage, then he poured the resulting mixture over rice and sprinkled it with soya sauce. But that wasn't his favorite food because rice wasn't meant to be eaten by real Italians. Yeah, yeah, some Italians loved risotto, but they probably had foreign blood in them. And soya sauce, to him, tasted like melted shoe polish.

No, real Italians were meant to eat pasta, glorious pasta, good Italian bread, and sausages with peppers and onions.

He checked the vegetables, removed them from the pan, threw in a handful of freshly sliced garlic, and then, like a mother with newborn babes, carefully placed his children in the hot oil. They immediately began sizzling, as Italian sausage was meant to do, and his stomach growled with anticipation. He could feel saliva gathering beneath his tongue.

The telephone rang. Snatched from his reverie, he grunted and picked up the receiver. "Yeah?"

"Meats, this is Bonano. I–"

"Paisan! Buona sera."

"*Buona sera,*" Bonano responded. "Meats, the governor is coming this afternoon. I don't know why, but we need you at the council chamber by three thirty. He wants to address the council."

"You know what for?"

"What for what?"

"What for he's com–I mean, what he's coming for?"

"I don't know."

"Oh, then why didn't you say so to begin with? Okay, I'll be there." He smelled the sausages; they smelled hot. "Mama mia, I gotta go, Frank. The sausages are trying to burn." He hung up and rushed across the kitchen.

Lila Mae sat with Kelsey Fawkins and Sally at Rain, enjoying one of PooPoo's superb salads. She had come in to have lunch and found the two of them already there, so at their invitation, she joined them.

Kelsey, ever forthright, put down her fork and looked at the older woman. "Lila Mae, do you ever eat at Southern Fried any more?"

"Tell you the truth, Kelsey, I'm so sick of fried chicken and fish that I probably won't set foot in the place for a year." She sighed. "I've taken to doing some of my own cooking again. It's been so long since I fixed a meal that I've almost forgotten how, except for breakfast."

Sally laughed. "That's the only meal I ever had to fix, too."

Lila Mae looked at the slight blonde with sympathy. "You really getting a divorce, Sally?"

"I sure am. My lawyer's got all the papers drawn up now, and we're just about ready to sign."

"You had a talk with Dee about any of this?"

"No, to tell the truth, I'm afraid of him."

"Can't say I blame you. I get so mad at him when he plays up to Melba and talks her out of all that money. We should have an in-house attorney; it would save the city a packet, but Madam Queen won't hear of it."

"Why don't you run for mayor, Lila Mae?" Kelsey asked. "I think you could probably beat Melba."

"Probably, but I couldn't beat Joe Tyler; he's got all those holy people behind him."

"Who do you want to win the election?" Sally asked.

"None of the above," Lila Mae said with a grin. "You get Joe, you're going to have to fight tooth and nail to live a normal life; he'll come down on fornication, liquidation, and animation, just to prove he's the boss. He'll try to stuff prayer down everyone's throat, and erect a pedestal for that Learned Speaker to stand on. And he'll have Jackson Fatigay over here every week to tell us how poor Sunshine is, because he and Jack are both members of the Stinking Sinners Society. I hate that bunch of men. And with Melba, you'll get more wigs. Lord, I wish she had some taste!"

Kelsey took a bite of chicken. "Yeah, did you see that emerald green number she was sporting the other day?"

Sally gasped. "No, but I forgot to tell you, she's moved into her condo. I saw the truck unloading there this morning, and I recognized that ghastly sofa she has."

A shrill noise interrupted them and Lila Mae jumped. "Lord, I keep forgetting this thing. I got myself a beeper." She pulled the thing from her handbag and read the number, then rose. "Got to go call Frank Bonano. It's not often he calls me, so I guess it must be important." She went to the desk in search of the telephone.

Rainmaker hurried up the city hall steps and into the elevator. He had an appointment with one of his constituents at one, and he was running late. As he headed down the hall toward the room where they were to meet, Bonano came from his office with his jacket.

"Teddy, I just left word with PooPoo. The gov is coming at three thirty and would like all the councilmen to assemble in the council chamber. He wants to talk to you."

"Governor Slate? What does he want? Did he give you any indication?"

"You know the man, as close as your skin. No, he just said he was coming here, and for me to get my act in gear to make certain you all were in attendance."

"Okay, I'll be there. On your way out?"

"Yeah, I'm having lunch with Al McDonald. He's buying."

"Enjoy. Just don't drink too many martinis. We don't want you falling on your face in front of His Nibs."

Bonano started down the hall, then turned back. "Teddy."

"Yeah?"

He went back to the councilman. "Do you feel something in the air?"

"You mean like, spring?"

"I mean like, something fishy."

"Yes, I do detect a certain odor, but I can't put my finger on it. It's like a shoe that doesn't quite fit–quite uncomfortable. Why?"

"I think there's some back room deal simmering, and I can't figure out who the cooks are."

"You mean, on the council?"

"Yes."

"Out of the Sunshine?"

"Yep."

"Well, let's hope they're stupid enough to go forward, Frank. If they do, we can blow them out of the water. Go have lunch. I have to see a constituent. See you later."

CHAPTER THIRTY

Lila Mae was seated in the front row of the auditorium, her long legs stretched before her. She and Rainmaker were the first ones to arrive.

"Do you have any idea what this is about, Lila Mae?" Rainmaker asked.

"Not a clue, Teddy. It can't be about supporting the governor, because he doesn't run for two more years, and the state has already given us so much money that I doubt more is on the way. You got any ideas?"

"No, I'm in the same boat as you." He studied her face for a moment, then cleared his throat. "Have you noticed a change in the alignment of the council recently?"

"You mean how thick Melba and Joe have become? Yes, I noticed it the first time it happened, when they got all polite between themselves. If they were countries suddenly polite with each other, I'd think nothing of it, but when rival politicians get sugary, there's something going on." She sighed.

"What's wrong?"

"I just hope she doesn't show up in that damned lime green wig she loves so much. You ever get embarrassed by her?"

"I stay that way," Rainmaker said morosely. He straightened, then rose to his feet as the governor came through the doors at the back of the auditorium.

"Keep your seat, Teddy," the big man boomed. He was followed by the slight figure of Irma Law, the Attorney General, and Blanton from the Florida Department of Law Enforcement. They came down the aisle and began shaking hands. Governor Slate introduced them.

"Where are the rest of the council?" Ms. Law asked.

"Late, as usual," Rainmaker answered. "If they run on schedule, Joe Tyler will be next, followed by Merlini. Last of all is Melba. It happens every meeting."

"Governor, what's this meeting about?" Lila Mae asked.

"You don't have to worry about it, Lila Mae," was the terse reply.

At the same time that Tyler came through the little side door near the dais, the doors opened in the back of the room to admit a photographer and Al McDonald, followed by the cameraman from the local television station. Several of the city staff trailed after the cameraman, curious because they had seen the governor come in unannounced.

The governor turned to the F.D.L.E. man and gave him some quiet instructions, then beckoned to one of the city staff. "Honey, go get Chief Hicks for me, will you? If he's not in his office, tell the officer to locate him and tell him the governor wants him pronto." The young woman hastened away.

"Governor, this is a surprise," Tyler boomed. He came forward, hand outstretched.

The governor ignored the proffered hand. "Yes, Joe, it's going to be quite a surprise."

Just then the side door was flung open and the mayor rushed in, all smiles and batting eyelashes. "Oh, Governor Slate, you should have given us more warning. To what do we owe this signal honor?"

The big man smiled. "You'll find out soon enough, Melba. Please have a seat, you and Joe." They both started for the dais. "No, Melba, you're not in session. You can sit right there next to Teddy and that'll do just fine."

Melba and Tyler sat down. She turned to him and whispered, "That's Blanton of the F.D.L.E., so he and the Gov must be touring the state on his new crackdown on crime."

"I thought he always did that with a lot of fanfare," Tyler whispered back.

"He's not running this year, so he doesn't need a lot of publicity," the mayor said in a final tone.

Merlini bumbled through the door near the dais and looked around in confusion. Then he spotted the governor and smiled uncertainly. Why was he here? he wondered, and what was going on? Legislature was still in session; so the governor belonged in Tallahassee, making sure the other party didn't cause too much trouble.

"Councilman Merlini," the governor said quietly, "please be good enough to sit there with the others."

"Yeah, sure." He wandered over and sat down next to Lila Mae. "You got any idea what this is about?"

"Not a clue, Meats. He did say we're in for a big surprise."

He looked long and hard at her legs, then mumbled, "I don't like surprises; I never did."

Bonano came through the side door, shook hands with the governor and the man from F.D.L.E., and then was drawn aside by the attorney general.

The mayor clutched Tyler's sleeve, and whispered, "Looks like Frank is in trouble. I told you he's not to be trusted."

"The governor and the attorney general wouldn't come down here if Frank had done something wrong, Melba. I think the county commission has been at him, and he's here to try and make us leave the annexation alone."

"Fowler Dayes doesn't even belong to Slate's party, Joe. That doesn't make any sense." She tensed as DeLeon Slugge came through the big doors at the back of the auditorium, looking puzzled.

Ms. Law stopped talking to Bonano and nodded toward Slugge. "I'm glad you could make it, Mr. Slugge."

"I just hope this meeting is quick," he replied coldly. "I have several briefs to prepare and I'm running behind."

"Just have a seat down there with the others, if you will," Ms. Law said. She turned back to Bonano, who reacted when Chief Hicks came ambling through the doors, his hat at a jaunty angle, and a wad of chewing gum in his mouth.

"Well, how do, Ms. Law," Hicks said amiably. "I got a message that—"

"Yes, the governor sent for you, Chief. Please have a seat down there with the other folks and we'll get down to business. I think everyone is here."

Rufus Hicks's eyebrows rose, he blinked a couple of times, and then started down the aisle.

"Who knows about this besides Al McDonald?" Bonano quietly asked Ms. Law.

"Only the activists, I suppose. Mrs. Slugge is a very brave woman; I wouldn't want to take a chance on that one losing his temper with me. Notice his eyes?"

"Yeah, they're ice."

Irma Law laughed shortly. "You ever read a book on Chinese face reading?"

"No, can't say I have."

"Well, according to the ancients, when the whites of the eyes show all around the iris when the eye is looking straight ahead, it denotes madness of some sort."

"Well, in this case, they're right. He beat the hell out of his wife for speaking out against the council, and she's in the process of divorcing him."

"Nasty customer," she whispered. "Well, let's get this over with." They walked past the city employees who were still in the chamber and joined the little group before the dais.

"If I might have your close attention," the governor said. "We are here because there has been an allegation that the Sunshine Law has been broken, and I–"

"That is a vicious lie!" the mayor objected. "Who told you such a thing?"

"Madam Mayor, if you will allow me to finish what I was saying," Governor Slate ground out, "I would be most appreciative. As you all know, burden of proof requires only a preponderance of evidence. I want you to listen to a tape I will play for you." He gave Blanton a nod and DeLeon Slugge went white as he heard his voice.

"Lost Horizon file, confidential, for my ears only. Mayor Melba Tosti and two councilmen, Josephus Tyler and Gianni Merlini, have instructed me to begin negotiations with the Folders and the Hymans on the purchase of their ranches. The purpose of these acquisitions on the part of the Lost Horizon Partnership is to build a subdivision to provide housing for those who have lost their homes to the sinkhole, to attract younger families into the city of Sunshine, to restore the lost tax revenues by this means, and to enrich themselves greatly.

"I have finished the negotiations, and made arrangements to purchase the Hyman ranch for two thousand an acre. The Folder property will be bought at three thousand five hundred dollars an acre.

"I met this afternoon with Farley Pruitt at the Sunshine TrustBank to discuss the financing of this package. He has spoken with Mayor Tosti, Gianni Merlini, and Josephus Tyler, and has made arrangements to take care of the money end of the deal for ten percentage points. He feels, as I do, that this is a win-win situation, as the three investors are empowered to annex the property into the city limits, which will make the housing more attractive."

Slugge rose, shaking with fury. "That is my property; it was stolen from my house by my wife. You have no right to air a memo on legal business; it's confidential and privileged, between attorney and client, and fur–"

"Sit down and shut up, Slugge," Blanton said, moving away from the tape recorder, which he had switched off.

Melba Tosti sat with her mouth hanging open, her skin a pasty white. Josephus Tyler had closed his eyes and his lips were moving, but it was impossible to determine whether he was cursing or praying.

Merlini jumped to his feet. "You don't understand why I had to have the money, Governor, it was for a good cause. I wanted to build a museum for Sunshi–"

"Councilman, you have broken the law," Irma Law said. "Immediately you will be charged with breaking the Sunshine Law, and when investigations have been concluded, I expect there will be further charges. This pact that the three of you have entered into is such a violation of the public trust that it leaves me speechless. You will be tried very quickly, that I can promise you. We don't want to drag this out."

The mayor's mouth snapped shut and she looked around wildly, then realized for the first time that the entire procedure was being taped for television. Her hands automatically went to her head to adjust her wig, and then she blazed forth. "Dee Slugge, we trusted you, and you have betrayed us. How on earth could you invent such a lie to entrap us?"

Slugge turned a very unhealthy red, clenching his fists. "How dare you!"

"It won't wash, Melba," the governor said. "You already voted to annex the land, the three of you. If anything, your haste has helped the case against you." He looked at the camera in the middle of the chamber, then back at the councilmen. "As soon as you are charged formally, you will be removed from office. Chief Hicks, will you take Mr. Merlini, Mrs. Tosti, and Mr. Tyler into custody long enough to charge them with breaking the Sunshine Law. I will wait in Mr. Bonano's office for your telephone call assuring me that the charges have been brought, and then I will proceed. I want to clear this rot out of government."

Ms. Law went to Slugge and drew him aside. "I am writing the complaint on your actions, Mr. Slugge, so I don't think it will be brushed aside by the Bar. You have aided and abetted the commission of crimes, sir. You're a disgrace to the profession."

"I did nothing more than—"

"What any decent lawyer would do?" the attorney general asked sarcastically. She laughed and turned away from him.

Rufus Hicks didn't know what to do. He stood, uncertain, while the press scribbled and the camera recorded his reluctance to take into custody his erstwhile bosses. "Lord, Joe, I hate to do this, but I have to," he began.

"For God's sake, man, get us out of here!" Tyler whispered. "Take us to the station. I don't want any more footage on film than we can help. I might be able to squelch—"

"You won't be able to squelch a damned thing," Melba said bitterly. "You and your rotten ideas, look where we are now."

"My idea! You were the mastermind on this one, you bitch!"

Their squabbling was interrupted by Merlini's quiet sobbing. "I had found an artist who would do the sausage," he cried.

Flag _ City _ Gazette

The best little newspaper in Florida

The best little front page in the state

Mayor and Two Councilmen Charged with Sunshine Law Violation
Special to the Gazette

Sunshine: Mayor Melba Tosti and two of Sunshine's city councilmen, Josephus Tyler and Gianni Merlini, were charged yesterday with violations of the state's Sunshine Law.

In an unprecedented move, Governor Slate and the Attorney General, Irma Law, as well as Blanton of the Florida Department of Law Enforcement, arrived in Sunshine yesterday for the sole purpose of having the three city leaders charged with breaking the law. After the mayor protested that there had never been any breach of the law in her city, Governor Slate had Blanton play for the assembled group a tape made by attorney DeLeon Slugge, who aided and abetted the three.

The plan was to purchase two ranches outside the city limits, put up cheap housing that would sell for big prices, then annex the whole into the city limits. They forgot that, in voting to annex the land, they would break the Sunshine Law. A vote to annex the land was passed at the last meeting of the council.

"I'm glad that Governor Slate has seen fit to nab those scoundrels," said Fowler Dayes, chairman of Banter County Commission. "Dealing with them has always been a pain, and they have shown little regard for what the county has done for Sunshine."

"At least we won't have to look at those ridiculous wigs any more," said Commissioner Christine Suggs.

The case against the mayor and two councilmen will be brought before Judge Manson "Cheeze" Burger on Monday.

The governor has removed the three councilmen from office. He has not yet decided whom he will appoint to fill out their terms. "I am determined to return Sunshine to its original form of government, a mayor and five council members," he said.

"That form of government was chosen by the people of Sunshine, and ignored by Josephus Tyler and his successor, Melba Tosti. Once again, the will of the people will be heard."

Anyone chosen to complete the terms of Melba Tosti and Josephus Tyler must agree to run in the next election. Both were up for reelection in November.

5 Florida/State _ The Tampa Tribune

SUNSHINE TRIO CHARGED

Sunshine: Mayor Melba Tosti, Josephus Tyler, and Gianni Merlini were charged yesterday with violation of the Sunshine Law.

The Governor, accompanied by Attorney General Ima Law and Trout Blanton of the Florida Department of Law Enforcement, made a surprise visit to the city in order to have charges brought against the three. "I am tired of the political wheeling and dealing so rife in the State, and I want this to be a warning against all elected scofflaws. This law is going to be enforced," said Governor Slate.

Immediately after the three were charged, the governor removed them from office. He has not yet named their replacements, who must agree to run for office when the term they serve is up.

3 Bay area _ Times

Little Melba Sunshine (revisited)
by Harmon Tacks

Little Mayor Melba's gone from our house, hip hooray!
The Governor done cotched her and chased her far away,
That she'll be doing time in jail, this writer has no doubt,
Cause arrogance will git you if you don't watch out.

Mayor Melba's dearest buddy, Sunshine's Holy Joe,
   Had his hand in the matter too—oh no, oh no, oh no!
And he'll be doing time as well, so there goes all his clout,
   Arrogance will git you if you don't watch out.

Poor old Meats Merlini has tumbled from his throne,
   He'll have to do with sausages made from meat alone,
There goes the crazy Meat Museum; the bronze sausage is out,
   Yes, arrogance will git you if you don't watch out!

Bonano grinned as Lila Mae and Teddy both arrived simultaneously. "Take a pew, folks. What on earth brings you to this office so early in the day?"

"Frank, I'm at a loss," Teddy said, pulling up a chair. "Have you heard anything?"

"Yes, I heard a great deal that I didn't want to hear. Melba was screaming at me. According to her, this is all my fault, I've been after her for years, I hate her, I should be kind to the world and commit suicide, preferably by hanging myself from my balls–shall I go on?"

"Why did you talk with her?" Lila Mae asked.

"I had to ask her to clean out her office, bring in her keys, and those other niceties. She refuses to leave her condominium, says she has been framed and she's going to sue."

"Is she serious?" Lila Mae sat down.

"Very."

"Have you spoken with Joe or Meats?"

"Joe's wife is taking all calls, and you can't get through to him. Sarah says he has gone into religious retreat."

"That means he's praying for deliverance," Rainmaker said. "Well, only God can get him out of this one."

"I feel sorry for Meats," Lila Mae mused. "Poor old man, all he wanted was to build his museum."

"For that he should have been arrested," Rainmaker declared. "The man can't be completely sane."

"No, he ain't, but he's not all that bad." Lila Mae laughed. "I'll miss his trying to stare down my blouse. He's such a dirty old man."

Bonano nodded. "Yeah, he is that. His eyes almost popped from his head the first time you showed up in that slit skirt. I suppose you're the only thing he ever saw that looked better to him than a sausage."

"Gee, thanks. You're so sweet, no wonder Mary Lee has taken a liking to you."

"I understand the State is going to ask for the maximum penalty on the Sunshine violation."

"Oh, my God, Frank, are we in violation here?" Lila Mae gasped.

"No, we're not discussing anything you might vote on."

She whistled with relief. "What is the maximum penalty?"

"What good is it, giving you a copy of the Sunshine Law book, if you never read it?" Bonano asked.

"Frank, you know perfectly well that I don't understand legalese, much less all that Flip versus Flop that they go into. Now, cow flop I know something about, but I don't know a thing about law."

Shrugging, Bonano said, "The max is five hundred dollars fine and sixty days in jail. It's only a misdemeanor. But the Gov can remove the person from office; that's the sting."

"Do you suppose they'll be charged with anything else?" Rainmaker asked.

"Hard to say; I don't know what they're investigating them for. But politically they are dead."

"Lord, I hope so. If I never see another lime green wig, I'll be the happiest woman on earth. I wonder who Governor Slate is going to pick to put in their places."

"Well, he's going to appoint an executive mayor, that much he has made plain," Rainmaker said. "It will seem strange, having a mayor who can't vote on council issues."

"Yes, but if we get a good mayor, then he'll come up with good ideas for the council to address," Lila Mae said. "That can't be all bad. Look at the nonsense we've had to put up with from Melba, Joe, and Meats."

"Did you hear that Farley Pruitt has been fired from the bank?" Lila Mae asked. "The Board dumped him yesterday."

"Well, I'll be da–!"

They were interrupted by the telephone on Bonano's desk. He grabbed the receiver. "Bonano. Of course I'll hold." He covered the mouthpiece. "It's the governor's office calling."

Both of the councilmen sat up straighter, intent on the instrument in Bonano's hand.

"Yes, Governor Slate. Good afternoon." Bonano nodded several times, then laughed. "They are both in my office at this moment, sir. Just a moment." He handed the telephone to Lila Mae. "He wants to talk to you."

Chairman Lila Mae Warner looked over the chamber, which was packed with people, and gasped with surprise. There was Henny in the first row of seats, still looking like an armadillo, his mouth gaping. Next to him, and a strange pair they made, sat PooPoo, who looked as proud as anyone could possibly look. She banged her gavel. "The meeting of the City Council of the City of Sunshine will now come to order. We will rise and say the Pledge of Allegiance, after which Councilman Strike will give the Invocation." She looked at each member of the newly formed council: Gavel Strike, Sally Slugge, Guy Fawkins, and Dustin Forbes, a local businessman, then rose and turned to face the new flag, which had been delivered the day before.

At the far end of the dais, Mayor Theodore Rainmaker stood up, his face solemn, his eyes dancing.

The citizens in the chamber stood as one and began to applaud. The loudest accolade came from the people who lived on Mosquito Row, who shouted and yipped as they clapped their hands.

Lila Mae smiled at them and when they quieted, she placed her hand on her magnificent bosom and began. "I pledge allegiance to the flag of the United States of America—" As the voices of the citizens come to watch their new government rang in faltering echo behind those on the dais, she reflected that she had never really aspired to anything in particular, especially to anything as great as being chairman of the Council. She had been floored when Governor Slate had given her the job, flummoxed and humble. Then she realized that her time had finally come. Who knew?–perhaps one day, she would run for the legislature.

True greatness had laid its claim upon her; she had been given untold power! She hoped that, someday, poor Henny would understand.

ABOUT THE AUTHOR

Gilliam Clarke is a water activist who has spent an inordinate amount of time working with politicians across Florida, in efforts both rewarding and frustrating.

A native of Washington, North Carolina, she worked in medicine, banking, and money management. She is married to a retired United Nations official, and spent some fifteen years in the Caribbean before moving to Florida. Contact with many Caribbean political leaders laid the ground for writing political satire, and Florida's politics has proven even more fertile territory than the Caribbean.

She is the proud grandmother of a boy named Griffin, who loves to read.